PACIFIC CREST

by J.R. Herman

This is a work of fiction. Names, characters, businesses, places, events, locales, and incidents are either the products of the author's imagination or used in a fictitious manner. Any resemblance to actual persons, living or dead, or actual events is purely coincidental.

Cover design by Jon R. Herman

PROLOGUE—AUGUST 12

The bastard was still in pursuit. She heard him crashing downhill through the thick brush. The young woman turned and plunged into a tangle of vine maples, rain-loaded branches whipping her in the face.

Faith didn't understand how he kept going with such a deep wound. She'd used all of her strength to jam the knife into his leg and remembered feeling the long blade deflect off his femur.

She peered up between dripping vine maple branches. The pre-dawn light revealed a shadowy grove of tall fir trees a hundred yards away. Once into that old growth forest, she could move faster, but at first she'd be exposed to view. She was willing to take that chance. She'd be able to outrun him then, as long as she didn't break a leg getting there.

She stumbled over duff-covered rotten stumps and slick logs to reach a creek that gurgled along the edge of the big trees. A brief pause to listen as the man thrashed through tangled vine maples, maybe 200 yards back.

She wiped water from her eyes and peered across the creek. Lichen-draped trees stood like shaggy columns in a temple, receding into darkness. Sunrise was coming but it would take a while for daylight to seep through the thick canopy. The ground was free of thick brush, easy to run through. If she hurried, got far enough into the trees, she'd be hidden.

Faith leaped across the creek and entered the forest, walking fast on a diagonal route uphill. After four months on the trail, she was strong. Training and experience in battle had given her confidence, but it also taught her to be cautious. She had to keep her focus. She'd been assaulted and drugged and was sleep deprived. She told herself to pay attention, put one foot in front of the other, and repeat. One careful step at a time, but quickly too.

The dark forest closed in behind her. Dewy spider webs tickled her face. Moving quietly, dodging around massive tree trunks, she heard small animals and birds scurry and flutter out of her way. She also heard her pursuer in the brush. Until she didn't.

Did he stop, or might he be in the forest now, moving in silence just as she was?

Faith continued uphill, determined to keep the high ground. She had no map, no GPS and no idea where she was going. But she was alive, in relatively good shape and had escaped with her clothing and boots. She needed distance now.

Memories surfaced, memories of being pursued through a wild landscape, heading into the unknown. This time there was no M4 carbine hanging on a sling, no M9 pistol strapped to her thigh, no comrades to watch her back. No radio, no helicopter gunship coming to her rescue. She was on her own, and no one knew where she was.

After a few minutes, she paused, held her breath and listened. Aside from birds, the forest was silent. She let out her breath, bent over and put her hands on her knees, shook her head. Long black hair fell in wet tendrils and hid her face. The flashbacks were disorienting. She told herself to save the traumatic memories for her VA headshrinker. *This is now, not then. This is real, the memories aren't. Focus on the current danger.*

Standing, she turned and listened. A varied thrush called, its sweet, multi-toned song clear in the cool air. Still no sound of her pursuer. Maybe she'd thrown him off her trail. Maybe the wound slowed him down. He likely had no idea which direction she'd taken once she reached the forest. She took a few deep breaths and moved on.

A few minutes later she reached a hilltop and paused in a grassy clearing. Mist drifted through the tall trees. She looked up to the clearing's circle of sky and saw thin, high clouds glowing red. Day was here at last and the storm had passed. She was soaked, chilled to the bone and longed for the sun's warmth.

There was still no sight or sound of the man. *Where was he?*

From far below a faint, hoarse shout shattered the peace. The shouting continued, eventually resolving into words, faint in the still air.

"Lila! Lila! Come back! I'm sorry! Just come back! Lila, I love you! Come back!"

A chill swept over Faith. *Lila?* That was her twin sister's name. Lila had disappeared from the Pacific Crest Trail 10 years ago.

What the hell? This man . . . this man who had assaulted and kidnapped her? He must've known Lila and mistaken Faith for her. Known her well, from the sound of anguish in his voice. Given what happened last night, was it too far fetched to think he was responsible for Lila's disappearance?

The voice grew fainter, still yelling "Lila!" over and over again. Heart pounding, Faith stood rock still and listened. Wild thoughts and feelings whirled through her mind. They soon spiraled into one hard knot of certainty.

She saw the mist thickening in the trees, even as the sky overhead grew brighter. More birds were singing. The sun was coming. Grim-faced, she turned and started downhill toward the distant shouts.

CHAPTER 1 — APRIL 10
FOUR MONTHS AGO

Snake! A hissing rattle shattered her walking reverie. A large grey diamondback was coiling in the trail a few feet away, preparing to strike. Without thought, Faith leaped up and over the writhing snake and landed beyond, out of striking range. The leap was a surreal experience that seemed to defy physics. Even with a heavy backpack, she'd felt weightless. Fear can cause amazing reactions.

Heart racing, she turned and watched the thick serpent unwind itself and slide off the trail into a pile of rocks. She closed her eyes for a moment, took a few deep breaths and then opened them onto the bright desert morning. A meadowlark called from a nearby bush. Below her, a Border Patrol SUV bumped down the road, trailing a cloud of yellow dust. High in the blue a red tail hawk screamed.

Faith Montaigne shook her head and laughed. There was irony in seeing that snake since she'd been thinking how incredibly serpentine the Pacific Crest Trail is. Only 10 miles north of the Pacific Crest Trail's southern terminus and she was already weary of the many twists and turns of the trail; mile after mile of up, over, down and around the rocky hills. It seemed like the trail wasn't interested in getting anywhere. Faith turned and resumed her journey, puffs of powdery dust exploding around her boots.

It was mid-morning on Day One and she was tired. The previous day had been a long busy one. The flight from Portland to San Diego, dinner and drinks with old Navy friends, a sleepless night camped in their back yard, a mild hangover, an early morning drop-off at the border. It was all a whirl. Faith took a deep breath and told herself that she could relax now. The months of planning and preparation, the training hikes in the Cascade Mountains, the logistics; they were all behind her. She was on the trail at last, free to walk and let her mind wander.

She thought about her parents, remembering how hard it had been to convince them that she needed to do this trip. It was a way to save herself, to restart her life. They didn't understand, and part of that was her fault. She hadn't told them what happened on that last mission in Afghanistan, nor did she tell them about the nightmares that haunted her since.

Several times a week the horrific dreams shocked her awake, sweating and frantic, usually in the early morning hours, and that would be her wake-up call. The nightmares' trauma poisoned her days, painting a dull brown film over her existence. She went to work tired and irritable, snapped at her co-workers, rebuffed attempts at friendship and inclusion. So it had gone for too many months.

Since her discharge from the Marines, she'd gone to weekly therapy sessions. They helped in the short term, but after two years and three different therapists, Faith knew that her PTSD was not going away. It was time to try something different. She was sure that she'd go crazy if she didn't get to the wilderness and find some psychological space, a chance to re-adjust to post-combat life at her own speed. Her VA counselor agreed and supported her plan.

Convincing her mom and dad had been challenging. They associated the trail with the loss of her twin sister Lila, who disappeared from the PCT in southern Oregon ten years ago. Lila was never found, her fate unknown. The only time Mike and Sally Montaigne ever spent on the trail was during the anguished weeks of searching for their daughter.

When Faith called her parents two weeks ago to let them know her plans, the shit hit the fan. Her dad's first response had been, "Are you out of your mind?" He berated her for quitting her job and upending her life, for not letting them in on her plans. "It was bad enough when you were overseas, doing God knows what, out of contact for weeks. After Lila disappeared, we were scared we'd lose you too, and thankful every time you came home in one piece. And now you're putting us through all that again?"

She tried to reassure them. "Mom, Dad? This is something I have to do, and you know I'm capable and smart enough to get through it. There's no Taliban on the trail. Nobody will be shooting at me. Probably the biggest things I'll have to worry about will be the littlest things like snakes, insects and parasites."

Her parents weren't convinced. A few days after that call, on her way south from North Bend, Faith stayed overnight at their home near Meeks Landing, Oregon. She'd grown up there with her sister, roaming the rolling hills and forests along the Willamette River. It had been an idyllic childhood and one that she looked back on with a strange mix of happiness, regret and sadness. On this latest visit, the excitement of embarking on a new adventure balanced that. She hoped that her mom and dad would see, maybe share, that excitement.

The evening of her visit, they gathered in the big living room to talk. Her dad sat on the left side of the couch, a big man in a blue plaid shirt, broad shouldered, broad-faced, with what he called "a bad case of cop belly" hanging over his blue jeans. Her mother sat on the other side, hands clasped together. She was an energetic, heavy-set dark woman, wearing a pastel rose pantsuit. Her oval face was framed by jet-black hair streaked with grey. She was the older version of her daughter, but it was easier to see the Native American heritage in her face.

Faith finally told them about her PTSD and the nightmares. She described that last terrible mission in Afghanistan. She said that the only way to get past it was to go on the long hike, and that other veterans had found relief and hope in the wilderness. "This is something I have to do. I've already been through a lot and got through it in one piece. This trip is about healing as well as for remembering our Lila."

Mike had been Meeks Landing police chief and was involved in a traumatic mass shooting. He grudgingly admitted that he understood her. "After that shootout at the church I spent a lot of time in the outdoors, took a lot of vacation days, fishing and hiking. It did help a lot, helped me come to terms with what had happened. I can relate. We just wish you'd told us about this trip sooner."

"I'm sorry I didn't, but this is something I had to decide and do on my own."

Sally got up and walked over to embrace her daughter. Tears in her eyes, she said, "I think we understand now. I'm glad you told us about your troubles and about what happened to you over there. I'm so sorry you went through all that. I really wish you'd told us sooner, but at least now we can understand where you're at, why you're going."

Mike cleared his throat and said, "Okay, well, tell us all about the trip!"

She told them about the extensive planning and training, the gear she was taking, how she'd be able to stay in touch with them via cell phone and a satellite communicator. That last point reassured Mike and Sally.

They went on to talk about Lila, as they always did when Faith visited. Even after ten years her absence hurt, but they wanted to keep her alive in their memories. So they told time worn stories and laughed again at the twins' antics.

Lila had been the rebellious one, the artistic type, wearing outrageous clothing and sporting bizarre hairstyles, dating boys who were social outcasts and misfits. Lila was always at odds with her parents, at odds with all authority. She wasn't happy, she didn't feel complete, unless she was rebelling against something, challenging some part of the status quo, engaged in a cause of some kind.

Faith was the quiet daughter, the good student and school athlete who never got into trouble. She went her own way as much as Lila did, but did so quietly. As a teenager, Faith wasn't concerned about being popular. She was an athlete because she loved it. She was a good student because she loved learning. She didn't drink much or party because she didn't like to. She rarely dated in high school. Although she and Lila were so far apart in habit and demeanor, they had remained close. Faith felt that they still were, even though Lila was gone.

Faith paused and drank water from her Camelbak hose. It was getting near noon and time for lunch. She found shade under a clump of tall brush. After checking for snakes and scorpions, she took off her pack and sat down to eat a granola bar. Her phone vibrated and she pulled it from a cargo pocket to check for messages. There was a text from her dad:

How is your first day on the trail? Just thinking about you and hoping your trip is off to a great start. Your Mom and I support you completely. Keep on truckin'! Love you, Dad.

Faith smiled as she tapped out a reply:

Eating lunch. Hot and dry. 12 miles so far and only 8 miles to Morena Lake Campground. Saw a rattlesnake but no problems. Talked to few other hikers. Only 2,638 miles to go! Love ya, Mom and Dad!

CHAPTER 2 — APRIL 10

Mike read Faith's text, smiled and set his cell phone down on the wooden rail. He hoped that being in regular contact with Faith would reduce his anxiety. Mike stood on his cedar deck and took a deep breath of the sweet fresh air. It was a sunny spring morning in the Willamette Valley. The maples and alders ringing the back yard were full with shiny new leaves.

For some reason he always thought of Lila on days like this. Maybe because it was around this time of year and on a similar day that he last saw her, just before she left for her PCT trip.

The scene grew blurry and Mike blinked, looked down at his hands resting on the deck rail. The grief never went away. He used to wonder if it would diminish, and it did eventually, but sometimes it would surge back and slam him out of nowhere like a massive tsunami bludgeoning his heart. It stopped him in his tracks and he'd pause and struggle for composure. Or just give in and let the tears flow. Let the tide of pain come in and pool up, then slowly drain away.

Mike let it wash over him this time. He wished he could be more like Sally. He knew that she felt the pain as much as he, but she somehow turned it into something better, a way of honoring Lila's memory and keeping her alive in her mind and heart. Sally would be home from work later, and just by her presence, she'd help the pain-tide recede.

Something else that might help would be to dig out the old files again. Mike had been Meeks Landing's police chief at the time of Lila's disappearance and was given full access to the case files. As a cop, he was also allowed to participate in the investigation. A lot of people, hours, hard work and brain power had gone into that investigation. Mike found no fault with how it was conducted, but he still felt like they should've solved the case, or at least come up with more than they did. By now, he was certain they'd never know Lila's fate. Continuing to work on it, to go over the evidence and interviews and diagrams and maps . . . it helped him feel like he was still doing something; that he hadn't given up on her even after ten years.

He went back inside the house and walked down a hallway to the home office. There was a tall steel file cabinet next to the roll top desk. Mike crouched down and pulled out the cabinet's bottom drawer. It slid open to reveal its only contents, a cardboard box. He used both hands to lift the box and place it on the desktop. The box edges were fuzzy from use, softened on the corners. Inside were file folders, DVD's and folded maps. He pulled out several folders and arranged them on the desk blotter so that he could see the labels, decide which one to go over first. One more time, go over the evidence, look for the tiniest clue, that one informational anomaly that would help him figure out what happened to his daughter ten years ago on the Pacific Crest Trail.

Lila had been 22 years old when she decided to hike the PCT. At the time, she was enrolled at The Evergreen State College in Olympia, but decided to take a break during spring and summer quarters to hike the full length of the trail. A photo taken before she left shows a tall, slim young woman with short black hair and brown skin, a wide white smile and piercing blue eyes. Her hair has purple streaks in it and she's wearing a bright red scarf, black sweatshirt, black shorts and leggings, athletic shoes. She stands a little lopsided, her right arm over the shoulders of a short and somewhat scared looking young man in overalls, sporting a mangy beard and wire-framed glasses.

A later photo, taken on the PCT and sent via her cell phone, shows Lila with longer, pure black hair, khaki shorts, muscular legs, green t-shirt. She's wearing a blue backpack, folded up sleeping pad strapped to the bottom. A happy and confident smile brightens her sunlit face. The photo was taken just a few days before she failed to check in. It wasn't a selfie, but no one knows who took it. It's the last known photo of her.

She'd started at the southern end of the trail in April. The trail didn't have good cell coverage in those days. Her parents and sister received occasional texts and rare phone calls as Lila hiked north through the semi-arid mountains and hot desert valleys, north into the heart of the Sierra Nevada.

Lila's text messages told of sharing hardships and campfires with new friends, enduring storms and heat, getting stronger the whole way and loving every minute of it. She kept at it, moving through the forested mountains of northern California, past snowy Mount Shasta, into Oregon, getting closer to home. Mike and Sally were to join her at Santiam Pass and travel with her to the Columbia Gorge.

That never happened. She vanished in mid-July somewhere south of Crater Lake. At first her parents thought she just forgot to check in or was running later than expected, so they didn't report anything for two days. But the continued silence filled them with a deep foreboding and Mike called Crater Lake National Park headquarters. Park staff alerted their field workers to watch for Lila. Her photo, that last one, was circulated throughout the park.

After another day, Mike called the Oregon State Police and officially reported her as a missing person. OSP contacted the Park Service, who in turn coordinated with the Forest Service, sending out officers to intercept and interview north-bound hikers wherever the trail crossed a road. Some people recognized Lila from the photo and were able to contribute information about her.

She was known on the trail as Tahca, the Lakota word for deer. She had made a good impression on the people who had contact with her. Everyone spoke of her with respect and admiration. She didn't hike much with other people because she was simply too fast and nobody could keep up with her. No one was aware that she'd disappeared or where she might've gone. They were all surprised at the idea that she might've quit and gone somewhere else.

The investigators couldn't find anyone who had seen Lila at the park's lodge or on the trail north of Crater Lake, so the search focused on the stretch of PCT between State Highway 140 (the Lake of the Woods Highway) and Crater Lake. They enlisted the help of U.S. Forest Service wilderness rangers and aircraft to search along the trail. There were various scenarios to account for Lila's disappearance, and ruling out voluntary departure from the trail, the search focused on criminal violence, accident or illness/incapacitation. National Park Service Investigative Services Branch (ISB) helped out with interviews and background checks on some potential suspects who were employed at the lodge as summer help. One was a registered sex offender who had lied on his job application. ISB and OSP detectives investigated and questioned him thoroughly but he turned up clean. The lodge fired him for lying on his application.

If Lila was ill or had an accident, she might have been visible from the air or ground, so known hazardous areas were searched and more hikers interviewed. After two weeks of extensive work, searchers didn't find any trace of her, or anyone else who had seen her. At that point, the investigation began to slacken off.

Mike and Sally were in on the trail search, and Mike's training and status allowed him, at his insistence, to take part in the planning as well as the ground and air search. No one was more thorough than those two. They kept at it after the official search was called off in September. Mike called in favors from his various contacts. With the extra help and support, Lila's parents kept searching and investigating for weeks, until snow and time made it seem futile. Even after they could no longer walk the trails, the distraught but determined couple kept going: updating social media, looking over records and aerial photos, re-reading search reports and interview transcripts, sometimes calling and re-interviewing witnesses.

As fall faded into a dark and snowy winter, Mike and Sally scaled back their efforts. Their health and work had suffered, as had their marriage. They had to re-group and take care of one another, return to their jobs and maintain their relationship with their other daughter, Faith, who was deployed overseas. It was a rough road, but after counseling, praying and talking, the road was smoother by spring. That didn't diminish the grief. Nothing would ever do that except time. When the mountain snow finally melted in late spring, the Montaignes resumed their search with the help of Faith and a couple of dozen friends. The group was organized, methodical and committed, but after several weeks, they found nothing. Mike continued to pursue the case and the search whenever he could. After a while, it became more difficult to get help. Eventually Mike and Sally had to admit defeat. The investigation was a different story. Mike continued with that, off and on, for years.

Sally strode through the door in a burst of cool air. Outside, the last of the spring sun gilded the rolling hills around their home. She carried a couple of cloth bags filled with groceries and set them on the Formica counter that divided the kitchen from the dining area. "Mikey!" she called out. "Help me with the groceries?"

Mike thudded down the hall and into the kitchen. His face looked grim and Sally asked, "Mike, what's wrong?"

She studied his face. “You seem down. You okay? Is Faith alright?”

Mike mustered up a smile. “Faith is fine. She sent that text today, the one I forwarded to you? She’s doing good. As for me, I started thinking about Lila and decided to look at the case files again. Going over it all one more time. Shit, I know I won’t find anything new, but I still have this flicker of hope.”

Sally sat on the stool next to him and took his hand, looked into his eyes. “I know it hurts, baby. It hurts bad, but don’t you think it’s time to let go, at least a little? What made you want to view those files again? Is it Faith’s trip?”

“Sure. It’s all hitting close to home. Our daughter, Lila’s identical twin, hiking the same trail, the same time of year, the whole nine yards. Don’t you feel the past tugging at you?”

Sally smiled and put an arm around his shoulders. She said, “I do. Pretty unavoidable, but we’ll help each other out, just like we always do, and we’ll let Faith do what she needs to do for herself to get right with the world. We’ll stay in touch, maybe meet with her along the way. We’ll cheer her on and keep her in our prayers and trust to God to get her through safely. It’s what we have to do, Mikey. It’s all we can do.”

CHAPTER 3 — MAY 8

Max took him down fast. One moment the stumpy, gnarled old man was drawing his pistol and the next he was on his belly in the dust, handcuffs clicking around his bony wrists. It wasn't much of a contest. Forest Service Officer Max Albricci was a tall, rangy young man and much faster than he looked. He'd done this many times.

"W-w-what the hell?" the man yelled in a high, gravelly voice. "Take yer goddamn fuckin' hands off me! I'm a sovereign citizen and you got no fuckin' right! Ya got no jurisidictionary over me, motherfucker!"

With the man's Colt 1911 pistol in hand, Max stood up. He popped out the magazine and pulled the slide back to eject a shiny brass .45 cartridge. It dropped to the ground with a puff of dust. He put the full magazine into a cargo pocket and jammed the empty pistol into his utility belt.

Max shook his head. "Come on, man. You said your name was Andy, right? Let me help you up, Andy." He put his hands under the man's sweaty armpits and effortlessly pulled him onto his feet.

"You son of a bitch, that hurt my goddamned shoulders," said Andy. His bloodshot eyes were wide and spittle speckled his grey stubble. "You fuckin' jack-booted fed bastard! I'm a free man, not beholden to any gov'mint asshole cop!"

Max sighed and dusted off his green uniform pants with one hand, holding one of his prisoner's arms with the other. Max was glad he had long arms so he could keep Andy at a distance. The old man stank like a leaking distillery filled with cigarette smoke.

"Look, it's a hot morning. Let's go sit in the shade and cool off. Deputy Kingsley'll be here by noon and we can hash this out."

"Why's that little prick coming? What's he got to do with you illegally denying me my fuckin' rights?"

Max sighed. "Andy, when I first arrived, you told me that you only acknowledge the authority of the county sheriffs, right?"

Andy nodded vigorously. "Damn straight. You got no goddamn federal authority over me accordin' to the God blessed, almighty Constitution."

"So there you go. Like I was trying to tell you before you tried to draw your weapon, I requested that the Sheriffs send somebody up, so they're sending Deputy Kingsley and he can take care of this situation. Now come on."

Max shuffled Andy over to the battered green Ford F-150 that was parked in the shade of a ponderosa pine. He told him to sit on the pickup's dented, open tailgate. Andy hopped up and sat, silent and frowning, legs dangling. The back of the pickup was a jumble of pine tree rounds, wood slivers, slabs of reddish bark, dented Hamm's beer cans and empty whiskey bottles. An ancient, battered blue McCollough chainsaw sat on the ground next to the truck, oozing tangy fumes of oil and gas.

Max walked across the dirt road to a spot where he could look south down the mountain and out across the vast valley far below. It was a clear day and easy to see the green water tower and dark trees of Ellensburg in the distance. Further away, beyond a series of tan ridges, the white hump of Mount Adams, draped with wrinkled glaciers, jutted into a pale blue sky. Max smiled at the view.

Movement below caught his eye and he saw a Sheriffs vehicle rolling up the steep road switchbacks, light bar flashing red and blue. This was Max's first week as a Forest Service law enforcement officer—an LEO, in cop parlance—and he was about to meet the Kittitas County co-op Sheriffs deputy for the first time. The co-op deputy was partially financed by the Forest Service and worked closely with the agency on enforcement and investigative issues on Forest Service lands in the county.

Max turned back to the pickup and saw that Andy had hopped down from the tailgate and was in a bowlegged, stumbling scramble toward a dense stand of trees. Max swore and broke into a run. "God damn it, Andy!" he barked. "Don't make me hobble you like a goddamned mule!"

If nothing else, the encounter with Andy was an interesting conclusion to an otherwise dull first week on his new job. Despite all the pre-employment paperwork he'd done and the office visits and phone calls, not to mention the three weeks with a Forest Service training officer in Oregon, the bullshit kept dribbling out of the butt of bureaucracy. Slogging through it took up a lot of valuable time. Computer profiles, multiple passwords for various government sites, online training, insurance documents, and more. There was a myriad of petty details arranged into a bewildering bureaucratic maze of baffling inefficiencies. Max thought the Park Service had been bad, but the Forest Service was worse.

He didn't get into the woods until Thursday afternoon. A light rain fell as Margaret Lin, the Roslyn District Ranger, took him on a tour of key areas he might be interested in. Places that included a cabin where there'd been a murder/suicide, a couple of former marijuana grow sites, illegally built cabins and hunting camps, vandalized signs, illegally built trails, chronic litter sites, poaching scenes, timber theft, dump sites with piles of old tires. The list, and places, went on. There were a lot more issues than Max had dealt with at Mount Rainier National Park.

Late that afternoon, Max and the District Ranger stood at the edge of an unofficial campsite along the Cle Elum River. Raindrops dimpled the smooth-flowing water. Broken and tattered black garbage bags were strewn over the trampled ground, spilling out their colorful filth. Max observed syringes in the dirt, along with old condoms, water-matted toilet paper, beer cans, broken glass, brass cartridges, cereal boxes, paper plates, red plastic cups and more. An old blue lawn chair squatted nearby, lopsided, its bottom cut out. Underneath that hole was a lumpy pile of human waste and soggy toilet paper.

Lin asked Max, "Was it this bad at Rainier? You were LEO there for a couple of years."

Max shook his head. "Not quite this bad. We had a smaller area and a lot more enforcement than here, so we could keep things in check. Still, the park got the same types of people, looking for a place to party and blow off steam. Campers have changed a lot over the years. I get pretty steamed about it sometimes. I guess we all do. Seems like people don't go to the mountains to commune or connect with nature anymore. They're not looking for peace and quiet. They don't know the difference between a national park and a national forest. They don't know what to carry in the woods when they hike or how to stay safe. They don't know about the wildlife or plants. All they know is to party, walk around like zombies with their tablets and cell phones and try to take selfies with a bear."

Deputy Kingsley rolled up in a grey Chevy Tahoe, sheriff's gold star on the door. Wording on the back panel said "Forest Deputy". Trailing dust surged forward and briefly enveloped the SUV before being nudged away by a gentle breeze. The lights went off and Kingsley stepped out the driver's door. He was a small, fit-looking man in his early 40's. Neat uniform, baseball cap topping a stern face. Not somebody to mess with. He glanced at Andy and strode over to where Max stood.

Max smiled and put out his hand. Kingsley paused, looked up at Max and then shook. His stern face broke into a small smile. "Einar Kingsley, Kittitas County Sheriffs."

"Max Albricci, USDA Forest Service. Glad to meet you, Einar."

Einar turned to look at Andy, sitting on the tailgate. Andy glared back at him. "So I see you've met Uncle Andy."

"Uncle?" said Max. "Actual uncle or metaphorical?"

Einar looked sheepish as he said, "Well, that guy is my actual uncle, believe it or not. Andy Quincy Kingsley. Every family has a black sheep, or a grey and grizzled one like that old reprobate. Let me go over and have a talk with him."

Max waited and watched while Einar and Andy began a spirited discussion. There was some hand waving and Max caught the occasional swear word from Andy, his gravelly voice plaintive. Max leaned against the side of his white and green Ford Explorer Interceptor. Einar's Tahoe ticked as the engine cooled. A squirrel chattered nearby and in the distant blue sky a raven croaked. Max inhaled the wonderful smell of pine needles warmed by the sun.

Eventually Einar shook Andy's hand, patted him on the shoulder and walked back to Max. "Well now, I think we're good," he said. "Uncle Andy regrets his disrespect and will hand over his driver's license. Go ahead and ticket him for whatever."

"Um, did he tell you that he tried to pull out his pistol?"

Einar turned to stare at his uncle. "Well now, that he did not. But if he did, I'm sure it wasn't loaded. We keep ammo away from him."

Max held up the Colt's loaded magazine. "It was loaded, with one in the pipe."

Einar scowled. “Shit! I don’t know what to say, Max, or why the hell he’d do such a stupid thing. Uncle Andy joined some secret militia group last year. Maybe he got the ammo from them, not to mention his awesomely crazy government conspiracies. What do you wanna do?”

Max thought for a moment. He handed the Colt to Einar. “How about you keep the gun for now, unofficially, and Andy gets violation notices from me for illegal firewood cutting and no spark arrestor on his chainsaw. And we confiscate the wood. Once he’s paid his fines, we forget all about the gun-pulling incident, but if it happens again, I’m charging him with assault on a federal officer with a deadly weapon and obstruction.”

Einar’s face relaxed into a rueful smile. He shook Max’s hand. “You got a deal, Max. And I know what a good deal it is, so thank you. By the way, he’s not getting this gun back.”

Einar took out a cell phone and started tapping his thumbs on the screen. He glanced at Max and said, “Andy isn’t fit to drive, so I’ll get one of my other uncles to come get him.”

“Yeah, I was wondering about that. Sounds good. And then let’s get the paper done, the wood unloaded and your uncle on his way.”

Einar looked up from his phone. “Sure thing. You want to meet in town later? I know a great coffee shop where we can have a cup and some cop talk.”

CHAPTER 4 — MAY 8

A couple of hours later, the two officers parked their vehicles along a tree-lined street in the city of Ellensburg and walked into a crowded coffee shop. The customers, most of whom appeared to be college students, tensed and stared at the two uniformed lawmen as they walked in. Max and Einar ordered their coffees up front and walked over to a corner table in the back of the shop. After they sat down, Max noticed that the other patrons relaxed.

The faded barn-wood walls of the Settlement Coffee House were adorned with large black-and-white photos featuring old-time logging, cowboys, mining and town scenes. There were rusty animal traps, a striped Hudson Bay Company blanket coat, sweat-stained cowboy hats, rusted crosscut saws and Indian artifacts.

Max said, "All this place is missing is a stuffed Jackalope."

Einar smiled and pointed behind Max, who turned and laughed when he saw it. "Okay! The décor is now complete. Jackalope duly noted."

A tall young woman whose nametag read "Doreen" brought them their drinks. Einar leaned back in his chair and sipped from a steaming cup of black coffee. Max held a large mocha and looked dubious. He said, "Ummm, you sure we're safe drinking the coffee here?"

Einar gestured toward the barista. "She's my cousin, so yeah, the coffee is good here. No spittle, no loogies, no pee, no dirt off the floor. Now, there's other places in town where that may not be the case." Einar leaned forward and said quietly, "I can email you a copy of a very secret, completely unofficial interagency safe list for county restaurants and coffee shops if you want. Strictly on the QT though! If my supervisor got wind of that, or even worse, if the local community found out, there'd be a shit storm."

Max laughed. "You got it. Mum's the word."

Einar put his elbows on the table and said, "So. What do you think of the Roslyn Ranger District so far?"

Max blew on his drink and took a moment before replying. "Well, so far, so good. I went on a tour with the District Ranger yesterday. Quite an eye-opener. The job isn't going to be easy, but everyone is really supportive. They seem pretty happy to have a LEO on duty again. Seems like a good place to work."

Kingsley nodded. "Well now, they are good folks. I've been working with them for many years and truly enjoy the job. So, how'd you wind up here?"

Max smiled. "That's a long story, but I'll try to make it short."

Even when he was a kid, Max had known he wanted to be in law enforcement. His dad was a university physics professor and his mom was a freelance features writer covering outdoor stories. Max wanted something more exciting, like what he saw on TV.

He told Einar, "All those terrible cop shows on TV somehow put it into my head. The car chases, the shootouts, the women. If I'd seen a series like *The Wire* when I was a kid, I might've chosen a different profession."

After getting a Bachelor's Degree in law and justice at the University of Washington, Max joined the King County Sheriffs Reserves and got enough training and certifications to get hired as a seasonal law enforcement ranger in Mount Rainier National Park. After a couple of summers there, he became a full-time NPS protection ranger and attended the Federal Law Enforcement Training Center in Georgia. After several seasons in the park, he started suffering from burnout.

"It gets very busy at Rainier. With Seattle, Tacoma and Portland so close, they get more visitors than ever. We dealt with every crime and situation imaginable, including vehicle accidents, lots of domestic violence, theft, lost or injured hikers and dogs, drug violations and vehicle break-ins. I got pretty tired of it all and wanted a change, so when this job opened up, I applied, and here I am. It's a good deal. I'm still close to friends and family in Seattle and I can live in a peaceful rural setting."

Einar nodded and said, "Well now, what do you think so far as compared to your parks job?"

"Out of the frying pan and into the fire, but it looks like I can spend less time sitting on my ass and more time in the woods. There's a lot more variety, too, and I can do more investigative work, hopefully." He sipped at his mocha and then asked Einar, "So, are there any current or open cases around here that are outstanding, interesting and something I can really sink my teeth into?"

"Funny you should mention that." Einar leaned back, dug into a cargo pocket and pulled out a worn, folded piece of paper. He handed it to Max. The paper opened out into a flyer with a color photo of a smiling young dark-haired woman beneath the word "MISSING." Below the photo was the name "Melissa Hampton" and a detailed description of the woman along with where she was last seen. The flyer included a request for people to be on the lookout for her or any of several described items she was last seen with. Max studied it carefully.

He looked up. "She's been missing since last August? No trace?"

"Nothing. This case has been eating away at me. She disappeared, and no clue about what happened to her. I met with her family a few times. It was heartbreaking. You know what I'm talking about. Didn't seem to be anything I could do to help them. Just vague promises that we'd do our best. A detective and I worked on this case as much as possible, in between other cases, but nothing."

"It says here she was hiking the entire Pacific Crest Trail. Any chance she got tired of it and bailed? Maybe decided not to go back to her old life?"

Einar shrugged. "We considered that, and suicide as well, but according to everyone who knew her, she was an upbeat, optimistic soul. We looked at her last texts to family and friends and there's nothing indicating she was tired of the trail, or tired of life. The texts were enthusiastic, joyful even.

"It's been over nine months now and still nothing. We had search and rescue crews covering about 20 miles of Pacific Crest Trail, gridding what areas we could. Helicopter and fixed-wing searches. Forest Service wilderness rangers checked known hazardous spots. We interviewed hikers and horsemen and followed hunches. Finding something in that wilderness is like trying to find a needle in a whole field of haystacks.

"The official search was suspended when winter hit. This spring, Hampton's family informally resumed the search and they hired a private eye to follow up. We gave the PI everything we had on the case, but she had no more luck than we did."

Max said, "So nobody knows if she was murdered, killed by an animal, fell off a cliff, had a heart attack or ran away. What if she was murdered? The killer has had almost a year to cover his or her tracks. A year to vanish."

"That's a big jump. Of course we looked at that possibility but found no evidence to support it. There's a lot of potential for accidents in the wilderness. My theory is that she fell off a cliff or into a river somewhere and died."

"You're probably right. But remember a few years ago, the two women murdered on a trail in the North Cascades? No one was ever caught. No suspect, no motive, no reason was ever found. Whoever did that got away with it. I often think of that and whether the killer has done it again somewhere else. It's rare that someone who'd do something like that doesn't do it again, eventually."

"True. But that single case doesn't indicate a pattern."

"You're right," said Max. "By the way, I should mention that I'm leaving on Monday to attend an advanced course on federal violent crime investigation. When I get back, I'd like to practice what I learned, so I'm interested in the Hampton case. It sounds challenging. If your agency doesn't mind, I'd like to look into this whenever I have free time."

Einar said, "Well now, that's fine with me. Might be good to have a fresh pair of eyes on it. Let me know if I can help. I'd like some closure on this, for the family and for myself."

CHAPTER 5 — MAY 5

"You gotta watch out on this stretch. I heard there's bandits and rapists! And gang bangers! They come out here from the cities to earn cred by robbing, raping and killing hikers!" The man's voice was strained as they trudged up a steep, hot section of Pacific Crest Trail. The heat made the trail ahead waver in the harsh sunlight.

Faith glanced back and said, "No reason to borrow trouble. Almost 500 miles now and I haven't had issues with anyone." Faith silently added, *except for you.* The tall young man with the trail name Slowpoke had attached himself to Faith the day before and like a remora, wouldn't let go.

Unlike a remora, he talked non-stop, his mind bouncing around like a water drop in a hot skillet. He talked about everything under the sun, from his lucrative banking job, which Faith was sure was a lie, to his rude neighbors to what a bitch his ex-girlfriend was. He complained about people treating him with disrespect, boasted of times when he got the best of people, described complete movie plots in excruciating detail, compared himself to Bruce Lee, and went on about his parents and how they'd mistreated him. The man could not, would not, shut up. Interspersed with the babble, he sucked on a vape pipe and blew out immense white clouds of sickening apple-cinnamon flavored vapor.

Faith thought she could outpace Slowpoke, given his trail name and the size of his pack and his belly, but he wouldn't let go.

"You're livin' in a delusional world," he gasped. "Women hiking alone are sittin' ducks and ya gotta watch your back all the time. I got your back, Faith! Don't you worry. I mean maybe you should worry, but not as much now that I'm with ya. Stop a sec, gotta show ya something."

Faith rolled her eyes and turned around. "What is it?"

Slowpoke made a show of looking up and down the trail, then reached into a belt bag and pulled out a small black pistol. "I got this in case I run into trouble." He waved the pistol around as he talked and the round, black muzzle swept across Faith's chest. Faith's right hand flashed out and snatched the gun away.

"Ow! What the hell are you doin'? That's my gun!"

Faith glared at him. "If you ever sweep me with that pistol again, I'll destroy it."

"What're you talking about? Why did you do that? What's the matter with you?"

"What's the matter is that you don't know what you're doing with that gun and you're going to hurt yourself or someone else. You never point a gun at anyone, ever, loaded or not, unless you're going to shoot them. Do you understand? You handled your loaded gun in a way that it was pointed right at me. I can't even begin to describe how incredibly stupid that was!"

"But it's not loaded!"

Faith held up the pistol and pointed to the top of the slide. "You think I'm an idiot? See that little red thingy sticking up behind the ejection port? Printed on top it says 'Loaded When Up'? On this model, that means the fucking pistol is loaded and ready to go." She turned the pistol in her hand. "At least the safety is on."

The man faced her, his chubby face mottled red under a floppy boonie hat. He was a couple of inches taller and a couple of dozen pounds heavier. He looked down and frowned. Unsure of his reaction, Faith braced herself. Slowpoke finally said, "I-I-I didn't know, Faith. I'm sorry. I really am. But Jesus, you don't have to freak out over it."

"Freak out? You could've killed me. You don't know what you're doing with that thing. It's more of a threat than any human or animal. Don't let me see that gun again. I've had enough of guns. And don't let any of that vapor reach my face." Faith handed him the pistol, turned and started hiking again. Anger gave her extra energy and she went faster. She heard Slowpoke trying to catch up, gasping in the hot air, still trying to talk.

"Faith, wait up . . . I won't get out the gun again, ever. Hey, is that where you got that long scar on your cheek? From a bullet? If so, I understand why you got so mad. Hey, maybe you can teach me about guns so I'm safer! My Uncle Clyde accidentally shot himself once. Blood everywhere! They had to amputate his leg. You shoulda seen the medical bill on that one! Don't get me started about insurance companies . . ."

Slowpoke—or as Faith now thought of him, The Remora—hiked with her the rest of the day, babbling continuously and puffing clouds of sickly vapor. At least he was being more considerate and blowing it downwind. Since The Remora didn't seem to require a response, Faith let her mind wander over the last several weeks.

The hike north from the Mexican border had been grueling. Despite all of her spring training, she found that the only true way to get in shape for the trail was to start hiking it. From the border north, the PCT wound through the arid, rocky, scrubby mountain ranges of southern California. The altitude gains and losses were sometimes severe, the heat intense, and the landscape was at times a blasted, desolate wasteland that reminded her too much of western Afghanistan. A couple of times she traveled over 20 miles without water and would hike at night to avoid severe dehydration. Most of the time, with the help of a smartphone app, she was able to find water caches and other sources near the trail. PCT support volunteers—"trail angels"—maintained caches at some critical points along the trail where there were long stretches between safe drinking sources.

The trail was chaotic, crisscrossed by roads, other trails, irrigation canals, power lines and highways. It ran through wide, desolate valleys, squiggled up grassy mountains covered in tall windmills, followed busy roads and highways for miles. In places it was difficult to find the trail due to people stealing PCT signs.

Despite the severity of the landscape, there were times when it displayed a barren beauty. At the end of a long day, Faith enjoyed relaxing in front of her tent, watching low light and hazy air paint the brushy hills in gold and then red before the sun winked out. In the cooling night, coyotes yipped and howled across the dark hills. An orange moon floated through a hazy sky sparsely dotted with dim stars.

Still, although the terrain had its charms, Faith was looking forward to getting into the Sierras. She yearned to see, smell and listen to the mountains, to wander in a landscape of conifer forests, creeks and rivers, waterfalls, snow and peaks. All of that was waiting for her a couple of hundred trail miles north.

Faith and Slowpoke camped that night at a spring, joining a small group of bearded young men who turned out to be veterans of Afghanistan and Iraq. They were on a mission similar to Faith's. As one of the men told her, "We all served together at one time or another, and we decided things weren't working out for us in the U. S. of A. Too much fuckin' crap to deal with, you know what I mean? So here we are, gettin' some breathin' room to figure things out."

Faith was happy to share their campfire and their stories. It felt like a weight was lifted as they talked effortlessly of their experiences overseas and at home, the struggle to re-adjust to what to them was no longer a normal life.

The Remora was silent at first, and puffed on his vape pipe until everyone told him to "put the fuckin' thing away" or to smoke it somewhere else. He opted to stay and put the pipe away. As the evening went on, he tried to insert himself into the conversation, struggling to find and relate similar experiences. The group was tolerant of his efforts and tried to make him feel included, but to Faith it was painfully obvious that Slowpoke was not one of them and should stop trying to pretend that he was.

When their small fire dwindled to glowing red coals and the air grew chill, the group broke up for the evening. Faith returned to her small red tent, crawled into the sleeping bag and fell asleep almost instantly.

Tiny beeps from her watch woke her at 4:30 a.m. She yawned, stretched and crawled out of the sleeping bag. Outside the tent, she stood and stretched again, shivering in the cool air. Thin clouds over the eastern horizon were turning red and gold as coyotes yipped in the distance.

Quiet and quick, Faith packed her gear and shouldered her pack. She meandered through the brush to the trail and paused, looking back at the camping area. Relieved to see no sign of movement from Slowpoke's tent, she turned and started down the trail. As Faith passed the nearby spring, a voice hailed her from the brush. She stopped and peered into the shadows to see one of the veterans, a red-haired man known as Ballistic, filtering water from a small, glimmering pool.

"You're headed out early," he said.

Faith nodded. "Sure, cooler now so it's a good time to start. When are you guys heading out?"

"I dunno. Peabody's got himself some bad blisters so we might hang out here for the day, let him heal up. Hey, where's your friend Slowpoke?"

Faith smiled and put a finger to her lips. Ballistic shook his head and said, "No, no, no. Please don't tell me you're dumping him on us. The guy is a shitbag, Faith."

"Sorry, but I've got to get away from him. He's driving me nuts. Don't worry, you'll be fine. You guys can take turns listening to him. Okay, gotta go now. See ya down the trail." Faith turned to leave and then turned back. "By the way, he has a gun. You might want to appropriate it for safety."

As Faith walked away, she heard Ballistic say, "Are you kiddin' me? Come on Faith, have a heart."

Faith smiled and kept walking, felt the blood flowing to her legs, the cool air in her lungs, in her ears the blessed silence of the dawn trail.

CHAPTER 6 — MAY 18

After a long, tiring day driving south on Highway 101, the man was relieved to be in a campsite at Harris Beach State Park, just outside of Brookings, Oregon. He relaxed in a chaise lounge next to his pickup and camper, enjoying a mellow evening on the coast. He felt the tension draining from his neck and shoulders. All the way down, it had been a day of low, rushing cloud, rain squalls and intermittent sunshine. Now the sky was clear and warm sunlight flooded the park. A light breeze blew in from the west, carrying that wonderful smell of the sea. The man heard gulls crying above the soothing soft roar of surf crashing on rocks a few hundred yards away. He popped open a can of Guinness and waited for the hissing and foaming to subside before taking a grateful sip.

Three cans later, he was feeling very relaxed. The sun hung above the horizon, shining directly in his face. He closed his eyes and lay back, remembering the long-distance Pacific Crest Trail hike so many years ago. What an adventure! And then he started thinking about the special woman that he'd met on the trail. His one and only true love, first seen rising naked from an alpine lake like some kind of wilderness Venus. This time he managed to stop himself. Nothing good would come of thinking about her. At least not yet. He always wound up feeling bad so it was better to drop it. Think about other things, like how many PCT hikers were going to enjoy his food this year and what a great summer it'd be. He started going over the logistics in his head and that helped him relax.

There were many stops to make as the main wave of PCT through-hikers headed north. He tried to position his kitchen trailer at trail/road junctions, places where it would feed the most people. There were so many things to consider such as weather, availability of food, how much food to have on hand at any given moment, where other trail angels could lend a hand, where other food trailers were positioned. And then there were road conditions and special use permits. Making sure he had enough food available at the right times was the biggest challenge. Although the trailer had two freezers and a large refrigerator, he could only store so much food. That's one reason why it made sense to supplement his supply from the field, to live off the land.

Another Guinness had him nodding off. A cool breeze woke him, made him shiver. He stood up slowly and gathered the empty Guinness cans, put them into a plastic grocery bag he'd tied to the chair. *Leave no trace.* The chant ran through his mind: *leave no trace, leave no trace . . . leave no fucking trace.* He giggled and wasn't sure why, but it made him laugh. Leaving no trace was what it was all about, wasn't it?

He took some deep breaths and tried to clear his head. No more Guinness for him! There was plenty of driving again tomorrow, so he better climb into the camper and get some sleep. Still many miles to go to his first PCT stop of the season, Tuolumne Meadows in Yosemite National Park. Maybe he'd see her there, or the one that would be just like her. It would be a grand reunion and a great way to start the season.

The man walked back to the large trailer that was hitched to his pickup. He opened the trailer's rear door and stepped into the darkness of the kitchen. A flick of a wall switch and the place lit up. Swaying slightly, he leaned against a polished stainless steel refrigerator and looked around. The space looked small now. When the kitchen is fully deployed, some of the components slide outward to create more space. The man grinned as he remembered some of the good times in the kitchen. Special times with special women. His women. He felt himself getting hard and chuckled. Another look around and he turned out the light, stepped out of the trailer, closed and locked the door.

He stumbled to the pickup truck and stopped at the camper's steps to look around. His eyes were moist, watering like crazy. He wiped them on a sleeve and looked toward the sea. The sun had disappeared and the western horizon glowed a wondrous deep gold, the last of the light fading up into blue darkness.

CHAPTER 7 — MAY 30

Faith paused to catch her breath. It was a refreshingly cool morning but the sun on her back was hot. A few mosquitoes whined around her head. She untied her hair and let it fall around her face to fend off the insects. Standing on a large patch of old winter snow, she slowly turned in a circle. The view from Donohue Pass was amazing; 360 degrees of snow-streaked peaks and deep valleys.

The Sierras were everything John Muir said they were in his book, *My First Summer in the Sierras*. He called the Sierra Nevada "the Range of Light" and Faith had to agree. The high altitude, deep blue sky, sunshine, sparkling lakes, patchy snow and bare white granite gave the high mountain landscape a pristine, otherworldly glow.

She compared the scene around her to that at the start of her journey and felt a great sense of relief to have all that behind her, to be in the wild mountains that had inspired Muir to write with such eloquence and enthusiasm. Now, after 900 miles and seven weeks of hiking, she felt strong and capable, happy to be hiking through sweet smelling fir forests and alpine meadows, along clear rivers and beside jewel lakes. The abundance of water was like a miracle.

The crowd that she'd started with had thinned, both by distance and attrition. Though not social by nature, Faith at times fell in with groups of other hikers, sharing meals and campfires, stories of their lives, plans for the rest of the long journey and beyond. She never said much about her own history. She didn't want to reveal it to people who she felt wouldn't understand. She was tired of hearing people say, "Thank you for your service" when they had no idea what it had been like, and when they didn't seem to care.

Where she had cell phone reception, Faith called her parents and updated them on the journey, but as time went on, she found those conversations out of sync with her wilderness experience. As a substitute, she texted when she checked in. Although there was a solar charger on top of her pack, she kept the cell phone off most of the time. She was tired of the mountain peace being shattered by someone's phone ringing, pinging and blaring music in a campsite or along the trail. It happened too often.

So far the weather had been exceptional, with occasional afternoon thunderstorms and rain. In places, the clouds of whining, whirring, buzzing mosquitoes and flies forced Faith to wear a net over her head. Fortunately they weren't very numerous at windy, snowy Donohue Pass, so she removed her pack and took a break on a rocky ledge. It overlooked a wide, U-shaped valley that curved to the north. In the middle of the valley, a river wound through rocky meadows and groups of trees. The valley was Lyell Canyon and it would lead her to Tuolumne Meadows, where she'd pick up a resupply package and stop for the night. After a quick snack, Faith hoisted her pack and returned to the PCT. She stopped to take a photo of a wooden sign bolted on a post next to the trail. It told hikers they were entering Yosemite National Park on the John Muir/Pacific Crest Trail. She put her camera in a belt pouch and began the descent into Lyell Canyon.

A couple of hours later Faith encountered a problem, and its trail name was Duster. She'd walked off trail, through a flowery meadow for a hundred yards and stopped along a creek to wash her extra change of t-shirt, bra, underwear and socks. The water was ice cold and she had to pause at times to let the sun warm her fingers. She thought she was far enough away from the trail to avoid people, but Duster found her.

He was of medium height and build, with long, stringy dark hair and a short scraggly beard. Despite the warm sun, he was wearing a long tan coat that trailed behind him. When she first saw him, he was stumbling toward her through the flowers, singing an aimless song. That song faded into silence when he spotted her at the creek. He paused and stared at her for a moment, his face blank. He didn't wave or say anything. Without acknowledging him, Faith looked away. Most people would've gotten the message.

She heard him approach and say, "Hello there!" in a deep voice. Faith glanced up and saw that the young man had a big smile on his bearded face. "I see here beauty amongst beauty. That would be you, fair one! A sight for sore eyes!"

Faith gave him a thin smile and went back to washing her underwear. Still not getting the message, he took off his backpack and squatted in the flowers across the small creek from her. He stared at her hands as she wrung out her underwear in the icy water.

"My name's Duster. They call me that because of my coat. It's a duster coat, ya know. So, I started out at the border back in April. What about you?"

Without looking up, Faith said, "Good for you. I hope you continue to have a great trip."

Duster said, "So what's your trail name? Are you doin' the whole trail?"

Faith draped her underwear over a sun-warmed rock and without looking at him answered, "Don't have a trail name and don't want one."

"No trail name? That ain't right! A beautiful girl like you hiking the Crest Trail needs a trail name!"

Faith said nothing. She looked up to see Duster staring at her underwear. She felt her irritation turning into anger.

Duster's eyes darted to her face and said, "You know, to be honest, you shouldn't wash your underwear in the streams like this. It's really whack. It can cause pollution. I mean, I ain't sayin' your underwear is dirty or anything, but you know? It's just uncool."

"Okay," she said, now looking directly at him. "Don't you have some miles to cover before the day is done?"

"Naw, I'm gonna take a break day at the Meadows. We're almost there, you know. Get me a resupply and a shower if they got one, some good food. Maybe we could camp together there, if you're traveling by yourself?"

"I'm meeting my boyfriend there and he's joining me on the trail after that, so no thanks."

Duster grinned. "Boyfriend eh? I saw that movie, too, ya know? *Wild*? Where Reese Witherspoon tells that old guy that her boyfriend is nearby? Ha ha! But if it's true, I shoulda known. All the good ones are taken." He stood up and sighed. "Well, it was nice seeing you and maybe we meet again down the trail. I sure hope so. Maybe you'll have a good trail name by then. Bye now!" He stood, shouldered his pack and turned away, but paused and turned back, a silly grin on his face. "You know," he said. "If you don't have a trail name next time I see you, I'll give you one. So you better come up with something."

Faith glared at him and said, "Go away."

Duster's smile faltered and he stood uncertainly for a moment before turning and walking away. She watched him as he headed back to the trail, coat billowing. He resumed his aimless singing. She hoped she wouldn't see him again. The way he stared at her underwear was creepy and his manner was false. She hoped he wouldn't become a problem, but if he did, she knew how to deal with him. When her clothes were dry, Faith packed up, waded through the lush meadow and back to the trail where she resumed the day's hike to Tuolumne Meadows.

By noon, Faith had set up her tiny red tent in a campsite at the Tuolumne Meadows Backpacker Campground. She went to the Tuolumne Meadows Store and Tuolumne Meadows Post Office for lunch and supplies. It appeared that everything there had the name 'Tuolumne Meadows' tacked onto it. The store/bar/grill/post office was an odd structure, a cross between a building and a tent, white canvas over a wooden frame. Weaving among the crowds inside, Faith said hi to several hikers she'd met along the way. Lunch was an expensive veggie burrito and a cold Coke, eaten at a rickety picnic table in the shade of pine trees.

After eating, she walked to the post office portion of the tent building. The small space was crowded with other hikers on the same mission. The sour, acrid smell of so many unwashed people crowded into a small, hot space was almost too much to bear. Most people made this stop first, eager to get their supplies. Behind the counter there were shelves crammed with taped packages of various sizes. After a long, odiferous wait in line, Faith picked up her pre-shipped food package from a harried, weary clerk.

Emerging from the tent building, she took a deep breath of the pine-scented air. Package in hand, she walked back to the campground and stashed the box in her tent. Next on her agenda was the short walk to the Yosemite National Park Visitor's Center where she got an update on trail conditions and took in some of the displays on local history and nature. After that, she wanted to get a shower, but learned that the nearest facility was almost 20 miles away in Yosemite Valley. A dip in a creek sometime soon would have to do. By late afternoon, Faith was walking back to the campground. Near the store, she was considering dinner from the bar and grill when a deep voice startled her from close behind.

"Hey, there's the trail beauty!"

Without thinking, she spun around with fists clenched and nearly decked Duster. He stumbled backward with eyes wide and hands up. "Girl, wha's up with you? Just sayin' hi."

Faith lowered her fists and said, "You shouldn't sneak up behind people."

Duster looked hurt. "I wasn't sneakin'. I just wanted to say hi, so here I am sayin' hi! Geez, you need to relax, Beauty! Hey, you up at the campground? Hooked up with your boyfriend yet?"

Faith sighed and said, "Look, Dusty—"

"Duster! The name's Duster. That's my PCT trail name. You got one yet? A trail name, I mean."

"Okay. Good. Duster, what I'm doing and what my name is, is really none of your business. I'm moving on now, and you're going somewhere too. Somewhere else, right?"

Duster took a step back and put his hands up, palms out. "Hey, Beauty, dudette, don't get all jammed up. I didn't mean to harass. You got some serious head shit; I can see that. If you need to talk sometime, Duster will listen. In the meantime, I'll just head over to the grill for some eats. Hey you know that TGI Monday's food trailer, with the free food? It's setting up for breakfast tomorrow. You should maybe try it out. Pancakes, omelets, sausages, hash browns. Good shit! Check it out. We could have breakfast together. That is, if your imaginary boyfriend doesn't show up."

Faith didn't say a word. She stared at him with narrowed eyes. Duster's eyes widened and he took another step back, started to say something and turned around. He hurried away toward the canvas building, long coat flapping. Faith watched him for a moment, trying to determine the long-term threat level he posed. She saw him pause by a tree 20 yards away and turn back to look at her. He appeared to stare at her, his shadowed face unreadable. Faith turned and walked away in the opposite direction. She decided the threat level was Moderate for the time being.

CHAPTER 8 — MAY 30-31

After retrieving a down jacket from her tent, Faith wandered back toward the Tuolumne Meadows store. The sun was low in the west and the evening air was turning chilly. She greeted a few hikers that she vaguely knew and looked around for a place to eat. Not wanting a repeat of the burrito, she asked a passing park ranger where to go for some good food.

The ranger paused and smiled. She was a tall, angular blonde woman in Park Service uniform, her narrow face dwarfed by the broad-brimmed Park Service campaign hat. "Place to eat?" said the ranger. "Well, you're in luck. There's a couple of food trailers set up nearby. You got The Chef's trailer up by the highway, but he just got in and isn't set up yet. And then there's Burger Boy's, which"—she turned and pointed into the nearby trees—"is right down there in a clearing behind the gas station. I can recommend Burger Boy. Best burgers around, maybe the best burgers anywhere!"

Faith thanked her and walked in the indicated direction. After a couple of minutes of moving through a shadowed pine forest, she entered a large clearing. Parked sedans and SUVs ringed the edges and in the middle was a meadow. Several kids were throwing a Frisbee across the grassy expanse and a barking dog chased it. Off to her right was the Burger Boy food trailer, a flashy, well-lit unit surrounded by several tall tables. Behind it, a generator murmured. There was a crowd of hikers standing at the tables eating, talking and laughing. More hikers were lined up at the trailer's serving window, white paper plates in hand. At the window a tall, lean, white-haired man was serving up food. A sign over the window stated in all caps, "WELCOME PCT HIKERS! YOUR FEAST AWAITS YOU! DONATIONS APPRECIATED".

Faith shuffled into line, mouth watering as she smelled the sizzling hamburger meat. The line passed a long, low table covered in stacks of paper plates and cups, boxes of plastic cutlery, a couple of coolers labeled "Water" and "Lemonade", stacks of napkins weighted with small rocks, a cardboard box filled with small bags of potato chips, and at the end of it all, a container labeled "Donations".

As Faith gathered up some of the items, someone bumped into her from behind and she felt a brief touch of fingers on her left buttock. She spun around to see a tall, gaunt, bearded young man wearing an embarrassed look on his face. "Sorry about that, ma'am!" His prominent Adam's apple bounced as he talked. "Too eager to get to the food, I guess. I'm real sorry."

Faith gave him a cool look and said, "Okay then. Just take it easy. The line will get there."

The man's head bobbed up and down. "Yep. I'm so wicked hungry right now I could eat a whole cow! Been averaging maybe thirty miles a day now. What about you?"

Faith nodded. The man looked and sounded familiar. She'd seen him somewhere before and tried to remember.

"That's great! Hey, my name is Slowpoke!" He stuck out his right hand. Faith hesitated a moment and then shook his hand. She barely recognized her talkative former companion. He'd grown a beard and lost a lot of weight. She thought it strange that he didn't recognize her.

Slowpoke held onto her hand as he said, "Ya know, you look real familiar. I've seen you before on the trail. Your name's Faith, right?"

Faith pulled her hand free and said, "You got it. We hiked together for a few days down south, several weeks ago." She paused and lowered her voice, said, "Hey, when you bumped into me, I could've sworn you groped my butt. Did you do that, Slowpoke?"

He drew back and his face turned brick red. "No! No way! I would never do something like that. My mom taught me to respect women and I do. It was an accident, I swear!"

Faith stared at him a moment and then said, "Okay, I'll give you the benefit of the doubt."

Slowpoke's face relaxed a bit and the redness faded. He was silent as the line of hungry hikers shuffled along. Eventually Faith was sidestepping alongside the serving window, holding up a plate. Above her, the white-haired man grinned and slid a giant hamburger onto it. He said, "You want fries with that?" and laughed.

Faith smiled back and said, "Sure. How many times a day do you say that line?"

"Not that many. I reserve that for only the prettiest hikers!"

"Uh, thanks, I guess."

"Here, have some more fries. You want more food, come on back. Don't be shy, I've got plenty."

Faith was trying not to drool as she carefully carried the floppy plate and paper cup of lemonade to a nearby table. She was irritated to see Slowpoke walk up and set his plate and cup down opposite her. Behind him, the sun was almost down, the tops of the pines glowing red. A breeze from Slowpoke's direction brought her the faint aroma of apple-cinnamon. She was thankful he wasn't vaping at the moment.

Cheeks bulging with food, Slowpoke said, "Again, I'm really sorry about that. Honestly, I just bumped into you. It wasn't on purpose. I know that someone as pretty as you probably gets hassled by jerks a lot. Well, you know I'm not a jerk."

Her own mouth full of burger, Faith mumbled, "Okay, so don't worry about it. Thanks for the compliment."

"Sure, well, you're as pretty as a sunrise, Faith." In the ensuing awkwardness, Slowpoke finally said, "I'm surprised to see you again, thought you'd be way ahead of me now. I took a wrong turn and got into some bad country. Lots of snow and hard to find the trail. I got lost for a week or so and ran out of food, lost a lot of weight fast! I finally came down out of the mountains and found a town, got stocked up and found a ride back to the trail. Like I said, been doin' around 30 miles a day to make up for lost time. I'm gonna have to slow down. That's too many miles!

"Hey, you know I missed you after you lit out that morning. Those guys that were camped there? They weren't all that nice. One of 'em took my gun. Can you believe it?" He looked up at Faith. "How did they even know I had one? Anyway, he took it and said I'd have it back when I was ready to move on. Turns out those guys were staying there for a day or two. So I stayed with 'em, but they weren't happy about it. Veterans are weird people, you know? I mean, sorry to say it, but they are. Think they're better than the rest of us or something? I dunno what. Combat got 'em messed up, I guess. What do they call it? Post trauma brain damage or something? They wouldn't talk to me and finally I'd had enough being treated that way, so I asked for my gun back and said I was leaving. The fuckers wouldn't give it back! Can you believe that shit? I said that gun is worth four hundred bucks . . ."

Slowpoke went on about the pistol and his conflict with the group of vets. Faith kept eating and tried to tune him out. Finally she put up a hand and said, "Wait! Stop!"

Slowpoke stopped, a fried potato wedge hanging out of his mouth.

"Slowpoke, quit dissin' vets. You know I'm a vet, right?"

"Oh, okay, but you're a girl vet. That's different. I mean, you never saw combat, right? Unless maybe that's where you got that scar on your face? I dunno. I guess it's not polite to comment on something like that."

Faith sighed and wadded up a grease-stained napkin, put it and an empty paper cup on her plate. "Slowpoke, your problem is that you don't know when to keep quiet. Learn to listen, okay? Learn to be quiet."

Slowpoke was quiet. He gave her a hurt look and gulped down the fry. Faith said, "Did you ever get your gun back?"

Slowpoke frowned and shook his head. "Nope. Fuckers took it apart and threw the pieces a long ways into the brush. One of 'em took my address and said they'd send me four hundred bucks. Yeah, right. I wished I could've called the cops on 'em. No cops on the trail though, right? At least I've never seen any. Kind of makes it lawless out here, so–
–hey, where you goin'?"

Faith had gathered up her litter and started to walk away. She said, "Sorry, got to go. Take it easy, Slowpoke. Remember what I said, less talking, more listening. Have a great trip."

She walked over to a dumpster, lifted a floppy rubber hatch and threw the plate, cup and plastic ware in. She felt Slowpoke watching her as she strode away across the meadow and back into the shadowy trees.

Her rifle is useless. It won't fire, but she carries it and the ammo for it anyway, running and gasping in the eerie brown half-light. Her load must weigh at least eighty pounds, straining her back and knees. Despite the semi-darkness, it's hotter than hell and she's soaked in sweat. Running and sometimes stumbling through the scrubby desert, she doesn't dare look back. She doesn't have to. She knows that her pursuers are gaining on her. She can hear them, can feel the psychic pressure of their hatred. She hears rocks being knocked loose and the occasional bullet rips past her, followed by the pop of a gunshot.

The landscape changes and now she's running through a maze of small barren hills, following a serpentine wadi. Ahead, hazy in the distance, is a massive mountain topped with ice and snow, the lower slopes clothed in forest. The mountain is luminous in bright sunlight. It means salvation if she can get there ahead of her pursuers. She pushes harder. Obstacles begin appearing in her path. She dodges around shapeless lumps of torn flesh and gore, around weapons lying in the sand. The bloody lumps were scattered at first, but as she continues, the lumps multiply and grow larger. They resolve themselves into horrific forms. Here a torn arm clothed in ragged camo, there a bent, shredded leg with a boot on the end. She stumbles past a Kevlar brain bucket and makes the mistake of looking into it. Horrified, she tells herself not to look anymore. Just run, keep moving, don't look down, don't look back. Run!

The body parts grow larger. Torsos, legs, arms, heads began to assemble themselves into complete, but not whole, bodies. It's impossible to ignore them now. Zombie soldiers, shredded and bloody, rise up and block her way. She screams at them to let her go, pushes them out of the way. There're more pops behind her and she hears bullets smacking into body armor and decayed flesh. Ahead is a wall of dead soldiers, their arms raised and pointing at her. The mountain, her salvation, is farther away than ever. She turns to see the Taliban fighters closing in. She raises her useless rifle, then drops it. She grasps a grenade, pulls out the pin. A dead man's switch. She'll take a few bastards with her.

Faith woke up in her sleeping bag, heart pounding, soaked in sweat. Eyes open wide, she gasped for air and listened, heard only the soothing whisper of a distant waterfall. She sat up and put her hands to her chest, breathed, looked around the dark tent, told herself there were no zombies, no Taliban. She was in the mountains, in the USA, safe and sound. As her breathing slowed and became more even, she focused on the smells of fir and pine trees, mixed with the odors of sunscreen and her sweat.

It was just the dream, just the same damn nightmare putting in an encore performance. Fortunately the nightmare's frequency was diminishing. The reality of the trail and the mountains was breaking down the memories and feelings into manageable pieces, and in the process diluting the nightmares.

Despite that knowledge, the aftereffects of the dream lingered, leaving Faith tossing and turning. Eventually she managed to drift off, but all too soon her stomach started convulsing, shattering sleep. She sat up and swore. It was time to sprint to the rest room. The expensive burrito must've been toxic. It certainly had tasted that way. Or maybe it was the Burger Boy's food?

By first light, after several sprints to the toilet, Faith was ready to pack up and leave. She crawled out of her tent, tattered and exhausted, her limbs heavy. She shivered in the cool morning air, breathed in the pine scent. Grey jays hopped and chirped in the branches overhead. An obese chipmunk squatted on the ground nearby, beady black eyes watching intently for any dropped tidbits.

Faith slowly packed up sleeping bag and tent, retrieved her food from a nearby bear-proof container, arranged everything in and on her pack. The rising sun was painting the treetops with gold as she shouldered her load and picked up the empty cardboard box her supplies had come in. People in the sites around her were stirring, voices murmuring. She dumped the box in a recycling bin and left the campground. She started out slowly to warm up and felt the blood flow into her tired limbs. The pack was heavy again and she tightened the hip belt to take the strain off her shoulders. Sun at her back, she walked west on the dusty shoulder of Highway 120, the Tioga Road, toward the turnoff onto National Parks Road.

At the junction, there was a long turnout where a small crowd was gathered around a large green pickup truck and a gold and white food trailer parked there. Up ahead, a small sandwich board sign pointed toward the trailer with the words "The Chef's Awesome Free Eats!" Faith smiled. She'd heard of the trail angel and chef Joshua Monday and decided that in at least one way, Duster was right about a good breakfast. Last night's purge had left her feeling empty and hungry. An omelet would be the perfect way to start the day. As she approached the group, she noticed a grinning Slowpoke standing at one of the tall tables, talking to a short red-haired woman. And there was Duster in his stupid long coat, carrying a tray loaded with food to another table.

Faith stopped. She didn't want to risk The Remora attaching himself to her again. As for Duster, the less she saw of him, the better. She walked by, turning right to plod up a dusty road toward the PCT trailhead. Breakfast would be a granola bar somewhere a short distance up the trail. Maybe she'd have another shot at the Chef's food trailer somewhere farther up state.

A few early hikers were ahead of her, striding up the road. She knew that some of them were racing north, challenging themselves to do as many miles per day as possible. She didn't understand what the hurry was, but figured to each their own. Despite the bad dreams and lack of sleep, she felt her heart lift as she headed back into the wilderness of the high country, heading north and following in her sister's ghostly footsteps. North under the dark blue mountain sky.

CHAPTER 9 — JUNE 9

It was early afternoon and distant thunder pounded the hot, humid air. Billowing clouds were crowding out the blue, their summits blindingly bright and their dark undersides heavy with the promise of rain. Looking through a windshield speckled with dead bugs, he saw a solitary young woman, bent forward under a large red backpack. She was walking slowly east on the shoulder of the Donner Pass Road near Soda Springs. She was medium height and slender, wearing khaki shorts and a light, long-sleeved turquoise shirt. Her long black hair was tied in a ponytail and threaded through the rear loop of a white baseball cap. As he slowed and rolled up alongside her, he could see sweat running down her tanned face, her eyes hidden behind dark sunglasses. She reminded him so much of someone else, someone special to him.

Despite the clattering of his truck's diesel engine, she didn't look up. She must be deep in thought. Maybe she was mulling over how many miles she should do, when and where she should camp. Maybe she was trying to make a plan for the rest of the day. He could help her with that.

She still wouldn't look up so he pushed the button that lowered the truck's passenger side window. He leaned toward it and said, "Hey, you need a ride to the PCT?"

The woman ignored him. She kept her head down and walked on. He kept pace with her, tires popping on the rough pavement, engine rattling. He tried to make his voice friendly and reassuring as he said, "Hey, it's okay! I was just asking if you needed a ride. Can I drop you off at the PCT? It'll save you some time and effort. I've hiked the trail too, so I know a ride might be welcome. You must've just picked up supplies in Soda Springs, am I right? And your pack is probably feeling pretty heavy again? And it's sure hot out. So hop on in, and I'll drop you off at the PCT junction."

The woman finally looked over her shoulder, down the side of the big truck to the attached trailer. Her face lit up in a smile.

She looked up at the man and said, "Sure! Thanks!"

CHAPTER 10 — JUNE 12-13

The intense pain came in waves, pulsing through her innards. Curled up in the sleeping bag, Faith groaned and grit her teeth as her writhing guts made horrific noises. She wondered if passing hikers would hear that over the rumbling roar of the Middle Fork Feather River. It rushed by a few yards below her campsite.

She didn't know what was causing the pain. It was similar to, but much worse than, the episode she'd experienced at Tuolumne Meadows. She was sure that had been caused by the greasy burrito, and maybe food was the cause this time too. Earlier the previous day, she'd eaten at another food trailer parked at the La Porte Road crossing. Pete's Eats charged five bucks for all you can eat, which wasn't a bad deal for hungry hikers. She took on the challenge and ate all she could. Her meal included a heap of scrambled eggs with bacon, a pile of hash browns, a huge Danish, sausages, a stack of pancakes with syrup and a small yogurt. She might've overdone it.

After hiking a few miles following the massive breakfast, the pain started building. It hit her hard in the afternoon, just as she was approaching a large iron footbridge over the Feather River. After crossing, she'd struggled up the trail a few hundred yards, bent over from the pain. Luckily, there was a campsite in the forest, not far below the trail. The pain had gotten worse as she struggled to set up her tent and hang her food. She barely managed to fill her water filter bag at the river, haul it back to camp and hang it from a tree branch. After that, she'd sought refuge in the tent and endured a sleepless night with several desperate and explosive trips into the trees behind camp. All she could do now was lie in the warm tent and watch sun patches move slowly across the taut nylon ceiling. Lie there and hope the pain kept fading.

The illness meant a day without her usual 25 miles. She wasn't on a tight schedule, but wanted to stick as close to her plans as possible since she was due to meet Jenks and Julia at Crater Lake on July 11. Still curled on her side, she pulled out the iPhone, turned it on and brought up the calculator app. After tapping in the number of days before July 11 and the distance to Crater Lake, she figured she had time to make up the lost miles. That was, if she was recovered by the evening and was able to get some sleep before returning to the trail the next day.

Not only was she concerned about falling behind, but also apprehensive about staying in one place so long, confined to her tent. The apprehension was due to recent incidents that had turned into an apparent pattern of harassment.

The first incident occurred a day or two north of Tuolumne Meadows. She got up in the morning after a night rain and noticed fresh boot tracks in the sandy soil around her tent. The tracks were only a couple of hours old and circled her tent, then went to the tree where her food bag was hanging and then went back to the trail. From there, the tracks had been covered by the boot prints of early hikers. She used her cell phone to take photos of the prints for future reference.

Two nights after that, someone had come into her camp and moved her food bag. It was near four in the morning when a noise awakened her. She wasn't sure what it was so she slowly exited her sleeping bag and grabbed a headlamp and can of bear spray. As fast as she could, she unzipped the tent fly and crawled halfway out of the tent. She turned on her headlamp and swept the bright blue beam around the campsite's perimeter. Movement caught her eye and she turned the light back to it. There was her food sack, swinging gently in the still, cool air. She was shocked to see it hanging from a different tree than the one she'd used.

Angry and afraid, Faith had searched the surrounding area with the light and then went over the ground to look for tracks or any other clues. There was nothing. It was already getting light, so she put on more clothing, along with a down coat, and made a wider search. Still nothing. There were no other hiker camps nearby and no sign of tracks. She packed up camp and moved on. When it was light enough, she'd stopped and pulled all of her food from the pack. She inspected everything to see if someone had tampered with it. Any loose or accessible food she wrote off as a loss and only ate food that was still sealed. It was possible that whoever was harassing her was also trying to poison her.

A couple of nights later, there was a third incident when someone made growling noises outside her tent late at night. Faith could tell it was a human and most likely a man. As she'd done during the previous incident, she burst out of the tent with headlamp and bear spray at the ready. Someone or something crashed through the woods away from camp. Using her light, she saw vague tracks here and there. They weren't made by boots and she later figured out that whoever was there had worn moccasins. She tried to remember if she'd seen anyone on the trail wearing moccasins, but recalled only one person, an older woman many miles and several weeks ago.

Who was harassing her, and why? Faith thought of two possibilities: Duster and Slowpoke. Both men, each in their own way, were strange and suspicious. Duster had obviously been putting on an act, pretending to be friendly and harmless when his actions painted a more disturbing picture of a man calculating and selfish, wanting something from Faith that she wasn't going to give. She considered that he might be a sociopath and could see him as the one behind the harassment, and willing to take things further if he could get away with it.

Slowpoke seemed more harmless, but also interested in Faith. She wanted nothing to do with him for a variety of reasons. Faith was no psychologist but experience had taught her how to read people. She saw Slowpoke as a man filled with resentment, jealousy, regret and longing; a man unpredictable, slightly paranoid and at times hard to read. She could see him as the harasser, but didn't imagine him going much past that.

Faith reminded herself not to get locked into assumptions. That lesson had been drummed into her head during Special Forces training and subsequent experiences in the field. Consider all options, all possibilities and evaluate as best as you can, and then be ready to re-evaluate as information and situations changed. With that in mind, her harasser could be someone, man or woman, unknown to her. Someone who got their thrills from random attacks on hikers. It could be another PCT hiker, or someone who lurked along this stretch of trail. It could be anyone, really. Faith had to be alert and observant, look for clues and try to think ahead.

She was angry with whoever was playing tricks on her. Angry that her trip now had an element of stress and threat to it.

The grinding pain diminished throughout the long, hot, boring day. By noon Faith was able to creep down to the river and splash cool water on her face. She sat on a boulder for a while with closed eyes, soaking up the warm sunlight, before returning to her tent for a series of short naps that lasted into the evening. Above her camp that afternoon, the trail was busy with thumping boots and the occasional conversations of hikers.

Just before dark Faith fired up her small stove and boiled water for a cup of chicken noodle soup. The soup stayed down but brought back some of the pain, so that was all she ate. In the half-light of late evening, she went back to the rocky shores of the river to filter water. As she returned to camp, she sensed something wasn't right. She stopped, water bag in hand, and looked over the site. There was no movement and everything seemed normal. Her tent looked undisturbed. The food bag hung motionless below the tree she'd chosen. Her pack and stove were in the same place. And then she smelled it.

A slight shift in the evening breeze brought her the stench of shit. She clicked on her light and swept the area around camp. And there it was, a pile of overlapping slimy brown turds right next to the tent. Faith winced at the sight and looked up. It was almost dark, so she swept her light into the woods. There was no movement but she thought she heard, over the noise of the river, faint laughter.

She started in the direction of the laughter, but changed her mind. It was too spooky, too strange. Maybe whoever it was wanted her to come after them. Maybe it was an ambush. She returned to the tent and pulled a plastic poop trowel from her pack. A few feet away, at the edge of the campsite, she used the trowel to dig a hole about a foot deep and half a foot wide. It was tough due to a lot of tiny roots, but she jabbed her way through them. Using a couple of sticks, she rolled the turds to the hole and pushed them in. The smell was awful and she held her breath as much as possible. Part of the awfulness was a faint sickening sweet odor of apple and cinnamon. In Faith's mind, that implicated Slowpoke. She didn't find it hard to believe. She concluded the turd roundup by scooping dirt into the hole and patting it down.

By then it was full dark and stars sparkled through the black trees. On consideration, Faith decided there was no way she would stay in that campsite. She was still weak from her illness and lack of food, but that didn't stop her from packing up. She'd hiked at night a few times at the start of her trip and she could sure do it again. There was no moon, just starlight, but she had her headlamp. Anything was better than staying there.

It took 20 minutes to take down and pack up camp. She ate a granola bar and waited a moment for any ill effects, but the bar tasted good and there was no pain. She shouldered her pack and stepped up to the PCT, hesitated a moment and then resumed her journey. She didn't need a headlamp yet. The dusty trail was visible in the starlight, a pale path through the dark forest. She hiked carefully, not in a hurry, happy to be leaving her violated camp.

Faith asked herself what kind of person does something like that, dropping a load in someone's camp, and why? The only answer she came up with was mental illness and the only near-rational reason to do it was to inspire fear, disgust and uncertainty. In short, it was a form of what the military called tactical PSYOP, or Psychological Operations. She'd seen it used in Afghanistan. Hell, she'd participated in it. It was designed to dismay, intimidate and otherwise confuse an enemy.

Faith wondered how she could be seen as anyone's enemy. Maybe rejection would inspire such a reaction in the likes of Slowpoke or Duster? If so, she would have to somehow get on top of the situation. As of yet, she didn't know how. She couldn't turn to law enforcement because there really wasn't any effective presence in the wilderness. She'd seen a few wilderness rangers and a backcountry cop along the way but they were few and far between. And what would she tell a cop if she came across one? That she suspected someone was harassing her, but she wasn't sure who, or where, they were? She had no proof of a crime, and belatedly thought that she should've taken a photo of the turds. That would've been some kind of evidence. There was always DNA too, but that idea made her shudder.

Twenty minutes after leaving camp, Faith's musings were interrupted by a distant scream. She stopped to listen.

There it was again, somewhere behind her, down in the river valley. Was it a cougar? No, it sounded human and agonized. Another scream, long and drawn out, ended suddenly and there was silence. She waited another couple of minutes, but there was only silence and the soft sound of the distant river. It likely was her persecutor, trying to scare her some more. Well, that was good. It meant that he thought she was still in camp and now the joke was on him.

Faith muttered, “Hasta la vista, motherfucker,” and turned to continue her journey.

CHAPTER 11 — JUNE 13

Joey wiped his knife on the man's pant leg and stood up. Turning the blade in the dim light, he didn't see any more blood, but obviously would have to wash the knife in the river. No problem there since that was where the dead man was going. Headin' on a little float trip down the river, maybe all the way to the Pacific Ocean. That would work for Joey. The farther away, the better.

Joey was surprised to feel such a rush. Killing the man had been so easy, and gratifying in ways different than killing a defenseless woman. Joey liked the *mano a mano* aspect even though it hadn't been much of a fight. The man was surprised when Joey showed up in the dark forest near the woman's camp.

Joey had observed him over several days as he stalked and harassed the woman, and that simply wouldn't do. She was meant for another, not some stupid rube with a twisted crush on her. And now, because of the harassment, she was on the alert. That might make it harder, when the time came, to take her.

Joey hadn't intended to kill the guy; just scare him off. But something happened when he confronted the man and he lost it, or as the Mentor might say, he found it. Such a feeling of power! And when the man screamed, Joey felt elated. Such a loud scream it was, full of surprise, fear and despair. Joey didn't blame him. Seeing a long knife buried in your chest will do that.

Well, enough reminiscing. The killer grabbed the man's legs and started dragging him through the forest, toward the river. It was dark, but Joey didn't want to risk a light. He'd seen the woman pack and head up the trail, but there could be other people in the area. As he struggled to pull the dead weight, Joey thought that next time, he'd try to lure his victim to where they'd be disposed of, instead of hauling dead weight. Live and learn!

The river wasn't cold. Joey waded toward the middle, his feet stumbling and slipping off round boulders, one hand hanging onto a leg. The current was moderate but still made it difficult to stand up. When he reached the swiftest part of the river and was struggling to stay upright, he let the body go. The current swept it away into darkness. Joey slipped and fell back into the water. His arms wind milled and splashed and for a moment he thought he'd join the dead man's journey. He reached out and grabbed the end of a log and used it to help him stand up. He worked his way up the log to shore, spitting water from his face and cursing.

Standing on the rocky shore, he started shivering. He could catch up with the girl later. It was time to build a fire and get dry, then get some sleep.

CHAPTER 12 — JUNE 29

It was almost July and Faith was following the Pacific Crest Trail north along the mountain ridges of northern California. There were switchbacks beyond counting, long descents and then long ascents, roiling rivers, placid lakes, the flash and rumble of thunderstorms in the afternoons, cleansing rains, wet brush, slippery snowfields, dark forests, shining volcanic peaks, busy and malodorous highway crossings.

To Faith, it was all good medicine. She felt incredibly well most of the time. The nightmares were almost gone. She no longer had the feeling that she was in enemy country. The stomach issues hadn't come back, and there hadn't been any more unusual incidents or harassment. She slept soundly through the nights and woke up knowing exactly where she was and what she'd be doing that day. Her life was simple and clear and filled with beauty. As the miles went by, she found herself looking forward to the company of others and started forming bonds of friendship with some of the hikers she encountered repeatedly.

Faith was looking forward to meeting up with her ex-husband Jenkins. She was happy that the divorce hadn't destroyed their friendship. They'd been a military couple, and as with so many military couples, the demands of the service had broken down their marriage. Jenks was still a close friend and confidant. As a former Army Ranger, he understood what she'd gone through overseas and how it had affected her. He was always there for her. That hadn't always been the case and Faith regretted the anger and arguing that preceded their divorce. It took a couple of years to heal the rift between them. Each had moved on to meet others. In Faith's case, her relationships never lasted and eventually she'd realized that her VA counselor was right; PTSD left her unable to maintain a healthy physical and emotional relationship. She found it easier to stop trying. It was less painful and traumatic if she just kept to herself. So that's what she did after she left the Marines, existing in a colorless bubble of existence. She held onto a few friends, but for the most part had been living as a loner. The trek had changed that and she welcomed the change, just as she welcomed the opportunity to spend time with Jenks again.

They were going to meet up at Crater Lake in Oregon. The only fly in that ointment was that Jenks' new wife Julia might be with him. Faith wouldn't mind, except that her impression was that Julia didn't like her. Faith regretted that. She liked Julia and felt she was a good match for Jenks.

It was late afternoon and cloudy. To the east, the summit of towering Mount Shasta was hidden in the murk. The grey sky drizzled light rain as Faith picked her way down a rough section of trail. A slide had left the trail littered with rocks and small boulders. Below and to her left was a rippling lake that her map app told her was one of the Deadwood lakes. A couple of yellow tents and a red tent were clustered near the lakeshore and people were gathered under a blue tarp stretched between the trees.

She entered the forested camping area along the lakeshore. As she wove through the trees and approached the tents, Faith was happy to recognize five middle-aged hikers that she'd encountered near the beginning of her trip. She'd forgotten their names but remembered them as being friendly and easy to talk with. The two men and three women greeted her with smiles and invited her to camp with them. She happily accepted.

The men introduced themselves as Ralph and Reacher, the women were Hobbit, Arwen and Eos. They were sitting under the tarp in tiny camp chairs, around a couple of hissing propane stoves that had large pots balanced on top. Steam curled out from the lids and Faith smelled some kind of meat stew.

"We're all old codgers," said Reacher, a tall, raw-boned man with a grey beard and long ponytail. "And we move slow, but we're gonna make it to Canada. It's just one painful step at a time, eh?" He laughed heartily.

Faith shyly introduced herself and the others complimented her on a great trail name.

"Faith? That's fuckin' great!" Reacher said. "That sums it up, don't it? We all gotta have faith that we're gonna fuckin' make it. Young lady, you couldn't have picked a better trail moniker."

Faith didn't tell them that was her real name.

The oldest woman, Eos, gave Faith a hug and invited her to join them for dinner. "So, we're going to get a resupply at the next road crossing, so we have to eat up the extra food! You're just in time to help! Now, okay dear, go set up your tent over there next to mine and when you get back, dinner will be ready." She had a breathless, excited way of talking that reminded Faith of one of her aunts.

The rain stopped just as she finished stowing her gear in the tent, the last few drops tapping the taught nylon of the rain fly. She put on a light green goose down jacket and joined the group under the tarp. Eos handed her a large steaming bowl of stew. As they ate, Ralph started a fire in the stone ring. He was a compact, quiet man and efficient in his actions. It didn't take long before a cheerful flame flickered and curled out from under the wood. Faith was content to sit next to the fire, eat the delicious stew and listen as the group bantered and updated her on their trail experiences so far.

"I remember seeing you at the beginning, Faith," said Reacher, "and you may be curious as to how we got ahead of you? Well, truth be told, we skipped a big section of trail that we'd done last year and bumped ahead. It was a relief to move ahead and I hope it means we can make it to Canada before the snow flies."

Hobbit, the smallest of the women, had a bubbly voice and bright eyes under a mop of curly grey hair. She said to Faith, "I remember you, Faith, and remember thinking, young attractive girl like you hiking alone seems kind of dangerous. Have you had any problems? Nobody bothers us, a bunch of elder hikers, but what about you?"

Faith shook her head. "No real problems so far." She decided not to mention the incidents of harassment. "Well, there was a couple of annoying guys along the way. Maybe you've run across one or both of them. Duster and Slowpoke?"

Ralph snorted and looked up as he put another chunk of wood on the fire. "Haven't seen that Slowpoke character, but Duster? That shitweasel? Yeah, we've seen him. Fucking leech."

Reacher laughed. "Yeah, you two didn't get along so well, Ralphy. Still, I think you were too hard on the rat."

Eos said to Faith, "Okay, so Duster was a little too persistent with us? He was hoping to travel with us and share our food. The key word is 'our' food. He didn't have enough of his own and seemed keen on taking ours, okay? At first we thought he was a charming, although somewhat false, young guy. We agreed to let him hike along and he did, talking incessantly. It got to the point where we'd tag team it on the trail, taking turns being the targets of Duster's verbosity. Well, you can imagine that wore thin pretty fast.

"The real problem came when Ralph woke up early one morning to find that Duster had lowered his, Ralphy's that is, food bag from a tree and was munching on his trail mix."

"Fucking leech!" said Ralph again. "I caught the shitbird red-fucking-handed. Swore and threw a goddamn rock at him and laughed as it hit him and he went down." Ralph smiled grimly at the memory. "Not my proudest moment, but Duster had driven us all to the edge. We couldn't take any more of him. My rock fixed that problem!"

Eos was shaking her head. "Okay, sad but true," she said. "The rock hit Duster in the belly and knocked him down, knocked the wind out of him? He didn't say a word at first. Just lay on the ground squeaking, trying to breathe. Then the poor guy got to his feet, scrambled over to his pack, gathered up his stuff, crammed it in and started to leave. He stopped and stared back at us and said in a menacing, weird low voice, 'You shouldn't dis Duster'. That's when Ralph threw another rock at him."

"Missed that time," grumbled Ralph, "but let him know I didn't give a rat's ass about what he had to say. You shoulda seen him scamper off!"

Faith used her spoon to scrape up the last bits of stew as she said, "Do you think he's an actual threat? Have you had any suspicious incidents or harassment since?"

Everyone shook their heads. Ralph said, "No, we haven't seen him since and that was several weeks ago."

Faith said, "My impression was that he was a liar and a wuss, with a dash of pervert mixed in."

That made the group laugh. Hobbit said, "Oh dear, I think you're absolutely right about him being a perv. I hung up my sports bra and panties on a line one day to dry and caught him staring at them, all blank-eyed. Gave me the willies, seeing that! I was afraid he was going to pull out his wiener!"

Everyone laughed and Faith said, "He tries anything around me, and he'll be looking for an aid station, if he's lucky."

"You're a girl who can take care of yourself, I can see," said Reacher. "Let me guess; either military or law enforcement. You look too young for either, but that's my guess."

Faith smiled and nodded. "Good guess, Reacher. I'm a Marine, retired from service and trying to get on with my life."

Ralph smiled broadly and said, "Semper Fi! Me too, Faith. I thought I recognized the look. Just not used to seeing it on such a young, pretty face."

Arwen spoke up for the first time, saying, "Ralph Dailey, you old flirt! Leave the girl alone." She turned to Faith and said, "Forgive my husband, but being a Marine, he can't help himself."

Faith got the message and smiled. "I'll take it as a compliment."

Ralph said, "It was! So, being a fellow Gyrene, I can see by your look that you've been overseas and likely in combat. Am I right?"

Faith touched the long, pale scar on her left cheek and nodded. She wasn't sure what to say. These were good people and everyone was having fun. She didn't want to bring them down with her story, but for the first time felt a strong, almost desperate urge to talk about what had happened over there. She knew Ralph would understand, and maybe the others had seen enough in their own lives to understand too. Besides, she was relieved that no one had given her the well-intentioned "thank you for your service" line.

Faith set her bowl down and Arwen took it and put it with the other dirty dishes. Eos had a large pot heating on one of the stoves, filled with lake water for washing. Darkness had overtaken the sky and the rain clouds had vanished. To the west, across the rippling lake, the horizon was a red and gold bar of light that silhouetted a line of dark pines along the shore. Overhead, a few stars flickered faintly. An owl called from the forest.

Ralph added more firewood and the flames wrapped around it, crackling and sparking and curling up into flickering points. He said, "Faith, if you don't wanna talk about it, I understand, but believe me, talking about it to people who know how to listen can work wonders."

Reacher spoke up. "Don't worry, you're in good company. Eos is retired Army. Intelligence if you can believe it! Ha ha! The rest of us, well, we're old enough to know how to shut up and listen."

Faith poked at the fire with a stick and nodded. "This trip has done so much to help with my . . . my . . . issues. But I'm scared about what will happen when the trip ends and I have to go back to the so-called Real World.

"You see, a little over two years ago, I was in some real bad shit in Afghanistan. About as bad as it gets. I can't tell you all of it since some is classified, but I can tell you the basics of what happened." She looked up and the firelight painted her face in waves of shadow and orange light.

CHAPTER 13 — JUNE 29

Outwardly, he was laughing at Milt Dinwiddie's jokes. The whole group was laughing. Dinwiddie was funny, as funny as his name, but inwardly the laughing man simply wasn't in the mood for frivolity. Still, there he was playing the jovial host to the park staff and some fellow volunteers. One must keep up appearances.

There were nine other people seated in lawn chairs around a small fire, drinking beer and telling stories. The get-together had become an annual tradition and he couldn't very well bow out of it, so he put up with it even though he was anxious as hell.

He glanced at his watch again. His apprentice was late. It was almost 5:00 and no Joey. There was no cell service so no way to tell when he'd arrive. The Mentor had agreed with the park manager to feed a youth group in exchange for free accommodations for three to five nights. He needed Joey's help to do that. And no doubt there would be PCT hikers stopping by for meals too. After all, that's why he was here. That was his *raison d'etre*; at least as far as the public was concerned.

He wasn't sure he liked mentoring. As much as he relied on the guy, he regarded his apprentice with distaste. The young man was a drifter, subsisting on the financial backing of a family that wanted him far away and out of their hair. They wanted nothing to do with him and he wanted nothing to do with them, beyond his monthly remittance check. A check that the Mentor now generously supplemented.

Despite how he felt, the Mentor needed the apprentice to help with his work, someone who shared his vision and his goals. Joey was that person. The Mentor hadn't planned on having an apprentice, ever. His true calling was a private and secret thing, beyond his food trailer service, but a couple of years ago, Joey had come across the Mentor disposing of the byproducts of his work. It had been a nasty shock. He'd been on an isolated forest road, miles from anywhere, when suddenly a bearded young backpacker stepped out of the trees and asked what he was doing.

Thinking that he would have to dispose of the guy anyway, the Mentor told him. Instead of shock, the man expressed fascination and offered to help. And help he did, without complaint or revulsion. At that point, the Mentor offered him a job. Joey, apparently recognizing a kindred spirit, agreed to be his apprentice. The Mentor wasn't sure if Joey realized what the alternative was. Luckily for him, the young man accepted the job offer with gratitude.

They'd been partners ever since, and Joey had proven himself a big help. Now the Mentor could harvest more every season. He'd been feeling the urge to do so. It used to be that one annual harvest was enough, but with Joey's help they did two last year and now he was hoping for even more this year.

He'd definitely need help to do that. Joey was his scout, his hound dog. He wondered if Joey had managed to track down the elusive young backpacker that he'd spoken of. She sounded like just the right candidate. From Joey's description, she sounded very much like his first, his one true love. More so than any of the others!

The party moved to the food trailer, where propane stoves were fired up. Food was retrieved from the refrigerator, dishes deployed and a feast was made. The Mentor was greatly relieved when Joey finally showed up just before dark and joined the festivities. The group greeted Joey with muted enthusiasm. Joey wasn't well regarded by the staff due to an unsolved theft the previous year. No one could prove anything but some food, an iPad and a wad of money disappeared from the park headquarters office right around the same time that the Mentor and Joey moved on.

When he had a chance, the Mentor pulled Joey aside and asked, "Well? Did you find her?"

Joey shook his head. "Sorry, Boss. No sign of her. I think she must be ahead of us somewhere."

The Mentor gripped Joey's upper right arm tightly. Joey winced.

"You find her, you hear?"

"Sure Boss, sure. Christ, you don't need to break my arm. We'll find her. You're gonna have to drop me off far enough north that we can't miss her. Look, we'll figure like the max number of miles she might be doing and get somewhere ahead of that. And then I'll wait, just like we've done before."

The Mentor released his arm. "Fine. But we have to find her, do you hear? I'm positive she's Her!"

"Well, duh she's a her. Most she's are."

"No, you moron. She might be the first one."

"But I thought you already took care of her."

"That was long ago. And I don't remember much about it. All I know is that she's out there somewhere."

Joey looked away and said, "Sure, whatever. You're the Boss."

CHAPTER 14 — JUNE 29

Faith looked at the others seated around the fire and began her story. "It was the start of the so-called Spring Fighting Season. To me that always sounded like some kind of sick chamber of commerce festival, but it meant that the snow was melting and travel was possible again. Fighting too."

They landed at night on a nameless snowy plateau. Faith remembered the blasting cold rotor wash pulsing through the open doors of the helo, snowflakes swirling as the pilot gently set the ship down. Fifteen soldiers tumbled out the doors past the watchful gunners, scrambling in the snow to set up a defensive perimeter. When the ship lifted up and thumped away into the starry sky, it left behind a profound silence. Captain Ernie Howell gathered his crew and quietly issued instructions. They shouldered their heavy packs and weapons and set out on foot for the nearest village. They moved silently, their gear taped or otherwise secured to make no noise.

Faith was proud to be part of the special Marine unit. Their classified mission was to gather intelligence on Taliban activities and weapons sources in Badakhshan Province, northeast Afghanistan. The highly trained unit was operating under the auspices of Naval Intelligence and the CIA. They were to make contact with villages along a suspected smuggling route. Villagers would be sequestered and questioned while buildings were searched. Faith would talk to the women through an interpreter, hoping they'd open up to her more than they would to her male colleagues. She hoped they'd reveal the location, names and actions of the Taliban.

According to the CIA, the Taliban were smuggling large amounts of weapons and munitions from northern Pakistan via the remote mountain village of Shogorabad. From there, the route went north through a maze of valleys and passes to Badakhshan. They were using long pack strings of mules and horses to transport the contraband through the rough mountain terrain.

The Marine unit, thirteen men and two women, was on foot and heavily loaded with supplies and weapons. They visited remote mountain villages, conducted searches and questioned everyone. Faith and her interpreter tried to extract information from village women but they were either surly or frightened, or both, and didn't talk. It didn't take long for the team members to realize that the mission was likely to be futile. In every village, they could see that the inhabitants were either too terrorized to talk, or were in league with the Taliban, profiting from them somehow.

Captain Howell decided they'd try one more village along the suspected smuggling route. After that, he'd call for extraction. He didn't want to risk his people any further, or waste their time. It was a fateful decision.

They didn't know the name of that last village. It was just another small collection of stone and mud huts along a gravelly river in the bottom of a deep valley. The community was surrounded by rock walls, lines of poplars and fir trees, small patches of stony agricultural land and irrigation canals. The team arrived in the early morning of what would turn into a hot day. Howell and the men questioned 23 male villagers while Faith and her interpreter questioned 30 women and girls. The village men didn't say a word other than to spin obvious lies, but Faith finally had luck with one of the village women. Her name was Delara

Delara was an angry and defiant old woman. The Taliban had killed her husband. Her two sons had died fighting for them. She had little left to live for, so she gladly revealed that the Taliban, or Devil Dogs, had indeed been smuggling large quantities of weapons into Afghanistan and large quantities of heroin out of that country. She revealed when and how often the pack trains came through, who some of the leaders were. Faith quickly scribbled the information in her tactical notebook. When Delara was done, Faith wrapped up the interviews. She noted that the other women were angry and afraid after Delara told her story..

Faith told the captain what she'd learned and was instructed to upload the information ASAP. Howell moved his tired Marines out of the village. They stopped to take five on a stone wall in the cool shade of some poplars while Faith used her satellite phone to send the information. It was 1300 local time and hot. Everyone was exhausted and relieved that they'd soon be heading back to base. They'd been on the go for a week, carrying 70 to 90 pounds each of food, water and arms, trudging up and down steep mountains night and day. Everyone, including the lookouts, was dulled by fatigue and the heat. They slouched in the shade talking about showers, pizza and some much-needed rack time. That's when the shit hit the fan.

Bullets started snapping through the air around the Marines, followed by popping gunfire, the whine of lead careening off of stone. A couple of Marines were hit. Everyone rolled off the rock wall and onto the dusty ground. The fire was coming from the village, from the men they'd just questioned. As they rose up to return fire, there was more popping behind them. It was coming from an apricot orchard 200 meters away. The Marines scattered to find better cover, returning fire in both directions. Faith had dropped her sat phone and was on hands and knees, frantically searching for it. Bullets were kicking up dust, shredding poplar leaves and chipping stone. Someone grabbed her collar and yelled, "Leave it, goddamnit! Move for cover!!" She was lifted off her feet and propelled toward a corner of the rock wall. Several Marines were already crouched there, rising up to return fire and ducking down.

The shooting from the village slackened and then stopped, as did the assault from the orchard. In the silence the Marines heard a man shouting in Pashto. Faith poked up her head and saw Delara stumbling from the village, heading toward their position. The old woman started yelling, her face frantic. The interpreter was on the ground at Faith's feet, hands on her helmet. She turned her head to look at Faith and said, "She's saying they forced her, that we need to shoot her, shoot her now! She's begging us."

Faith watched as Delara's robes billowed open to reveal a suicide vest; wires and packets of explosives tied together, a corset of death. Without thinking, Faith raised her M4 carbine and fired three quick rounds. Other Marines opened fire and Delara writhed and twisted with the bloody impacts. She fell and disappeared in a brilliant flash of light followed by a shock wave of dust and black smoke. The explosion knocked people down and blew leaves off the trees. Faith's ears were ringing and tears streaked her face. A muted voice was shouting at her to "Go, go, go!!" She went.

The Marines retreated to a melon field as the enemy gunfire resumed. Three of them were wounded and one of those three had to be carried. They continued past the melon field and through a line of fir trees, returning fire as they went. Howell led them up a stony tributary stream, making for the closest high ground where their return fire would be more effective. Adrenalin propelled them up the steep canyon, the rearguard pausing to take careful aim and fire at their pursuers.

Their one long-range radio was shot, literally. Faith had lost her sat phone. Howell's sat phone simply wasn't working. They all had GPS transmitters, but those often didn't work in deep canyons, like the one they were in. Since the mission was top secret, there were no scheduled radio check-ins, no orbiting relay drone. The enemy was rumored to have frequency scanner locaters. The Marine's radio silence wouldn't cause any concern back at Base for at least two more days. They were on their own.

They kept moving to keep the high ground, struggling up the rocky canyon, setting up ambushes to slow down their pursuers. The enemy numbered in the dozens and weren't giving up. They dodged from boulder to boulder, firing their AK's. Howell speculated that a large group of Taliban must've been following them for days and finally caught up with them at the village.

Eventually the Marines made it to the primary ridge top between their creek and the main valley. They struggled up and down along the rough, rocky ridge, through patches of old drift snow, gaining altitude. The Taliban still weren't giving up. More Marines were shot, some killed. The dead had to be left behind, the living took their grenades and ammo.

By day three, nine men had been lost, their bodies left behind with the intention of recovering them later. Two Marines were wounded but mobile. The female interpreter, a young Pakistani working for the CIA, was killed when a bullet plowed across Faith's cheek, blew off her lower left ear lobe and smacked into the interpreter's head. A couple of Marines grabbed Faith and pushed her on, one of them improvising a dressing as they went.

At that point, there were only four Marines, including Faith, still able to fight. Captain Howell was dead and Lieutenant Bruck was in charge. Along with two walking wounded, that made six remaining Marines that struggled up the high ridge. They were low on ammo, out of water and food, exhausted. They kept moving, pausing to snipe the enemy when they had good cover. The Taliban were tiring too, and appeared to be falling behind. Faith couldn't believe they were still in pursuit. She'd dropped at least three of them herself and the other Marines each shot at least as many, if not more.

As darkness fell on that third day, the tattered group was gasping and struggling with thin air and increasingly large snowfields. They followed the ridge as far as they could, until it ended in a series of sheer cliffs leading to impassable snowy summits towering into the evening sky. They couldn't go up any more, but they could go down. Under cover of darkness, Bruck led the surviving Marines down a loose, gravelly moraine and onto a broad glacier. They moved slowly, careful to avoid crevasses and snow bridges, and tried to keep to the darker areas, where rocks and gravel had accumulated on the ice. Eventually they came to a medial moraine and a cluster of large boulders. The lieutenant led them into the rocky maze and to a protected spot where they could see the ridge behind them, but not be seen.

With one person on watch at a time, everyone got some sleep despite constantly shaking from the cold. Faith's bandage was changed and she helped treat the other two wounded. None of the wounds were life-threatening. At least not as compared to their current situation. They yearned for dawn and when the eastern sky lightened behind the dark peaks, Faith felt a blend of relief and fear. As red and then golden sunlight crept down the steep, snow-streaked slopes to the west, small figures appeared on the rocky moraine the Marines had descended. They were about a kilometer away. Bruck watched them through binoculars and counted out loud up to twenty-seven. Once the Taliban had gathered, twenty of them began descending the moraine, trailing dust as they slid and ran down the loose slope. The others spread out along the ridge.

Bruck lowered the binoculars and told his troops to look to their weapons, take an inventory of ammunition and make every shot count. Faith had twenty rounds left in her magazine and no spares. Everyone else was in the same boat.

As they prepared for the final fight, Faith felt rather than heard a rhythmic thumping. Everyone looked up, heads swiveling as they scanned the sky. Bruck's strained face broke into a grin. "Cavalry, boys and girls!" He rummaged in his shoulder bag and pulled out two smoke grenades. When the thumping turned into an unmistakable roar, he pulled the pin and pitched one of the grenades into the open. Red smoke boiled out of it, signaling the helo pilot that there were hostiles in the area.

Sunlight flashed off the plexiglass of the huge helicopter as it lifted over the western ridge and swooped down across the glacier and toward the red smoke. Faith saw flashes from the Taliban on the moraine and a second later heard gunfire. The Sikorsky MH-53 lifted and veered to the north in a wide curve toward the Taliban. Faith heard one of its mini-guns growling and watched as the moraine exploded into flashes and gouts of snow, dirt and dust. The ship hovered at a safe distance and its guns hosed the entire ridge. Debris and body parts were flying in every direction. Bruck watched through binoculars for a moment and then he lowered them. He closed his eyes and shook his head, saying, "Shit, I kinda wish I hadn't seen that!"

The helicopter destroyed the Taliban group. The marines left the boulder field and walked to an open, level spot on the ice that was crevasse-free. Bruck popped a green smoker and the tired crew watched as the helicopter descended toward them. Within minutes, everyone was aboard and the doors were closing as the ship lifted off, blowing the green smoke into swirls.

They flew one low pass along the moraine and saw no movement, no whole bodies. Satisfied, the pilot turned and headed for base.

Faith poked at the fire's coals with a stick as she finished her story. She was silent for a few moments, looked up at her audience and said, "That's about it. That was it, for me. I was done. We lost too many good people, and having to shoot the old woman . . . ? And for what? Turns out the intel we got wasn't really worth it. The spooks already had most of it from informants so our efforts were mostly for nothing. Somebody just wanted further verification to cover his or her ass. The two wounded guys had full recoveries, eventually. The bodies of our dead were retrieved. Those of us who survived were treated for exhaustion and dehydration and given some time off once the After Action Review was done. I used that time to do some thinking and realized I was truly done. After 12 years and several deployments, I wanted out. So, I was given an honorable discharge, some medals and the thanks of the nation. I guess the medals, aside from the Purple Hearts, were for surviving. None of us felt we deserved them. The guys we'd lost certainly did, and they got 'em, but medals weren't worth much to them then. Maybe to their families.

"Something I didn't fully realize at the time, but later when I talked to a shrink? I found out how hard that mission had hit me." Faith stirred the coals some more and sparks flew into the air. "I thought I was tougher than that. There's a mythology around the Corps that appeals to you when you're young and feeling strong; that we're somehow some kind of super soldier automatons, unaffected by combat, but Marines are like anyone else. And like anyone else, they, we, find out the hard way how violent and traumatic combat is. I will say we're awfully good at it, thanks to training, discipline and attitude. It's the aftermath that hits us. You know, it hits us in ways we didn't expect. At least it hit me."

Ralph spoke up. "Thanks for sharin' your story, Faith. Man, that was one hell of a Charlie Foxtrot! I was lucky to never see anything that bad in Iraq, but it had its moments. I hope you realize how lucky you are to have survived."

Faith simply nodded.

Eos said, "Faith, that was a story that you needed to tell and we're honored that you told us. Most people can't imagine what you and your comrades went through, but I think we can. You're not alone. No one who ever served is alone if they just reach out."

"Especially if they reach out to nature," said Arwen. "Hiking the PCT can be a powerful antidote for what ails a person."

"Amen to that!" Reacher said, slapping his knees. "Well, it's gettin' late and I think we're all pretty tired." They talked some more about plans for the next day; distances, sights to see, how everyone was doing. Faith excused herself and walked over to her tent amidst a chorus of goodnights.

Minutes later, as she lay cocooned in her down sleeping bag, she felt drained but somehow better too, and was thankful for the people who had invited her to share their fire and to share her pain. Faith smiled and closed her eyes, drifted off into a peaceful sleep. A sleep without worry or nightmares.

CHAPTER 15 — JULY 4-5

Faith had seen a lot of human strangeness along the trail but she was caught by surprise at what she saw when she rounded a corner below Black Marble Mountain. It was another hot, blue-sky morning and she was hoping to do 20 more miles before sunset. Sweat dripped off her face and she felt it trickling down her back and chest. It wasn't even 0930 yet and already hot. She wiped her brow with a blue bandana and trudged the last hundred feet to the top of a spur ridge below the mountain.

There was tree shade where the trail rounded the ridge and she stopped to take a water break. Looking back at the route she'd just traversed, she saw the PCT as it threaded through a green meadow basin dotted with stands of fir trees. Looking ahead and to the north, more ridges, meadows, forests and a bank of dark cloud. The cloud looked odd, with a brown tint to it. After staring at it for a couple of minutes, she realized that the distant cloud was smoke from a forest fire.

That might be something to worry about, she thought. And then she thought that maybe she could choose not to worry about it until she had more information. *It's a deal*, she told her brain. Besides, there was something odd moving slowly on the trail ahead of her, through a brushy meadow. She couldn't tell what it was at first so she shouldered her pack and resumed hiking. As she got closer, she realized it was a man, 'hiking' the trail on his hands. Basically he was hiking upside down, with some kind of strange pack on his back.

She caught up to him five minutes later. After she said, "Hi!", he carefully lowered his feet to the ground and righted himself. The pack hardly shifted. The man staggered and steadied himself with one hand on a tree. He shook his head, looked at Faith and said, "G'day!"

The man was tall and skinny, a bushy blond beard covering most of his face. Faith learned that he was from Australia and had a bet with his mates that he would hike two miles or more a day on the PCT, on his hands, all the way to Canada. He said he could hike on his feet as far as he wanted but that he had to do those two miles on his hands every day. His trail name was Drongo.

"I know, I know," said Drongo. "It's a stupid bet and a stupid way to travel. We were drunk when the bet was made. Imagine that!" He explained that being from Australia, hiking upside down would be the natural thing for him to do in the northern hemisphere. "Anything but!" he said.

They talked a while longer and Faith finally said, "Drongo, it's been a pleasure talking to you. I admire your commitment. Have a great trip and hang in there, upside down or right side up!"

Faith continued on, remembering the other strange things and strange people she'd seen on the trail so far. There was the man hiking along in a kilt and playing bagpipes, a group of little people carrying large backpacks, the woman playing guitar and singing, the group of ten young men hiking to the beat of a loud boom box, the numerous people absorbed in their smart phones and ignoring the scenery, a preacher trying to convert hikers, the athletes who were running the trail, the horsemen re-enactors dressed as Old West mountain men, the camo-covered survivalist with an AR-15 slung over his shoulder. The list went on. It was quite the parade at times and Faith had to marvel at the diversity of people she saw on the trail.

And then there was the wildlife. So far she'd seen numerous elk and deer, squirrels, eagles, a condor, weasels, a few bears, a bobcat, several coyotes and a cougar. The latter was a close encounter that happened one evening when she left camp to find water. It was almost dark and she regretted leaving her headlamp in the tent. The darkness seemed to swell out from the dim forest. Following the sound of water, she found a small creek and deployed the filter. As she was pumping water into a CamelBak, she saw a furtive movement out of the corner of her eye and looked up to see a large mountain lion 25 feet away. It stopped to look at her looking at it. The big cat sat on its haunches and continued to stare while the end of its long tail twitched. The stare-down went on for a couple of minutes. Finally, keeping her eyes on the big cat, Faith resumed filtering. She had to remind herself to breathe. The lion lay down, long tail flicking back and forth, and continued to stare at her until she finished and stood up. The cat stood up also, stretched and disappeared into the dark forest.

Faith smiled to herself and shook her head. That cat was the most beautiful creature she'd ever encountered and she remembered feeling both blessed and frightened by its appearance. After the encounter, looking back frequently, she made her way to camp just as full dark hit. After a careful 360-degree sweep with her headlamp, she crawled into her tent thinking that she'd never get to sleep, but she did. Exhaustion overrides fear. She woke up in the morning alive and whole, uneaten by the big cat.

The smoke she'd seen in the morning grew into a towering, dirty brown column by early afternoon. The top of the column billowed white with water vapor. Faith wasn't sure how close the trail would get to the fire so she stopped, took off her pack and got out a map and compass. She preferred not to use the GPS on her phone. Old-fashioned map and compass seemed to work just fine, and they didn't need batteries or a cell tower. After getting the map and compass oriented on the ground, she determined that the fire was about 15 miles away and to the east of the PCT. For the time being a west wind was pushing it away from the trail, but that could change. She'd have to be very watchful.

That night she camped in some trees at the edge of a ridge top meadow. At sunset, while filtering water from a small tarn, she watched the ominous smoke column. The edges of the smoke flared orange, fading into red with the last rays of the sun. As darkness settled in, the cloud flattened and the bottom glowed as the fire continued its forest-eating march. Faith saw orange flare-ups flash bright and as quickly disappear.

The next morning the air was filled with smoke and so hazy that visibility was reduced to about a mile. The sun rose as a red ball and the acrid, smoky air grew hot. Faith trudged on, boots kicking up clouds of dust. The wood smoke felt harsh and dry in her throat and nose. It made her eyes water. She wondered what the day would bring and hoped to get past the fire without any holdups or detours. There were still some miles to make up from the day and half she lost while sick at Feather River.

After ten serpentine miles, she descended toward a pass and approached a trail junction in a meadow. It was almost three p.m. Her heart sank as she saw a small group of men and women wearing yellow shirts, green pants and red hardhats. Sunlight glinted off of a Huey helicopter that squatted in the meadow beyond the group. In the murky orange sunlight, the firefighters were putting up red hazard signs, including one with an arrow that read "PCT DETOUR".

Faith stopped and talked with them for a few minutes. One of the firefighters, a tall bearded man with a radio strapped across the front of his yellow Nomex shirt, handed her a small map and said, "You'll have to take this other trail and detour around the next 20 miles of PCT. It's gonna add about 10 miles to your trip. Sorry, but it's better than getting burned up in a wildfire."

Faith took the map and said, "Okay. I understand. So how big is this fire? How far away is it? What direction is it going?"

"It's up to around 30,000 acres and growing, burning east for now, about five miles away from here and about a mile and a half from the PCT. You never know what a fire's gonna do. The wind might shift and send it toward the trail, so we can't take any chances and we can't let you take any chances either."

Faith thanked the firefighter and turned toward the detour trail. She didn't have any information on the new route and would have to get out her map to see what it was about. As she approached the trail junction she saw a small group of backpackers resting in the shade of fir trees. A weathered wooden sign on one of the trees read "Sheep Gap Trail" and had an arrow pointing west and down-valley. Faith walked over to the group of hikers, said hi and took her pack off.

She was startled when a deep voice from beneath the trees answered back, "Hello yourself, Beauty."

Faith peered into the dimness and saw Duster lying on the ground, leaning against his pack, legs crossed. His trademark coat was bundled into a pillow. Faith stared at him for a moment before saying, "Oh, hi." She turned away and moved to the other side of the small group, stepping over people's legs and around their packs. Warning bells were going off in her mind. What was Duster doing there? Faith had been sure he was a few days behind her, so how did he get ahead of her? Maybe he was hiking at night and had passed her camp sometime? That thought was disturbing. Just as she was beginning to feel safe again, he shows up. At least Slowpoke wasn't there. Of course that made Faith wonder where he was and what he was up to.

One of the hikers, a short, stocky, hairy man she knew as Thoreau, said, "Faith, some of us are thinking maybe we'll take our chances with the fire. Maybe hike through at night. You with us?"

Faith took off her pack and set it on the ground, looked at Thoreau. "I'm not sure that's a good idea," she said. "The firefighters were clear about not going that way."

Thoreau frowned and said, "Look, I used to fight fires and I think that guy is full of shit. The fire's burning east, away from the trail. At night the wind dies down and the relative humidity goes up. The fire won't be goin' anywhere. We could make it through in three or four hours and the fire guys would never even know it."

Duster appeared out of the shade. "Thoreau, old buddy. Not a good idea. We should take the detour. If they catch us, they'll throw us in jail. That fire dude is right, you can't tell what a fire's gonna do. Like right now there's no wind. Did you notice that? What if it starts blowin' again and blowin' the wrong way? What if it blows the fire right at ya?"

Thoreau squinted up at Duster and said, "You can do whatever the hell you want, Duster. This isn't a team or a crew. Everyone here is their own boss. Take the fuckin' detour if you want. I'm hiking through tonight. Those fire guys will have to fly out of here before dark and when they do, I'm outta here too. Anybody that wants to hike with me, fine. Anybody that doesn't, fine too."

Duster shook his shaggy head. He said, "You're gonna burn up, dude. Or you're gonna inhale a lot of smoke and get sick or die." He turned to Faith and said, "'Faith?' Great trail name, by the way. I knew you'd get one eventually. What're you gonna do? Better take the detour. That's the way I'm goin'. That's the smart thing to do."

"Haven't decided yet, but I'm going to rest here a while. You should get started on that detour. It adds some miles to the trip."

Duster's eyes narrowed. "Trying to get rid of me, Faith? Don't worry about moi. I'm just a harmless hiker dude who cares about other people, tryin' to do you a favor." He looked at the others. "Tryin' to do everyone here a favor. But you're right, I better get going. Hope I don't read about you guys on the internet, all burned up into crispy critters."

Duster retrieved his coat and pack. After one last, pitying look at the group, he strode off down the Sheep Gap Trail, a small cloud of dust in his wake.

Watching him, Thoreau snorted and said, "Piece of stinky shit. Man, that guy reeks! He must be sweating like crazy under that fuckin' coat. So good riddance to him. I don't really want to hike by that fire, but if that's what it takes to shake that fuckin' dingleberry loose, I'll do it."

"And a creeper!" said a woman Faith knew as Owl. "There's something about that guy. It's like he's hollow inside or something? Like he doesn't have a soul. He's all fake, no matter what he says? And the way he looks at you? Cree-ee-py!"

Faith nodded. "I know what you mean, but I think he's right about hiking through on the trail. Not a good idea. I'm gonna give him a couple of hours to get ahead and I'll follow on the detour."

Thoreau settled back on his pack and pulled a desert camo boonie hat over his eyes. "Do what you need to do, Faith, but it's gonna slow you down. Me, I'm gonna take a nap and wait for those firefighters to fly on out of here."

The orange orb of the sun was low in the sky and Faith was thinking she better make camp soon. Because of the smoke, her eyes were watering and she was coughing at times. She was hiking on the detour trail, about a mile down from the junction where Thoreau, Owl and the others had been waiting. A few minutes previously the Forest Service helicopter had flown overhead, rotors slapping the air with a staccato beat. She watched and listened as it gradually diminished into the west. Thoreau and the others were probably shouldering their packs and strapping on their headlamps.

Faith was having second thoughts. The detour would add at least a day and a half to her trip. She wanted to stay on the PCT itself, but she didn't feel that she knew enough about fires to take the chance of hiking through. Thoreau seemed to know what he was talking about, but she'd known plenty of men and women like that and it seemed that at least half the time they were full of shit. Faith only trusted her gut and that trust had saved her many times. So, she was trusting it now.

But still . . . she looked up and saw something moving on the trail ahead. It was hard to make out in the thick, filmy air, against the glare of a setting sun. She stopped in the shade of a tree to block the light and squinted. About a quarter mile ahead, where the trail wound back out of a small valley, she saw a figure stop walking and begin to climb up a rocky bluff above the trail. She couldn't tell who it was or what they were doing.

Faith pulled a small Lumix camera out of a belt case and held it up to her eye. The camera had an excellent zoom lens and doubled as her telescope. Looking through the viewfinder, she zoomed in and muttered, "Fuck!"

The figure was Duster. He'd just reached the top of the rocky bluff and was taking his pack off. He sat down at the base of a tree and it looked like he would be hidden from anyone hiking the trail below. Faith lowered the camera and squinted her eyes. What in the hell was he doing? She put her camera back and thought a moment.

Her gut was telling her that this was wrong, that Duster was wrong. Was he waiting for her? Why else would he be sitting there doing nothing but looking around? Sitting in a hidden location where he could see back along the trail? Faith considered her options. Going ahead, she'd have to deal with the creep and it wouldn't be pretty. She wasn't afraid to use violence, but she didn't want to. Her trip was about finding peace, about healing.

Faith hated to let that pervert deflect her from the detour, but she decided that was what she'd have to do. On the plus side, she wouldn't be losing many more miles if she went back to the PCT. She looked around and considered her options. She was currently hidden from Duster and could backtrack on the trail a short distance where it crossed a gully. Using that gully as cover, she would travel cross-country uphill, through the forest, up to the ridge where the PCT was.

After one last look at the distant figure on the bluff, Faith turned and hiked back a short distance to the gully. She paused, looked around to make sure she was alone. She turned left and stepped off the trail, started trudging uphill through a maze of boulders and trees, always keeping to cover as she went. When the red sun finally sank behind the hills, the forest darkened quickly, made even darker by heavy smoke. The air grew cooler. She avoided using her headlamp and cautiously continued up the steep hill. As total darkness arrived, she stumbled onto the Pacific Crest Trail. She took a short break before turning on the headlamp, shouldering her pack and continuing north on the trail. Maybe she'd catch up with Thoreau and the others. Occasionally she looked over her shoulder and saw an orange glow through the trees. Faith wasn't sure, it was so hard to tell in the darkness, but it seemed to be getting brighter and closer.

CHAPTER 16 — JULY 5

"I think we finally found Melissa Hampton's remains," Max said into the satellite phone. He was standing in a sun-dappled meadow of waist-high flowers, surrounded by aster, columbine, bleeding hearts and Queen Anne's lace. Slow bumblebees hummed around him in the flower-sweetened air. Max felt the sun's warmth on his back. On a nearby trail two young hikers, a man and a woman, were standing in shade and looking on. The woman held tightly to the taut leash of an impatient black lab. A pileated woodpecker drummed on a nearby snag. It was a beautiful, peaceful setting that made the gruesome discovery even more unsettling.

Max waited through a slight delay and heard Deputy Kingsley reply, "Are you sure, Max?"

"No, but I can't think of anyone else it could be, given the missing persons case from last fall."

"Well now, we'll get that figured out later. The lab people can tell us. DNA, teeth, whatever. So talk me through what you've got, what you're looking at."

Max kept the phone to his ear as he walked closer to the ominous hole in the meadow. He was careful to stay on the beaten-down track the hikers had left when they pulled their dog away from its grisly discovery.

A patch of sunlight on the dark hole made several exposed bones seem to glow. Max sniffed the air and detected a slight odor of decay. "Okay Einar. Here's what we've got." Max paused as he leaned in to get a closer look. "The remains appear to be mostly bones, in a shallow hole, surrounded by pieces of a plastic bag. The bones are in bad condition, look to be partially burned. Blackened ends and patches."

Kingsley's voice crackled on the phone. "How can you tell the remains are human?"

"I can see half of a jawbone with teeth and there's some shiny material there too. Maybe fillings? On the long bones, there's linear scratch marks, gouges, visible on what looks like a leg or arm bone. Man, this is some spooky shit. So when can your forensics team get here?"

"Hang on a sec." There was a pause, and then the deputy said, "Probably by late afternoon, so another four hours?"

Max sighed. There went his plans for the day, but right now, this was more important than anything on his to-do list. The hikers had contacted him at the Deception Pass trailhead an hour ago and he'd hiked with them the short distance to view the remains and secure the scene. "Okay. I'll be here until they show up. There's two trails that take off from the trailhead, so make it clear that I'm on the Deception Pass Trail. Have 'em contact me on the Search And Rescue frequency when they get to the trailhead. The site is about 400 yards up from there. I'll tape off the trail and put up some flagging."

"Sounds good, Max. Hey, if you can, enjoy the day up there. Did you take a book?"

"Yeah, and a chaise lounge to relax in. It's gonna be great. Send me a pizza and some beer and it'll be perfect."

Kingsley chuckled and signed off. Max tapped the End button and returned the small satellite phone to his utility belt. Despite the banter with Kingsley, Max felt a heavy sadness lowering over his mind, dimming the bright day. He could handle the visuals. He'd seen death before. What he had trouble handling was the sadness that would wash over him. Sadness and regret over a life lost and the grief of those left behind. Max scratched his chin, raised his head, looked around and figuratively shook himself. No sense dwelling on it. There was work to do.

He turned and waded through the lush meadow, back up to the trail. The young couple looked at him expectantly. They were both dressed in cargo shorts, sweatshirts and hiking boots and had small rucksacks on their backs. The man was tall and spindly, his brown hair bound up in a bun. The woman was shorter and frail looking, her narrow face framed by long blonde hair. The Labrador lunged at Max, tail wagging vigorously. The woman had tears in her eyes. The man held his phone up and said, "Shit, there's zero signal here!"

Max told him, "Yeah, no signal anywhere up here, and even if there was, I'm asking you to keep this off public media, okay? This is officially a crime scene and the information associated with it is part of an active investigation. We don't yet know what we have here and any public speculation might damage the investigation and be traumatic for the family of the deceased, okay?"

The woman put a hand on her friend's arm and said, "Sure, we understand. This is so awful. I've never seen anything like this." She started crying. Her companion looked at her and rolled his eyes. He said, "Oh come on, Abbie. It's just a bunch of old bones." Then the bearded young man looked at Max and asked, "They're human, right? I heard you mention her name, dude. Did we find that Hampton girl?"

Abbie turned to him, wiping at her eyes. "That was a person, Jason! An actual person! And just think about it. Somebody killed her and she died all alone out here."

Max put a hand on the woman's shoulder. "Hey, it's tough finding something like this. Believe me, I know. Why don't we all sit on the big log over there and take a moment, okay?"

They sat down and Max advised them that counseling might be in order, that this sort of experience can be more traumatic than they realize. The man seemed skeptical but

Max didn't care. He was doing his part and what they did with the information he gave them was their business.

Abbie was eager to get out of there, but Jason was stubborn and at first insisted they be allowed up the trail.

Max took him aside, out of the woman's hearing, and quietly said, "Hey Jason, Abbie has had a hell of a shock today. For her sake, the best thing you can do, the best way to take care of her, is to get her out of here. It's up to you to do that for her, okay?"

Jason grimaced and said, "Yeah, I guess so. Women don't take these things very well, do they? Not like us dudes."

Max suppressed the urge to lecture Jason and instead patted him on the back, saying, "Good man. Find her another trail, or take her somewhere for a good meal in town. Get her mind off of this."

Max walked with them back to the trailhead and they paused at Max's Explorer. He asked them to wait a minute as he retrieved a metal clipboard from inside the SUV. He took out a form and clipped it in, handed Jason the clipboard and a pen.

"What's this, dude?"

Max pointed at the form. "Just a simple witness statement I need you two to fill out. What time you found the remains, how you found them, What time you contacted me. Just a brief statement and your names and addresses will be fine. And I'll need to see some ID to verify your identities. Thanks."

After some muttering, Jason and Abbie walked to a nearby picnic table and sat down to fill out the form. Max rummaged in the back of his Ford and pulled out a thick roll of crime scene tape and some thinner rolls of red tape. Ten minutes later, the young couple handed Max the clipboard and showed him their driver licenses. Max thanked them and gave them both his card. Abbie and

Jason got into their Subaru and drove off down the dusty road.

Using the trailhead bulletin board as an anchor, Max stretched yellow tape across the start of the trail and tied it around a tree trunk. Bold black lettering on the tape repeatedly made it clear that it was a "CRIME SCENE DO NOT CROSS". Satisfied that the trail was properly cordoned off, he picked up his daypack and trudged up the trail to the site of the remains. There he used a roll of narrow red tape to cordon off the trail and the section of meadow where the bones were. That done, he sat on a log where he could monitor the site. Taking the sat phone out again, he called his patrol captain at the Forest Service supervisors office in Wenatchee and brought her up to speed. She was busy, so it was a short conversation. After that phone update, he looked at his watch and sighed. At least three and a half hours to go. Max didn't like downtime.

Max had been plenty busy in the weeks since he started his new job. A three-week federal investigations course took up a big block of time. The rest had been spent familiarizing himself with the area and the people. The Roslyn Ranger District was comprised of some 375,000 acres, with many hundreds of miles of roads and trails, over a dozen campgrounds, hundreds of dispersed camping areas, a portion of the Alpine Lakes Wilderness area, several large lakes, rivers and more. All of that was patrolled by only three law enforcement officers: Max, Deputy Kingsley and a state game warden. Max's predecessor had left a lot of details about issues, pending criminal cases and persons to watch for. Enough that Max sometimes spent evenings at home reading the notes and reports, hoping to get caught up before the summer season, and the summer crowds, arrived on the Wenatchee National Forest. Most of the cases were crimes and incidents common to federal lands. They included wood theft, timber theft, littering, permit violations, destruction of natural resources, illegal cattle grazing, poaching, firearms violations, dumping, fireworks violations, drug use, arson, domestic disputes, DUI, abandoned vehicles, oversized groups, minors in possession; on and on and on.

Out of all of the ongoing cases within the boundaries of the Roslyn Ranger District, only a few stood out from the usual. One of those was the missing person case that Einar Kingsley had introduced to Max a few weeks ago. Since then, Max had requested and been mailed a copy of the case file from the State Patrol's missing persons unit.

According to that file, Melissa Hampton was a 30-year-old graphic artist from Seattle. She was 5' 8", Caucasian, long dark hair, outgoing, athletic. She'd worked for a computer game company in Seattle. She vanished in late August of last year along the popular stretch of PCT between Snoqualmie Pass and Deception Pass. Melissa had been a 'through hiker', one of the few who attempt to hike the entire 2650 miles of PCT from the Mexican border to the Canadian border in one season. She was reported missing on August 27 by her fiancé when she failed to check in via her satellite phone from Deception Pass. The fiancé called the Forest Service, who referred him to the Kittitas County Sheriff's Office. After another day had passed with no word from Hampton, KCSO sent out their search and rescue team.

After two weeks of concerted effort, the search was suspended due to lack of results, resources and time. Melissa's family and friends continued looking until early November. As Deputy Kingsley had said, the search was formally ended in the spring. Hampton's case was designated a cold case, her status still listed as missing. Max was sure that the remains were Hampton's and that her case status was about to change.

The forensics team showed up at 5:43 p.m. By then Max had contacted over 25 hikers, including a troop of ten boy scouts, who had ignored the crime scene tape and ventured up the trail. It was the Fourth of July weekend and the crowds were out, hoping to hike to several popular destinations in the Alpine Lakes Wilderness. He turned them all back. One group of five middle-aged men tried to argue with him, claiming that they had a right to hike up the trail. After repeated efforts to calmly explain the situation, Max had to pull out his ticket book and ask for their IDs. The men balked at that and said they'd go back to the trailhead.

The arriving team was led by the county coroner, Dr. Alvia Stone. She was a middle-aged heavy-set woman and Max was surprised to see that she was neither sweating nor winded by the hike in. She smiled, introduced herself and shook Max's hand before getting down to business. Max described what actions the hikers and he had taken, where they'd gone and what had been disturbed. Dr. Stone thanked him for the information and gave him an evidence chain of custody form to sign and date. She then joined her team as they donned protective clothing and carefully entered the scene.

After finishing the form and adding a brief narrative of his actions related to the crime scene, Max gathered his gear and started back to the trailhead. The late afternoon sunlight painted the forest and mountains in rich, golden light. Max was glad to be moving again, and moving in the right direction, toward home.

Two hours later, Max steered the government Ford into the rutted driveway in front of his cabin. He parked, called dispatch on the radio and went out of service. Gus, his big yellow Labrador, stood still and silent inside the fenced yard. He stared as Max got out of the SUV and opened the rear hatch, slung his pack on a shoulder and walked to the gate. Max figured that Gus was angry about not having been fed yet. The sun was behind the ridge to the west and the air was cooling. Robins were singing in the cottonwoods that lined the river behind the house. A blue Steller's Jay hopped in the branches of a nearby aspen and complained.

Max opened the gate and Gus continued to stand and stare. "Come on, Gus!" said Max. "I'm not that late. Get over here and say hi! Come on, boy, you can do it!"

The dog's tail started to swing while Max kept cajoling him. Finally he trotted up to Max and rolled over in the grass to get a belly rub. All was then forgiven and Gus loped across the green lawn as Max walked up a stone walkway toward the log cabin that was his new home. Ernie the black cat crawled out from under a lilac bush and streaked toward the front door.

This was Max's family these days. His now-former fiancé, Annette, had moved to Portland to pursue a career as a painter and art broker, so it was just Max and the two creatures holding down the fort. On the enclosed front porch, Max pulled out a cell phone and texted his patrol captain to let her know he was back safe and sound. She called about five minutes later and asked for a verbal report. He filled her in, trying to keep it short but sweet but she interrupted a lot. Captain Savannah Allen liked to talk and always asked a barrage of questions, many of them revolving around procedure and making sure Max had dotted the i's crossed the t's. It was annoying as hell, but Max remained outwardly patient and answered all of her questions while he moved around the small kitchen, dishing up dinner for Gus and Ernie.

Allen finally wound down and ended by telling Max she wanted an Incident Report in her inbox by end of day tomorrow, along with a copy of the WSP missing persons report and any other files related to Hampton. After she hung up, Max sighed and found a notepad to write down tomorrow's tasks. After that, he was able to take a shower and get some food.

After a late, makeshift dinner of Kraft Mac and Cheese with salad, Max settled in on the couch in front of the big screen TV and watched a Mariners versus Angels baseball game recorded from the previous day. He already knew how it turned out, which wasn't well for the Mariners, but Max found that having a baseball game on the TV, sound turned low, was relaxing.

Gus rested, head on paws, on his floor bed in front of the TV, brown eyes staring at Max. Ernie was sound asleep on his little bed in a window nook, so all was quiet on the home front. Max had the windows open and the sweet, fresh smell of summer cottonwoods wafted through the house.

Just as he finished eating, the house phone rang, startling him. Max chugged down the last of his beer and answered.

"Hey big brother!" a deep voice boomed out from the phone. "*Cosa sta succedendo?*"

Max smiled. "Hey Bruno, not much. How's my *fratellino*? How're things in Spokanistan?"

"Oh man, I'm doin' great but busy as hell, as usual, let me tell you. Mostly I-90 speed traps and accident scenes; it never ends. Also? You probably heard, we got some new hires? A whole batch of rookies, and now they're doing field training. So I gotta do some training days with one of 'em, introduce her to the joys of highway patrol. This gal is way too serious, eager and by the book. I'm tryin' to teach her how to pick her battles, *capisci*? Officer discretion? Undo some of the academy bullshit."

"Hell yeah! I used to be that person, and you were too when you started out. I hope you're going easy on her."

"Just some mild hazing, Bro, to keep her on her toes and teach her some important lessons that the academy neglected. Hey, reason I called, wanted to tell you. I saw your name today on a file request list for that missing person's case? Hampton, I think it was. It says you checked that out a couple of weeks ago?"

"Okay . . ." said Max.

"So there's been another request on that list. Alice in records, knowing you're my brother, showed me the list and it shows some FBI dude sent in a request from the Seattle office for that same file. She sent him a digital version. I just thought you should know they're looking into it also."

"You're talking about the Melissa Hampton case, right? Any idea why?"

"Must be something about the case that goes beyond local jurisdiction. Maybe kidnapping? Or something to do with the sub's status prior to her disappearance? I dunno. Anyway, might be worth giving them a call when you can."

"Sure, Bruno. Thanks for the tip. Now I'm really curious. Maybe they're doing some statistical analysis of missing persons. Do you know how many people go missing every year in this country?"

"If I told you that I do have a vague notion of that, would it stop you from lecturing me about it?"

Max laughed. "Nope! Listen up!" Max told his brother that just last year, there'd been 635,000 missing persons cases in the U.S. Most of those were runaways and resolved eventually. But at year's end, there were still over 85,000 active missing person cases. "Some of them are kidnappings. And some, as you know, are homicides. As of today, I know that Melissa Hampton is one of those."

"What? How? Why do you say that? She was never found, so there's no way to know, right?"

"I'm glad you asked." Max told his brother about his strange, sad day in the woods, guarding the charred bones.

When he was done, Bruno whistled and said, "Holy shit, Max. How's that for timing? I call to tell you about the FBI on the same day you find her. So now we're pretty sure

Hampton is dead, and that she was likely murdered. Do you have a cause of death yet?"

"There was no way to tell. I didn't touch anything and couldn't see much. The remains weren't in good shape. The techs and pathologist will tell us more, along with an ID, but that'll take awhile."

"Yeah, good luck with getting the DNA results anytime soon. Maybe, if you're lucky, there's dentals. But hey, it's all the county mounties' case, right? And maybe the FBI's? So no real worries for you, other than being curious. Maybe the FBI has some more info on it. Hey, you know what? I gotta get going. Sara and I are taking the baby to the park before it gets dark." Bruno was silent for a moment and then said, "So, uh, have you talked to Annette lately?"

Max hesitated before answering. "No, not really. We hardly ever talk anymore, just brief texts every few days. Sometimes days without anything. It is definitely over, man. She doesn't want to live in a small town, or be married to a cop."

"Well duh! She grew up in Paris, for crying out loud. Hard to expect a French city girl to take to your rustic country ways."

"Yeah, right. Well, not much more I can do about that. I finally admitted to myself that there's no hope. I do miss her a lot." He paused and said, "I'm pretty sure she's seeing someone else these days. Some jerk fuckwad artist named Chad."

"Hanging Chad?"

"All I need is a rope."

Bruno laughed, told Max to hang in there, laughed again and said goodbye. Max hung up the phone, a sad smile on his face. He looked at the wall clock. It was time to take Gus outside for his evening pee.

Bright pinpoints of stars flickered in the darkening sky and Max was grateful to see them. No light pollution where he was, just the sky as God made it. A broad splash of infinity. Gus sniffed what appeared to be every blade of grass and every bush in the yard before deciding to lift his leg and grace one with his precious urine. Max looked upward and breathed deep, relaxing.

He'd call the Seattle FBI office tomorrow and ask about the Hampton case, find out what their interest was in it. Past experience with the Bureau indicated that they might not be very forthcoming but it was worth a try.

CHAPTER 17 — JULY 5

The acrid smoke was getting thicker, rasping her throat. Faith's headlamp projected a wavering white cone of light on the trail that she could barely see through watering eyes. To her right, a sickly orange glow silhouetted nearby trees. She was on a grassy ridge where stands of firs dotted the meadow. In the dim light, Faith saw dense forest ahead of her.

She berated herself as she slowly walked up the trail, coughing. She used a bandana to wipe tears and mucus from her face. This was not a good idea after all. She still hadn't encountered the others and doubted that would happen at her current pace. Maybe they got through before the wind had shifted out of the southeast and sent fresh smoke surging over the trail. That happened about an hour and a half earlier. Faith stopped and checked her cell phone. 2:36 a.m. How fast would a fire travel with the wind behind it? She figured the wind was blowing 10-15 miles per hour. It wasn't much, but it was enough to turn the flickering, tree-eating beast around and point it in her direction.

She turned and looked to the east. The fire was getting brighter as it advanced uphill toward the ridge she was hiking on. The orange light was almost enough to see by. Time to get going again. She put her cell phone away and resumed walking. The headlamp cast a vague, bobbing circle of light on the dusty trail, but it was enough for her to avoid obstacles such as rocks, roots and dips in the ground.

The smoke got worse. Mucus hung from her nose in a long thread. She flicked it away and stopped to use her

CamelBak hose to soak the bandana. She tied it around her lower face. Breathing through it seemed to help. The firelight suddenly brightened and she looked over her right shoulder to see a nearby stand of pines burst into flame, roaring like a jet engine. Wobbling columns of black smoke shot skyward and disappeared into the darkness. The flames were only about 300 yards away. Faith felt their warmth. She increased the pace, panic starting to scrabble through her thoughts.

Dumb, dumb, dumb. Dumb to not take the detour! She could've dealt with Duster, but this fire? There wasn't anything to do but keep moving; maybe faster now. Maybe a whole lot faster.

The light was such that she no longer needed a headlamp, and that enabled her to increase her pace. Soon she was running intermittently, coughing and stumbling at times through the orange night. She entered thicker forest. The firelight grew dim and she turned on her headlamp again.

Faith was stopped by a wall of branches and prickly fir boughs. They were connected to a large fallen tree lying across the trail. She'd have to go around it. She turned her head and the headlight beam darted through the smoke. To the left was thick brush and dirt-encrusted tendrils of tree roots rising above it. To her right, the tree and its wilting branches faded into darkness. She went right, cursing and stumbling over rocks and branches. Boughs whipped her face and arms. She found a spot to cross where the log narrowed. She boosted herself up onto the trunk and then gently down to the ground on the other side. Her pack caught on a branch and she started to panic. She boosted herself up and pulled the pack loose. Back onto firm ground, she turned left and stumbled back to the trail, coughing.

The fire was getting louder; a muted roaring and crackling interspersed with the occasional thump as a tree crashed to the burning ground. Light flickered through the forest, exploding into brightness as another tree was eaten by soaring flames. Faith decided that it was time to run. No more fucking around. She removed and re-wet her bandana, tied it around her face, checked her pack straps and started trotting down the trail.

It was a living nightmare. It reminded her of that other nightmare she'd brought home from overseas. At least this time there was no enemy trying to kill her. If she got killed, it would be her own damn fault. Her stupidity was the enemy.

She felt the fire's warmth on the back of her neck. Every few steps, she glanced over her shoulder. It seemed to be gaining, bright flames searing stands of trees and exploding up into dark smoke laced with red sparks, roaring and crackling. It had a terrible beauty to it. She started running again, pack bouncing on her back. The warm, smoky air scratched at her throat and lungs.

She briefly considered throwing off the weight and running full out, but everything she needed in order to survive was in that pack. She tightened the shoulder straps and hip belt.

Fifteen minutes later, the trees gave way to more meadows. Faith was glad to feel the wind shift, this time from the west. She noticed the smoke thinning. Breathing got easier. The firelight faded too, so she stopped and turned on her headlamp. She looked back and saw the curtain of smoke peeling back into the fire. Once again, more trees flared up, flames licking at the smoke, but the fire was leaning away from her.

Faith slowed her pace, but pressed on. The wind might shift again. She started uphill, following the trail as it wound up and across a steep, open mountainside, through sparse meadows and rocks. Breathing heavily, still coughing at times, she reached a summit and turned to look at the fire.

"Faith? What the fuck?"

Startled, she turned and flicked on her headlamp. The beam swept over the squinting faces of Thoreau, Owl and the other hikers she'd talked to earlier. They had their packs off and were sitting on rocks, looking toward the fire. Faith turned off her headlamp. The faces of the other hikers glowed red in the faint light.

Thoreau said, "Holy shit! You came through that? You okay?"

Faith nodded, coughed and spit, wiped her nose with the bandana. "Yeah, barely. It was close though. Too close." She rubbed at her eyes.

Owl pointed beyond her. "Oh my god, more than close. The fire burned over the trail. You were just there! Oh my god!"

Faith turned and saw that Owl was right. About a mile back, the ridge that she'd walked along was now a sea of dancing flames and billowing smoke and embers. She muttered, "Holy shit . . . "

Thoreau invited her take her pack off. "It's safe here," he said. "No fuels to burn on this mountain and the wind has shifted in our favor. Besides, you look like you could use a break. Sit and enjoy the Fourth of July fireworks!"

Faith had lost track of time and forgot that it was the Fourth of July, or was that the previous day? She couldn't remember. All of the days blended together. Human designations of time didn't mean much after so much time on the trail. The rising and setting of the sun was what mattered. Every sunrise and every sunset was its own wonderful event to be witnessed and enjoyed, no dates or numbers needed.

Faith set her pack down. She looked at Thoreau, coughed some more and said, "I thought you said it was safe to go through, that fires always die down at night."

The man shook his head. "That's what I thought. That was my experience. I don't know. I guess fire behavior has changed because of the drought or something? Honest, I didn't think the fire would be going like this at night. It ain't fuckin' natural, I'll tell you that. Not natural at all. Look, I'm sorry, but if you'd come with us, it woulda been better. Sometimes timing is everything, know what I mean?"

Her face in shadow, Faith gave him a faint smile that he couldn't see. "You're right, Thoreau. All's well that ends well." She turned and sat on a flat boulder to watch the spectacle. Nobody said a word. It was a strangely beautiful vision of hell. Multiple layers of dark smoke flowed over the fire, their lower edges glowing red or orange, jets of bright flame shooting up through them. Pockets of orange light dotted the dark mountainsides, looking like the flickering campfires of a vast army. They heard the occasional freight-train roar as trees ignited, and the faint thud as burning trees crashed to the ground.

Thoreau finally said, "What made you change your mind? Why did you decide to stay on the PCT?"

Faith didn't want to mention Duster, so she said, "I decided I didn't want to lose the time doing that detour, so decided to cut up from the Sheep Gap Trail and catch up with you guys."

Thoreau said, "Again, I'm sorry, Faith. Sorry that this was my stupid fuckin' idea and that you almost died following us. I've never seen a fire do this. Usually they settle down and get quiet at night. The temperature goes down, the humidity goes up, so the fire's supposed to turn quiet. It's been maybe ten years since my last wildfire though. Like I said, things have changed. I thought it would be safe." He looked around at the others. "I apologize to you all."

Owl and the others told him that it turned out all right and to forget about it. Faith said, "Don't worry, I've seen worse and been closer to the Grim Reaper than this."

Owl said, "Whadda ya mean, Faith? Where? What happened to you?"

Faith looked around. "Nothing, really. I was just kidding, exaggerating. Trying to sound tough when I'm still shaking."

They sat and watched the fire until, after what seemed a very long time, the eastern horizon began to lighten. Eventually a coppery sun climbed up through the smoke and the hikers ate breakfast together. After the meal, they prepared to leave. A faint thumping noise to the west made everyone turn in that direction. The sound grew in volume and through the haze, a helicopter appeared.

"Probably those firefighters again," someone said.

The chopper was a Huey, like the one from the previous day. As it approached, it turned in their direction, ruddy sunlight flashing off plexiglass, and circled around the group. Faith saw the helmeted pilot looking down on them. After the sounds of the wilderness, the thumping roar was overwhelming. Faith put her hands to her ears and squinted as grass and other light debris swirled in the rotors' wind. The helicopter peeled away and drifted north, down to an open saddle where it settled onto wind-beaten grass next to the trail. Faith and the other hikers shouldered their packs and started hiking down the trail toward where the helicopter had landed. They heard the machine's turbine engine winding down and finally stop.

Faith coughed and kept rubbing her eyes as she hiked. They were gritty and sore. Her throat was sore too, and she felt like she'd been dragged behind a Humvee. She was hoping to take a nap sometime soon, maybe after getting clear of the smoke, if that was possible.

Owl said, "Oh my god, I bet we're gonna get a ticket."

"Why would they give us a ticket?" asked Faith. "How many other hikers do you think did the same thing? And maybe that's a different helicopter and different firefighters."

Thoreau said, "You never know with those dudes. Some are real hard-asses, authoritarian pigs, by-the-book assholes."

Faith shook her head and said, "No use speculating. We'll find out soon enough."

Ten minutes later, they reached the saddle and followed the trail toward the silent machine. One of the crew was tying down a rotor blade. Four other firefighters were unloading supplies from a rear cargo compartment, stacking taped bundles of pulaskis and shovels and cardboard cases of MREs. A blonde woman in a green Nomex flight suit stood off to the side, holding a bulky helmet in one hand and smoking a cigarette. She watched the hikers approach and wished them a good morning.

Faith answered, "Good morning yourself. Nice helicopter you got there. Can we hitch a ride?"

The pilot blew out a cloud of smoke and said, "If I had a nickel for every time somebody asked me for a ride, I could buy my own ship and make money hauling weary hikers. You people all headed for Canada?"

All of them said they were. Owl asked, "Are we in trouble?"

"Trouble? You mean because of the fire?"

"No, because we—"

"Yeah, we were wondering if the fire's gonna be a threat as we head north from here," Thoreau said.

The pilot dropped her cigarette butt in the trail dirt and ground it out with a boot heel. "Not if you keep hiking and get some miles behind you today, pronto. The fire's changed direction so many times, I can't even keep count. Just keep on hiking. Tomorrow could be bad around here."

"Yeah, keep hiking," said a man's voice behind them, "and this time follow the damn directions." The group turned to see the tall, bearded firefighter from the previous day. He pulled off a dusty red hardhat and ran a hand through his matted hair. "I oughta write you dumbshits some goddamn violation notices. Jesus, did you think I was messin' around yesterday? Did you think I was kiddin'? Hell, did you all make it through? Anyone missing?"

Thoreau answered him, "Everybody that was there when you left yesterday made it through. I dunno about anyone else."

The firefighter kept glowering at them. "Good. We got our hands full with this fire and watching out for our own people. For god's sake, just use your fucking heads and follow the goddamn instructions, okay? This fire, any fire, is nothing to fuck around with, do you understand?"

The hikers sullenly nodded their heads. The pilot said, "Take it easy, Todd. I think they get it now."

Todd said, "I damn sure hope so" and stalked off to help his co-workers.

The pilot told the group, "Todd lost a good friend a couple of weeks ago. Got burned over in a fire shelter and didn't survive. He's a little sensitive right now, so you folks might as well move on. Been good talking to you. Remember what he said, fires are nothing to fuck with!"

Faith silently agreed. She'd learned her lesson and swore to herself to never again be caught off guard by a wildfire. As the small group moved out, Thoreau invited Faith to hike with them for a few days but she declined.

"I'll hike with you guys today, for a while," she said, "but once we get clear of the smoke, I'm finding a creek and taking a bath, and then I'm going to get caught up on some sleep!"

CHAPTER 18 — JULY 9

He managed to keep most of the blood inside the large stainless steel tub. The Mentor nodded with approval and said, "You've really gotten the hang of our process. Well done. So now on to the grinding and packaging. After that, we'll respectfully dispose of the bones."

Joey nodded and wiped his brow with the back of a blue-gloved hand. The other hand held a large, bloodstained butcher knife. He said, "What about the head? The usual?"

The Mentor nodded. "Yep, just make sure you remove some locks of lovely hair before we place the head in the incinerator. It has to be completely turned to ash so that there's no DNA or teeth, no structure of any kind either macro or microscopic."

"Dude, I dunno what you just said, but I get it about the ash thing." He picked up the head by its hair and made a face at it.

The Mentor's face reddened under his beard and he said, "Knock it off, Joey! Show some respect. She was lost and lonely. Now she's safely mine, and soon she'll be a part of so many other people."

Joey's face grew solemn as he said, "Sure man. Sorry. I understand, I guess."

The Mentor laughed gently as he gazed at the dismembered body in the steel tub. "Yep, at least I know you try to understand. She needs to be spread out through her community, to live on in their strivings. We're the ones that help her do that. I own her, and then if she's worthy, I share her. She would've wanted that. She always wanted to share herself."

Joey shook his head and looked at the Mentor. "But she's a stranger, right? Like the other ones? You act like you know her."

Thunder boomed overhead, rattling the space and the two men. Joey looked up at the trailer's ceiling as rain began tapping on the roof. The mentor smiled calmly.

"I do know her. She always comes to me to be shared, over and over."

Thunder hammered the air and lightning flashed at the same time. It was late afternoon and the old guy looked scared. Joey had never seen that before and was intrigued. Over the roar of the rain, he yelled, "We have to get going! We have to get the hell out of here!"

"Why?" asked Joey, his voice muffled by a respirator. He was standing near the middle of the trailer, next to a square metal box about four feet high by three feet wide. It was capped by an intricate steel device that sprouted a round gauge, some switches and a hose. The latter spiraled out and led to one of the trailer's propane ports. A low hissing noise came from inside the box. "I'm not done with the disposal yet. The incinerator's still workin'."

His companion ran to a window and looked out. Then he ran out the back door and stood in the rain, turning in a circle. He came back into the trailer, water dripping from his beard. "Well, done or not, we need to go! It's like I thought. That last bolt of lightning? Started a fire in the trees nearby. I can smell the smoke. We could burn up, or worse, be visited by a nosey group of firefighters. Shut down the burner, bag what you have and be quick! We'll bury it in the forest. I'll head out to dig a hole. We gotta move fast!"

"Maybe we should just get going, bury the bones somewhere down the road?"

"No! No, I've never done that. I picked this spot for the operation and this is where we'll get it done."

"But we'd have more time to burn the bones and get rid of 'em—"

"No, goddammit! We need to get rid of them here, now and fast!"

"Sure, boss. But . . . okay, sure. Still, if we're in such a hurry, like I said, we could just drive off now and bury them someplace else."

The Boss grabbed a shovel and was on his way out the door. He yelled, "Just do as I say! I know things you don't so just listen to me. Bag the bones!"

Joey shrugged. Maybe the old guy had a point. It wasn't his place to decide. He flicked a switch and the hissing roar stopped. After carefully disconnecting the hose, he lifted the lid and leaned back as a cloud of bitter smoke and steam puffed out. He peered into the box and shook his head. There was a lot left in there. Wearing insulated gloves, he carefully lifted the partially burnt bones and placed them on the steel table located in the middle of the trailer kitchen. As they cooled, he opened a drawer and removed a plastic bag, shook it open. It took only a few moments to sweep the bones into the bag. Some of the bones were still hot and melted holes in the bag. Joey shrugged and muttered, "Fuck it."

He removed the respirator and goggles, lifted the heavy bag and staggered out the door to stand in the cold rain, looking around. He heard the man shout from the forest, "Over here, and quickly!"

Joey swung the bag over his shoulder and lurched in the direction of the voice. Rain pelted his face and he grumbled. Bones are a lot heavier than people think. Usually the remains they processed were much lighter, almost completely turned to ash before he disposed of them. This reminded him of what happened last year in Washington State, when the old guy made a mistake and thought there wouldn't be any people. Boy was he wrong! Sure it was far up a lousy road, but that didn't stop the hordes of hikers from showing up on Friday afternoon. Boss said to shut down the incinerator because of the fumes and smoke venting from a hidden chimney in the roof of the trailer. And then they waited until two in the morning to haul the remains a short distance into the forest where they hastily buried them. It was a rushed job, but so far so good. Nobody found the bones. Joey hoped that would also be the case this time.

His moccasin-clad feet hurt from small rocks and sticks as he covered the final 20 feet and lowered the bag to the ground next to the new hole. The old guy, digging frantically, was soaked by rain and sweat. The hole looked to be about three feet deep by two feet wide. He looked up at Joey and said, "Another few inches and then dump the bones in. We'll cover them up and get the hell out of here."

They worked fast and within minutes were on their way back to the trailer. A distant pounding could be heard, more of a feeling in the air than a sound. The old guy said, "Hear that? Here they come. The firefighters in a fucking helicopter. We gotta hurry!"

They broke into a run. At the trailer, Joey secured the incinerator by sliding it into a cavity under the kitchen's double sink. He heard the pickup's diesel engine clatter to life and within moments they were rolling down the muddy road. The rain slackened even as the pounding grew louder. The old guy stopped at the gate and waited while Joey jumped out of the truck and dragged the heavy metal gate open. He drove through, braked to a stop and watched in the side mirror as his apprentice closed the gate. Joey threw open the passenger side door and leaped into the seat. The Mentor shifted the truck into "Drive" and they moved slowly onto the highway and drove off. The sound of the helicopter diminished.

Despite his agitation, the older man kept their speed to the posted limit. He pounded the steering wheel with one hand and said, “That was damn sloppy! This makes two years in a row now that this has happened. We gotta more careful. Order and cleanliness and consistency of operations is the key that’ll allow us to continue our activities. Are you with me, Joey?”

Joey looked at him. “You know I am, Boss. So what’s the plan now?”

“Okay. I’m going to drop you off shortly. Your job is to get back on the trail and be on the lookout for her. Let me know if you see her and where. We’ll plan from there. And this time I want it to be *Her*! Not another substitute, another wanna-be. She’s gotta be the real deal. We’ll plan the harvest real careful and we’ll take her. I’ll take her. She’s special and this time it’ll just be me once you help me catch her.” He looked over at his apprentice. “Don’t worry, we’ll take another one for you later so you’ll get your reward.”

Joey turned to look at the old guy. He grinned through his beard and said, “Sure, Boss. Lookin’ forward to it.”

CHAPTER 19 — JULY 11

Crater Lake looked like an inland sea. It was the biggest lake Faith had seen for a while and reminded her of something out of a fantasy tale. All around, mountainous walls encircled the lake in a giant rocky bowl. To the northwest, the symmetrical cone of Wizard Island poked up from the serene and unbelievably blue waters. Far to the north and faint in the hazy distance, Mount Thielsen's white, pointy pyramid rose from a sea of low, forested mountains.

Faith wondered if Lila ever got to see this view. If she got this far before . . . before whatever happened to her happened. Lila had disappeared somewhere between Lake of the Woods and Crater Lake; about a 60-mile stretch of trail. That was only three to four days of hiking.

Faith had been thinking about her sister for the last week, wondering about her fate as the miles went by. She remembered her parents describing how they'd searched that stretch of trail ten years ago, back and forth, from the ground and from the air, until the winter drove them off. Faith herself had covered some of the same ground the following spring, helping in the search while she was on leave. She recalled seeing the maps that her dad kept in the cardboard box with the rest of the file records. They were the same maps they'd used in the search, stained with coffee and crumpled, marked with various colored lines showing search patterns, potential locations, aerial versus ground grids. To Faith the lines were marks of desperation and anguish, a record of grief and futile determination.

By the following summer, they'd given up the search and hoped that someday, somewhere, somehow, Lila would turn up. Ten years gone and she never did. Faith doubted that anyone would ever know what happened to her sister.

She stood on the rim of the old crater for a while, looking over the rock wall at the vast expanse of shimmering blue lake, and the steep cliffs beyond. Eventually she set her pack down and sat on the wall, still gazing out. It was a good place to sit and wait. She practiced mindful breathing like the therapist had taught her, letting go of the thoughts and feelings, focusing on what was in front of her.

Billowing white cumulus clouds towered in the sky, looking like mountains themselves. Faith imagined that's what Mount Mazama must've looked like before it blew up. Tall and shining white in the blue sky until a massive volcanic explosion pulverized the rock and ice and spread the mountain dust across North America, leaving behind a gaping crater that gradually filled with crystal clear water.

Faith wiped a bandana across her face, mopping up sweat. Although it was not yet noon, the air was hot and humid. It felt like a storm was brewing.

She was waiting for the shuttle bus from Klamath Falls to arrive with Jenks and his wife Julia. Back in March, Jenks had booked two lakeside rooms for them in the lodge, which was a great opportunity for Faith to get a rare shower and sleep in a bed. At the same time, he made dinner reservations for the three of them at the lodge dining room that night. She was certainly looking forward to that meal. She knew it must be expensive, but she also knew that Jenks was doing well as sales rep for a large Portland brewery. He could afford it.

Faith looked around her, up at the three to four story stone and wood building with its line of dormer windows and green roofing. The Crater Lake Lodge was over 100 years old but still looked good. She smiled as she thought, *I hope I look that good at 100.*

Knowing that Julia would be with him, Faith felt her heart sink. Although she had no claim on Jenks anymore, she still felt sad and a little angry that she wouldn't have him to herself. It wasn't his fault. Julia was his wife and wanted to see Crater Lake and hike part of the PCT too. Faith had met her and liked her, but still . . . well, so it goes, she thought. It was almost time for the shuttle to arrive. She shouldered her pack and started back toward the lodge. Thunder rumbled in the distance.

On the way, a familiar voice called out from behind her, "Hey Beauty!" She turned and saw Duster striding toward her, his namesake long coat flapping behind him. Faith could see the handle of a large Bowie knife on his belt. She turned around and continued on her way, wincing as she heard footsteps behind her and Duster's deep voice said, "Hey, hey! Wait up. Good to see you too. Geez!"

Faith stopped and turned to face him. He looked much the same except that his hair and beard were even longer. To Faith, he looked a lot like a Taliban fighter.

He stopped and grinned at her. "Good to see you, Faith! I was wondering if I'd run into you again someday, especially after that forest fire. I never saw you on the detour and was afraid you got burnt along with Thoreau and his bunch. Glad you made it!" He looked around, eyes wide. "Hey, you still on your own? No fantasy boyfriend? So why don't we hike together? I can be good company. I'm a fun guy!"

Faith glared at him, thought *you're definitely a fungi.* She said, "Duster, what are you doing? I don't know why you keep thinking that I want anything to do with you. Really, you need to back off. Just go away, okay? Have a great trip."

She started to turn away but noticed the hurt in Duster's eyes. It looked genuine and she was surprised to feel a pang of regret. She sighed and said, "Look, I'm just not interested in your company. There's dozens, maybe hundreds of other women on the trail and I'm sure there's some interested in hiking with you. I'm not. I hope you do have a great rest of your trip, and if I see you, I promise to say hi, okay?"

She started to turn away again but Duster grabbed her right arm, snarling, "Don't give me that false pity bullshit, Faith!"

She wrenched her arm loose, spun around and almost decked the man. He fell back a step or two, eyes wide in surprise. Faith could only wonder what was on her face, in her eyes, but whatever it was, it gave Duster pause. It didn't stop him though. He had to keep talking, his face contorted by anger.

"Shit! You beautiful bitches are all the same, aren't you? Too good for a regular guy like me. Always go for the beefed up macho guys, the rich fuckers with their money and their fancy cars. Whoever makes you feel good about yourself. Well, let me tell you something, bitch—"

Duster paused and his eyes focused on something over Faith's left shoulder. She turned to see Jenks striding up, his angular face tight with concern. "Hey, what's going on here?"

Jenks was a big guy and although he'd put on some weight, he was still muscular and could be intimidating. Duster fell back another step and his mouth jerked around before he managed to say, "Nothing. None of your business. Just having a little talk with the lady here. Trying to get some stuff straight."

Jenks stopped next to Faith and gave her a questioning look. She shrugged and looked back at Duster before saying, "I was just telling this guy that I didn't want his company and was wishing him a good trip. He was a little upset, but I think he'll be all right now."

Duster looked from one to the other. They looked back. Jenks finally said softly, “Time to be on your way, friend. Go in peace, or wind up in pieces. It’s up to you.”

Duster put up his hands. “Hey dude, no need to get your panties in a bunch. Jesus, I was just talkin’ to the lady here. Okay, okay, I’m goin’. See you around, Faith?”

Jenks lunged toward him and Duster scampered off, looking back over his shoulder. Faith said, “Thanks, Jenks! Good to see you.”

He clapped her on the back and gave her a quick hug. “You too, Faith. So who was that guy, and is he a problem?”

She looked at the retreating Duster. “I’ve run into him a few times. I think he’s a harmless perv and a bit of a thief. He thinks he likes me even though I haven’t encouraged him at all. Quite the opposite.”

Jenks looked at her in disbelief. “Harmless perv? No such thing, Faith. No such fuckin’ thing! Any guy wearing a long coat on a hot day is up to no good, that I can tell you. You want me to have another word with the shitweasel before we check in?”

She shook her head. “No. If he’s a problem later, you know I can take care of it.”

Jenks grinned. “Oh yeah, I do know that. That’s why I want to talk to this guy again, give him a friendly warning!” She laughed and Jenks said, “Come on, Jarhead! Julia’s waiting out front with our packs. Let’s go check in!” He took her pack and effortlessly slung it over his shoulder. Together they headed for the lodge parking lot.

As they walked, Faith turned her head to look up at Jenks and said, “Seriously? ‘Go in peace or wind up in pieces’? What movie did you get that from?”

Jenks’ face twisted into mock outrage. “Hey! I came up with that myself, just now. I thought it was pretty good! Very Schwarzeneggian! I should’ve said it with an Austrian accent.”

Faith laughed and punched him lightly on the shoulder, said, "Glad to see you're still a big goof."

Faith, Jenks and Julia were seated at a round table in the lodge's stone walled dining room. The table was covered by a white linen cloth and positioned next to tall windows that provided a perfect view of the lake. Shafts of rich sunlight flowed in under the storm clouds and painted the mountain walls with golden light. There had been a hell of a wet thunderstorm that afternoon and the land was rich with fresh color from the rains.

Faith thought it was the best meal she'd ever had. The lodge chef, whoever it was, sure knew what he or she was doing. The three of them shared an appetizer of Oregon mushrooms and polenta cakes, followed by salads and entrees. Faith had the grilled Caesar salad, followed by an 8-ounce filet mignon with baked potato, accompanied by a draft Full Sail Ale. After all that, she was still hungry and asked about dessert, which made Jenks crack up.

He turned to Julia and said, "This is a woman who used to eat like a bird. A very small bird. Probably a wren. Look at her now; eating like an eagle!"

Faith smiled sheepishly. Julia laughed. She was a petite woman but had managed to put away her fair share of food too. "It's okay, Faith," she said. "When I'm training for an Ironman, I consume millions of calories. You need those calories! So how many miles a day are you averaging?"

"I'm up to around 25 miles now. I probably put in an eight to ten-hour day hiking but I'm not hurrying like some people do."

"Holy shit!" said Jenks loudly. "You know, I read about some woman doing over 40 miles a day. Fucking insane! We didn't even do that in the Rangers. Well, at least not very often. Only when we fuckin' had to!"

Julia said softly but sternly, "Jenks. Language. Remember you've got a loud voice and people can hear you."

Jenkins looked around. Other diners were glancing in their direction. He grinned, hunched forward and whispered, "I'm fuckin' sorry, ladies. My goddamn language skills have been permanently perverted by my service to your country, so pardon me all to hell."

Faith laughed and shook her head. "Jenks, you haven't changed a bit. Julia, did you know what you were getting into?"

Julia looked at her and nodded. "Yes, yes I did, but his boyish charm and rugged good looks won me over. As long as he keeps his mouth shut, he's not so bad."

They decided against dessert and instead ordered more beers before moving out to the patio. The sun was down and there was a slight chill, but the air was sweet and fresh and the view was stupendous. The storm clouds were fading away now. Far above in the vast sky, their remnant tatters still glowed red. Nighthawks soared in the deepening blue.

Faith, Jenks and Julia sat in rustic wicker chairs, looking out at the land and sky as they talked and enjoyed their drinks.

Julia said, "Faith, you mentioned that you're doing 25 miles a day? Not sure we'll be able to keep up with you, at least at first."

"Not a problem. I don't mind slowing down for a few days. I have to keep moving though. People say that the last 200 or so miles through the North Cascades can be bad after mid-September. Snowstorms and winds, rain; that kind of thing."

Jenks looked at her. "You've changed, Faith. Used to be the worse it got, the more you liked it."

Faith nodded and was silent a moment. "Yeah, that's true enough, but you know what happened over there. That clusterfuck changed me, Jenks. I'm older now and I thought I was wiser, but just a week or so ago, due to poor judgement, I had a close encounter with the reaper."

"Over where, Faith?" Julia said.

Jenks said, "Afghanistan. I didn't tell you about it, Sweetie. Some of it's classified. I don't think Faith wants to talk about it right now."

Faith nodded. "Sorry, Julia. I'll tell you about it some day; just not today. Anyway, last week . . ." She told them about her hellish trip to escape the wildfire, including why she decided not to take the detour. When she finished, Jenks looked concerned.

"This fuckin' Duster guy? I don't know. I think he's a problem. The way he keeps runnin' into you? I think he's stalking you. Makes my Spidey sense tingle. And the fact that he caused you to make a lousy decision? Not good. In a way, the fucker almost got you killed."

"Not really. It was my lousy judgement that did that. But that's not gonna happen again. As for Duster, I just don't know about the guy. It's normal to encounter the same people over and over. That's the way it is on the trail. Sometimes you get ahead of people and later they pass you, and then you meet 'em when you get a resupply. People leapfrog each other all the time on the PCT."

Jenks shook his head and leaned forward. "This feels different. I can read people pretty good and just that brief encounter today gave me some bad vibes. I think the guy's got some kind of obsession with you. I think we should deal with him."

Julia's eyes grew wide and she whispered, "What're you talking about? You mean kill him?"

Jenks laughed. "No, no, no. I mean maybe just rough him up a little. You know, give him a friendly warning, maybe even disable him slightly. Nothin' permanent. Maybe just a broken leg, by accident? I could make it look like an accident."

Faith shook her head. “No, I don’t like that. Not a good idea. My trip isn’t about that. It’s not about violence. I’ve had enough of that shit.”

“I can’t believe you two are having this discussion,” Julia said, looking from one to the other. “It’s scary. You can’t just beat someone up like that, without provocation. How can you sit there and calmly talk about breaking somebody’s leg as if it’s just a project or something?”

“Now, Julia,” said Jenks, patting her arm. “We won’t do anything like that. Don’t worry, Sweetie. We were just speculating. Neither Faith or I will put the hurt on anyone.”

Julia stood up, frowning. “Well, I’m going to bed. I don’t like this talk. I don’t understand your world, the world you live in. It’s like you two are in some kind of special club that I can never be a member of.”

“Julia, now wait a sec!”

Julia started to walk away and turned to say, “Goodnight, Faith. I’m sorry.” She shook her head. “I’ll be all right. Sometimes I just get . . . well . . . look, I’ll see you in the morning.”

“That’s okay, Julia. Good night.”

They watched her walk away. Jenks shrugged and turned to Faith. “She’s a little sensitive about the things we did in the service, about violence and guns and war in general. She doesn’t like to hear about it. About that I did things, you know, that we had to do things, that we had to fight. I think she understands why, but the idea of hurting any human or animal really upsets her. It’s the way she is, and it’s one of the things I love about her.”

Faith smiled. “Well then, soldier. You better go right now, go to her and tell her that!”

Jenks stood up and stretched. “You’re right, Faith. Thanks for understanding. Sweet dreams, Jarhead.”

He paused at the door and said, “So what time tomorrow do we head out? Zero dark thirty?”

"Hell no! I've got a real bed for a change and I'm going to sleep in. We can leave at 0700, after breakfast at 0600."

Jenks laughed and shook his head. "You call that sleeping in? You PCT hikers are a crazy bunch. Okay, we'll be ready to go at 0600. Goodnight, Faith."

"Goodnight, Jenks."

Faith stayed a while longer on the patio. It was growing dark and getting cold, but she felt good, content to have had a great meal, the company of friends and the prospect of a soft bed to sleep in. She was very relieved to find that despite her perception that Julia didn't like her, they seemed to be getting along well. Tomorrow the three of them would head out. Faith was glad to have company for a change.

A boisterous family appeared on the patio, excited children running everywhere. Faith watched them for a while, smiling at their antics. She wondered what it would be like to have children, wondered if she even wanted children after the things she'd seen. Even in this day and age, there was subtle social pressure on young women to have kids. That pressure caused Faith to feel a slight guilt for not wanting any, but she felt too damaged by the experiences she'd had to consider herself mother material. Maybe that would change, maybe not. She decided not to worry about it. That was something that the trail had taught her. Don't worry about things that you don't need to deal with right now. Focus on here and now.

Faith decided that right here and right now, she was getting very sleepy. She pushed herself out of the wicker chair and stretched. Had she taken a moment to look down onto the road that ran below and parallel to the lodge's patio, she might've seen a dark figure in a long coat standing in the shadow of a tree, watching her as she turned, walked to the lodge doors and disappeared into the building.

CHAPTER 20 — JULY 24

Faith felt lonely for the first time on her long journey. Standing high on breezy Park Ridge, she looked south, down toward the lumpy meadows of Jefferson Park. A pair of ravens flapped by, wings swooshing. Small mosquitoes whined around her face and an intermittent light rain pattered on her raincoat and pack cover. Low grey cloud and shredded mist allowed only glimpses of the massive Mount Jefferson volcano that loomed beyond the meadows. Zooming in with her camera, she saw Jenks and Julia heading back down the trail, toward the Whitewater Creek trailhead. One of Julia's friends was picking them up there. Reluctantly, they both had to return to their jobs and obligations in the outside world.

Faith smiled. It had been a good journey with those two. Faith was happy to find that she liked Julia more each day. It helped that Julia didn't hook up with Jenks until some time after the divorce, so she had nothing to do with their marriage breaking up. The breakup was caused by a lot of things. Too much time overseas, away from home, moving from base to base. Jenks couldn't deal with it, or deal with her when she'd come back from an operation, silent and messed up in the head. She didn't blame him. At one point, she wanted to divorce herself too. Well, that was water long gone under the bridge. These were new days, brighter days, and Faith was happy that Jenks was her friend and that she had a new friend in Julia.

The weather had been hot and dry the last two weeks, with occasional evening thunderstorms. Slow at first, with blisters, aches and pains, Jenks and Julia had recovered from their afflictions and gotten stronger every day. By the time they were due to leave, both wanted to continue hiking with Faith. They were hooked on the Pacific Crest Trail.

Even though they couldn't see her, Faith waved toward her departing friends. With a sigh, she turned and looked north. The pyramid of Mount Hood was somewhere ahead and would've been visible but for the low clouds. So many volcanoes, thought Faith. She'd never seen so many, from Crater Lake north. Even before that there'd been Mount Shasta and Lassen Peak, not to mention numerous cinder cones and lava fields. Oregon had more than its share of cinder cones, hills of pumice, vast rugged lava fields, towering volcanoes with snowfields and glaciers on their flanks. It was fascinating, but by now she was looking forward to reaching Washington and its more varied terrain. And looking forward to more forest. The PCT in Oregon wound through never-ending stands of silver snags, killed by fire, always reminding Faith of her close encounter with death in California.

She stopped and turned around to try for another glimpse of Mount Jefferson. The dark clouds still hid it and were threatening to engulf her as well. She looked down on the Park and saw movement. A small figure walking north on the trail, weaving through small stands of ragged firs and hemlocks, long coat flapping in the breeze.

She zoomed in with her camera. It focused on the figure of Duster, pack on his back, trudging up the trail. Faith felt a surge of anger and a faint, tingling fear. How does he keep turning up? She would run repeatedly into other hikers but eventually wouldn't see them anymore. But Duster kept appearing, always alone. He was either behind her, or ahead of her, so how does he manage to do that? And why?

She'd last seen him a few days ago at Elk Lake, where she, Jenks and Julia spent the night at the campground and picked up their resupply packages. The TGI Monday's food trailer was parked there and serving meals, so they decided to try it out. Faith had been hoping to sample The Chef's food since she first saw his trailer down in California.

The trailer and truck with camper sat in a clearing near the resort and was surrounded by hungry hikers. The smell was wonderful and the trio walked up to the serving window where trays of steaming food waited. That night's selection was hamburgers, salad and fries, with a choice of meat or veggie patties.

When Faith stepped up to be served, the tall, heavyset, bearded man behind the counter fumbled a spatula and staggered back. He turned away for a moment and then turned back, a ghastly smile pasted on his pale face.

Faith asked him if he was okay. The man answered, "Fine, thank you. Um, not feeling well suddenly." He turned to a grey-haired woman in the trailer and said, "Shasta, could you take over? I need to go lie down for a bit." Turning back to Faith and her friends, he said, "Forgive me, um, I need to go rest now."

Shasta cheerfully took over and served them delicious hamburgers and homemade fries. They ate standing up at one of several folding tables set up in the shade of pine trees.

Julia said, "This food is awesome! And it's free? How can they afford to do that?"

Wiping his mouth with a napkin, Jenks said, "I hear The Chef is loaded, as in he's a fuckin' billionaire! You remember! Josh Monday? Former tech lord and billionaire? He was bigger than Bill Gates a few years back. There was a recent article about him in some outdoor magazine, said he was a retired tech dude that loves the PCT and this was his hobby –"

Faith saw Jenks' face tighten up. He was looking over her shoulder and she turned to see what had caused such an abrupt change.

There was barely a glimpse, but it was enough. A bearded man with long dark hair, wearing a long coat, darting behind some trees.

Jenks wadded up his napkin and said to Faith and Julia, "Okay, I am going to mess up that pervert motherfucker. He knows to stay away from you, Faith. He knows! Remember what I said? There's no such thing as a harmless perv."

Faith grabbed his right arm. "Jenks, he IS staying away. What we saw was him staying away. Please don't make trouble."

Julia echoed that. "Really, Jenks! Faith is right. Let it go. You need to learn that not everything can be handled with violence or aggression. Besides, it wouldn't be a fair fight."

Jenks laughed. "Fair fight? When I have to fight, it's to win. Fairness has nothing to do with it. Still, I know we talked about this, Jule. I know. Okay, I'll let it go. I'll let him go. But if we see him again, I'm not holding back."

Faith remembered Jenks' words as she stood on the windy ridge and watched the distant Duster through a gauzy curtain of rain. He somehow avoided running into Jenks and Julia, or he wouldn't be hiking right now. He'd be crippled up. So that means he hid from them? Or maybe was camping nearby and somehow missed running into any of them? Faith had no way of knowing, but she was thinking that maybe it was finally time she turned the tables on Duster.

CHAPTER 21 — July 24

Faith picked a spot two miles farther up the trail, where it descended into a landscape of rocky meadows and bands of fir and hemlock trees. The fog was thick there, with occasional beams of weak sunlight burning through. At times Faith saw patches of blue overhead. She hiked into a stand of trees, took off her pack, leaned the hiking poles against a rock. After making sure her folding SOG knife was in a cargo pocket, Faith sat on a boulder next to the trail.

She wasn't entirely happy with the situation and was almost afraid of hurting the creeper walking into her trap. At the same time, he was making her mad enough to not care. She waited and listened to the cool wind whispering through the trees, the staccato hammering of a woodpecker, the sharp chirps of tiny birds. All the while she stared back down the trail, across the misty clearing she'd just hiked through, waiting.

After a few minutes, her straining eyes saw a dark form taking shape in the fog. It was a walking man, a man in a long coat. As it got closer, the shape resolved itself into that of Duster. He was hiking with his head down and hands gripping the pack's shoulder straps. She could hear his boots thumping on the trail, getting louder. Faith waited until he was about 10 feet away before saying, "Yo, Duster, what're you doing?"

Duster jumped, his head jerked up and he stopped. Staring at Faith, his eyes grew wide for a moment, and then narrowed. His mouth twisted into a smirk as he said, "Hello, Beauty! Didn't expect to see you here. Were you waitin' for Duster? Are you finally ready to spend some time together?"

Faith sighed. "Duster, why are you following me? Why do I keep running into you? What do you think you're doing?"

He shook his head, eyes wide in feigned innocence. "I don't know what you're talkin' about, Faith. I'm hikin' the PCT. Simple as that. It's not my fault you keep showing up, that our paths keep crossin'. Maybe it's fate, though. You ever think of that? You know, you've never really given me a chance. I'm a nice guy and I dig you. You got a problem with that?"

"I do if it means you're stalking me, sneaking around."

Duster laughed. It sounded forced. "So now Duster is a stalker? You want me to change my trail name to Stalker? Would that make you happy?"

Stone faced, Faith said, "What would make me happy is that I not see you again on the trail, or anywhere else, ever. What would make me happy is if you keep on walking and you don't stop. Right on up to Canada."

"Aw, Faith, that's not fair. Then I'm gonna feel like I'm bein' pushed. I'll keep lookin' back over my shoulder, afraid that you'll think I'm a stalker if I take a rest day and you happen to catch up. No, it's not fair."

Faith stood up, pulled her hands out of her pockets. "I'm telling you right now to quit following me, and that I better not see you again."

Duster looked around, his bearded face twisted into mock concern. "Well now, Faith, you're starting to scare me. By the way, where's your big boyfriend and his cute little blonde friend? Boy, has she got a fine ass! Um, are they around? Close by? I don't see 'em. Maybe they're getting ahead. Maybe we should get goin' and catch up to them. Or maybe they left you all alone out here. Maybe they thought you needed some Duster time."

Faith could feel anger and adrenalin surge, sparking a fierce primal joy at what might happen next. She stood staring at Duster, her face without expression. He began to look concerned, but once again could not shut up.

"Faith, I should tell you I've taken quite a fancy to you. And I like your spunk too. You're spunky. That's a weird word, but it's you. I think we could really hit it off if you gave me a chance. We could hike together all the way to Canada, you and me. Long days on the trail, beautiful nights together in a tent. Whaddaya say?"

Faith felt her control slipping but she kept her voice level. "I say you get moving, Duster. Now! Just quit talking, turn around and keep on walking. Away, that is."

"Or what?" Duster laughed. "Little girl gonna get mad and beat up poor old Duster? Or maybe your boyfriend will come swooping in? I don't think so, on either count." Moving slowly, he took his pack off and set it on the ground. He sighed, saying, "I think maybe Duster needs to teach Faith a lesson in respect. Know what I mean?"

He started toward her. He was leering and holding up his hands as if to grab her breasts. Faith stood still as a rock and waited. When Duster was close enough, she lashed out with her right foot, fast as a lightning bolt, and booted him in the groin. He staggered back and doubled up, almost fell over.

"Uhnn . . . Uhnnn . . . H-h-holy . . . shit . . . Jesus fucking Christ!" he gasped. "Whaddaya do that for? Fuck!!"

Faith stood silent and still and watched. Bent over, Duster staggered around in a circle and groaned, then stopped and glared at her through ragged locks of stringy hair. "You fuckin' bitch!" he wheezed. "Sucker kick me in the balls, will ya? I'll teach you a fuckin' lesson you'll never forget!"

He managed to straighten up enough to pull a long, shiny knife from his belt. Waving it around, he started circling Faith. "Sorry to do this, Faith, but yer gonna pay for that. Yeppers, I'm gonna have me some of yer sweet honey and teach you a lesson too. Yep!"

Faith waited as Duster kept waving his knife and moving in a circle around her. It became obvious that he didn't want to get much closer, so Faith spoke up. "Duster, what're you doing? What's with the knife and the dancing around? You going to do something or what? I've gotta get my miles in today."

"You fuckin' cunt. I'll do somethin'! I'll do you!" He jumped and lunged at her with the knife. Faith calmly avoided the flashing steel blade and grabbed his wrist with her right hand. In one fluid motion, she twisted and pulled the knife out of his hand and flicked it away. Using his momentum, she grabbed his arm with her left hand and pulled him toward her, raised her knee and drove it into his solar plexus. Duster stumbled a few steps and crumpled to the ground. He curled up into a ball, croaking.

Faith kneeled next to his head and pulled out her knife, flicked it open. She held it close to his scrunched up face, where he could see the steely five-inch blade. His eyes opened and then opened wider. "Duster, I really don't like hurting people. I didn't want to ever do it again, but here we are. Shit. If I see you again anywhere within a hundred meters of me, I will kill you. I'll kill you and hide the body where no one will ever find it. Do you believe me?"

Duster croaked and wheezed some more.

Faith cocked her head to one side and calmly said, "What? I'm having trouble hearing you. Try again."

He managed to gasp, "I believe you, bitch. I believe you. Goddamn, I think you broke my balls and my fuckin' arm!"

"No, they just feel that way. You'll be fine . . . eventually. By the way, why all the harassment in California? Messing with my camps? Shitting on the ground next to my tent? What the hell was that about?"

"What? Shi--, no! Christ, it hurts! Uhhnnn . . . no, wasn't me. Someone else? Not my style to harass like that. I didn't do it!"

Faith remembered the peculiar odor from the shit she buried; the apple and cinnamon odor she associated with Slowpoke. Maybe Duster was telling the truth. She hadn't seen Slowpoke in a long time, and the harassment had stopped at Feather River. She shook her head and said, "Okay, whatever. Just leave me alone. Stay away from me or I'll hurt you bad, maybe permanently. Do you understand, Duster?"

He nodded and gulped, groaned and said, "Fuck, yeah. But you already hurt me bad, bitch. I'm sure you broke my fuckin' arm, goddammit!"

Faith stood up and said, "No, but I should've. Maybe I should've done worse." She shook her head and looked around, folded the knife and returned it to its pocket. "I really hate violence. I hope you believe that, Duster, but you forced me to take drastic steps." She walked over to her pack and shouldered it, grabbed her hiking sticks. "Why don't you rest here a bit? You're not permanently damaged, but I'd give it a day or two to recover."

She walked a few yards and looked back. Duster was sitting up now, clutching his wrist and hugging himself. He looked up at her and snarled, "You cunt bitch! Yer gonna pay!"

Expressionless, Faith turned and started back toward him. Duster rocked back, mewling. "NO, no no! I was jokin', Faith. For God's sake, don't hurt me anymore. Please!"

She paused to stare at him for a long moment, then turned and walked down the trail. She looked back once to make sure Duster was still down. He was; a dim, lumpy shape in the mist.

CHAPTER 22 — JULY 27

He'd waited patiently for several days, but now his patience was wearing thin. Fortunately it was a beautiful place to wait, parked under the mighty Mt. Hood; a nice place to wait for her to stop by and fulfill her fate. No, rather it was their fate; she and him. To be together. But where was she? Joey had called and told him she was on her way. Hopefully that was true. The Mentor was getting restless and feeling the need for another harvest, and sooner rather than later.

That very morning, he'd seen one that was so much like her, over by the visitor center. She looked so vulnerable, smooth, soft and delicious. He wanted to take that one and have her, then share her, but without Joey, it was too dangerous. Besides, he might miss the real deal when she showed up and the freezer would only hold so much.

No, he needed to save himself for her, the actual *Her*. After all these years, he couldn't believe it when he saw her at Elk Lake. He'd nearly fainted. He'd felt nauseous with relief and joy and yearning. Joey's photos hadn't lied. It was *Her*. She'd come back at last! They wanted to take her that night, but she wasn't alone and the campground was crowded. It would've been too risky. And then she was gone again. Joey followed but had to be careful. They'd had to bide their time. And then when the big guy and his blonde companion had finally parted with her, Joey hadn't been able to keep up with Lila. The Mentor wasn't sure why and had a suspicion that Joey wasn't telling him everything.

None of this was easy. He'd waited ten years for this moment and had to proceed carefully. All the effort, the planning and the execution of those plans would make taking her all the more satisfying. He was getting an erection just thinking about what it'll be like with *Her*, the actual *Her*, again. He giggled. It'll be just like old times.

CHAPTER 23 — JULY 29

Max was looking forward to seeing Agent Bernard Battles again. Bernie was a mentor, friend and the best instructor he'd had at the Federal Law Enforcement Training Center in Georgia.

A few days after the phone conversation with Bruno, Max followed up on his brother's tip and called the Seattle FBI office. After punching through the automated phone tree and waiting on hold for several minutes, he was finally able to talk to an actual person. Max told her what his credentials were, including his federal law enforcement ID number. She thanked him and put him on hold for another few minutes. The hold music was awful; a looped fragment of an orchestrated version of a popular Bee Gee's song. Eventually the musical torture ended with a click and a man's voice appeared. He asked Max what he wanted to know. Max mentioned his interest in the Hampton case and that he was the one who found her remains. He then asked about the FBI's interest in the case. The agent he spoke to said, "We'll get back to you on that" and took down his contact information.

Another week passed before he got a call back from the FBI. An agent told Max that it was Special Agent in Charge (SAC) Bernie Battles who had made the request for the Hampton file. The agent then switched him over to Battle's phone. Bernie was pleased to hear from him, but didn't say much about the case other than, "You know what? We gotta meet and discuss this. I'm thinking, maybe this is right up your alley, Max. You're gonna love it! Let's set up a lunch date, okay?"

That date was today. Max ducked out of the cold, drizzling Seattle rain, through iron-bound wooden doors into Delbert's Publick Ale House. It was crowded, as it always was anymore. Young men and women sat on stools lining the long, polished antique bar and on benches in dark-stained, high-backed wooden booths. Most of the customers were professionals. Delbert's had been discovered by the Seattle techie crowd. It was no longer the slightly shady, quaint neighborhood pub and brewery it had once been when Max was a student at the University of Washington. The smell of stale beer, cigars and cigarettes was gone, as were the battered old pool tables with the ripped felt and stains. The bathrooms no longer gave off the faint aroma of beer piss and urinal cakes. Now the pub was filled with ambitious chatter, people tapping on cell phones, people staring at their tablets, smells of coffee and micro brewed beer. It felt sterile to Max, like something meaningful had been lost.

He felt out of place. Most of the patrons were younger than his 35 years, and were dressed differently. Plaid shirts, black t-shirts and high-water skinny jeans dominated the room. Max was wearing dark green baggy Carhartt cargo pants, a grey t-shirt and a brown leather bomber jacket. Hidden underneath the jacket was a small shoulder holster containing a Sig Sauer P229 .40 caliber pistol. That was not the prevalent wardrobe in Delbert's these days.

As he always did in any crowd situation, Max observed the demographics of the customers. Most of them appeared well off, judging by their clothing and tech accessories. They were young and white, although he did spot a few East Indians here and there.

Behind his back, a perky, high-pitched woman's voice startled him. "Is everything all right? Do you want a booth, a table or a seat at the bar?"

Max turned to see a small, energetic blonde woman holding menus and looking up at him expectantly. Under a mop of unruly golden hair, her over-bright blue eyes were dilated and she was breathing rapidly through her too-bright smile. Small beads of sweat sparkled on her pale face. She looked ill, but Max suspected there was another cause. He'd seen those symptoms too often.

Max smiled back and in his slow way said, "I'm here to meet a friend. He should be here by now. Short, sturdy black guy, very serious looking, probably in a cheap dark suit? Thin tie?"

The hostess giggled. Her words tumbled out fast and blended together so that Max had a hard time understanding her. "I saw him! He's in the back, in a booth by the big rocky fireplace. Do you want a menu?"

"Sure." He took the menu. He thought about saying something to her about her drug habit, but what good would that do? "Just say no" didn't seem to have much affect on people. He let it go. Instead he smiled and said, "Thanks."

She said, "You're welcome!" turned and walked briskly away. Menu in hand, Max wove his way through the busy throng, heading toward the big stone fireplace where a gas fire flickered cheerily.

Bernie Battles was a short, blocky man, mid-40s. Max noticed that his close-cut curly hair had thinned and there were hints of grey in it. He also saw that Bernie's face had sagged a little; probably because of too much time indoors as the head of Seattle's FBI office. Battles looked up from a menu as Max approached. His square face lit up with a smile.

"Hot damn!" he said as he stood, right hand outstretched. "If it isn't my favorite student! How the hell are ya, Max?"

"Good. Pretty good, Bernie" said Max, smiling as they shook hands across the table.

"Sit and order some food. It's good here, despite the overabundance of youthful, distracted energy."

They looked over the menus in silence, made their decisions and set the menus down on the table. As if by magic, a skinny young man with a goatee and a man-bun appeared next to the table, an overly broad smile on his lean, pale face. "Hello, Gentlemen. My name is Nathan and I'm delighted to be your waiter today. Are you ready to order?"

Bernie ordered the halibut fish and chips and Max said, "I'll have the same." They both ordered beers and handed the menus to the waiter.

Nathan's smile stretched to the breaking point as he said, "Excellent choice, gentlemen! Wonderful! I couldn't have made a better selection myself. I will place your order immediately. Anything else you need, I will assist you with. Just ask me!" His stretched smile remained fixed in place as he looked at each of the two men. Both shook their heads.

"Excellent, gentlemen! Your delicious meal will be here shortly!"

As the waiter walked away, Bernie looked at Max. Max looked back and suppressed a laugh. "What the hell was that about?" he asked.

Bernie grimaced and shook his head. "That, my friend, was about the new Seattle. Nathan the Obsequious Waiter is but one sign of how things are changing in the Emerald City.

"But enough about that, I wanted to tell you that I was sorry to hear about you and Annette."

Max gave him a tired smile. "Where did you hear about that? How the hell did you hear it?"

"Hey man, I'm the Special Agent in Charge! I see all and know all. So what happened? I only met her a couple of times when you two were down in Georgia, but I was sure impressed. Smart, talented and what a beauty! Thought you two were made for each other."

"Yeah, I thought so too, but things haven't been right for awhile now. Taking the Forest Service job and moving here finished off our relationship. She said she was tired of living in small towns. She capped that off with telling me she took a job offer to manage a fancy art gallery in Portland."

Bernie shook his head. "Sorry to hear that, Max. Maybe you two aren't done forever. Seriously, don't give up on her."

"It's beyond salvation, Bernie. She was serious. And she knows I'm not cut out for big city life. She made it clear that the cord is cut. And there's another guy in the picture now. Some artist named Chad."

Bernie shook his head. "Chad? Holy shit, who names their kid Chad? Anyway, sorry to hear it, Max. Long-distance relationships are difficult. Dorothy and I had some tough times while I was in Anchorage. It took a lot of work to keep our marriage going!"

Max sighed, looked at his old friend and said, "Okay, enough about me. Time for more upbeat conversation. So how's your family doing?"

Bernie's face brightened. "Doin' good! Damn good! I'm a blessed man, Max." Bernie told Max that his wife Dorothy had a new job at a bookstore, his two sons Ed and Elliot were studying law and justice at a university and his daughter was enrolled in culinary school. "Brenda uses us as guinea pigs for some amazing meals she cooks up. Seriously, you need to join us for dinner some night when Brenda is cooking. You will not believe how good good food can be. You'll enjoy a great meal and more importantly, you'll save me from myself by helping to eat the food." Bernie laughed. "Okay, enough about that. How's your family doing?"

Max smiled. "Pretty good. Dad's still teaching physics at the U-Dub and is as enthused about it as ever, which is what makes him such a great teacher. Mom was downsized and let go by the paper. Now she's a freelance features writer, writes mostly about the outdoors, doin' better than she did at the paper. My little brother Bruno, who isn't so little, as you know, is still with the State Patrol, working out of Spokane. He and his wife have a new kid, so I'm an uncle now."

"Congratulations, Max! Your family is growing. You need to get out there and find the right woman, have some kids of your own. Family is everything, my friend."

Max shook his head. "We'll see, we'll see. So, I hadn't heard that you were the SAC here. Congratulations! When did that happen?"

"Thanks! It was about four months ago. Still getting dialed in. It's a change from Anchorage, but not a big one. Wetter, warmer, worse traffic, fewer moose, more interesting cases, or at least more of them. How about you? How's Smokey the Bear treating you?"

Max frowned. "Well, I've already figured out that we're underfunded, understaffed and overworked, and it's supposed to get worse before it gets better, if it ever does get better. There's a lot of discontent in the ranks. Not me, I'm too new, but my older colleagues aren't very happy."

"Grim times, my friend, but take it in stride. Learn your new job, do your work and don't worry about it. If you people were more into counter-terrorism, you'd likely get more funding." Bernie paused, clasped his hands together and leaned forward. "So, how'd you like a change of pace, my sylvan friend?"

Max was surprised. "Hey, I don't wanna be a G-man. No offense, but I like working outside, in the mountains, away from this city crap. That's why I signed up with the Parks and the Forest Service in the first place."

Bernie smiled and shook his head. "Fine. Good. You can still do that. Just hear me out. I'm not asking you to join the FBI. But what I am asking is, do you want to work with the

FBI on a potential case that concerns possible crimes on Forest Service and Park Service lands?"

Max shrugged. "Sure, despite the 'potential' and 'possible' aspects. But how can you make that happen? I'm pretty new to the job and the patrol captain is pretty strict about my duties. Working for the FBI? I don't know. She'd take some convincing"

Bernie slapped the table and grinned. "Done, and done! Already talked to her. She's cool with it. The detail, that is. Took some fast talking, but she came around, so we drafted and signed a MOU. When I pointed out that we'd be paying you out of our budget for several weeks, and that I'd get her a free MRAP, she was all for it."

Max laughed. "Holy shit! A free MRAP? What the hell can we do with a monster vehicle like that? We can't even afford to buy gas for one of those things, and it won't be able to get up most forest roads."

"Hell, I dunno. Park it at Rainbow Family gatherings or something. Intimidation factor. Keeps people in line."

Max laughed again and waved his hands. "Okay, okay. Fine. So what is this assignment and why should I accept it?"

Bernie pointed a finger at him. "Because you're the best goddamn field investigator I ever taught and that's what I want for this case. We need you for this."

"Thanks, professor. So what's this case about? Sounds a little hazy."

"It is, but it's related to your Hampton case and I'll tell you about it after we eat lunch. I see our waiter Jason, or Kevin, or whatever the fuck he said his name was, headed this way with our fish and chips."

CHAPTER 24 — JULY 29

Nathan delivered the food, grinned obsequiously, asked them if they needed anything else, and left. Max and Bernie dug in and were silent for a few minutes as they enjoyed their meals.

Still chewing some breaded halibut, Battles finally said, "Best goddamn fish and chips this side of Victoria! That's why I come here. Okay. Anyway, the case! It's basically a multiple missing persons case. Multiple missing persons over several years and in several geographic locations; most of 'em on Forest Service land. Of particular interest: the missing persons, all women so far, vanished from or near the Pacific Crest Trail in California, Oregon and Washington."

Max was about to take a swig of Brookside beer and suddenly stopped, glass halfway up. He stared at his mentor, set the glass down. "You mean like the Hampton case."

"Bingo, Sherlock!"

"Multiple cases? How many? How come we haven't heard about this? Something like this would stand out, especially on the PCT."

"Oh, you'd think so, but the cases were scattered over wide locations and times, the victims often not reported missing for days or weeks. One of my new whiz kids . . . he's probably eating lunch somewhere in here. Fits right in. Anyway this kid, William, he built a new computer application that looks for patterns within and without our own databases, including media stories and reports. Supposed to be the shit. The application, that is, not

William. Well, two days after he cranked it up in early June, we got an automated email notice regarding a new pattern of missing persons. When I say 'new', I mean newly noticed. Some of the cases go back almost ten years. Most of 'em are in NCIC and NIBRS, but a pattern was never detected. Probably because some agencies don't subscribe to NIBRS and some cops don't bother to submit full reports to the NCIC files. I'm talkin' about some of the sheriff's departments that resent the FBI. Hell, some of 'em don't even acknowledge federal authority."

Max nodded his head. He said, "How many victims are we talking about?"

"Not sure. So far we've come up with eleven. I wish it had been noticed before. Like I said, different times, different locations and maybe most telling, different jurisdictions. All that Homeland Security bullshit was supposed to streamline interagency communication and make us all one big happy family. As you know, that didn't happen, and we're still handicapped when it comes to sharing information or having access to it. This computer application seems to be the remedy. Ha! Some asshole in D.C. will probably shut it down once they realize it actually works. Anyway, we have it now and this is what it gave us."

"I'm interested. What role would I play in this investigation?"

Bernie replied, "First thing, tell me what you know about the Hampton case. I read the file, but I want your take on it."

"My take is that there's still a lot of information pending. The case was mentioned in my predecessor's files and of course I've been over the state patrol file. The same one you read. A case like that, it gets your attention. Talented, strong young woman with her entire life ahead of her, off on a great adventure, and then she's gone, just like that. Dead and gone, as was finally confirmed by her dentals. I spent a sad day in the wilderness guarding her remains until the forensics team got there. Had some time to think and wonder."

"Any cause of death yet?"

Max shook his head. "She was out there a long time, over the winter. There was a lot of decay and disturbance by wildlife and insects. And it appears the bones were subjected to high heat, partially burned. It did a lot of damage. Preliminary report said that the bones had a lot of nicks and knife cuts on them too, indicating she was butchered. But there's no COD yet. I hear they're going to try to do tissue analysis at the state patrol lab. Look for intoxicants and drug residue. Given the condition of the remains and the scarcity of soft tissue, I guess they don't expect to find much, if anything. It'll be several weeks before there are test results. So as of now, who knows what happened or how? Something like this leaves behind a lot of grief stricken people and a mountain of sadness. It's not right, especially when it's caused by another human being. I gotta tell you, I was relieved that the Sheriffs did the family notification."

Bernie stared at the flickering gas fire. "Yeah, that's the worst. I still do some, even as SAC. Sometimes people feel better if it's someone higher up on the chain. It lets the family know that we thought the victim had value and that we did all we could. Anyway . . . "

"So, there are ten similar cases, all along the PCT? That means a person or persons is committing kidnappings and murders and getting away with it because we had no comprehensive means of tracking crime nationwide. How many other unknown cases are there like that?"

Bernie nodded and paused as his cell phone made an odd whistling sound. He pulled it out from a jacket pocket and checked a text message, then put the phone away.

"Sorry," he said. "Had to check that. It's about our new potential victim; number 12. Did I mention that? A young woman hiker disappeared near the PCT at Crater Lake. She's another through-hiker and her photo, well, she looks a lot like the others. That's one of the key points that ties all of these cases together. The victims are all hikers and they all look very similar. And this is the second such case this year. Another one vanished from Donner Pass in mid-June. That was case number 11, and *she* matched the vic profile too. Anyway, this Crater Lake case? We have remains, discovered by a hiker's dog on the 19th. Just like with Hampton. I tell you, I'm never hiking with dogs again. They can ruin your day. Anyway, more about her later. First the Donner case.

"We don't know much yet. The victim disappeared along a highway at Donner Pass in California; reported on June 10 but she apparently vanished on the ninth. Search didn't turn up anything except we have an eyewitness that puts her hitchhiking on the highway on June 9. Nobody's seen her since. She was hiking the Pacific Crest Trail, just like the others. You'll see what we have when you read the task force report.

"The Melissa Hampton case was what triggered the pattern discovery in early June and now we know about the pattern, but we don't know much. What did Rumsfeld call that? Known unknowns? Anyway, right after the pattern was discovered I decided to form a task force. There was too much information from too many sources and we needed help, so I called the Assistant Director. I made as strong a case as I could for approval and funding. Potential serial killer operating out of sight, eleven known cases at the time, likely will strike again this year, popular scenic trail, possible good publicity if we catch the asshole, yada, yada.

"I can't believe I just said 'yada, yada'! Anyway, the AD said okay, you got three weeks to come up with something. If you don't have any good leads by then, no more moola. So, I put out the call through our Office of

Partner Engagement. We managed to form up pretty quick, within days. The team was me as lead, Special Agent Del Franklin as second, a woman from the National Park Service ISB, another woman from Fish and Wildlife , a guy from Washington State Patrol CID and a guy from U.S. Marshals.

"They're good people, but weren't used to working together, and we really didn't have time to come together as an effective team. A couple of them were rookies and I think they happened to be people who were available at the time. Anyway, long story short, we came up with zip in terms of a suspect and what the fate of these vanished women was. We compiled a huge file of all the cases, possible intersections, all associated missing persons reports, potential suspects and alibis, all kinds of stuff. Most of it is in spreadsheets now. It's pretty comprehensive but it's just the foundation for further investigation."

"So the task force was disbanded?" said Max.

"You got it. We didn't develop any solid leads that pointed anywhere. I wish we'd had the evidence that later turned up with the two skeletons. True to his word, the AD axed us, said we had more important things to spend our time and money on than on a series of incidents that may or may not be crimes. Again, bear in mind this was before we had any new evidence, such as the remains you found and the ones at Crater Lake.

"So we had the start of an investigation. A lot of the background legwork was done, the heavy lifting accomplished. The files sat in their box in a corner of my office. There was plenty of other work to do, funded work that involved counter-terrorism, organized crime, human trafficking, you name it. You wouldn't believe the shit that goes on around here!

"So, I let it go for a while, real busy, basically forgot about it until late June, when William's clever software pinged us with another pattern-matching missing persons case, the one in California at Donner Pass. I asked the nearest local FBI office to look into it. They sent a couple of agents who hung around a few days until the search for the woman was suspended. They didn't learn much and filed a report to that effect.

"So then I hear about the remains, the new evidence at Crater Lake, and I'm gettin' pretty upset. There's definitely this fucking psycho out there and he, or she, has just struck again, and he's probably going to do it again and again if we don't catch him. The missing person looks just like the other victims, and a friend at NPS told me there's positive ID on the remains. She fits the victim profile. When I got word about that yesterday, I started thinking hard about how we can catch this guy. I called the AD again, but he still says I have to have solid leads, and a suspect would help too. But how in hell can I do that when I've got no budget for an investigation?"

Max sat back and whistled. He raised his hand for the waiter and ordered another couple of beers. Nathan nodded vigorously, grinned widely and promised that their beers would arrive post haste. After the waiter hurried away, Max said, "Okay, Bernie. I gather you're asking for my help."

"You got it. I've finagled my budget to come up with some funding for you to pursue this case. I can't spare any other personnel, so you'll be working mostly on your own, aside from any local help you can drum up. You'll be our field investigator, going on scene to get whatever fresh evidence you can. I also want your take on the task force files. Go through them thoroughly and see what you can come up with. In my mind you're the best man for this job. This is a chance to use those great skills and talents you have."

Their beers arrived and they stopped talking until the waiter was gone.

Bernie took a sip of his Guinness, leaned forward and said, "Max, this case is perfect for a guy like you. You have greater access and knowledge of the terrain and the activities. And you have greater mobility. And, maybe you know a lot of people that can help us out; mountaineer clubs, trail volunteers, people like that. Your captain is fine with you traveling as long as we foot the mileage and motel bills, so basically all of Washington, Oregon and California awaits you. We can meet at the FBI office on Friday to brief you. Gives you a couple of days to look at the task force files. After that, we discuss your next step. Maybe a trip to Crater Lake, or re-interview some of the players if you see a need. So whaddaya say?"

Max thought a moment, raised his glass and took a big swig of beer. He wiped his mouth, nodded and smiled. "Sure, why not? It sounds like a hell of a challenge, and it would be a nice change from the routine. I already felt invested in the Hampton case. Now maybe I can help catch her killer."

Bernie leaned back and said, "Whew! Wasn't sure you'd take it. Good deal, and you have my thanks. So . . . " He reached down next to his chair and pulled up a thick brown accordion file, plopped it on the table.

"Here's what we have from the task force work. It's pretty thorough and will save you background time. This is a great foundation for your investigation. So, study these files over the next couple of days. We'll meet at my office on Friday at 0900 and talk about it."

Max hefted the file and smiled. "Sure thing, as long as you pay for lunch."

CHAPTER 25 — JULY 31

"Bernie, I'm definitely a country boy now. I had a hell of a time navigating downtown and finding the damn FBI parking entrance. One-way streets, new bike lanes, new buildings, fog and rain. Shit. I thought I knew this city. And you guys should have a sign or something showing where the parking garage is."

Max and Bernie were walking side by side down the carpeted hallway of the Seattle FBI field office. It was Friday morning and very busy. Off to either side were glassed-in cubicles where men and women were talking on phones, tapping on computer keyboards, poring over documents. At the end of the hallway was the conference room where they were to meet with Agent Will Darzi to go over the PCT case.

Bernie laughed. "Max, I'm not sure I'd call you a country boy. After all, you grew up in this town."

"Yeah, but it's changed so much I barely recognize it anymore. And I do live in the country now."

"I envy you that. This town has changed, is changing, a lot. Giant cranes everywhere looming over the streets, makes it look like a scene from *War of the Worlds*. More homeless people than ever, inflated housing prices, traffic tie-ups, lack of parking, old landmarks being torn down. It's sad."

Bernie pushed through double doors labeled "Strategy Den" and ushered Max into the conference room. It was large and filled a corner space, illuminated by ceiling lights and long windows. A light rain was falling outside, streaking the windows with meandering water drops. At the end of a long conference table stood a small, dark-skinned, slightly overweight young man in navy Dockers and a black FBI polo shirt. He was arranging some file boxes when they walked in. He looked up, smiled and strode forward with hand outstretched.

"Agent Albricci! I'm special agent Will Darzi. Very glad to meet you! Bernie's told me a lot about you. Thanks for helping us with this case."

Max shook his hand and said, "I can't guarantee that what Bernie told you was true, but thanks. I'm not an agent, though. Merely a lowly LEO on loan to the FBI."

Bernie said, "Max, you're on the rolls as a . . . what was the phrase again? I think it was 'Special Federal Agent', or something like that. Anyway, it sounded pretty important. Okay, let's get to it. I've got another meeting in two hours, so we should get movin'."

Darzi stood at the head of the conference table and pointed to a large flat screen monitor behind him. It showed a FBI log-in page with the acronym PRS at the top.

"I wanted to name the software 'DataDiscover'," Darzi said, "but Agent Battles overruled me, so instead we're calling it PRS, or Pattern Recognition Software. I gather from Bernie that PRS is also an acronym for a popular brand of electric guitar that he owns. Anyway, it took almost four months to build and test the application. I worked with Amenable Solutions Corporation to use their software as the base platform, a means of transcending the usual barriers between apps, databases, platforms and language. Without Amenable, we wouldn't have PRS. On June 2nd we officially put PRS to work and in less than five minutes, we had our first ping, which was based on your Melissa Hampton case in Kittitas County."

Darzi's round face lit up in a broad smile. "The app worked like a champ. It recognized the similarities between

Hampton and another case in California, which led to tie-ins with even more cases from other databases. In a very short time, it identified and built the pattern of related cases that we have now, with the addition of the Donner Pass and Crater Lake victims."

Darzi demonstrated the web interface for the app. "Any new information or observations will go onto this site. All the case files you've been reading are also referenced in this database as read-only docs. Anything you add will be updated by me, as admin."

Following Darzi, Bernie presented an overview of the evidence they had with a Powerpoint that included maps and photos. Once revealed by Darzi's software, the pattern and case similarities were glaringly obvious. As Battles had said, they were hidden from view by chronologic and geographic distance, along with lack of effective communication between agencies. Another factor that obscured the pattern was the overwhelming number of missing persons cases every year. Bernie said, "Over 85,000 unsolved cases a year makes it damn difficult to spot any kind of pattern, especially over a ten-year period and in different states."

He summarized the evidence that the task force had compiled during its three weeks of effort, most of it from the local and state agencies who handled the missing persons cases. It was a mixed bag with varying levels of competence, thoroughness and even literacy. Some investigators went all out, others just went through the motions.

Bernie said, "Hell, one detective didn't even interview friends or family of the missing; just wrote the case off as an 'adult runaway' who wanted no further contact with her family."

The basic data was cleverly condensed into a sophisticated flow chart that Battles tacked onto a wall-mounted corkboard next to the conference table. The chart was in landscape format and large, around four feet wide by two and a half feet tall. On the left of the chart was a map showing the PCT as it passes through the states of California, Oregon and Washington. Along the red squiggly line of the PCT were small colored circles with a date written in each one. Four green circles for Washington, three for Oregon, three for California. There were also two brown circles, one for Washington and one for Oregon. Each circle on the chart's map represented a promising young life vanished, and given what they'd recently found, two deaths. The circles were positioned on the map to show each person's last known location. Max stood back to get a broader view.

Bernie pointed out fine lines leading from each circle to photos and brief bios of the disappeared. "As you can see, the chart is a comprehensive, concise summary of the case as we know it so far. The print's pretty small, but you can see that each photo includes a caption indicating date of birth, physical description, family and investigative agencies. Two photos associated with the brown circles are marked "Deceased". That would be Melissa Hampton in the upper Cle Elum River Valley and Tamara Ivanova at Crater Lake National Park."

Reading the chart, Darzi said, "So, Ivanova was 32, missing as of July 12. Last known location was near Crater Lake. This was over two weeks ago." He pointed to the bottom of the chart. "If you look at the timeline here, you'll see that the human remains, initially suspected to be hers and later confirmed, were found by a hiker and his dog in Crater Lake National Park on July 19, less than two weeks ago. The relative freshness of the remains was a plus for the investigation. We should be getting a report from the Park Service's Investigative Services Branch soon."

Max nodded. "Hopefully that'll shake some things loose. You know, I'm still amazed at the similarity between the victims. It's remarkable."

The women were all in their mid-twenties to early thirties at the time of their disappearance. The photos and descriptions showed that all had long black hair, were 5 feet 4 inches to 5 feet 6 inches tall, slender, athletic. Their faces were similar too. Most were oval shaped with blue or brown eyes, a strong nose and chin, full lips.

Bernie said, “I know. They all look related, but none of them are. We haven’t been able to find any connections between them beyond being PCT through-hikers. The big question in my mind is, how does the killer find these look-alikes? It must take a lot of searching and then some logistical planning to kidnap them in just the right place at the right time.”

“Do you think he has help?” said Max.

“I don’t know.” He gestured at the chart. “Maybe the answer is in that maze of information somewhere.”

Max leaned forward and studied the chart. “I see more fine lines radiating out from the photos, leading to more text boxes and small maps. Different colors being used. I’ve never seen anything like this. Does the chart map the entire case?”

Bernie nodded. “Indeed it does. The software that produces these is phenomenal.” He swept his hand across the chart, left to right, from the map to the complex maze of text, maps, timeline, suspect profiles, search information, location descriptions and more. “You know, the TV programs show investigators painstakingly pasting up photos and handwritten labels, using a spider web of colored yarns, covering a hell of a lot of wall space. We don’t do that anymore. This digital version is much easier to manage. And it’s updatable and easy to print or email. That being said, maybe it’s time to sit and go over some hard copy files.”

Darzi walked to the table and rummaged in a file box, removed several folders and set them on the table. He looked at Max and Bernie. “Max, this can give you a more detailed view of the task force work that was done. And we can give you a current copy of the chart to take with you. As we update it, we'll email those to you."

Max said, "Sounds good! Let's get to it."

The task force had acquired a lot of information in a short period of time. Max had no doubt their efforts would've yielded results had they had access to the recently found evidence and been given more time. There were printed spreadsheets noting the specific commonalities of age, appearance, gender, as well as the victims' various hobbies, activities, employment, education levels. These were also summarized on the chart. There were profiles of families and friends, potential suspects, physical evidence (or lack thereof), media coverage, search and rescue records, reports from law enforcement and private investigators.

Also included was a preliminary FBI profile of the perpetrator. The profiler said that the individual is likely a young to middle-aged Caucasian male, thought to be organized because up to now his crimes hadn't been discovered. The modus operandi, signature and demographics were unknown. Location was unknown. The subject has a fixation based on a specific woman, but it's unknown what the original relationship, if any, had been. The task force had plenty of unknown unknowns.

Max read the profile, shook his head and dropped it on the table. "Guys, this profile is worthless. Hell, I would've come up with the same assessment."

"I know," said Bernie, "but it's the best we could do with the data we have, which isn't enough. Hopefully we can get an updated profile based on the new evidence."

Darzi said, "Don't hold your breath. The profilers are backed up. Not enough of them for all the whack jobs coming out of the woodwork these days."

They discussed a spreadsheet listing the potential suspects from each independent investigation, but every single one had eventually been ruled out. Almost all of them fit the profile, but the profile was so basic, that fact was meaningless. There were no solid suspects. There weren't even any tentative suspects. Their best hope was that the new evidence would give some direction to the case. Max would learn more when he read the NPS file on the Crater Lake remains.

Using the map on the chart for reference, Max read a brief summary on the status and history of the Pacific Crest Trail. The report stated that the Pacific Crest National Scenic Trail is 2,650 miles long and was designated as an official National Scenic Trail by Congress in 1968. This was after years of piecing together sections of old trails with new. At first only a few hikers went the entire length, but these days, it's thousands a year. The Pacific Crest Trail Association reported that in the previous year over 4400 permits were issued for through-hikers. The summary concluded, "That was a record, possibly because of a popular movie and book about the PCT.

Max used his index finger to trace the trail on the map. "Okay, so, people typically hike the trail from south to north, starting in April at the Mexican border and finishing up at the Canadian border in late August, September or early October. The trail manages to stay mostly on federal land throughout its length, managed by the Forest Service, National Park Service and BLM. As a result, crimes on or near the trail are under both state and federal jurisdiction, depending on the type of violation or crime. And in this case you guys would be the lead due to the nature of the cases, being possible kidnappings and with the perpetrator acting across state lines. Or so we suspect." He looked at Battles and Darzi. "All we really have right now are a lot of *possibles.*"

Bernie said, "Yeah, that's what derailed us in terms of funding. I guess the AD was being generous in granting us what he did, considering that we had no definitive proof of much of anything." He pointed at the chart. "But anyone who has a lick of sense can see that pattern now. We need to find more evidence to justify an intensive investigation!"

Max nodded. "I think we'll be getting that when we get the full reports on Hampton and Ivanova. If there're enough similarities in how the remains were disposed of, and it certainly appears that there are, maybe a case could be made to your boss for further funding. We'll not only have definitive proof of murder, but also that the same person is behind both."

Bernie said, "Max, dig into this and figure out what we missed. Feel free to contact me or Will to discuss. As for the Ivanova and Hampton cases, I know it's early yet for the investigators to come up with anything solid, but find out what you can. Preliminary conclusions are fine. We're not trying to build a court case. At least not yet. Time is of the essence, both from a funding standpoint, and more importantly from a public safety standpoint. As you know, there were two possibles last year, two so far this year and the profiler thinks there might be at least one more. The son of a bitch is likely escalating."

Darzi said, "So Max, what are your thoughts and plans?"

Max looked at the map and rubbed his chin. "I'll spend a few more days in my office back at the ranger station, do a thorough review, follow up on some of the task force work and start making more connections. That chart is a good basis to work from. What the task force came up with is great, but as you know there's some gaps in the investigations by individual jurisdictions. I'll do my best to fill those in. Within a few days, the NPS should have a report to us, right? About Ivanova?"

Bernie nodded and said, "Should be something within a day or two. The investigator is Ellen Plante. She was on the task force so she's up to speed on the situation and personally invested in working it."

Max said, “Good to hear. By the way, how do we want to deal with the media?”

Darzi said, “Media interest evaporated when that small town in Eastern Oregon burned up. Killed some people, and it killed the Ivanova story too.”

“Yeah,” said Max. “That was horrific enough to knock all other news out of the way. So the media is off the Crater Lake story? Just as well, given that if they went into it too deep, they might discover that pattern of disappearances.”

Bernie nodded. “Agreed. We really don’t want that to happen just yet. That kind of exposure could drive our psycho underground. So keep a low profile. If you’re contacted by the media, play dumb for now. If it’s just one media source, maybe we can work out an exclusivity deal with them. Hell, they might even be able to help out. Some of those people aren’t stupid. Somebody’s bound to put two and two together eventually.”

Max nodded, rubbed his chin and said, “And what about the Hampton case? Has State Patrol gotten anywhere with their report?”

Will shook his head. “No. As I’m sure you know, there’s a huge backlog at the state crime lab. Once they got a positive ID, Hampton’s case went on the back burner. Even the media has been quiet about it. We’ll just have to wait.”

“Can you guys light a fire under the state, get the case moved up?”

Bernie shook his head. “I doubt it. And anticipating your next question, we can’t just move in and take it over either. Not with what we have right now. We have to maintain good relations with our state brethren. Besides, our crime lab is backed up too. It would be out of the frying pan and into the fire. Although maybe out of the refrigerator and onto the ice might be a better analogy for the glacial pace of evidence processing.”

They talked for a while longer before Bernie had to go to his next meeting. As they stood up from the table, Bernie said, "Max, what's your impression of things here? What d'you think of the assignment? Did you get your travel voucher squared away? Got your travel and gas cards?"

"Yep. I made it through the bureaucratic maze, thanks to your personnel department. I'm set up and will keep you posted as to my schedule, where I'm going and who I'm talking to. Maybe I'll have something solid by end of next week?"

Battles said, "I wrangled up enough funding, including expenses, for you for six weeks. So unless somebody cuts loose more money, that's all the time we have to come up with air-tight evidence, and/or catch the killer. Get onsite help where you can, call me if you need FBI assistance. I might be able to spare some agents at times, but only if it coincides with another case, or I can fudge it to look that way."

Will helped Max gather up the hard copy files and fit them into one cardboard file box. Max hefted the box in both hands. He looked at Bernie and Will.

"The answers have to be in here. There's got to be something in all of this evidence, maybe something at Crater Lake, that will spark this case."

Bernie said, "If there is, I'm sure you'll find it. It's in your hands now, Max."

CHAPTER 26 — AUGUST 2

The Roslyn Ranger District office was quiet on Sunday mornings but Max had his office door closed for added privacy. Most of the people who had weekend shifts were already out of the office, tending to the campgrounds, patrolling the trails, watching for fires and keeping tabs on the throngs of outdoor enthusiasts out to enjoy a sunny summer day on their public lands.

Max was sitting at his green and grey government-issue metal desk, staring at the computer monitor, reading the Park Service's initial report on the remains found at Crater Lake. It was written by Ellen Plante, the Investigative Services Branch detective that Bernie had mentioned. The report was concise, well organized and detailed. Max sipped a cup of coffee while he read.

According to the report, Tamara Ivanova, age 32, was first reported missing on July 12 after failing to check in the previous day from Crater Lake Lodge, as had been arranged with a friend. After waiting another day for her to check in, and after repeated attempts to contact Ivanova, her friend reported her as a missing person. An intense search was launched by Park Service personnel but failed to locate Ivanova. There was no cell signal or GPS detected from her phone.

A week later, on July 19, an elderly hiker named Marco Guzmann was hiking a trail near a national park administrative road when his dog, an energetic blue heeler, ran up to him with a long bone in its mouth. Being a retired emergency room nurse, Guzmann immediately recognized the bone as a human femur. He ordered the dog to drop it and after looking more closely, realized it was of recent origin and exhibited signs of tool marks. Unable to phone in the discovery due to lack of cell service in the area, he hiked out and reported the find at park HQ. Two seasonal law enforcement rangers returned to the scene with Mr. Guzmann, arriving at 7:38 p.m. They visually examined the bone, taped off the area around it, took Mr. Guzmann's statement, and reported by radio to their supervisor. The supervisor instructed them to release Mr. Guzmann, but to remain on site to protect the evidence. He then contacted Agent Plante at the NPS Investigative Services Branch Resident Office in Medford. She responded immediately and organized a crime scene team.

At the direction of Plante, the team assembled early the next morning and was on site by 8:00 a.m. on July 20. Team consisted of Agent Plante, crime scene investigators Dr. Nora Devary, Rich Dempsey and Imelda Chang. Several Park Service LEO's provided site security and helped with evidence search. Site was located along a trail near the gated administrative road. The gate was closed, but the lock was broken (and had been for some time) leaving it accessible to the public. Fresh tire tracks had been seen at the gate, but were obliterated by responding emergency vehicles.

Dr. Devary confirmed that the bone was a human femur from a young adult female. She said that the bone had been in its present state for at least a week. Dirt adhering to the bone and its remaining tissue indicated that it had been under dirt at a different location prior to discovery by Guzmann's dog. Plante wrote, "It had smears of blood and some gristle on it and was lying on top of the grass and pine needles. Yellow jackets were circling around it. There was a faint odor of decay in the air. The bone exhibited several linear scrapes and cut marks, indicating that a knife or similar cutting tool had been used on it, perhaps to remove the surrounding tissue and muscle. One end of the bone had been charred, suggesting that the femur had been exposed to intense heat."

Given that the bone implied a source of additional evidence nearby, NPS K9 Officer Angus Finlay and his tracker dog Alan were called in to assist in a further search of the area. Team search operations were suspended pending Officer Finlay's arrival at 5:15 p.m.

Once onsite, and after consultation with Plante's team, Officer Finlay put Alan to work sniffing out a trail from the bone. Plante and ranger Jimmy Chaplin accompanied Finlay as he carefully flagged out Alan's route. At 5:47, Alan indicated to officers that he had located the source of the bone.

Plante, Chaplin and Finlay observed a recently worked pit that contained a pile of bones, including ribs, vertebrae, leg and arm bones and a scapula. More bones were partially visible underneath soil. The visible bones were mostly free of tissue and exhibited marks similar to those on the femur already discovered. Some also showed signs of being partially burned. Agent Plante summoned the crime scene team and led them to the new site.

Finlay's K9 Alan followed a scent trail from the bone cache to another segment of the admin road. It was there that the officers observed two different sets of freshly made tire tracks indicating a large pickup or SUV had been there with a trailer. There were also two sets of footprints, but they were very vague, as if the persons had been wearing moccasins. Officers immediately secured the bone pit and pattern evidence scenes pending further investigation the following day.

Early on July 21, the NPS CSI team documented and processed the bone pit. The bones were carefully removed, photographed, tagged and bagged for further evaluation at a medical facility. A second team of LEOs documented and processed the tire tracks scene using drone photography, close-up photography and casting. The tire track pattern evidence was gathered and Agent Plante determined that for expediency, evaluation and identification of the tracks would be farmed out to a private agency, Excelsior Investigations, in Seattle.

Identification of the remains occurred within two days, thanks to the presence of a skull with teeth. Dental records confirmed that the remains were those of Tamara Ivanova. The search was suspended. After family was notified, a press conference was convened on July 24 and the information given to the media. What was not given to the media was the information regarding the tire tracks, or the condition of some of the bones.

Excelsior was able to quickly identify the make, model and size of tires for both the pickup/SUV and the trailer. On July 24th, an alert was issued to federal, local and state law enforcement for the tire combinations, to be checked when possible during stops and at parking lots. Given the abundance of recreational vehicles and trailers on the road at what was a peak vacation time, and that law enforcement had more immediate priorities, ISB considered the effort a long shot. Plante wrote in her report, "Chances of finding the same combination of tires on a vehicle and trailer is astronomically low, but I was determined to follow all possible paths. Sometimes we get lucky. I had also hoped to begin researching tire purchases across Washington and Oregon for the last three years, but am already over-booked and there are no personnel on my team available to implement that effectively. Any efforts I made would be time-consuming, inconsistent and haphazard. This is a task for either the OSP or FBI." So far, no such effort was underway.

Max continued reading. Plante included media reports from Oregon newspapers and TV news. As usual, the TV stations went all out, with reporters on the scene, most dressed in what they regarded as outdoor wear. Speculation was rampant, but neither the media nor the investigators had anything concrete to relate regarding a suspect or motive.

Plante and several LEOs canvassed the park and points north looking for witnesses who might've seen Ivanova on the trail or at the lodge. They also enlisted the help of Forest Service law enforcement in locating possible witnesses.

There were no hits until July 27, when a U.S. Forest Service wilderness ranger interviewed two young female hikers on the PCT near Mount Hood. One of them recognized a photo of Ivanova and recalled an encounter with her around the date of her disappearance. The hiker couldn't recall a specific date, but had encountered Ivanova at a road turnout near Crater Lake Lodge where all three were eating dinner at a food trailer parked there. According to the hiker, Ivanova had talked about quitting the trail because she felt she was being stalked by a male hiker.

After dinner, the witnesses saw Ivanova sitting on a rock wall near the lodge and overlooking the lake. They said she looked despondent. Witnesses went to camp after that and didn't see the victim again. That was the end of the interview. The wilderness ranger didn't ask any follow-up questions, nor did he record the witness full names or contact information. Plante reported that as an opportunity lost and recommend that the ranger, who was a Forest Protection Officer, be given more training. Locating the hikers again would be nearly impossible.

Plante, and Max agreed with her, wanted to know more about the possible stalker as well as the food trailer where the witnesses talked to Ivanova. Max made a note to look into the food trailer angle. He had already heard that there are several located along the trail, most run as nonprofits by Pacific Crest Trail volunteers.

Max swiveled in his office chair and winced as it squealed. He stared out the window. He was supposed to always leave the blinds closed, something to do with security. Max thought, *to hell with that.* It was a beautiful sunny morning and he had a fine view from his second story office. Below him was the ranger district's fenced equipment yard where lines of white Forest Service pickups and SUV's were parked, along with some heavy machinery. There were piles of lumber next to the main warehouse. Four firefighters were out there with a large fire engine, washing it and checking the stock of hoses and other equipment. Beyond that was the town of Roslyn, a motley collection of squat old brick buildings, two-story wooden false-front buildings and refurbished miner's homes. Smoke drifted up from the local barbecue joint, which was hidden behind the brick post office building.

Roslyn had been a coal mining town up until the mid-1960s and now tourism was king. Visitors were fed glory stories of the mining days as well as stories about the 1990's era TV show "Northern Exposure". Most of that popular series' exterior and outdoor scenes were shot in Roslyn and the surrounding area. Roslyn was known world wide as Cicely, Alaska. Even after more than 20 years, the show's fans flocked to Roslyn to see the various places they'd seen on TV. As a result, the main downtown streets were crowded with all kinds of vehicles and pedestrians. Tourists were everywhere, mostly walking, taking in the small town ambiance. Max heard the deep rumble of Harley Davidson motorcycles cruising up the main road through town. The sound was almost constant on summer weekends and a disturbing reminder that Roslyn wasn't the quiet little mountain town it used to be.

Max rolled his chair back to the keyboard and clicked the mouse to open a folder on his computer desktop. It contained the digital versions of the files that Agent Battles had given him. He clicked on the report about the June 10 disappearance of PCT through-hiker Bonnie Middaugh, age 28, at Donner Pass. The report was generated by the task force in June, during the unsuccessful search for Middaugh. The search was suspended on July first. Witnesses reported seeing Middaugh stop at the Soda Springs Post Office at 11:00 on the morning of June 9 and pick up a resupply package. After that, she was observed walking east on the Donner Pass Road. Last witness sighting was around 11:45 when she left the populated part of the community. Traffic on the Donner Pass Road was light but steady that day. Most traffic went over the pass on nearby Interstate 80. Residents ignore the summer traffic, and no one reported anything unusual. In short, there was nothing to go on other than the similarities to the other cases; young, single female PCT through-hiker, remarkably similar appearance to the other missing women. Maybe the biggest similarity to the other cases was that there were no clues. Middaugh simply vanished.

Max looked at Middaugh's photo. Whatever started the kidnapper/killer on his rampage likely started on the PCT and with a woman similar to the victims. So the place to start looking would be the first case.

Max straightened up in his creaky chair and tapped more keys. He brought up the file of the first known case in the pattern. It was from 2008 and involved a 30-year-old woman named Kasey Wamsley, of Ojai, California. Wamsley, like the others, was hiking the entire Pacific Crest Trail and had vanished near Mount Hood, Oregon around September 4. As with most of the other cases, she disappeared near a road junction, indicating that whoever was kidnapping the women had a vehicle and planned the abductions, or at least planned on the possibility. How was he finding the women and than arranging an abduction? Was he a hiker who had a co-conspirator with a car? Did they communicate by cell phone? There wasn't enough information yet, so Max put those questions aside and kept reading.

What followed was all too familiar and sad. Wamsley failed to check in with her parents via text message. The parents waited a day or two and when they didn't hear from her, contacted authorities. Authorities in Clackamas County started a search and rescue operation around Mount Hood. That lasted for over two weeks and yielded no clues or signs. Oregon State Police detectives were brought in to the case and they investigated further afield under the assumption that Wamsley had either been kidnapped, or had decided to quit the trail. Nothing was found. OSP detectives did the usual interviews of family, friends, employer, co-workers. Once again, nothing stood out. Wamsley had a boyfriend, but everyone maintained they were on good terms. Detectives determined that the man had a solid alibi for the time of her disappearance. He proved that he was vacationing in the Bahamas with another woman. *So much for true love*, thought Max.

There was a more promising suspect but he also provided a solid alibi for the time of the disappearance. He was Wamsley's co-worker at a coffee shop in Ojai known as Bean There, Done That. Max grimaced. According to the file, the young man had often expressed interest in Wamsley, indicating that he liked "hot older bitches". Other employees reported several incidents where Wamsley had to use physical force to discourage the guy. Max smiled as he read on. Wamsley had been a MMA fighter and was well able to take care of herself. Eventually, because of the incidents, the man was fired from the coffee shop.

Max looked out the window and wondered how someone gets the best of a fit MMA fighter. If she was kidnapped, how did she get taken? The perpetrator must've used a weapon or drugs to subdue her. A woman like Wamsley would not go quietly and it would likely be difficult for someone to surprise her.

Max rubbed his eyes, looked at his watch and decided to take a walk. Sitting in front of a computer was tiring. Constantly seeing investigative dead ends was tiring too. Somewhere there should be a clue, a small detail, something to link to a suspect, a person who was a common factor in all of the disappearances. Once they had a suspect for the initial crime, they'd be able to build a better profile and a picture of possible opportunity, means, motive, links to the other women and locations. They could find connections in time and space to the other cases as well as the reasons that he kept attacking the same type of woman. Max hoped that the evidence from Crater Lake would give profilers enough information for a more detailed report. Max didn't trust profiles, but at this point, any potential insight was welcome.

He stepped outside and took a deep breath of fresh air. It was a sunny day, cool for August and very pleasant. Max decided to walk downtown and get some lunch at Roslyn Burgers and Shakes. He was in plain clothes and hoped that nobody would recognize him. And then he wondered who he was kidding. He'd talked to a lot of locals over the last several weeks and some of them had gotten tickets for various minor violations. On the other hand, his observation was that most of the people in town on weekends were tourists. He'd take a chance.

Max was almost to the cafe when a shrill, gravelly voice from across the street yelled, "Thanks for the ticket, asswipe!" He turned to see old Andy Kingsley, notorious alcoholic, troublemaker, scofflaw and longwinded gasbag, starting across the street toward him. Max sighed, stuck his hands in his pockets and braced for the coming verbal storm.

CHAPTER 27 — AUGUST 3-7

Monday morning in the office was busy. Everyone was back at work, people rushing up and down the hallways. There were meetings, crews were getting organized, emails were filling up inboxes and demanding attention, new directives were trickled down to employees. Because of this, Max arrived at work before most of the personnel and sequestered himself in his office once again, door closed. He was making a to-do list for the investigation when his cell phone rang.

He picked it up, looked at the screen to see who was calling and answered the phone with, "What's up, Pop?"

His father, always an early riser, was calling to remind him of the upcoming Albricci family reunion and to make sure that his work wouldn't interfere with attending. The reunion was six weeks away, but Vincenzo Albricci was excited and wanted to talk about it.

"Just think of it, Max! Your Uncle Umberto is coming all the way from Firenze. And your cousin Felisa too! She also is of the *carbinieri*. You two will have much to talk about. And she's your *secondo* cousin, a real looker! You know what I say, Max? Not a *problema*, eh? And your mother, she likes her too."

Max smiled and rolled his eyes. His father went on to enthusiastically describe the food that he and Max's mother Geneva were going to cook. Max checked his watch a couple of times and felt hunger gnawing at his stomach. He'd skipped breakfast, which he now realized was a mistake. He loved his father, but all the talk about delicious home cooking was making his hunger worse. Plus, he had to get back to work. He finally resorted to a white lie by saying, "Hey Pop, damn! I gotta go. Just got a call on the radio that I have to respond to. I'll call you and Mom tonight, okay?"

Vincenzo said, "Okay, Max. You remember dinner this Sunday, yes? Your mother is going all out. Bruno, Sara and the new baby will be there. You have to be there too! It's been too long, *mio figlio*."

"Sure, Pop, I'll be there. I promise."

"Okay, *molto bene!* You be careful out there, *capisci*? Like Sir Isaac said, some bad apples that don't fall far from the tree, they make you trip and fall. Gravity, eh?" He rang off.

As good as his father's English was, he purposefully mangled phrases and old sayings to get a laugh, and it always worked with Max. He chuckled, set the phone down and rummaged in his desk drawers for something to quell the hunger. He finally dug out a lumpy old protein bar and chewed open the wrapping, started eating.

Max resumed writing out the to-do items for the day. When he finished the lengthy list, he picked up the cell phone again, tapped the screen's keypad and held the phone to his ear, waiting. Investigative Services Branch Agent Ellen Plante answered on the sixth ring. Max introduced himself and asked her if she had time to talk about the Ivanova case.

"Sure. I got about ten minutes or so before the Monday morning maelstrom of bureaucratic mayhem descends. Who did y'all say you were with?"

"Well, it's complicated. I used to be with the Park Service at Mount Rainier, but now I'm a Forest Service LEO on detail to the Seattle FBI to investigate cases like Ivanova's. Like the ones you worked on with the task force."

"Okay, let me get this straight; a former Parkie, but now a Smokey working as a Feeb" said Plante. "Okay, got it.

Sounds like Bernie Battles roped you in to work his PCT pattern. Is that right?"

Max laughed. "I wouldn't say 'roped'. More like enticed. You know Bernie! He can talk the rattles off a snake. Anyway, I read your report—great job, by the way—and I had a few questions for you."

Max explained in more detail how he came to be investigating for the FBI. When he was done, he said, "So like I said, I was reading up on your case at Crater Lake and found similarities with a case on my own district last year." Max told her about Melissa Hampton and his discovery of the partially buried bones.

When he was done, Plante said, "Yeah, I remember the Hampton case. We covered it in the task force report. I'm glad to hear about your evidence recovery. Sure sounds like the two cases are linked. The way the bones were disposed of, near a road, the condition of the bones as regards heat degradation, the similarities of the victims."

"That's right. I'm hoping the new evidence will get us some solid clues, but as you know it'll be some time before we learn much. Look, I wanted to ask you if you have anything to add about the Ivanova case, anything you might've heard about since your task force work that's relevant to the PCT cases?"

"I can't think of anything right now. Like you said, the lab is still studying the remains. I'm currently working with my team on reinvestigating accidents at Crater Lake over the last dozen years or so. Maybe I'll run across something there."

"What do you mean? Why reinvestigate accidents? Weren't they already investigated?"

Plante coughed out a laugh. "Yeah, they were, but guess what? We found one that *wasn't* an accident. A fall from a cliff. The wife claimed her husband slipped and fell. Sure, something tragic like that happens at least once a year, y'all know what I'm sayin'? Initial investigation says it was an accident. Everyone shrugs their shoulders and says, 'Oh well, accidents happen.' Very sad, but so it goes, right? And then, about a year later the guy's young son contacts us, says it wasn't an accident. We say what? Sure, says the kid. 'My dad was pushed off the cliff by my mom'. Of course we ask why and the kid says it's because his mom was bangin' some guy named Conrad and Conrad is now his step-dad and Conrad is an asshole. So we did some investigatin' and to make a long story short, we find out the kid was right. There was a conspiracy to kill this poor guy, get his life insurance and live happily ever after. They almost got away with it."

"So they got convicted?"

"Not yet. The court case is pending. In the meantime, we're re-openin' any and all accident investigations for incidents that might be not accidents. Other parks are doin' the same thing. I declare, this job sure does lower one's opinion of humanity."

"You got that right," said Max. They talked a while longer and Ellen promised to let Max know if she found anything of interest.

Max spent the rest of the day reading the task force's files, including the original missing person reports, follow-up interviews, search and rescue reports and more. He made a list of possible gaps in various investigations, things to investigate further with involved parties; detectives, witnesses, friends, relatives. As Bernie told him, a few of the cases had been poorly documented or were incomplete, which was a nice way of saying that people had fucked up. Although the task force had done some of the follow-up on the cases, Max was starting to see that his efforts could be very time consuming and possibly futile due to the limited time and funding. He needed a key, something that would open up some of the secrets, accelerate the investigation to the point where he wouldn't need to re-do previous efforts. He sat back in the chair and closed his eyes. He'd been reading and taking notes since early afternoon and it was almost 5:30. Time for a break. Maybe he'd go home, get some dinner and work through the evening. He felt the pressure of time, the pressure of figuring this out and stopping the perpetrator before another young woman disappeared.

The remainder of the week was more of the same. The tedious, methodical process of investigation was nowhere near as exciting as in most movies and TV shows. Max worked both at home and at the office, using email, telephone and Skype; contacting investigators, re-interviewing witnesses and family, re-examining data. Most of the witnesses were surprised, and not pleased, to be interviewed again. The most common response was "That was so long ago, who can remember anything? Don't you have the old transcripts of what I said?" He must've talked to 25 people and no one could tell him anything new. Talking to family members was much the same. They were more inclined to help, but as with the witnesses, they didn't have much to add. Several said they were glad to see that the FBI hadn't forgotten them or their family members. Max didn't tell them what had made the cold cases hot again.

Calling various investigators proved to be more of a challenge. He focused on the ones that had, in his opinion, done a crappy job. Their work had serious gaps and omissions. There were six of those and Max felt that he didn't have time to be nice. He called each and asked pointed questions about their work. Two hung up on him and wouldn't respond to further attempts to talk. One was deceased. Three investigators talked to him, but they all maintained their work was good and implied that Max was an asshole for challenging them. He was unable to get any new information out of them despite several questions regarding their omissions. Max made notes to contact and interview some of their witnesses.

Wednesday was a bust as far as the PCT investigation went. Max had to go to federal district court in Yakima for a tire dumping case. Back in early June, Max had caught the perpetrator in the act, having just dumped over a dozen used truck tires near a popular trailhead, with another two tires remaining in the back of his large U-Haul truck. The subject never showed up at court, so the judge issued a warrant for failure to appear. All in all, the day was a bust and Max arrived home in a bad mood. He called Bruno to vent his frustration at the waste of an entire day.

By Friday afternoon, Max felt like he was spinning his wheels. He wasn't any closer to finding a suspect, and the damn clock was still ticking. Despite the feeling of urgency, he knew he needed some time off to clear his mind. When 6 p.m. rolled around, he stood up and stretched. He was so tired of sitting. A short evening hike with Gus would be a good idea, and then tomorrow morning maybe go fishing with his neighbors Jimmy and Roberta. He was reaching for his briefcase when the desk phone rang. Sighing, he sat down and answered it. He was pleased to hear Agent Plante's voice on the other end.

"Hey Max, I've got somethin' for y'all here. Somethin' good! You wanna hear it? Okay, so there's this old missin' person's case from 10 years ago? I came across it in Crater Lake's SAR files while I was researchin' those accidents and the searches and recoveries, right? So I went lookin' for any case files related to it? Couldn't find anything in the database, so I looked in the physical files. The boss is adamant about maintaining hard copy files. He's old school and doesn't trust digital files, which is good. So I looked through those and still couldn't find anything, which is strange. So all I got here is a basic paper report about the search and rescue ten years ago for a missing woman named Lila Montaigne, missing along the Pacific Crest Trail. Most of it is just documentation of hours, personnel, equipment and stuff like that. There wasn't much about the person other than her name, gender, age and a photo. And guess what about the photo?"

"She's the same as the others? Her looks and age are the same?"

"Ya got it. She could be a sister to the other victims. They could all be sisters. I don't know, but this could be the initial case, the catalyst. It pre-dates the Wamsley case by a year. There might be others from even further back, but given the time and the length of the trail, they'd be hard to find. By the way, there's no digital version of the Montaigne SAR file. Nothing. Anywhere."

"No shit? Well, the FBI's PRS app would've found anything related to the pattern if it was in any of the databases."

"Exactly, Max. From what I saw on my end, there was nothin' to find. No files for that case on record anywhere. The only mention of her is this hard copy SAR report. So what's goin' on?"

Max rubbed his chin and thought a moment. "Okay," he said. "So who else would have a file on the woman's disappearance? The county? State police? Who investigates things like that at Crater Lake?"

"For Crater Lake? It's all done in-house. NPS handles investigations into incidents on park land. But for cases like this, we usually send a file to the Oregon State Police and they keep it in their archives in Salem. I'm talkin' cases involving missing persons, assaults and homicides; anything that might overlap into state or county jurisdictions."

"Homicides? Do you get a lot of them in the park?"

"No . . . well, the answer to that is pending. Like I said the other day, we're currently revisiting those accidental death cases. That's why I was looking through the SAR files."

"Yeah. Well, so what's the next step? Visit the OSP archives in Salem?"

"I think so, Max. One of us could call, but they're closed already, until Monday mornin'. What with the lack of a paper trail for the Lila Montaigne case, I think it would be better to show up in person and see for ourselves. Can you make it down there on Monday? If not, I might be able to and I'm closer."

Max thought a moment and said, "Sure, I can go, but it'll have to be in the afternoon on Monday. I've got some family obligations over the weekend that I can't ignore. Hey, how about we both go? I could meet you there Monday afternoon, around two? Do we need to call first?"

"Sure, okay, I can do that. As far as I know, no need to call. We just show up with our credentials and get access. So I'll see you there Monday, 1400 hours? I'll be in uniform so you'll know who I am. Don't look for the Smoky Bear hat though. I've never cared for that hat and I look terrible in it."

Max laughed. "I understand. Sounds good. When you get there, look for a tall, Lincolnesque guy in civvies; that'll be me."

Max's next call was to Agent Battles in Seattle. When Bernie answered, Max heard seagulls in the background, along with the woosh and rumble of road traffic.

"Down at the piers again?"

"Hey Max! Great to hear from you. Yeah, my late afternoon walk. Dorothy is adamant, and between you and me, I think she's tracking my phone. Hell, she might even be listening in on this call!"

Max laughed. "Well if anyone could do that, I suppose the wife of a FBI special agent could. Anyway, I've got some good news." Max updated Bernie on the information about the "new" case and told him he was heading to Oregon on Monday.

"That sounds good! It's very strange that PRS didn't pick up that case. Stranger still that the NPS doesn't have a file for it. If that file is anywhere online or in a database, I'm sure PRS would've found it. Shit. Okay, checking this out is paramount. I hope there is a file there. If this is really the first victim, we need to know a lot more. This might be the break we need. Keep me informed."

"Will do, Bernie. Oregon or bust!"

CHAPTER 28 — AUGUST 4

Her shout of "Shit!!" echoed off the snow-streaked mountainsides around Cispus Pass. Faith watched her iPhone rattle, slide, tumble and tap its way down the rocky slope below the trail, disappearing between some boulders with a final flash of reflected morning sunlight. Faith took off her pack and set it down on a large rock. She stood at the edge of the trail, looking down, hands on hips, swearing. She'd just finished a conversation with Jenks and was putting the phone back into her pants' cargo pocket when it slipped out of her hand, skidded off a trailside boulder and went down over the edge.

Carefully placing her hands and feet, Faith crawled down the steep boulder slope. About 50 feet below the trail, where she thought she last saw her phone, she reached down between the rocks, fingers questing. Tiny turds from pikas and marmots were her only rewards and she swore some more. After about 15 minutes of searching among the rocks, she finally gave up and started to clamber back up the slope. It was getting hot and the effort made her sweat.

When she finally climbed back onto the trail, there was a man sitting on a large lichen-covered rock next to her pack. He was smiling as if amused by her recent antics. Faith glared at him as she dusted off her pants. He was a tall, lean older man with a salt and pepper beard and ponytail. Faith knew him from somewhere. She searched her memory and finally smiled and said, "Reacher!"

"Faith!" said Reacher. He reached out and shook her hand. "Good to see you again. Um, looks like you lost something? I heard your shout and was hoping it wasn't trouble. Then I saw you down there and decided to wait and make sure you're okay."

Faith sat down next to him and sighed. "Lost my goddamn iPhone is all. Fumbled it and down it went. It's probably in the grubby little paws of a marmot by now."

Reacher laughed. "Well, don't deny God's wee creatures a shot at technology too. Hey, having a cell phone is overrated anyway. I haven't had mine since California and don't miss it a bit. When I was a young man in the mountains, I never had any way of communicating with the outside world. Didn't even think about it. Didn't want it. Part of being out in the wilderness was to get away from humanity for a while. I survived somehow."

Faith pulled hair away from her face and said, "You might have a point. Where's the rest of your bunch?"

Reacher pointed south. "Back there somewhere. We were moving so slow, we finally realized that none of us would make it to the finish at that pace. So, I volunteered to represent our group and make a push for Canada. I skipped most of Oregon and regained the trail at the Columbia. Not sure where the rest of them will end the journey for the year but the plan is for them to make it to Cascade Locks, then come back next summer and finish up in Washington. In the meantime, I'm to do this last stretch so that as a group, we can say we did the entire PCT this year. It's like a relay."

"I was just in Cascade Locks a few days ago, spent a rest day there with my mom and dad."

"How was that?"

Faith smiled. "Fun, but strange to be around cars and roads and crowds, even for just a day. I felt pretty restless."

Faith had arrived in Cascade Locks five days after her encounter with Duster. The weather had been sunny and hot and she was able to do well over 20 miles each day. Once past Ollalie Lake, much of the trip had been easy hiking, but monotonous. The trail wound its way over low, rolling mountains, through a mixture of old growth forest and logging units studded with stumps and small firs, across several power-line corridors, past a few lakes and finally to the white pyramid of Mount Hood.

Hood was magnificent enough to make up for the monotony that led to it. Faith stopped at rustic Timberline Lodge to pick up a small resupply package and then pressed on a few more miles to make a hidden camp in alpine meadows along a ridge. The location gave her a view back down the trail as it traversed the slopes of Mount Hood.

All along the way, Faith had kept an eye out for Duster. Given his behavior at their last meeting, she didn't think she'd seen the last of him. She carefully considered reporting Duster's attack on her, but decided against it. If she had to take more severe action in the future, it would be good if her name wasn't attached to the creep. She knew she could handle him if he turned up again. Her threat to him hadn't been idle.

Because of her training and experience, it was second nature to be alert and observant, but even more so after any unusual event. She often paused to look ahead and then look back along the trail and she tried to camp in hidden locations. None of this bothered her much. She didn't feel particularly paranoid or scared. She was just taking precautions that seemed sensible and made her more comfortable.

Two days past Mount Hood, she stepped back into the 21st Century at Cascade Locks, Oregon. She walked on a dirt road to cross under Interstate 84, traffic rumbling overhead. The acrid odor of exhaust made Faith cough. Her lungs weren't used to it. She felt bewildered as she made her way through Toll House Park. There was a lot of noise and hustle; the roar of the freeway, the whoosh of cars driving through the town. People were at picnic tables in the park, eating lunch, talking and laughing. A group of hikers was sprawled on the grass, sleeping in the shade. Their large packs were stacked up against a tree. Faith's destination was the Best Western Columbia River Inn and it wasn't far. She could see it through the trees ahead. To her left, the steel framework of Bridge of the Gods dominated the scene. That would be her path across the Columbia River. As she walked across the hotel parking lot, she spotted her parent's blue Toyota Highlander and smiled.

Reacher asked, "So how was it seeing your mom and dad again after so long?"

"It was good. We had a great time. Toured the small town, ate a lot of food, took some walks along the Columbia, and had some laughs. My parents hadn't approved of this trip, but I think when they could see for themselves what it's done for me, they felt better about it. My mom said I finally seem happy."

"Was she right?"

Faith thought for a moment before answering. "Yeah, I think she was. This trip is more than I expected or imagined. Having a goal, and being away from the hassles, noise and hurry has helped a lot. I've met some great people, been immersed in beautiful nature, gotten back into condition. Yes, I'm definitely happier. Definitely just happy. What about you, Reacher?"

"Well, I just remembered a quote that made a huge impression on me, and that sums up my wilderness experience. Let's see, I tried to memorize it. It's something like this: 'We were rich in memories. We had pierced the veneer of outside things. We suffered, starved and triumphed, groveled down yet reached for glory, we grew bigger in the bigness of the whole. We had seen God in His splendors, heard the text that Nature renders. We had reached the naked soul of man.'"

"Wow. Who said that?"

Reacher squinted up at the sky and said, "It was Sir Ernest Shackleton, written after his two year ordeal of survival in the Antarctic and South Atlantic, sometime in the early 1900's. Perhaps not a valid comparison to hiking the Pacific Crest Trail, but it sums up how I feel about being in the wilderness. It strips away the bullshit of modern life and leaves you feeling clean of mind and soul, immersed in nature's beauty." Reacher held up a finger. "The secret is to hang onto that when you return to your so-called normal life and to civilization."

"Yeah," said Faith. "That's gonna be a toughy, but I'm in it to win it. I think this trip has made a deep enough impression that it'll stick."

They sat in silence, gazing out at the mountains and sky. Directly to the south, rising out of blue valley haze, the huge, broad snowy hump of Mount Adams towered into the blue. To the southwest was the truncated volcano of Mount St. Helens, its broad summit rimmed with strips of old snow. It was the most prominent mountain between them and the Pacific Ocean. To the northwest, Mount Rainier and its crevassed glaciers loomed in the blue sky.

Her eyes focused on the distance, Faith sighed and said, "I thought I'd get tired of this, of being out here, but I'm not. Every day is amazing."

"You got that right. Hey, not to belittle what we've been talking about, but I was wondering if you encountered that dipshit Duster any more?"

Faith looked at him and said, "Yeah, I did." She told Reacher about the encounters, including the most recent one.

Reacher stared at her and said, "Holy shit, Faith! I admire a woman that can take care of herself like that. So did you report Duster to any authorities? Did you call 911?"

"Thought about it, but I figured it wouldn't do much good. And given how it turned out, Duster could make himself out to be the victim."

"Are you afraid that he might contact the authorities and do just that?"

Faith shook her head. "Not him. I think he's got too much to hide, maybe even a record for all I know. Plus it would hurt his pride too much. Even pervert shit-weasels like Duster have their pride. He'd never admit to anyone that a woman got the best of him. Besides, if I encounter him again and have to take more drastic action, I don't want the authorities to be able to associate me with him."

Reacher gave her a gentle smile. "That's kind of cold, Faith. Cold, but pragmatic. I'll forget you said that, just in case."

She shrugged. "Guys like Duster? Sometimes they have to be dealt with. It's just a fact of life. Anything I give him, he'll deserve. I don't ask for trouble, I don't look for trouble, but if someone brings it to me, I deal with it."

"Faith, I've never been in the military or in combat, but I've seen what it does to people. Some get beaten down, some spend years getting over it, and some take from it what they can, move on and leave the rest behind. I'm happy to see that you're the latter."

"I hope so," said Faith. "I really hope you're right."

Reacher stood up and stretched and said, "Don't worry, I am! So, where you headed today?"

She turned her head, scanning the vast mountain landscape. "White Pass. It's still early and I think I can make it. I'll order a new cell phone there and have it shipped to Snoqualmie Pass, pick it up there."

"Sounds like a plan. Want some company along the way?"

"Sure! Why not?"

The Pacific Crest Trail, true to its name, kept to the high snow-streaked crest of the Goat Rocks Wilderness. Despite high elevation and snow banks, the day turned warm with sunlight beating down from a hazy blue sky and sometimes up from the snow. Reacher and Faith took a lot of water breaks and moderated their pace.

As they walked along a narrow, rocky ridge, Faith said, "I have to ask about your trail name? Is it from that character in the Tom Cruise movie, *Jack Reacher*?"

"You're not the first to ask, but yes it is. From the Lee Child books, actually. My real name is Melvin, so please continue calling me Reacher. That moniker was imposed on me by our little group. Arwen said that aside from the beard, the pony tail, the grey hair and the fact that I carry a lot more than a folding toothbrush, I somehow resembled her image of Jack Reacher. So the name stuck. It's not a bad name and I wear it proudly. So, what about your trail name?"

"It's my name, my true name, if you can believe it."

"I do, it's a good name."

Reacher led the way as they walked on in silence, boots crunching on fine rocks. High above them, ravens rode the thermals and called to one another, black silhouettes floating in the blue void.

Reacher looked back at her and said, "So, Faith, what're your plans for after the hike? A lot of people talk about what they're going to do after. About how the hike has changed their lives and the direction they want to go. So if you don't mind me asking, what're your thoughts?"

"I don't really know. I've avoided thinking about the future. Dealing with the past has taken up a lot of my energy, as has learning to live in the present. The future feels brighter now, but also intimidating. Do I use the GI Bill and go back to school? Return to my warehouse job? Join a veterans organization? Move back in with my mom and dad and mooch off of them? Hunt down a rich old man and marry him for his money?"

Reacher laughed.

"Seriously, Reacher, I don't know. Any suggestions?"

"Do what you love, what you're good at. Given your training, your experiences and how you can handle yourself in tight situations, I'm thinking you might have a future in law enforcement, security or even private investigation."

It was Faith's turn to laugh. "A private eye? Law enforcement? Seriously? I don't want to wind up in hazardous situations ever again. I don't want to shoot anyone, or be shot at. I don't even wanna carry a gun."

"If you're a PI, you usually don't. In fact most investigators never carry a firearm or find themselves in hazardous situations. A lot of it is pretty tedious work doing background checks, assisting clients and defense attorneys with cases involving child custody, insurance fraud, investment schemes, financial chicanery, elder abuse, harassment claims, you name it. The only hazards are getting hemorrhoids or diabetes from all the sitting around in the office or on stakeouts."

"How do you know so much about it?"

"Glad you asked! After I retired from 20 years in the insurance business—yeah, I was a corporate guy—I worked another 10 as a freelance fraud investigator for insurance companies. I had to have a PI license for that and it led to other work for some lawyers I knew, including my wife. Still doing it part-time, mostly working on cases for her in the Portland area. There's worse jobs out there. It's interesting and sometimes you get to do some good, help people out. And I've never had to carry a gun. Pay ain't bad either!"

"So what about those hemorrhoids and the diabetes?"

Reacher smiled. "That's what hiking the PCT is for, to make up for all that damn time sitting on my ass, and to get back in shape!"

"I bet you've got some great stories though."

Reacher raised his long arms toward the sky. "The only great stories I have are from out here, walkin' the world."

"Well thanks for the advice, Reacher. I'll take it into consideration when I ponder my future. For now, I wonder if we're going to make it to White Pass before nightfall?"

"Ha! The answer to that is in your name. Have faith, Faith."

CHAPTER 29 — AUGUST 4

Willie Nelson was singing "On the Road Again" as the big pickup roared down the highway, camper on the back and trailer in tow. Traffic was light on I-5 and it was a beautiful blue-sky morning. The Mentor was definitely feeling better.

He'd been very upset and depressed about missing her at Mount Hood. She never showed! So much disappointment. At first he wanted to take it out on the messenger, his faithful apprentice Joey. But that wouldn't be fair, and he needed Joey's help. There was no one else to help, was there? He needed help to continue his work at the level he was used to now. One thing he learned from Joey's company was how vital teamwork was.

Luckily, there was another chance to intercept her. He'd dropped Joey off along the PCT in the Gifford Pinchot National Forest. Joey hid along the trail and waited. Waited, and sure enough, finally saw her heading north. According to his last text message, he was following, but was having trouble keeping up with her. He was at least a day behind. That was okay with the Mentor. Better to follow at a discreet distance. Mustn't spook her! Cell phone coverage was good, if spotty, so the Mentor got updates periodically. Updates that helped him to pick a good spot to meet her. He'd used that place before. It was a great location, right along the Crest Trail. The road was off the beaten path too. A place to park and have a reunion with his one and only true love.

How long ago did they first meet? Maybe ten years or more now. What a wonderful time that was. Pure bliss really . . .

It was eleven years ago that he sold his software company and retired at age 40, a wealthy man with plenty of time and energy to enjoy his billions. He felt like he'd earned it after so many years of hard work and sacrifice. All he remembered before retirement was constant hard work, from when he was a teen in junior high and high school, through university, right up to the sale of his company. He hadn't minded. When he was young, hard work helped distract him from a lonely and miserable childhood. When he was older and out on his own, hard work felt good. It empowered him. Especially when it led to raking in tons of money through the sale of his revolutionary application. He'd been the toast of the town, the envied and admired Seattle software mogul that for a while stole the limelight away from Bill Gates. There'd been parties, charity events, media appearances, all of it accompanied by a seemingly unending selection of willing and beautiful women.

He owed it all to Amenable Solutions. That application had been his baby, his reason for being. Over a long year, he'd worked day and night and on weekends to build it, perfect it, test it over and over again until it was ready for release. Amenable provided application monitoring and compatibility software which allowed disparate programs and databases, even those on different platforms, to function smoothly together with the click of a mouse. His investors paid for a huge release party, with plenty of local and national media in attendance.

He continued working hard to promote and adapt Amenable to the ever-changing application environment. It paid off. He finally went public with Amenable and the stock shares soared. He hired a staff of developers, an accountant and a lawyer. He was riding a wave of phenomenal success.

That success came with a price, as his doctor pointed out to him. The Mentor was on the road to a variety of diseases caused by a bad diet, obesity, smoking, drinking, sleep deprivation and stress. The doctor advised him to take some time off and relax, get a grip on his bad habits and enjoy life. After careful thought, he agreed and, to the surprise of his friends and company board members, took it even further. He decided to sell Amenable. He told people it was the best decision he could make. The company sold for $2.1 billion, leaving him a substantial nest egg, and he continued to hold stock and receive royalties from his patents.

He sold his massive Mercer Island home and had a modest custom getaway built on Lopez Island. He bought a sailboat to go with the new house. He hired a nutritionist and personal trainer to help him get fit. He even had a steady girlfriend for a while, but she eventually broke up with him. They always did, but he didn't care. He always got what he wanted from them and there was always another one to take her place.

After 10 months of hard work, he was fit and healthy once again. He was ready to look for something else; something that would be a challenge to his newfound fitness and freedom. A friend had recently hiked the entire Pacific Crest Trail and told him about how much good it had done him. The Mentor liked the idea of taking on another big challenge. This time, it would be for him and no one else. He would challenge himself and there would be no money involved, no competition, no comparison. Just him and the wilderness.

It had been rough at first, especially for a guy who for many years hadn't spent much time outdoors. Very rough indeed, both physically and mentally. At one point, he thought he was having cardiac issues, but a trip to the emergency room revealed that he was just pushing himself too hard. So he learned to slow down. After all, what was the hurry?

And along the way, he met the girl of his dreams. He thought it a hackneyed phrase, but that was just how it felt when he first spotted the raven-haired beauty, skinny-dipping in Blue Mirror Lake. Long black hair trailed down her tanned back as she swam in the clear, sparkling water. When she turned to swim back, she saw him staring at her. Instead of getting angry or embarrassed, she smiled and waved. The Mentor smiled and waved back and took her glowing smile as permission to keep looking. She didn't seem to mind as he watched her step onto shore, dripping sunlit beads of lake water. He took it all in; her beautiful oval face, long hair, perfect breasts, tanned skin, the triangle of dark hair between her long legs.

He was transfixed, and instantly in love. He'd never before felt love alongside the lust. Up until that point, he'd been convinced that his abusive father had beaten the capacity to love out of him when he was a kid. Now, it felt so crazy and wonderful, it must be love. He turned away as she put on shorts and a t-shirt. And then she walked up and introduced herself, started asking him questions about his trip so far. He was surprised to find himself tongue-tied at first, but the two of them hit it off and hiked together that day and for several weeks after. And they spent nights together too. Nights like he'd never known; filled with love and passion. It was like a wonderful dream.

And like most dreams, he thought bitterly, it came to an end. He finally did something he'd never done before with any woman. He professed his profound and complete love for this free spirit. What was her response? She . . . she told him that what they'd experienced together had been fun, but it was time for her to move on. Just fun? Move on? He had a hard time accepting that. Surely what they had was more than just "fun"! Her rejection crushed him. He was mad with dismay. He frantically tried to persuade her to relent and stay with him. How could she not see what they had?

He tried so hard to persuade her. He tried too hard, but once it was done, he felt an odd, fierce joy. He owned her then and forever. He shook his head. He still couldn't remember exactly what happened, but he knew that eventually she was completely his. At first he felt bad, so horrible. But he'd also felt incredibly empowered and victorious. He couldn't understand the odd mixture of sadness, rage and power. Seems like it took him days to get his shit together. Everything from that first time was hazy. He remembered that she diminished. Was that the word? She shrank as he made her his, as she shared her very essence with him. What an odd experience that had been. Odd but somehow addictive. She disappeared but he still felt she was out there somewhere and that he should search for her again, find her again.

Sometimes he thought he'd see her on the trail, at his food trailer, in a grocery store, driving by in traffic. His heart would leap in his chest and hope would fill his mind with light, but it was always someone else. Sometimes that didn't stop him from meeting the new her though. He knew it wasn't really her, but they always looked like her and reminded him so much that he had to meet them, get to know them in the most intimate way. In the end, they would prove somewhat satisfying, but he was always disappointed. None of them were *Her*. Until now.

Seeing her at Elk Lake had been such a delicious shock. Part of his mind screamed, "Impossible!" but another part of him felt such hope. He knows what he saw, who he saw! And the photos were additional proof, direct from Joey's phone to his tablet. No possibility that they'd been Photoshopped. It was *Her*! Somehow . . . he couldn't imagine how . . . it was Her. She didn't recognize him though. After all those years, she'd forgotten him. He wasn't surprised. To her, he'd been a fling, a good time for a while, something to be used and thrown away. Well, she was going to learn different, wasn't she?

Next encounter, he'd have to be careful. If she remembered him, she might run, but after so many years? Maybe not. Once she was sedated, she'd stay. Anyway, he'd play it cool, be polite, try to get to know her again, and then he'd take her and he'd tell her why and what she'd done to him all those years ago, how she ruined his life. Tell her that now they'd be together forever. How satisfying that would be! And when he was done doing that, he'd take ownership and share her with others. Mustn't forget the sharing. She didn't want to be with just one guy. She wanted to move on, and he'd help her do that after he took ownership. He would be the one making that decision then. Sharing. That was so important.

CHAPTER 30 — AUGUST 10

The Oregon State Capitol Building was not what Max expected. Instead of an elaborate and stately government structure in the classic style, it was a newer looking, plain white block building with a round, dome-less rotunda in the middle. Capping the rotunda was a pedestal topped off by a statue of what looked like a golden lumberman holding an axe. He had a cloak or long coat slung over his shoulder and looked like maybe he was headed home after a hard day of chopping down trees. Aside from the statue, the rest of the building was very utilitarian, or maybe totalitarian, in appearance. It looked like it could've been designed by the Third Reich's architect, Albert Speer.

Max arrived in Salem an hour early, so he used the time to take a walking tour of the state capitol campus. As he ambled along, he realized that all the buildings on the state capital campus, including the Public Safety Building, were in the same utilitarian style. Plain, blocky white structures made of square-cut marble.

He looked at his watch and then looked around for a Park Service vehicle, the one that would be carrying ISB agent Ellen Plante. There wasn't one in sight. He walked over to a shaded stone bench outside the front doors of the Public Safety Building and sat down to wait. It was a hot, humid day. Max took out a bandana and wiped the sweat off his face.

Footsteps on the sidewalk to his left made him look that way. He saw a young, short, somewhat stout African American woman in a Park Service uniform. She turned toward the doors of the Public Safety Building and looked at Max uncertainly. He stood up, smiled and walked toward her, hand outstretched.

"You must be Ellen Plante!"

She looked up, smiled in return and shook his hand.

"Nice to meet you, Max. How was your trip down?"

"Pretty easy once I got south of Tacoma. I left early, took my time." He looked around and said, "I've never been here before and was wondering about the architecture. I've never seen such a plain state capitol setup. What gives?"

Ellen laughed. "Well, plain as it appears, it surely cost plenty to build in the 1930's. It's Art Deco design. One of the few state capitols that is."

Max shook his head. "So instead of being plain, it's actually artistic. Okay, got it. Well, shall we go inside and see what we can find?"

Their federal law enforcement credentials allowed them to bypass the security line and proceed directly into the building's main lobby. It was refreshingly cool inside. Distant phones rang, quiet voices and footsteps echoed in the big space. Max and Ellen walked over to the building's directory and saw that the OSP offices were on the fourth floor. Moments later they stepped out of the elevator, looked for directional signs and followed them down a long, carpeted hallway to a door labeled "Oregon State Police, Public Records".

The clerk behind the counter was a stooped, gaunt elderly woman wearing a pastel rose dress and a black sweater vest. She gazed impassively at the visitors over glasses balanced on her narrow nose. A uniformed security guard stood in the corner to their right. He was a beefy, middle-aged man with a bushy white mustache who nodded to Max and Ellen as they stepped up to the glassed-in counter. The clerk didn't smile when the two introduced themselves. Her nametag read "Linda". When Max told her they were looking for a hard copy of a National Park Service missing persons file, she frowned and shook her head.

"This is the archives for State Police, not Park Service. You've got the wrong place, young man."

"No, we're looking for a hard copy of a missing persons report that was sent here by the Park Service about ten years ago."

Ellen stepped up beside Max and said, "If I may, Linda. I'm with the Park Service? We routinely send copies of files to the OSP for cases of interest where jurisdictions might overlap, such as with missin' persons cases? So the file is likely here somewhere."

Linda stared at her a moment before saying, "I don't know about that. Do you have a file number?"

Max and Ellen looked at each other. Ellen said, "Uh, no we don't."

Linda pursed her lips and lowered her glasses further before saying, "Then how am I supposed to find this file? You need a file number. We have a system. The files are organized in numerical order."

Ellen said, "Do file numbers coincide with the date they were filed? This file would be from ten years ago."

Linda leaned back and crossed her arms. "Possibly, but I simply don't have time to go back in the rows and open files, looking for names or dates."

Ellen gave Linda her brightest, most sincere smile. "Well maybe we could go look? We're cops, you know."

Linda's eyes narrowed. "So? You still might mess up the files. You might not put everything back right. In my experience, cops can be very cavalier about records once they find what they want."

Max spoke up. "I assure you, Linda, we will leave everything exactly as we found it. We just need to look at that file. It's part of an important and current criminal investigation. A matter of public safety."

Linda stared up at him. "So you say. You still need a file number. It's the only way to find—"

A man's voice interrupted her. "Oh for heaven's sake, Linda!" Max and Ellen turned to see the security guard stepping forward. "Let them go look for the file. I'll go with them and make sure all is well."

Linda looked down and straightened some papers as she said, "Very well, Roger. But I am not responsible for this violation of the rules." She looked up. "And what if someone comes in here waving a gun or a bomb and you're not here. What am I supposed to do? Die?"

Roger sighed. "Linda, let's not be overly dramatic. I'll be gone for only a few minutes. Kevin is just down the hall. You'll be fine." He turned and said to Max and Ellen, "Come with me and I'll help you find the file."

Roger walked to a door that was labeled "Authorized Personnel Only" and opened it, ushered the two feds through.

As they walked down a hallway, Roger introduced himself as, "Roger Fender, Retired OSP. Well, semi-retired, obviously."

Ellen and Max introduced themselves and shook his hand. They thanked Fender for intervening.

He waved a hand, said, "Not the first time. Poor Linda has worked in this office for almost 35 years now. She's burned out but won't or can't retire. She gets a little grumpy, but she's a good employee and at heart a good person."

They came up to a door with marbled glass. Block letters across the glass proclaimed it "OSP FILE ARCHIVES". Roger opened it and led them in. As befits an archive, the room was musty and closed in. There were no windows. Lines of florescent lighting flickered above long rows of multi-tiered metal shelving. He asked, "What was the name on that file?"

Ellen said, "The missin' person is named Lila Montaigne. Disappeared from Crater Lake National Park ten years ago?"

Roger rubbed a stubbly chin. "Montaigne? Crater Lake? I remember that case. Yeah, ten years ago. I think some of my OSP buddies looked into that. Her father was Mike Montaigne, police chief in Meeks Landing. Here, let me see if I can find it."

Max and Ellen glanced at one another as Roger led them down an aisle between rows of metal shelves. Files and cardboard boxes lined each shelf. Numbers were pasted on the shelves they rested on as well as on the boxes and file holders. Some of the boxes were labeled with names too. Roger muttered to himself as he slowed and started looking closely at the labels, checking dates and names. Finally he stopped and said, "Here it is."

As he pulled the box off the shelf, he said, "Uh oh! Feels kinda light."

He opened it and looked inside, said, "Shit" and showed the box to Max and Ellen. It was empty.

Max and Ellen both said, "Shit!"

"What gives?" said Max. "No files? What's going on here?"

Roger shrugged. "File's gone. I don't know what happened, but obviously this ain't right. So what now? Have you looked in the databases? Maybe online somewhere?"

Ellen shook her head. "There're no other files anywhere aside from a SAR report I found. I looked. Nothin' digital, no hard copies. Nothin' in NCIC or NIBRS. It's nowhere."

Roger said, "Somebody must've cleaned house then. Somebody with a lot of clout, maybe a lot of dough. I know there was a case and obviously there must've been a file. This is going to mean an internal investigation. Shit."

The three of them stood in silence for a moment and then Roger snapped his fingers and said, "You know what?

I bet Chief Montaigne has a copy of the file! He was pretty involved in the search and the investigation. Yeah, he's gonna have a copy."

Max asked, "Can you get us his contact information? We need to call him. Today."

Roger nodded. "Sure, sure. He's retired but I can look up his home address and phone. Come on back to the front desk and let me get on a computer."

Back at the front desk, and under the stern eye of Linda, Roger used her computer to access the state law enforcement personnel database. He found Michael Montaigne's contact information and printed out two hard copies for Max and Ellen.

As he handed them the copies, he asked, "What's this all about anyway? You said a criminal investigation? Public safety? Have the poor girl's remains finally been found? I know Mike and his wife would want closure."

Max took his copy and said, "Sorry Roger. We can't talk about it right now. I can fill you in later, once it's resolved."

Roger looked disappointed but nodded. "Sure, sure. I understand. I used to be a detective. I know how it is. But yeah, let me know when you get a chance. Mike's a good guy, and I know the entire law enforcement community would like closure."

They shook hands all around and Max thanked Roger for his help. Ellen thanked Linda, who stared over her glasses and nodded, tight-lipped. Back outside the building, the temperature had cooled enough to be comfortable, so Max and Ellen sat side by side on one of the stone benches.

Max said, "This is getting really weird. Who would have the resources to wipe out secure files like that? They were likely in multiple databases, like NIBRS and NCIC, not to mention the Park Service and OSP. Not to mention the hard copies. Who the hell could do that?"

"Like Roger said, someone with a lot of money and resources. And someone with some serious hackin' skills. Those databases are as secure as you can get."

"Well, at least I can give the FBI profilers a couple of new clues. We now have strong evidence that the subject is wealthy and that he's got computer skills, or he can afford to hire someone who does."

"So, Max, what's next?"

"I'm going to call Michael Montaigne and ask to see him, see his files, ASAP. Isn't Meeks Landing near here? Somewhere on the Willamette?"

Ellen took out her smartphone and said, "Let's find out." She tapped the screen a few times and shaded it with her hand. "Yep, it is." She showed him the phone. "About halfway between here and Portland, right on the river. It's way out of the way and on some back roads. Might be tough to find."

"I'll find it, that is after I call Montaigne and make sure he's around, and that he has a copy of the file."

Max walked back to his SUV, got in, started it up and got the AC going. He called Michael Montaigne's cell phone but there was no answer. He left a message identifying who he was and that he was hoping to see a copy of Lila Montaigne's missing person file as soon as possible. Max decided to get some dinner while he was waiting for a call back.

An hour later, he checked in to a nearby Holiday Inn. Max entered the darkened third floor room, tossed the key card onto the desk, dropped his overnight bag on the floor and flopped onto a king size bed. With a sigh of relief, he closed his eyes and then winced when his cell phone rang. Eyes still closed, he reached out, fumbled with the phone and answered it.

It was Bernie. "Max, where are you and what did you find out today?"

Max sat up and told Bernie about meeting Ellen Plante, about the missing file and that he'd left a message with Michael Montaigne. "He still hasn't called back. It was getting late, so I got a room here in Salem. Hopefully I'll hear from Montaigne soon."

"Great!" said Bernie. "Maybe we're making some progress at last! That was a stroke of luck that the security guard remembered the case and knew who Montaigne was. The file deletion gives us a clue, maybe the beginnings of a trail, however nebulous. Now we just wait to find out what Montaigne can tell you. I'll forward any new info to the profiler, but not sure when he can come up with a revised profile. Just like all of us, those people are busy as hell these days and there's not much chance of expediting this."

"I understand. I don't know about you, but I feel like we're running out of time. This guy, whoever he is, he's losing it, becoming disorganized after ten years of getting away with it. He's going to go after more women and I just hope to hell we get to him first. "

CHAPTER 31 — AUGUST 10-11

Mike Montaigne called later that evening. Awakened by his buzzing, glowing cell phone, Max sat up on the edge of the motel bed, rubbed his eyes. He struggled to get his brain into gear as he answered the phone with a mumbled "Yeah?"

"Agent Albricci? Hey, this is Mike Montaigne. Got your message and am curious as hell as to what this is about."

"Uh, yeah, this is Max Albricci. Sorry, sir. I was asleep. Um, thing is that I was wondering if you have a file on the investigation of your daughter Lila's disappearance ten years ago?"

"Sure, sure I do. But why are you asking me? Why are you looking for the file? Is there new evidence, new clues? Has something turned up about my daughter?"

"We're not sure. So far there's nothing in particular. This is in relation to another case."

"What case?"

"A woman vanished at Crater Lake National Park a few weeks ago. You probably heard about it?"

"No. No, we didn't hear anything about it. Must've happened when we were gone. Took a two-week cruise in Alaska. So this new case is similar to my daughter's?"

"It is."

"So why ask me for the file? There's one in Salem, and the Park Service has a copy too. And it's online, right?"

"I'm in Salem right now, sir. I visited the OSP office with a Park Service agent today, hoping to find a copy but it's gone. The NPS doesn't have a copy. There are no copies anywhere in any databases either. It was only by pure luck that we found out about your daughter's case. Agent Plante came across a SAR report at Crater Lake."

There was silence on the other end. Montaigne finally said, "What the heck? That doesn't make any sense. What happened to the other copies then?"

"We don't know yet. Look, can I come see you tomorrow morning, get a look at the file? I can give you a complete, coherent update then. I'm sorry, but I'm exhausted tonight. Would that be all right?"

"Sure, sure. I'm very curious as to what this is about. You can meet my wife and I at a small cafe in downtown Meeks Landing. Cousin's Kountry Kitchen? They got good coffee and they serve a great breakfast. How does 9 o'clock sound?" Montaigne gave him the address and directions to Meeks Landing and the cafe. Max rapidly wrote it down on a hotel notepad. After he hung up, Max set his phone on the bedside table, lay back on the bed and was asleep almost instantly.

Early the next morning, Max pulled into a turnout at the crest of a hill and looked down and across the valley. What he saw made him wonder if his Ford was some kind of time machine. The scene looked like an old oil painting of an idealized, rural America from days gone by; a green oasis of beauty under a blue sky, soaked in morning sunlight. A small town nested in the middle of a landscape of trees, green fields and rolling hills. Two white church spires rose above the tree-lined city streets. Beyond the town, the lazy Willamette River was an intermittent blue ribbon winding through acres of cottonwoods. Max could see what looked like a covered bridge amidst the cottonwoods. There were no strip malls, no giant McMansions looming on the hills, no freeways roaring through.

Max stepped out of his vehicle and listened, the sun warm on his back. He could hear a dog barking, the rattle of a woodpecker, a train whistle far in the distance, a tractor chugging in a field somewhere, birds singing in the towering firs behind him. He shook his head and smiled, listened a moment longer and got back into the SUV. He turned the key, pulled back onto the county road and headed down the winding road to Meeks Landing.

CHAPTER 32 — AUGUST 11

Mike and Sally Montaigne sat on red vinyl-cushioned benches in a window booth at Cousin's Kountry Kitchen. Sally wrung her hands and Mike checked his watch. They kept turning their heads to look out the large window at the end of their table. Across the street was the old Sears Roebuck store where the portly young manager was currently unlocking the front door. They watched him step inside and flip the "Closed" sign to "Open". That store was going to be missed. After 80 years, it was being shut down, and Mike wondered why. There weren't any big box stores in the area to compete with it. He and Sally and many other people did a lot of business there.

Sally broke into his reverie. "Mike, are you sure he didn't tell you anything more?"

Mike sighed and stirred his coffee. "Honey, I told you everything. He identified himself as a Forest Service investigator working for the FBI, whatever that means. All he said was that Lila's disappearance might be tied to a new case, that one we looked up on the internet last night? He needs to ask us some questions and review the case files. He told me that the original files and all other copies are gone, vanished. All of which is very strange. I'm sure we're about to find out what's going on."

"Well, he's five minutes late, and I have to get back to the college soon for my ten o'clock class. He better show up."

Mike reached across the Formica table and held her hands in his, looked into her brown eyes. "Baby, this might be very important. It might be the break we've always hoped for. Let's focus on that. Your class can wait."

A raspy woman's voice from behind him asked, "'nother cup of coffee, Chief?"

Michael turned around and smiled at the stooped, elderly waitress. "No thanks, Alma. And I'm not the Chief anymore, you know. Just a regular Joe now."

The waitress winked and said, "Whatever you say . . . Joe." She shuffled away, chuckling to herself. Michael and Sally smiled at each other and shook their heads. A flash of reflected sunlight made Sally turn to look out the window.

She said, "There he is. I think."

Michael squinted. "Forest Service law enforcement, it says. Yep, that's him."

Across the street, Max's green and white Ford Explorer Interceptor pulled up and diagonal parked in front of the Sears store. They watched as Max got out of the vehicle, looked around and started across the street.

"Hopefully we're about to find out what the heck is going on." said Mike.

"Max, it's good to meet you, and thanks for coming here."

"Sure," said Max, sitting across the booth from them. "Thanks for agreeing to see me and to show me the case files on your daughter."

Sally spoke up. "I can't believe we have the only copy now. What happened? How did the original and others disappear?"

Alma appeared and asked Max if he wanted to order anything. He looked up and said, "Just coffee for now. Thanks." He turned his attention back to Mike and Sally. "That's a great question. My preliminary assessment is that the man who is responsible for Lila's disappearance is the one that made the files vanish. That in itself is an important clue. A gap in his, or her, armor of anonymity."

"But how? That would require some resources and some gall."

"Not to mention skill," added Mike.

Alma came back and set a steaming ceramic mug in front of Max.

Max nodded as he stirred cream and sugar into his coffee. He looked across the table at Mike and Sally. "Yes, a lot of money and computer hacking skills to make those files disappear. This might be the break we need. So I need to look at your files."

"You will. But we're wondering what this is all about," said Mike. "Why the renewed interest in our daughter's case? I mean, we did look up the recent Crater Lake story and it is, on the surface, similar to Lila's case. The victim even looks like her."

Max sipped his coffee and set it down. He wiped his mouth with a paper napkin and said, "Okay, I shouldn't be revealing this, but what the hell . . . you deserve to know. Just keep what I'm about to tell you to yourselves." Max lowered his voice. "It turns out that your daughter was probably the first in a string of at least 12 potentially related disappearances over the last ten years along the PCT. The new Crater Lake case of Tamara Ivanova is the latest one." He went on to give them an overview of the investigation, how the pattern was finally detected, the FBI task force work and how there were two new potential victims this year. Sally started to interrupt him at several points, but Mike put a hand on hers and shook his head.

It took almost 15 minutes for Max to describe the history of his investigation. When he was done, the Montaignes looked at one another and back at Max. Mike's face was pale and Sally's hands were trembling.

"Look," said Max. "I can see you're upset. I'm very sorry to bring this all back to you. I can't even begin to understand your pain, but we need to—"

"Max! Just . . . shut up and listen," said Mike. He paused and wiped his broad face with a napkin. "Just listen! Our other daughter, Faith, is out hiking the trail this summer. You say that you're expecting more disappearances? More murders this year?"

"Well, yeah. But that's more of a supposition than anything. It's the FBI's assessment that the killer is becoming disorganized and will increase his activities. And as I said, the victims all fit a very particular physical profile. They all closely resemble Lila. I don't know if your other daughter would be at risk, so—"

"Max!" said Sally. "You don't understand. Lila and Faith were identical twins!"

Max leaned back and stared at them. "Okay. Shit . . . uh, where is she now? Have you heard from her? Is she okay?"

Mike said, "We spent the 30th and part of the 31st with her at Cascade Locks. Then she called us two days ago from White Pass and said she'd lost her cell phone. I ordered her a new one, had it sent to the post office at Snoqualmie Pass for her to pick up. She's supposed to be there in three or four days. We don't have any contact with her right now."

Sally's voice shook as she said, "We have to find her, Mike! Max, we have to find her now! We have to get her off that damn trail!"

Max looked at each of them and nodded. "Okay." He paused. "Look, I'll go find her. I've got detailed maps, mileages, everything about the PCT in my rig. We can figure out generally where she might be, based on when she called you from White Pass and how many miles a day she's averaging, if you know that. I'll try to get some people to start looking and I'll head up there too."

"She's been averaging around 25 miles a day," said Mike.

Max stood up, hands flat on the table. "Okay. Look, I'm going to get my maps. I'll be right back. I'll need your help getting this figured out. I'll still need to look at your files too."

The Montaignes watched Max dash across the street, open the rear hatch of his SUV and start rummaging around.

Sally was shaking her head. Tears rolled down her cheeks.

"Michael, I can't go through this again. I just can't. This can't be happening. Our daughter is out there alone with a murderer!"

The old waitress shuffled up to their booth and said, "Sally, are you okay? What's wrong, dear? Was that young man bothering you two?"

Sally shook her head. "No, not at all. I'll be okay. Could you bring us the check? We need to go."

Alma bent down and patted Sally's shoulder. "You bet, dear. You let me know if you need help, you hear?" Sally nodded and Alma walked away.

Mike leaned forward and said in a low voice, "Look, we're going to find her, okay? Max seems like a solid fella and sounds like he can help. And I'm going with him, so don't you worry."

"You? Michael, you're not a cop anymore."

"No, not officially, but I am Faith's father. And I've got a lot of SAR experience, and I won't let Max say no."

CHAPTER 33 — AUGUST 9-11

She was being stalked. It was more than just a feeling. It was knowledge. She *knew*. It wasn't speculation or supposition or paranoia. She never understood how it was possible to know something like that without logic and supporting evidence, but experience taught her that it was so. Sometimes you just knew that you were being scrutinized, evaluated, followed; perhaps with ill intent, perhaps not. That knowledge didn't bring much more with it. She had no idea who or what was stalking her, but suspected it was a human and that the human was likely Duster. The feeling was a warning, a nudge to the mind. Be alert, be aware, take precautions even if they seem silly, just as she'd done for days after the last encounter with Duster.

The feeling had appeared a day north of White Pass. After camping overnight at nearby Sand Lake, she and Reacher parted company. He'd decided to spend a rest day in camp due to arthritis and told Faith that he planned to keep going north, but was going to slow down. She moved on. At first Faith missed Reacher's company, but she felt her mind gradually ease back into the landscape, quiet and at peace within her solitude. That didn't last long.

Near the end of the day, she became increasingly uneasy. As she hiked north along the low mountain ridges, the trail took her through vast old clearcuts where she could pause at strategic points to look back. She encountered a few other hikers along the way, but never saw anyone suspicious. Yet the uneasiness persisted.

By mid afternoon of the third day after Sand Lake, a high layer of pale clouds flowed in from the southwest. Faith was glad of it since it moderated the heat. Hiking along an open, logged-over ridge near Bearpaw Butte, she looked southwest and saw shredded low clouds around the base of Mount Rainier. Combined with the advance of the high clouds, that meant rain was on the way.

It had been a long day of hiking from Green Pass north. She was hoping to camp at Stampede Pass, but was getting tired and hungry. She was ready to stop for the night. In the central Washington Cascade Mountains, the PCT winds its way through brushy, stump-studded old clear-cuts and then through small patches of old growth trees, and then through clear-cuts again, crossing several overgrown logging roads. Some of those road junctions had campsites but there were no water sources. Faith kept going.

It was almost 7:30 in the evening when she stepped onto a road and was happy to see, next to a PCT marker post, a small sandwich board sign for “TGI Mondays!” There was an arrow on the sign pointing right. Stampede Pass was only two miles away, but Faith was spent and needed food and rest. She walked down the road for a couple of hundred feet. It passed through an old clear-cut and was lined with stunted alders and willows. Huckleberry bushes, grey stumps and small fir and hemlock trees covered the rolling landscape around her. She looked ahead to a large turnout on the left and there was the gold and green food trailer. Faith smiled as she approached it. The front of the trailer was marked with the words “TGI Monday’s!”. A cartoon script underneath proclaimed “Awesome Eats by The Chef!”. There were two hikers eating at one of the stand-up tables and a third at the trailer’s serving window.

The trailer had a festive look, with brightly colored Christmas lights lining the wide serving window. The faint hum of a generator came from the far side of the trailer. Faith greeted the three hikers and dropped her pack.

Sighing, she stretched and then walked up to the serving window. There was the big bearded man she remembered from Elk Lake; The Chef. Jenks had mentioned his name. She remembered realizing that it explained the 'TGI Monday's' written on the trailer. The guy's last name was Monday, but she couldn't remember his first name.

He was dishing up a healthy serving of burger and fries to a tall, emaciated, bearded young man. Monday glanced at Faith and said, "Be with you in a min—" and stopped, looked back at her. Once again, just as at Elk Lake, his face turned pale and his eyes widened. He stuttered a moment before saying, "Be right with you, miss." He finished serving the man. His hand was shaking and the serving spoon rattled against the hiker's plate. Faith noticed an odd little smile on the man's face wondered what was going on, but she was too tired and hungry to worry about it.

The young man stepped away with his food and Faith walked up to the window. Monday told her, "Hang on there. I'll be right back with some more burgers and fries!" He disappeared back into the kitchen.

Faith turned and looked at the other three hikers while she waited. They smiled and one asked how her trip was going. She exchanged small talk with them for a few minutes. As those minutes went by, she grew impatient. Her stomach was growling like a cornered cougar and she felt a dire need to feed. She was about to knock on the counter when Monday reappeared, smiling and carrying a tray heaped with hamburgers and paper bags filled with French fries. His face wasn't pale anymore and his hands were steady.

He beamed at her. "Sorry about that. I had to cook up some more patties, but here they are." In a louder voice, he said, "Seconds anyone?"

It was almost a stampede as the hikers rushed forward with their plates.

"Hang on people. This lady was next. Miss, here you go. What's your trail name?"

"I don't really have one, but people are calling me Faith." Monday smiled and nodded as she took the full plate and walked a few steps to a tall table. She set her plate down and inhaled the wonderful steam curling up from the food. She dug in. The juicy burger tasted like heaven.

As Monday served the other hikers, he said to her, "Faith. That's a great name for a hiker. So is it because you have faith that you're going to finish the trip in time? I mean, before the snow flies?"

Faith took another bite of the burger, closed her eyes and smiled. She opened them and said, "Sure, whatever. I know I'm going to make it. What is it, another 300 miles or so? Piece of cake after what I've already done."

One of the other hikers, whom Faith remembered was named Conehead, shook his head and said, "Faith, you're hella strong! Me, I'm about to call it a day. Just gettin' more and more tired, more and more ready to just be done."

Monday shook a spatula in Conehead's direction and said, "Now's not the time to give up, man. You've made it this far. Don't stop now! I felt like you do when I hiked the trail ten years ago and I was 40! But I kept going and the less I thought about the goal, the easier it got to get to that goal." He nodded his head and continued, "One day at a time, that's the key."

Conehead grimaced and said, "Whatever, dude. Can I have some more fries?"

The meal and the friendly conversation continued for another half hour. Monday finally said, "Time to close up folks! It's gettin' dark soon. I'm sure you all want to find campsites. I've got bottled water for everyone, so come and get it."

He handed out two one-liter bottles to everyone. The other three hikers thanked Josh and said they were moving on to camp at Stampede Pass for the night. Faith wanted to join them but she was just too tired. She felt uneasy about staying near the trailer and decided to camp up the road, out of sight. She couldn't explain the feeling but she knew better than to ignore it. It had saved her life in the past. She thanked Monday and said she'd find a campsite elsewhere.

"Sure, Faith. You know, there's a couple just west of here." He pointed up the road. "Couple of hundred yards, I'd say. Just around the second corner. I camped there myself when I came through. No water, but good views and out of the way."

Faith thanked him and shouldered her pack, started hiking west on the road. It felt good to have a full belly for a change and Faith was looking forward to a good night's sleep. She looked back once and saw Monday standing next to his camper, staring after her. He raised a hand and waved. She waved back, turned and walked on, feeling uneasy.

CHAPTER 34 — AUGUST 11

Max tried to decline Mike's offer to go with him, but it was only token resistance. Sometimes family members were the key to finding someone. They knew the missing person better than anyone and could predict their behavior—the choices they might make, who they might seek out, how they'd react. Mike could be a valuable asset.

Alma poured more coffee and walked away, her face pinched with concern. Max, Mike and Sally leaned forward on the red vinyl bench seats and looked over the maps Max had laid out on the table. He made notes of dates and mileages and finally said, "So according to the dates and numbers you gave me, Faith is likely somewhere along the trail between a place called Green Pass, here, all the way up to Snoqualmie Pass. That's about 30 miles of trail. She called you early on the morning of the 9th, from White Pass. So, if she traveled that day in addition to yesterday and today, that would get her roughly 72 miles from White, which would put her here." Max put his finger on the map. "A few miles north of Tacoma Pass."

Mike stood up. "Makes sense to me. We should get going. To the house for a go-bag and then let's head north. I'll get the case files too. Didn't want to take them out of the house until I knew what was going on."

Mike walked up to the cafe's long counter and took out his wallet. Alma waved him off. "Your money's no good here, Chief. My hearin' ain't so good anymore but I heard what you're doin'. You just go and find that dear child of yours. And you let me know when you found her, okay?"

Mike nodded but took a twenty from his wallet and laid it on the counter. “Thanks, Alma. I really appreciate that, but I always pay my way. I’ll be back in a couple of days, with Faith.”

Max followed the Montaignes’ blue Toyota Highlander for three miles to their rural home outside Meeks Landing. He waited on the sunny back deck while Sally and Mike threw together a go bag. Max sat on an old-fashioned wooden picnic table bench. He pulled out his phone, checked the signal strength and called Bernie in Seattle. Bernie answered on the first ring and Max filled him in on what was happening.

After he finished with the update, Bernie said, “Max, sounds good. So your plan is to go look for Faith Montaigne?”

“Yep, and I’d like to get SAR out on this, either King or Kittitas County, or both. The trail straddles both counties.”

There was a pause. “Max, I don’t think we can do that. I don’t have any search and rescue resources and I’m not sure I can find anyone at the county level who will go out.”

“Shit! Aren’t you the agent in charge?”

“Max, like I said, we don’t have our own resources for that. And we’d have to ask the counties involved to step up, and frankly they are not fond of us feds, and more to the point they don’t have a lot of funding. Faith isn’t lost or known to be in immediate danger, is she? There’s been no crime committed against her. You know the protocols here.”

“She may be in great danger!”

“I know, I know. I understand how you feel, especially with the parents there, but realistically there’s not much I can do. Doesn’t the FS have resources?”

“No. I mean there are people who could help, but they’re not law enforcement and I don’t know if they’re available on such short notice. I’ll try to contact some of them. Anyway, I see Mike is ready. He's got the files too. I'm going to review them as we head north."

"We?"

"Yeah, Mike's going with me. Look Bernie, I can't stop him, and I think his help would be invaluable. Besides, he's a former cop. I might need backup."

There was silence on the other end. Finally Max heard Bernie sigh. "Okay. Fine. You guys go for it. For god's sake make sure nothing happens to him, or to you. The paperwork would be killer. I'll see what I can do on this end to at least get a couple of agents headed your way for backup."

A half hour later, they were heading north on Interstate 5 at 80 miles per hour. While Mike drove, Max sat in the passenger seat and made another phone call, this time to his patrol captain, to ask for some help. Captain Allen wasn't very helpful. Most of Max's end of the conversation consisted of a series of "yes," "I see," "uh huh," "but what about—" "okay," "do you think—" After the call was ended, he stared out the window.

Mike glanced over at him and said, "That didn't sound encouraging."

Max sighed. "Everything's about budget these days. I was hoping Kevin, the LEO in Naches Ranger District, could bring his canine up and help look for Faith, but the captain said there's no money for overtime and he's working on a case right now. She said there doesn't appear to be a public or officer safety issue here and that I should get help from the FBI since I'm officially working for them. And then when I asked her what about our county co-op deputy, she said he could possibly help, but would the FBI cover his cost? I doubt that. Lordy, everything is budget, budget, budget."

"Welcome to my world, Max. Or should I say my former world? I dealt with that crap for years, constantly fighting to get enough money to run an effective department. Every time my department got enough funding and was successful in lowering the crime rate, city and county would cut our funding. And then because our funding and resources were cut, the crime rate would go up, so then we'd get more funding. It's ridiculous! The battle never ends."

Max said, "Yeah. I hear ya, except in the case of the Forest Service, the crime rate keeps going up while the enforcement budget keeps going down. Anyway, no sense worrying about that now. I better look over these files. What's in 'em might determine our course of action."

Mike continued to drive while Max reviewed the Lila Montaigne files. Traffic was thick and Mike had to concentrate, so he didn't say much. After 20 minutes, Max turned to him and said, "I'm reading about this Josh Monday guy, the one who traveled with Lila for a few weeks? According to the file, Monday was background checked, came up clean. Two witnesses, a married couple, claimed to have been hiking with him during the time of Lila's disappearance." There was a pause. "That name really rings a bell. I'm trying to remember where I've seen it lately."

Mike nodded. "I remember Monday. I talked to him myself. The guy is practically a saint in the Seattle tech scene. I can't remember all the charities he supports. It's a lot. Anyway, I liked the guy. Very personable and he tried to be helpful. I don't know. I like to think that after all my years in law enforcement, I can spot a liar. That guy did not strike me as a liar, and his alibi checked out."

"I suppose, but I'm still trying to think of why that name rings a bell." After a pause, Max snapped his fingers. "I've got it! Joshua Monday. There was an article in a magazine recently. An article about Josh Monday the trail angel. He operates one of those food trailers for PCT hikers. I planned to do more research on the food trailers and the trail angels." He swiveled the vehicle's dashboard mounted computer so he could use the keyboard and monitor. "Let me find that article. *Adventure Trails Magazine*, I think it was." He tapped some keys, waited a moment and tapped the trackpad. "Okay, here it is. The title is 'The Archangel of Trail Angels'.

The article covered a springtime visit and interview with billionaire Josh Monday at his modest home on the shores of Lopez Island. The writer gave background on the Pacific Crest Trail and went on to discuss the role of trail angels in helping long distance hikers realize their goal.

The writer described Monday as "a tall, stout man of 50 with a short, neatly trimmed red beard. He moves and talks deliberately. Pointing to a tall green and white Ford F-350 pickup with a large camper on back, Monday said that it was his summer home. The shining camper is painted with a bewitching pattern of subtle PCT emblems; the same emblems seen on signs along the trail." Hitched to the pickup was a shiny gold and green food trailer. Emblazoned across the front and on the sides are large letters with the clever name, "*TGI Monday's*". And under that a cartoonish, funky script reads, "*Awesome Eats by The Chef*".

Max said, "In the interview, Monday says he hiked the PCT ten years ago, soon after retiring at 40. And he goes on to say he's been a trail angel every year since then."

Mike pounded the steering wheel with his palm and said, "Well shit! That's gotta be him, Max! That son of a bitch had me fooled. The timeline matches. And this trail angel business gives him the opportunity. I mean, he's out all summer along the trail, meeting lots of hikers at road crossings, lookin' like a goddamn saint, or angel, or whatever. And means? The guy is filthy rich and doesn't work, so he's got all the time and resources he needs. As for motive, his brief relationship with Lila must be it.

Maybe she rejected him and he lost it, killed her and made her disappear. Maybe that drove him even more off the deep end and he started killing women that reminded him of Lila. Jesus!"

"But what about his alibi witnesses? How do you account for that?"

"Oh hell, a guy with that kind of money? He must've paid the witnesses off! As in 'here's twenty grand if you'll say you were hiking with me at so and so time'. Maybe he even threw in a threat with it." Mike shook his head. His face had turned red, his lips were tight and he was squinting at the road ahead. His hands gripped the steering wheel tightly.

Max asked him, "You okay, Mike? You want me to drive?"

"No . . . no, I'm okay. Let's figure this out. Let's work it. All right, so how does this guy operate? Let's say he moves up the PCT, setting up his trailer at road junctions, sees his victim, plays it cool and moves further up the trail to the next road junction and waits for her. He's got the perfect cover. He's above suspicion! Who'd suspect this guy? The guy is affable as hell, rich, popular, makes a good impression. His victims would never have a clue until it's too late."

Max said, "Given what I've learned about some of the missing, Monday must use drugs to subdue the women when the time comes. Some of the women were into martial arts, so would put up a hell of a fight. So he catches them off guard somehow, but he has to physically subdue them. My guess? He puts something in the food that conks them out and then he physically restrains them in a secure location, such as his trailer. Motive, means, opportunity . . . it's all there.

"And as for covering his tracks, he's got plenty of money to pay someone to make the first case files, your daughter's, disappear. And no doubt the skills to hack into databases. It all fits!"

"We gotta find Faith, make sure she's safe and then we gotta find Monday and put him out of business."

Max told him, "We'll need solid evidence, some proof. I don't think we have enough probable cause for a search warrant. Maybe we can get him to talk, inadvertently show us enough evidence for a search. A confession would be even better. If that happens, don't get any ideas about dealing out your own justice on this joker. Anything we do has to be court-worthy. We need to play this cool and by the book, okay?"

There was silence as Mike stared at the road ahead, mouth set in a thin straight line. He finally said, "Max? I have never, ever dealt out my own justice, as you put it. Throughout my entire career, I've been by the book, followed the DA's lead, keep everything tight and legal." He turned to glare at Max. "But by God if he's done anything to Faith, I will fucking kill him and plant a gun on him. It'll be self defense and you can damn well look the other way!"

"I can't promise anything, Mike." Max understood how Mike felt and wasn't sure how to respond. He didn't want to endorse what Mike said, but was pretty sure he would look the other way if Mike did what he promised to do.

Mike glanced at him and said, "You ever shoot someone?"

"Thankfully, no. And I hope I never do."

"It ain't pretty, that's for sure. I had to shoot a couple of guys during my career. One of 'em died on the spot. I had no choice but to shoot. He was stoked on meth and on a rampage with a machete, a lot of people around. He'd already injured two. After several verbal warnings, I gave him a double-tap and down he went like a water-logged towel. I'll never forget it. It was justified, plenty of witnesses, video, all the verification you could wish for.

But . . ." Mike paused. "But it's always haunted me. I found out a few things about the guy afterward and if it hadn't been for the drugs? He could've been a good guy. He was a good man before his life went to shit. And then I came along."

"You did your job. You protected the public, maybe saved some other lives."

"I know, I know. But still, if you have any humanity, something like that haunts you. It's a strange feeling, a dark feeling. So I guess what I'm saying is avoid it at all costs, but if you have to do it, be prepared for some inner flak."

"Are you prepared for that? If you take the law into your own hands?"

Mike drove in silence for a few moments. The only sound was the rumbling of tires on the pavement, the muted smooth hum of the engine. He finally said, "If Monday's the guy who killed my Lila, if he's done anything to Faith, I think I can deal with the flak."

Max nodded and looked out the window. Abruptly, he said, "Hey shit!" and pulled out his cell phone. He looked over at Mike. "I got an idea. I'm gonna call Bernie. I think our job just got simpler."

CHAPTER 35 — AUGUST 11

Faith found an open grassy spot near the road and set up her small red tent. The sky was darkening and the air felt humid and heavy. The view was pretty good, despite the murky evening. Forested ridges receded into blue distance, where massive Mount Rainier rose up, partially obscured by cloud and looking like a ghost mountain in the fading light. On an anonymous distant mountaintop a tiny red beacon flashed. Pale curls of mist floated over the westernmost mountains.

It felt like rain was on the way, so Faith stretched the rain fly over her tent. When that was done, she walked into nearby brush to pee. She returned to her pack and fished out toothbrush and toothpaste, along with a headlamp and water bottle. Sitting on a stump, she brushed her teeth and gazed at the vast mountain scene. Aside from a distant, very faint train whistle and a jet passing high overhead, the evening was silent. She felt lonely. Faith wished she had a cell phone and could call her parents. She was looking forward to picking up the new phone at Snoqualmie Pass.

Her head jerked up at the sound of footsteps grinding on the gravel road. Moments later a dim shape appeared. Monday's voice came out of the semi-darkness. "It's just me, Josh! Hey, I thought you might like a delicious dessert. In my haste to close up, I forgot to offer it to everyone, but I remembered you. Can I come into your camp?"

Faith stood and beamed her headlamp at him. Fifty feet away, the big man squinted and held up a paper plate with a large piece of chocolate cake on it. Despite her uneasiness, she said, "Sure."

Josh walked through bear grass and up to Faith. He smiled and held out the plate. A white plastic fork rested next to the cake. “Here ya go. You can give me the plate and fork in the morning. I’ve got a litter bin for it.”

“Thanks,” said Faith. She looked down at the multi-layered chocolate cake and felt her appetite return.

Nobody said anything for a few awkward moments. Josh finally said, “Okay then. Good night! Be sure and rig for rain tonight! If it gets too bad, you can camp under the trailer awning. So, breakfast tomorrow is scrambled eggs with veggies and hash browns and toast. There probably won’t be many other diners at that hour, so plenty of food if you want it. See you then?”

“Sure,” said Faith as she held up the plate. “And thanks for the cake. Looks outstanding.”

She watched the dim shape of Josh fade into the darkness, listening to his crunchy footsteps grow fainter. When she was sure he was gone, she turned off her headlamp and set the cake plate on the flat top of an old tree stump. Working quietly, she pulled her sleeping bag and pad out of the tent, pulled up the stakes and lifted the tent. After some searching, she found a hidden flat spot behind nearby trees and re-set her tent there, pressing the stakes into the ground. She went back and re-loaded her pack, grabbed the chocolate cake, sleeping bag and pad and returned to her new campsite.

Sitting in the darkness in front of the tent, she devoured the cake. It had five layers of rich chocolate frosting and was delicious! She ate every bite and licked the remnants of frosting off the plate. After putting plate and fork in a plastic bag, she threw that into her food sack and walked to a nearby group of small fir trees. Using parachute cord, she hung the bag as high as she could in one of the trees. She was reaching up to tie the cord when she noticed something was wrong with her balance. She managed to secure the bag high enough to keep rodents out and then abruptly sat down on the hummocky grass. Something was definitely wrong. She felt dizzy and disoriented. It was difficult to focus her eyes. She blinked, shook her head, tried to focus but the darkness and something else kept her vision blurry.

Grunting with the effort, she managed to stand and lurch toward the tent. She made it there and crawled inside, collapsed onto her sleeping bag and lay still for a moment, trying to gather her wits. They would not be gathered. She struggled to sit up and couldn't, lay back down, the dizziness growing worse. She heard the sound of gravel popping and the rumbling clatter of a vehicle engine nearby. The clatter stopped and a car door slammed shut. Muted panic raced through her whirling mind. Faith was trying to sit up again when she heard a man's voice out in the darkness. He muttered, "Now where the hell did she go?"

Faith's head dropped and her eyes shut themselves. She just had time to curse herself for being so stupid before her thoughts faded into nothingness.

CHAPTER 36 — AUGUST 11

"Good work, Max!" Bernie was on speakerphone and enthused over Max's revelation about Josh Monday. "I think you're right. It all fits. Like you said, motive, means, opportunity, it's all there. We'll dig into his background and see what comes up. We don't have enough for a search warrant yet, so find him and see what you can get out of him. Anything I can do on this end?"

"Yes and it's the main reason I called. Could you get some real-time visual satellite coverage of the trail and the area I described? Could somebody like Agent Marzi search for that truck and trailer combo? Could he do it ASAP?"

They had a bad connection and Agent Battles' voice sounded shaky over the cell phone. "Okay, look, it's hard to get sat time but I'll sure as hell try. For a one-time focused surveillance, maybe 15 minutes of sat time? That might be all we need if we just search the area where Faith might be, where she's likely to run into Monday. I'll work with Will myself. The truck and trailer should be easy to spot, but we better hurry. The weather is due to close in soon and there'll be cloud cover. That'll make a satellite search more difficult. Text me the previous and projected location information on Faith and we'll sat check it. We'll take a look at each road and trail junction, plus the roads around them. I'll grab a couple of agents to help and get back to you."

After the call ended, Max sent a brief text to Bernie, indicating Faith's last known location was at White Pass and that her present location was likely from Tacoma Pass north. Next on the list was a short email with a photo of

Faith and a description of Monday's food trailer. This was sent to contacts at the World Trails Foundation and Pacific Crest Association, to be forwarded to any work crews in the area. Max sent instructions to report the location of both Faith and/or Monday's food trailer. He also advised no contact with Monday, but to contact Faith and let her use a cell phone to call her father.

When he was done sending the emails, Mike said, "That's great! The more eyes and ears on the ground, the better."

Max nodded and got back on the computer to Google search 'Joshua Monday'.

A minute later, he said, "Holy shit, Mike!"

"What did you find?"

"Monday has a website, and the website has a schedule for his stops along the PCT throughout the summer. I just checked and he's supposed to be at Stampede Pass right now."

"So we don't need the sat intel after all?"

Max shook his head. "No, we'll need it in case his plans have changed. We need to get a real-time assessment, but we're headed in the right direction. I'll let Bernie know about Stampede Pass and they can check that area first."

They rode on in silence for a few moments while Max examined Monday's website. He said, "Here's a weird thing. Monday's site doesn't show any info on where he's been. No record of his previous stops this year, or any year. He mentions a few locations in a summary, but there's no actual record that matches his schedule. He only says where he'll be, not where he's been. I'd think his entire summer calendar would be on the site.

"Not if he's covering his tracks." Mike peered out the windshield, squinting as he looked up at a pale sky. "That weather is coming in fast. You sure the satellite will work?"

Max said, "I think so. They have infrared capabilities that'll work as long as the cloud cover isn't too thick. They can spot a campfire or camp stove and possibly something as small as a cigarette, if it's an isolated heat source."

Mike shook his head and said, "Things sure have sure changed since I started in law enforcement. Pretty amazing when you think about it."

Max nodded and they rode in silence. The SUV's radio crackled now and then as it scanned law enforcement frequencies.

Mike said, "Max, I sure appreciate you lettin' me go along. It means a lot."

"Hey, I need the help! Thanks to you and those case files, we might solve this."

An hour later, Max's phone buzzed and he picked it up, looked at the screen. "It's a text from Bernie." Max paused and then said, "Great! They spotted the trailer, sent some images, along with coordinates and direction. In the photo, it sure looks like Monday's setup. There's an infrared image along with the visible light one. Looks like people are lining up to have dinner. A square bright heat source inside the trailer indicates a grill or stove. I count at least four people, with one inside the trailer and one more approaching the set-up."

"Do any of the images show facial features? Can they be used to identify people?"

Max shook his head. "No, the normal image is fuzzed out by the thin cloud layer, and the IR image shows primarily heat, not external features. And I'm not sure the images we're getting are of sufficient resolution. Sorry, Mike."

"Sure. I was hoping, had to ask. So where is the trailer? How do we get there as fast as possible?"

"It's north of Tacoma Pass, south of Stampede. Looks like our fastest route is to continue up I-5 to I-90 and over Snoqualmie Pass." He scrolled the phone's screen. "We'll take an exit for Stampede Pass and go from there onto a maze of Forest Service roads. I haven't been up there yet, but I know the exit. We're looking at probably another two hours of drive time to there. We should be there before dark. Pull over at the next rest stop and I'll drive. You wanna hole up somewhere, maybe Snoqualmie Pass, and wait for next morning before we tackle those forest roads?"

Michael shook his head vigorously. "Hell no. Are you kidding? My daughter is out there somewhere and so is that fucking psycho murderer."

CHAPTER 37 — AUGUST 11

He wasn't surprised that she'd moved her camp. She'd already demonstrated unique perception and survival skills. Still, it irritated him that she made him look for her. But he had a powerful flashlight and found her soon enough. Her little red tent was tucked back in the trees, but not far enough back. He approached the tent, crouched down and slowly slid aside the unzipped entry flap. He aimed the flashlight inside and saw her. She was unconscious and sprawled on her back on a sleeping bag. Drool slid from her open mouth. He took out a bandana and gently wiped it off.

S*leeping Beauty, at rest in her tent.* It was a struggle to drag her back to the road, but he did it, even without Joey around to help. And he got her up into the trailer and across the floor. He reached under her armpits and lifted her onto the stainless steel center table.

Trembling with joy and anticipation, he positioned her so that she was on her back, lying along the length of the table. He removed most of her clothing, except her panties and bra. Seeing her like that, so vulnerable and almost naked, he wanted to do things to her then and there, while she was asleep, but he restrained himself. It wouldn't be fair, would it? She had to be awake for that, sharing in the experience, knowing that it was him being with her again, loving her whether she liked it or not. Showing her that she had no choice but to submit and to be shared.

He lit some candles and positioned them around the trailer so that they cast a rich, warm glow on her. He folded her clothes neatly, set them aside along with her boots and socks. He turned to look at her, to drink in her beauty and to reassure himself that it was really *Her*! He still couldn't believe it, after all the years and all the others, the substitutes, he finally had the real thing again. He walked up to the table and felt her face with his hands, closed his eyes. Yes, it was Her. He felt the long scar on her left cheek and opened his eyes to look at it. Following the scar with a finger, he brushed her hair aside and discovered that the lower part of her ear lobe was gone. She'd been shot? He couldn't believe it. Josh wondered how and when that had happened. He'd have to ask her when she woke up. He looked more closely at her face. It was different than he remembered. Of course she was older now and there were fine lines at the corners of her eyes. They didn't look like lines generated by mirth and laughter. They looked like stress lines. He was surprised to feel a moment of compassion and concern, and curiosity. That moment made him pause but it passed quickly. It had made him uncomfortable, afraid that it might interfere with the reunion and his revenge. He had to stay focused.

Josh Monday bent down and lightly kissed her slack lips, placed his hands on her breasts. The touch was like a jolt of electricity. No! Not yet, he told himself. He pulled his hands back. She needed to be awake for the consummation, for the moment when he took ownership of her again.

She wouldn't wake up for another hour or two. He could wait. Sometimes the anticipation was almost as good as the consummation. In the meantime, he needed to go to the camper and get restraints. When she woke up, she might try to leave. She might not like what was happening to her. They never did. They didn't appreciate what he had in store for them, and they would try to escape. Josh didn't want to take any chances. *Yes, go to the camper and get the restraints, take them back to the trailer and tie her down like a sailboat to a dock.*

Outside, it smelled like rain. He looked up and saw no stars, felt a cool wind and heard it stirring the brush and trees. Inside the camper, he had to hunt for new restraints. The last ones had been thrown away afterward, too soaked with blood to keep. He finally found new ones in a sliding drawer below his bunk. He took them out of the plastic bag and held them up. They were red velvet restraints that he'd purchased at a so-called adult shop. They wouldn't hurt her if she struggled. He didn't really want to hurt her, at least not so soon. The hurting would come later, after the loving. Then she'd pay for what she did to him so long ago, for what she made him into.

Josh's eyes glazed over and he sat down on the bunk, staring into nothing. Flashes of memory swept through his mind like a slide show. Lila laughing with him around the campfire. Lila swimming naked in mountain lakes, covered in goose bumps from the cold water. He and Lila holding each other and watching the sun set. Lila happy and laughing on the trail. Lila and he making love under the stars. The look on Lila's face when he told her that she'd never leave him . . . the slideshow stopped. His thoughts jerked back to the present. He sighed and stood up, the restraints dangling from his hands. He looked at them and realized that he better get back to the trailer and get her secured. There was still plenty of time, but better safe than sorry!

Outside, a few small raindrops hit his face as he walked back to the trailer. The air smelled good. He liked the smell of rain, especially in the mountains, all blended with the scent of fir trees and huckleberries. He was glad Joey wasn't there yet. It was better to have her all to himself. She was special. This reunion was special. He muttered to himself, "Goddamn finally got her. Got her back at last. He's gonna miss out, but she's all mine anyway. Always been mine, and now she's come back to me. Wonderful.

It'll be wonderful! Better get to her. I can't wait, can't wait . . ."

Josh was smiling as he opened the trailer's rear door and started up the step into the kitchen. He quit smiling when his right leg exploded into a massive fireball of intense pain.

CHAPTER 38 — AUGUST 12

They were lost. No doubt about that. It was dark and rain was drumming on the roof of the Ford, streaking down the windows. One minute they could see the large trees on either side of the road, the next they'd be engulfed in a thick mist. Max had to flick the headlights to low beam so they could see through the fog and rain. The Forest Service SUV bounced down one muddy road after another, wiper blades thumping. The watery potholes were terrible, and to add insult to injury, most of the Forest Service road markers were gone, or vandalized to the point of being illegible. At one point, Max had to brake abruptly to let a small herd of elk cows and calves trot across the road. They materialized from the darkness, trotted through the bright headlight beams, and disappeared back into darkness.

Mike had the passenger side dome light on and was trying to correlate the GPS with Max's oversized Roslyn Ranger District map. He cursed as he wrestled with the huge map, trying to fold it just right so it would sit peacefully in his lap. So far the GPS had led them down three dead-end roads. Two had been engulfed in alder brush and were impassable and another had a huge washout that they almost didn't see in time. Max had to back his way out of that one for about a quarter mile. In the process, he discovered just how inadequate his SUV's backup lights were. Both men were getting tired and discouraged.

Max finally braked to a full stop in an open area and put the shift lever into Park. It appeared they were on a small mountaintop, surrounded by the skeletal steel structures of cell and microwave towers. There were small metal shacks at the towers' bases where feeble security lights bathed the scene in yellow light. The tops of the towers disappeared into misty darkness where a single red beacon flashed. Max rubbed his eyes. He said, "Well at least now I know where we are. This is called Microwave Hill by the locals, for obvious reasons. I've seen it from the freeway. We're really close to the PCT at this point. Mike, can you find this on the map?"

Mike looked at the map and put his finger on it. "Yeah, here it is. You're right, the PCT is close, but we need to backtrack. I think the road we want is back down a ways. I remember seeing the junction, but there was no marker." He put down the map and said, "Shit, I gotta take a break, and a leak. I'm not a young man anymore."

Max sat up and gripped the steering wheel. He glanced at the dashboard clock. "Yeah, you're right. It's almost 0300. I'm beat too. Can't keep my eyes open. There's a big turnout back down the road. Let's go there, catch some shut-eye, and wait for daylight. I'd rather not spend much time around all of these towers. They're probably putting out a lot of radio emissions. If you're hungry, I've got some MRE's in the back."

"Ha! Faith calls those 'Meals Rejected by Ethiopians'. I'm not sure I'm that desperate yet."

Max smiled. "Let me know when you are. I high-graded the good stuff from a whole box of meals, so they ain't so bad."

Max shifted back to Drive and turned the vehicle in a circle until they were pointed back down the road. "Okay, let's find the turnout and get some sleep. And then at first light we can head up that other road."

Both men slept fitfully until sunrise. The Ford's front seats couldn't be reclined because of the security screen behind them, so slumping and slouching were the only choices for Max. Mike slept curled up on the cold vinyl of the back seat. Max had to periodically start the engine and turn on the heater. The rain stopped and occasional peeks at the sky revealed bright stars sparkling through holes in the cloud cover. Once it started to get light, Max retrieved a couple of MRE's from the back. Mike had the hash brown potatoes with bacon and said, "Not bad, not good. I'm not that hungry, but I guess it fills the void. Cousins Kountry Kitchen does a better breakfast though."

Max grinned and said, "Well it's like that guy said, you don't go to the woods with what you want, you go there with what you got, whatever that means."

Mike replied, "Yeah, and now I have to go to the woods with what I got to get rid of. Is there any toilet paper in this rig?"

While Mike was off in the trees, Max stood next to the Explorer and stretched, yawned, checked his phone signal. It was still weak. When Mike finally trudged out of the trees, Max smiled and said, "I thought you'd fallen in. Everything okay?"

Mike's face was tense. "Yeah, yeah. Did you hear that yelling?"

"What? Where?"

Mike lifted the rear hatch and set the toilet paper roll inside, closed the hatch. "I couldn't tell where it was coming from. It was echoing off the mountainside off to the north there. It was a man's voice, hollering something. I couldn't tell what. It was very faint."

"I didn't hear it. I wonder what's going on. Berry pickers maybe? Although it seems early in the day for that, especially with how wet everything is."

"Yeah, well, I guess I'm ready to go now. How about you?"

Max gave him a tired smile. "As ready as I can be, considering. Let's hit it."

As Max drove, he glanced over at Mike and saw him struggling to text on the bumpy road. "You updating Sally?" he asked.

Without looking up, Mike said, "Yeah, there's just enough signal here to get a text out." After a moment, he said, "She got it. Told us to find Faith and stay safe."

"We'll definitely do both," said Max.

Max took the first left turn below Microwave Hill. Light from the sunrise reflected off of scattered fog and illuminated the forest with a peculiar golden glow. The Ford's heater was on, rattling as it blasted warm air at the two men. "This road feels right", he said. The gravelly road had no marker, but according to the map and the GPS, it led in the right direction. As he turned the steering wheel, Max automatically used his turn signal. He laughed as he flicked it off.

"No need for that out here, I guess. That's what exhaustion does for ya."

As they gained more elevation, sun-brightened mist billowed up from the forest below the road and faded away into a blue morning sky. Max's cell phone rang and he stopped to check it. It was Bernie.

"Bernie! We were just about to call and give you a progress report. I think we're finally closing in on the location."

"That's great, Max! Been worried . . . two . . . around the woods . . . night. I wanted . . . that I've got a couple of agents on . . . DOT office at Snoqualmie Pass. Sent 'em up early this morning. It might be good . . . another team searching for Faith. What do you say?"

"You're pretty broken, but I got most of that. Sounds good, but this place is a convoluted maze of old roads. GPS is almost worthless up here and cell service is spotty. I'm not sure the agents will get here in a timely way. We're real close. I think we finally found the right road. Go ahead and send them this way, have 'em call me on my cell when they get to the Stampede Pass exit off of I-90. Hopefully I'll get the call and have a better idea by then of where they'll be most defective."

"Okay, got . . . that . . . you meant to . . . effective, right?"

"Yeah. Yeah, I do, I did. Shit. I'm running on empty. The little grey cells are not working right."

"Okay. Well, keep me post . . . safe, Max. Be . . . on a swivel. Running on empty is not . . . to run."

Max and Mike continued up the road, watching the GPS screen and the waypoint as it got closer and closer. It was now obvious they were on the right road. Within five minutes, they drove out of the big trees and into an old clear-cut. The low angled morning sunlight made the sodden brush and small trees sparkle.

After a few hundred yards, Max stopped at the indicated location, but there was nothing there. Both men got out of the SUV and stretched, looked around. Max studied the ground and said, "Here's some tire tracks, Mike. Looks like from last night."

Mike nodded. "Yeah, and there's two sets. Second set here is smaller. This is a truck and trailer combo. This is what we're looking for."

He looked up the road. "They went that-a-way. I wonder why he moved?"

Max walked around to the driver's door and said, "Let's find out."

They rolled on past the Pacific Crest Trail junction and continued to follow the tire tracks up and around a corner. Beyond the corner, they saw the pickup/camper and food trailer parked in a large, level open area to the right. Sunlight flashed off of chrome and glass. The huge white mass of Mount Rainier rose in the near distance, its bright glaciers partially shrouded in mist.

Max drove past the vehicles and turned around. He parked the Ford across from the trailer, facing back down the road. There was no mistaking the paint job on the green trailer with the faint gold PCT symbols all over it. Wording on the side said "TGI Monday's, Awesome Eats by the Chef".

Max said, "I think we found it."

Mike's face was grim as he stared at the trailer and said, "Yeah. Pretty hard to hide that rig."

"Hang on a sec." Picking up his cell phone, he sent a text and GPS location to Bernie. Reaching up between the seats, he unlocked the gun bracket that held an AR-10 automatic rifle and a Remington twelve gauge tactical shotgun.

"Just in case," he said to Mike. "Keep an eye on me, okay? Pick whichever weapon you want and be ready. You're my cover officer. I'm going to make contact with Monday, if he's here."

Mike stared at the trailer and didn't say anything.

"Yo, Mike! Are you okay? Did you copy?"

Faith's father shook his head and said, "Not really. I've been working and waiting years for this. And here I am, about to find out what the hell happened to my Lila. Not sure I want to know now, and I'm afraid of what I'll do when I do find out. So help me God, I might want to kill that bastard, slowly."

Max put a hand on his shoulder and said, "Mike, you've got to hold it together. I can't imagine how tough this is for you, but we need to be professionals. We need to take that asshole alive and interrogate him, find out what happened, what he's done over the last ten years. Not just for us, but for all those other families who lost daughters and need closure. *Capisce?*"

Mike closed his eyes and nodded. He said, "I can do that. Okay. I got this. I'll take the AR, cover you. But you need to be careful. Things are off here. Moving his setup away from the PCT, not coming out to see who's here? It's abnormal behavior. Remember that yelling I heard earlier?

Things are amiss. You sure you don't want me to come with you?"

Max shook his head. "Probably better that we keep an element of surprise, which is you armed, watching and in reserve. I'll be careful."

CHAPTER 39 — AUGUST 12

Lila must not have eaten the entire piece of cake. Josh would be surprised if that was the case. Nobody made a chocolate cake as delicious and beautiful as The Chef did. Still, she regained consciousness too soon. Maybe he made a mistake with the dosage?

He had searched for her until the pain in his leg was too much. Searching was useless anyway. He wasn't a tracker. Everything was dripping wet and he was soaked, as well as in pain and feeling weak. Probably time to get out of there. If Lila got away and told someone, they'd be after him. Maybe he could ditch the trailer in some out of the way road turnout. He hated to abandon it, but maybe it was time. Ditch it and go to Canada. But maybe Lila would die out there in the forest, and no one would ever know about the trailer, or about Josh and Joey. And then they could continue doing what they do, search for her again, find her, and then make sure she didn't get away. Josh shook his head. That didn't make sense, if she died in the forest . . . but she died once before and came back. What was to stop her from doing it again?

Too many maybes made his head hurt almost as much as his leg. He struggled up the mountainside and made it back to the road. The stab wound was bleeding a lot. Another five minutes of limping brought him back to the trailer and camper. He had time to think that Joey was right. He'd mentioned in a text that she was dangerous, but didn't say why. What happened to her to make her that way? Something to do with her being shot? He couldn't imagine. It didn't make sense, did it? None of it did. He remembered doing things to her that a person could never come back from, but ten years later, she did come back. It made him sweat thinking about it, which is why most of the time he tried not to remember. How he'd cut her up, and then he . . . never mind that. Where was she? Never mind that either. He had to take care of the knife cut that bitch had made. It was deep and it hurt like hell.

He searched the trailer and finally found the first aid supplies. He always had a well-stocked first aid kit in case some hikers needed help. Because that was the kind of trail angel that Josh was. He was a guy who helped people.

Now it was time to help himself. He turned up the lights and sat on a chair, stretching out the wounded leg. He placed a large trauma dressing over the wound, wrapped it right around his pant leg and taped the shit out of it, hoping that direct pressure would slow the bleeding. He noticed that the wound was swelling now that he wasn't moving. A big old nasty hematoma was forming, blood pooling under the skin. Shit!

What was that noise? A vehicle engine, tires on gravel, the squeak of brakes as the vehicle stopped. Who could that be? Josh winced as he stood up and peeked out of a crack in the serving window shutter. A white and green Forest Service SUV was turning around. It parked across the road and shut down. The words "FOREST SERVICE LAW ENFORCEMENT" were visible on the side of the vehicle. Josh cursed under his breath, limped to the center table and leaned on it. He pulled out his phone and tapped out a quick text, hit send. A reply text came back just as someone knocked on the door at the rear of the trailer.

CHAPTER 40 — AUGUST 12

Max walked around the pickup and trailer before approaching the camper door. He stood to one side and knocked, waited a moment and knocked again. There was no response. He looked around, focused on something out in a grove of small trees. It was red, maybe the top of a tent?

He knocked again and listened. Still no response, so he went around to the back of the trailer and found a door there. He knocked on that, waited, knocked again. Finally he heard footsteps inside and saw the trailer rock slightly. He stepped back to the side and put a hand on his holstered pistol, unsnapped the retention strap.

The door opened and there stood Josh Monday, the tall, bearded Santa-like man from the magazine article photos. He didn't look so cheerful or Santa-like now. His clothing was soaked and there was a bloodstained white bandage wrapped around his right thigh. Monday mustered up a grimacing smile and said, "Good morning. Can I help you?"

Max stood back and said, "Yes sir. I'm officer Albricci with the U.S. Forest Service. Could you step out of the trailer please? I have a few questions to ask."

Holding tightly to the doorframe, Monday carefully stepped down and groaned with the effort. Max said, "What happened to your leg? You're bleeding pretty bad."

Monday tried to laugh. "Oh, just a kitchen accident with a knife. It happens in my line of work." He held out his right hand. "I'm Josh Monday, proprietor of the TGI

Monday's trailer, trail angel for the Pacific Crest Trail hikers."

Max shook his hand and said, "Max Albricci."

Josh nodded. "Yeah, yeah. Saw your vehicle and the symbol. It says 'Law Enforcement'? Have I broken any laws? I assure you, I've got a special use permit and can show it to you."

Max said, "No, that's okay. Right now I'm more concerned about your wound. It's bleeding a lot. Let me go get my medical kit, okay? I'm an EMT."

Josh gave him a strained smile and shook his head. "No, no. It'll be all right. Really."

"I dunno about that. It looks bad. That bandage is rapidly turning red. What the hell happened?"

"It was a stupid mistake. I was cutting some meat and slipped. The knife struck my thigh. I'll be all right."

Max whistled. "Must be a hell of a knife. Look, I'm going to get my kit and we'll patch you up, okay?"

Josh's strained smile faded to a strained frown. "NO! I really must get going on preparing meals for the hikers. Some will be along any minute. It's my job to feed them and I'm always there for them."

Max gestured back down the road. "But you moved your trailer away from the trail, out of sight, so how are they going to find you?"

Josh closed his eyes and shook his head. "I . . . I needed a break, to get ready. Look, will you leave me alone? I'm fine." Josh stepped back and sat down hard on the door sill, right leg stretched out in front. He groaned again.

"Okay, that does it, Mr. Monday. You're not fine and I'm going to get my kit. Don't move!"

Mike turned around in the seat and asked, "What's going on, Max?"

Max had the SUV's rear hatch up and was rummaging through his gear for the medical kit. He looked up, glanced over at the trailer. All he could see of Monday was his leg still stretched out. He looked at Mike and said, “It’s Josh Monday alright, and he has a severe bleeding leg wound. Claims he slipped with a knife, but I doubt that. It looks pretty bad. And his story doesn’t make any sense. His clothing is soaked. He’s been wandering around in the woods.” Max quickly recounted the conversation he’d had with Monday.

Mike looked grim. “Max, this stinks. I better come with you.”

“I’ve got another mission for you right now.” He reached into a file box and pulled out a single sheet of paper, walked around to the passenger door and handed it to Mike. “This is the information on the tire pattern evidence from the Crater Lake case. There’s a pair of binocs in the glove box.” He paused and glanced back at the trailer, still saw Monday’s leg. “While I’m digging out my med kit, could you use them to scope out the tires on the trailer and truck and see if the make, model and size match?”

Mike retrieved the binocs and squinted through them at the nearby tires, referring to the sheet that Max had given him. Max finally found his orange med kit and pulled it out of the back. He left the hatch up and moved around to the passenger side. “What’s the verdict on the tires?”

Mike shook his head. “The sizes match, but not the make or model. Inconclusive, except for one thing.”

“What’s that?”

“The tires on both the pickup and trailer look almost brand new. I think he ditched the old, incriminating tires and replaced them with new. “

“That makes sense. We know this guy isn’t an idiot. Okay, I’m going to treat his wound, try to get some more information out of him.”

“I don’t like your plan, Max. You sure you don’t want me to go with you? I don’t know about you, but I’m about

90 percent sure this is our guy, our serial killer. Come on, we should cuff him and stuff him, and then ask our questions, treat his leg."

"I want to get that wound treated before he passes out. I doubt he's an immediate threat. You should see him. He looks exhausted and weak. The guy can barely move. Stay here, Mike. Hold down the fort. I want to talk to Monday some more, get a look inside that trailer. Also, I spotted what looked like the top of a red tent off in the trees. We need to get a closer look at that."

Mike's face turned pale. "Red tent? Faith has a red tent. It's in her photos. Shit, I better go take a look."

Max put up a hand. "Take it easy, Mike. A lot of hikers have red tents. We just don't know yet, so stay calm, stay focused here, okay? Be my cover officer. Let me talk to Monday some more."

"Sure, sure. Come on, Max, I'm no rookie. I know what to do. But if we find out that is Faith's tent, I'll be talking to Monday myself. You be careful."

Max approached the trailer and noticed that he could no longer see Monday's leg. He pulled out his pistol and turned right to walk a wide arc around the back of the trailer. Monday was no longer visible anywhere. Max dropped the medical bag and used both hands to hold his pistol at the ready. He approached the trailer's open back door.

CHAPTER 41 — AUGUST 12

Mike sat in the SUV, the AR10 carbine on his lap, and watched Max walk toward the trailer. When he saw Max draw his pistol, drop the med kit and change direction, Mike opened the door and stepped out, jacked a .223 round into the chamber of the carbine.

He saw Max pause and look around, then move around to the back of the trailer where he turned toward the trailer's open door, pistol held at the ready. Mike started walking toward him and was startled by two muffled pops. He saw Max fall back onto the ground.

"Shit goddamn!" said Mike as he started jogging toward the rear of the trailer, rifle at the ready.

He saw Monday hobble out of the trailer, pointing a gun at Max. Mike stopped and brought up the rifle, shouted at Monday to "Stop!" Monday turned and saw him, raised his pistol. Both guns went off at the same instant. Mike felt the rifle kick and then something else kicked him in the gut. He went down to his knees, hunched over and then fell onto his right side. It felt like a sledgehammer had punched him and embedded itself, a terrible pressure.

He raised his head and watched Monday stagger up to him, kick the rifle aside and bend over to stare blankly at his face. Monday asked, "Who the hell are you? You look familiar."

"What've you done with my daughter, motherfucker? Where is she?"

"Your daughter? I don't know your daughter? Who?"

"My daughter Faith! What've you done with her?"

Monday's eyes lost their focus, like he was staring into the far distance. "I don't know Faith. Maybe you mean Lila. I know Lila. She was with me and then ran off, but I know she'll be back. We're meant to be together you know. If you're her dad, you gotta understand, man. I keep finding her and losing her, but this time is the real deal. This time it's her destiny. My destiny too."

Mike coughed. "What the hell? What the fuck are you talking about, you bastard! Leave my daughter alone!" Mike tried to get up, but the pain in his gut was too intense, like the sledgehammer was now glowing red hot. His left hand groped for the rifle, but Josh leaned down and grabbed it. He pushed Mike over onto his back and searched his pockets. He removed Mike's cell phone, tossed it into the roadside alders.

"You won't be needing that, or much of anything else," said Monday in a calm, emotionless voice.

He limped past Mike and over to the SUV. He opened the driver side door and looked inside, started ripping wires and cables from the computer and radios. When he was done, he shuffled back to where Mike lay on his back, clutching his stomach. He paused briefly and pointed the AR10 at Mike.

Mike grunted, "You stupid bastard! We've got backup coming. If you know what's good for you, you'll give up right now."

Monday reversed the rifle and held the butt over Mike's head. He smiled and said, "Maybe someone needs to take a little nap, wake up less grumpy." He brought the rifle butt down hard on Mike's head.

CHAPTER 42 — August 12

Faith opened her eyes and blinked. The first thing she noticed was that she was cold. The second thing was the headache, throbbing in her skull with every labored beat of her heart. Her vision was blurry but she could tell she was inside a room of some kind. She must be lying flat on her back because she was staring straight into dim ceiling lights. She closed her eyes. All she could hear was the hum of some machinery, maybe a generator. She tried to move but her limbs felt like they were filled with wet sand. She opened her eyes and turned her head to see shelving, pots and pans, a refrigerator or freezer, containers in the faint light. There were lit candles placed here and there, orange flames wavering. She got dizzy. Thinking was so difficult.

She asked herself a series of questions, trying to clear her mind, bring it out of the abyss. Where was she? Inside a room. How did she get there? Unknown. What's around her? She looked again. In the dim light were shelves, containers, pots and pans. The candles; what was with the candles? She could hear that generator. She was in a kitchen? Yes, a kitchen. How? And that final question made it all click into place.

Josh Monday and his TGI Monday's trailer. The chocolate cake, poisoned! She'd been drugged by Josh Monday, the friendly trail angel. What the hell was going on? She managed to raise her head and see that she was wearing only her sports bra and panties, lying full length on a steel-topped table. She gripped the edges of the table and her fingers explored the gutters there. On her right, a tray next to the table held a large knife, some folded towels, white zip ties and two small, flat packets. The packets looked like condoms. That made her sit up. She almost passed out with the effort but was feeling stronger and more clear-minded by the second. Her mind was waking up, and it offered her the obscure memory that she'd always been resistant to anesthetics. At the dentist office, they always had to shoot her with more anesthetic and they always marveled at how much it took. She was thankful for that now.

Faith slouched, shaking her head. She looked at the tray more closely. Those were condom packets, that was a knife, and those were absorbent towels and zip ties.

It was time to go.

She swung her legs off the cold table and stood, leaning against the table's edge. For a moment, she thought she'd black out. She looked around, listened. She didn't hear any sounds of movement or detect the presence of anyone else in the trailer. There were her clothes, neatly folded on a counter. There were her boots, side by side on the floor, socks sticking out the tops.

Even though her mind was still swimming, she dressed quickly. *Focus and move efficiently*, she told herself. No need to panic. Cargo pants on first, then her Smartwool top and green fleece vest. *Pull on the socks, insert feet into the boots*. Faith was shaking as she tied her bootlaces. She straightened up, looked around and saw the knife. She lurched over to the tray and grabbed it. It was a long knife, maybe ten inches and broad of blade. She gripped it tightly in her right hand and stood there, head moving side to side, searching for the door to freedom. There it was, located down the length of the trailer, a thin tall rectangle of a door with a small dark window in it. She dragged her feet that way, trying to keep her balance, trying to keep her boots quiet on the tile floor. She got to the door and moved to one side, peering out through the small window. It was dark outside. She listened and heard a man's voice, indecipherable at first but growing louder as he approached the door. It sounded like Monday.

"Where's that dipshit Joey? Goddamn finally got her. Got her back at last. He's gonna miss out, but she's all mine anyway. Always been mine, and now she's come back to me. Wonderful. It'll be wonderful! Better get to her. I can't wait, can't wait . . . "

The door's latch clicked and it swung open, bringing a puff of cool, fresh air that smelled like rain. Monday's right leg stepped up through the door. Standing to one side of the doorway, Faith gripped the knife handle in both hands, raised her arms and jammed the blade down hard into Monday's thigh. She felt the tip hit bone and slide off to one side, going deeper into the flesh. The man screamed and jerked his leg back, pulling the knife with it. Faith followed him out the door and into the darkness, punching and kicking. She was still under the influence and her blows were feeble and off the mark. Faint light from the open trailer door showed Monday falling backward.

He put up his hands as she flailed at him. He was screaming and twisting around on the grass, knife handle protruding from his thigh. Faith stood over him and tried to grab the swirling handle but he was writhing too much. His screaming turned to words. "You fucking bitch!! Jesus! What the fuck?!? Oh my leg! My fucking leg! You stuck a fucking knife into my fucking leg!!"

She leaned down, reaching, and almost had the knife. Josh kicked up with his left foot, struck her in the chest and sent her flying backward. He sat up and grabbed at the knife handle with his right hand and jerked it out of his thigh. He roared and started to get up. Faith was already on her feet. She kicked his bloody thigh as hard as she could. He fell back howling.

Faith came at him and screamed, "What the hell are you doing? I'll fucking kill you if you don't stay down!"

Monday, on his back, slashed the knife at her. She jumped back.

He got up onto his left knee, right leg splayed out to the side, knife held toward Faith. A cold rain started falling.

He growled, "Stay back! Jesus, I give you my love, my soul, and this is how you repay me. After all these years? I'm going to make you love me, bitch, even if it's from the grave. You're not leaving me again. Ever!"

Faith shook her head, wide eyed and gasping for breath. "What're you talking about, Monday? What the hell are you talking about?"

Josh managed to heave himself up onto his left leg and use his right for balance. He waddled toward her, slashing back and forth with the knife. He was crying and laughing at the same time. Faith felt her blood run cold.

She stepped back onto uneven ground, back out of the trailer light, and felt the ground start to fall away behind her. She must be on the edge of the road turnout. Monday was silhouetted by the light from the door; a looming, lurching shape, hobbling toward her, blubbering and swinging the knife.

Bewildered and fearful, Faith turned toward the darkness and peered downhill. The darkness was less than she thought. She could see. She could see enough to run. With one more backward glance at Monday, she plunged down into the brush.

Faith, free and in the woods, paused in the hilltop clearing and listened again, arms clasped around her torso. His cries were getting fainter now, but the words were still clear.

"Lila, Lila! I'm so sorry! Come back! I love you! Come back!"

Faith now knew what had happened to her sister. Joshua Monday had happened to her, ten years ago on the PCT. And now he was hunting Lila's twin sister, probably thinking she was Lila. Kidnapped, drugged and hauled into the TGI Monday's trailer, Faith had seen enough to have an idea of the fate he intended for her. It made her skin crawl. She was lucky to have escaped.

Now it was Faith's turn to be the hunter. Find Monday and make him talk, tell her what he did to her sister. The sun was up now, burning off the morning mist, but it was still cold. Faith shivered, soaked to the skin. The wet wool and fleece warmed her enough that she could still function. Although the headache persisted, she felt recovered from the drug that Monday had given her. Faith was sure she'd never eat chocolate cake again.

She started downhill toward the distant shouts, but after a few minutes of fast walking realized she wasn't hearing Monday anymore. The shouts had stopped. Faith paused. What now? Should she keep going, hunt the bastard down? Or should she try to escape, get the hell out of there. But escape where? She'd lost track of where she was, didn't know how far away the road or the PCT was. Didn't know which direction to go or how far away help might be.

No, she had to find the pervert son of a bitch, make him talk, and then? She wasn't sure. She hadn't thought that far ahead. Everything was so sudden. He must be heading back to his trailer. The man was wounded and likely losing blood along with his ability to walk. He'd be weak, slow and easy to deal with.

Varied thrushes sang in the trees. A raven flapped by, wing beats audible in the still morning air. Beams of sunlight sliced through the fog, making splashes of sparkling gold in the wet forest. Faith inhaled the sweet smell of a Northwest forest morning. She was feeling better. Cold, thirsty and hungry, but better.

Moving carefully downhill, back through the big trees, she reached a small creek and dropped to her knees on its mossy bank. She bent forward, cupped her hands and dipped them into the current, raised them and drank the icy water.

Wiping her mouth, she looked up and across the creek. There was the brushy hillside that she'd stumbled down in the near dark. It was still sopping wet, so Faith searched for a better route back up the hill. Moving along the creek bank, it took her only a minute to find an old skid road that went straight up the slope. Loggers had used it to drag trees up to the road with cables. After so many years, it was hemmed in by alders and vine maple, but had fewer logs and trees to stumble through. She jumped across the creek and started climbing up the lumpy, grassy route; at times pulling herself along by grabbing small trees.

She was relieved to finally move up out of shadow and into the sunlight. She paused, closed her eyes and felt the welcome warmth on her face. All around her the landscape steamed and brush sparkled with a thousand rain diamonds. In the glaring light, she could barely see and shaded her eyes with one hand while continuing to scramble uphill. She looked up when she heard an unseen vehicle rumble by on the road above. It was close, but she couldn't tell which direction it was going. Was it Monday, fleeing?

A few more minutes brought her up to the road, gasping for breath. She pushed her way through stunted alders to the edge of the road opening and looked both directions. The trailer and pickup were nowhere in sight. Faith held her breath and listened. Somewhere off to her right, there'd been a sound like a couple of taps, but she didn't hear anything more. She shrugged and moved out onto the road. Faith was worried that Monday had escaped, that it was his truck and trailer she'd heard going by. There was a set of fresh vehicle tracks in the road, but it was a single vehicle, no trailer. A visual sweep of the area revealed that she was probably down the road from where the trailer was. She turned west and uphill. A short walk brought her to the turnout. She recognized it as the same place she'd eaten dinner at. There were tire tracks leading up the road from where the truck and trailer had been parked. Monday must've moved the trailer up the road, closer to her camp. She had a faint memory of hearing an engine before blacking out in the tent. Faith started walking, wet clothes steaming in the morning sun.

Two loud pops shattered the morning peace. Gunfire!

CHAPTER 43 — AUGUST 12

Josh was feeling better now. A little light headed, but better. Things were going his way again. True, he had a lot more work to do, but he was in a good place. As long as Joey showed up to help, they could get it done. He should be here soon. Josh had texted him when the Forest Service vehicle pulled up and Joey texted back immediately to say he was about a half hour away. Once he got there, all they had to do was find Lila and everything would be as it should be. At least it would be once these two men, whoever they are, were disposed of properly.

He approached the trailer and looked around, surprised. The tall ranger cop was gone. Josh couldn't believe it. He'd shot the man twice in the chest and saw him go down. He must've been wearing a goddamn vest. So where the hell was he?

Josh hobbled over to the spot where he'd seen Max on the ground. He looked around, confused. And then he heard a voice behind him yell, "Freeze, Monday! Drop the weapon!" He turned and there was the cop by the front of the trailer, pointing some kind of pistol at him.

Max aimed his Taser at Josh and repeated the command. Monday shook his head. He turned and started to run, only to feel hammer blows of electric shock as the Taser probes struck his back. He fell hard, twitching and writhing on the wet ground. The rifle skittered out of his reach.

Max ran up to him, one arm reaching behind his back to pull the handcuffs out. That was when he heard a woman screaming, "Look out! Look out!"

Max barely had time to turn around when someone body slammed him and knocked him into the side of the trailer. He fell to the ground and something struck his head. His vision went dark, filled with pinpoints of light and then there was nothing.

CHAPTER 44 — AUGUST 12

The shots sounded like a semi-auto pistol and an AR10, sounds she knew well. Faith picked up her pace. Another five minutes brought her around yet another corner and there was the trailer and truck. It was 50 yards away. Another vehicle was parked near it in a wide spot across the road, pointed in her direction. Sunlight glaring off the windshield made Faith wince. It was a white SUV with green stripes. It had a law enforcement light bar on top. Did Monday call for help? Why would he do that? What about those gunshots?

Faith started toward the vehicles, keeping to the inside cut bank of the road, mostly out of sight and in the shade. She moved slowly, watching the scene ahead. She paused in thick alders and carefully surveyed the area. There was a man lying prone near the SUV. He was moving, trying to crawl to the vehicle. And there was Monday at the SUV. He was just leaving it and shuffled past the prone man, said something to him and kept going. Monday was carrying what looked like an M4 carbine. She watched him limp to the rear of the trailer and pause. There was a bloodstained white bandage on his leg. A tall man in a leather jacket and jeans appeared out of nowhere behind Monday and said something to him. He was pointing what looked like some kind of yellow gun. Monday started to bolt and suddenly went down, twisting and rolling on the ground. The tall man approached, reaching behind his back.

Faith heard boots thumping on gravel, approaching her position. Concealed by the alders, she turned and saw a bearded man in a long, flapping coat running past her, breathing heavily. As he went by, the man threw off a large red backpack and picked up speed. He was heading straight for the tall man. Faith couldn't believe it. Couldn't believe that it was Duster. She stepped out of the brush and yelled, "Look out! Look out!"

She started running. The tall man was bent over, pulling Monday's arms around to put on the handcuffs. He looked up just as Duster body slammed him, bowling him into the side of the trailer. The tall man groaned and slumped to the ground, clutching his chest. Monday scrambled to his feet and lurched over to lean against the trailer.

Duster raised his right hand and struck the tall man once in the head. The man went all the way down and was still. Duster stood up, panting. He dropped the bloody rock he was holding and turned to Monday, started to say something when he noticed Faith. She'd changed direction and was running toward the SUV. She darted behind the vehicle. Eyes wide, Duster screamed at Monday and pointed across the road. "Josh, over there. It's her!! It's her!!"

Faith heard Duster's shout and scrambled to hide behind the Forest Service SUV. The passenger door, which faced away from the trailer, was open and Faith crawled to the opening. She looked inside and her eyes widened as she saw the shotgun resting in the between-seats rack. She felt a wave of relief when she noticed that the rack was unlocked. She reached in and grasped the butt of the Remington, carefully pulled the black shotgun down and out of the SUV. Squatting next to the vehicle, she quietly worked the pump to put a shell in the chamber.

She tensed when she heard Monday's voice call out, "Lila? Lila? I knew you'd come back! It's your destiny, my love. Our destiny!" There was more, but anger and revulsion roared through her thoughts. She felt a red rage blossom in her mind. Her inner voice kept saying, "Now he pays! Now he pays!" Another part of her said that she needed to know what happened to her sister, that she needed to get answers out of Monday first.

Looking under the Ford, she saw Monday's feet approaching. He was limping badly, dragging his right leg. The feet went around the wounded man. The wounded man looked familiar. What the hell? Faith's mind went blank with shock for a moment. The man looked like her father, but that was impossible! But no, that man was her father, Mike Montaigne. Faith was bewildered. Something bumped into the SUV and Monday's voice startled her. He was only a few feet away. She heard him say, "Lila? Come out. Come to me. Where are you, my love?"

He was shuffling around the front of the SUV. It was only a matter of seconds before he saw her. She gripped the shotgun and tensed her legs, ready to stand up and fire.

CHAPTER 45 — AUGUST 12

Josh's face lit up with joy as he pushed himself away from the trailer. He bent down and picked up the rifle, started limping toward the SUV. He was grinning. He barely heard Joey say, "Go get her, boss. I'll take care of this guy."

Josh called out, "Lila? I knew you'd come back! It's your destiny, my love. Our destiny! Give up and fulfill it. You were meant to be with me, forever!" He limped closer, going around the wounded man, who reached out, trying to grab his leg. Josh ignored him. He grabbed the hood of the SUV and steadied himself, peered through the windshield. "Lila? Come out. Come to me. Where are you, my love?"

He lurched around the driver's side of the vehicle, right hand on the hood, left hand carrying the rifle.

He carefully sidled around the front of the vehicle until he saw Faith crouching behind the open passenger side door, peering up at him. Leaning against the grill, he took the rifle in both hands and pointed it at her. He smiled.

"Hello, Lila. Time to come out and play. Time to fulfill your destiny. Lila, Lila, Lila. I so love saying your name!"

He was thrilled to see Lila stand up, but she had a shotgun in her hands, braced against her shoulder. That wouldn't do. He was surprised to hear her say, "I'm not Lila, you asshole. I'm Faith. Lila was my sister and you killed her, didn't you?"

Lila? Faith? She wasn't making any sense!

Josh stared at the black muzzle of the shotgun. "There's no need for the gun, dearest Lila. No need at all. You know what's about to happen? You won't be needing that gun. Remember last time? You didn't have a gun then. And we had so much fun. You wanted to leave, but you stayed and we had a hell of a good time."

Faith's eyes filled with tears as she said, "What did you do to my sister, you sick fuck? What did you do to her?"

Josh's eyes glazed over as he replied, "You don't remember? I convinced you to stay, and you did. And then I made you mine forever. It took awhile, but you nourished me."

Faith felt her finger tightening on the trigger. She could hardly see through the tears. She whispered, "You, you killed her, didn't you? And you . . . Jesus Christ . . . you ATE her? You sick fuck!"

Josh said, "But it all worked out! I made you mine forever, and now that you've come back, I'm going to do it again. Put down the gun and come with me, Lila. There's no other way."

Faith squinted through the tears. "No, no, no . . . my god."

Behind Josh, a man's weak voice said, "Hey motherfucker."

Josh turned around, his face blank, and saw the gut-shot man sitting up. He was bent forward, holding something in his hand. He coughed and frothy blood dribbled from his lips. Josh grimaced and raised the rifle. He said, "Time to put you down for good, old man!" He struggled to pull back the slide and jack a .223 round into the chamber, but there was already one there. It partially ejected and jammed up against the new round. Josh cursed and tried to pull back the slide and remove one of the cartridges.

He looked up in surprise as the gut-shot man said, "Go to hell, fuckwad!" Josh was shocked to see a small stainless steel revolver in the man's right hand, even more shocked at how loud it was.

The bullet caught him in the right cheek and his head snapped back, blood spraying. Josh screamed through his mangled mouth and dropped the rifle, grabbed at his bloody face with both hands. The pain was overwhelming. Josh felt two impacts against his chest that made him stagger back against the Ford's hood. He somehow stayed standing, screaming, grabbing at his face, red spots blooming on his shirt.

Mike was going to pump two more rounds into the bastard, but flinched as a loud explosion pounded his eardrums. Monday's chest erupted in a blasting cloud of red mist, shredded tissue and white bone. His body collapsed like a puppet with its strings ripped out.

Next thing Mike knew, his daughter Faith was kneeling down next to him, smoking shotgun in hand. "Dad! Dad! Are you okay? Holy fuck! What're you doing here? What is happening? Oh shit, you're bleeding! God damn it, Daddy! What's going on!?"

Mike lay back and grabbed her arm, tried to smile. "Thank God you're safe, Faith. Been trying to find you, to warn you. Shit, this hurts, but I been shot before. Not crazy about coughing up this blood though. Fucker slammed me in the head too. You gotta listen. Monday's a serial killer. So's the other guy. You gotta save Max. That fucker in the coat has him, dragged him behind the trailer. Go!"

Faith looked bewildered. "Who's Max? That tall guy?"

Mike nodded and waved his pistol toward the trailer. "That's him. Gotta save him from the coat fucker. I'm all right for now. You gotta save Max. Go!"

Faith set down the shotgun, dropped to her knees and gently grasped her father's shoulders. "Dad, Dad? You gotta do something for me, okay? I want you to roll over onto your injured side and stay there, okay? And cover the wound with your hand, tightly. It's gonna hurt like hell, but that'll make it easier to breathe while I'm gone."

Mike nodded and groaned as she helped him roll onto his left side.

Faith stood up and pumped the shotgun. An empty red case flew out and landed in the dirt. She looked down at her dad, said, “I’ll be back” and started running for the trailer. Max and Duster were nowhere in sight.

CHAPTER 46 — AUGUST 12

The tall man was heavy and Joey, aka Duster, was having a hard time dragging him. He grabbed the man under the armpits and pulled, huffing with the effort. He managed to drag the guy around to the back of the trailer where he dropped him to the ground. The man was still breathing. Joey paused a moment before reaching down to remove the pistol from its holster. He hefted it in his hand and smiled. It was a Sig Sauer P229, caliber .40.

A series of gunshots ending in an explosion made him jump and whimper. He turned, ran around the corner of the trailer and froze in place. There was the SUV, there was that guy in the dirt and there was Faith, kneeling next to him and holding a shotgun. Behind her was a jumbled red heap. For a second, Joey couldn't tell what it was. And then he realized it must be Josh. The bitch shot him! She fuckin' blew him away! Joey stared at the mess. It didn't look like Josh anymore. It didn't look like anything recognizable. While Faith knelt next to the man on the ground, Joey popped back out of sight, hoping she didn't see him.

He collapsed onto the rear step of the trailer and closed his eyes against the bright morning sun. Well shit! Josh was dead. D . . . E . . . A . . . D. Dead! Hard to believe. He was going to miss his mentor, but with any luck, he could continue their work. Maybe even do more than Josh had ever dreamed. Joey wouldn't be constrained by the limited parameters that Josh had worked under. No sirree! For Joey, the prey could be just about any woman, and oh the things he'd do with them. He could start with Faith, finish

Josh's life work and get his revenge on the bitch, and then move on from there.

And what about Faith? Where was she? Joey leaped to his feet and peered cautiously around the corner of the trailer. He was shocked to see Faith jogging across the road toward him, shotgun in hand. Joey stepped out, raised the pistol and fired a wild round. He heard glass break somewhere. Faith dodged to her left, toward the front of the trailer and out of sight. Joey backed around to the rear of the trailer and stuck the pistol in his belt. He made sure the trailer door was open and grabbed Max around the shoulders again, heaved him up the step and inside. Joey pulled him along the smooth tile flooring and stopped at the steel kitchen island. He let go and heard Max's head thump on the floor. He hurried over to close and lock the trailer door. He pulled off his coat and threw it into a corner, crouched and waited.

Faith was lucky the shot went wild. As close as Duster had been, he could've sent a bullet right into her brain. She jumped to her left and got between the trailer and the camper, carefully stepping over the hitch. She glanced back at her father. He was pulling himself along the ground to get behind the SUV. Shit! He was supposed to stay still, on his side.

Where was Duster? She leaned against the front of the trailer and put her ear to it. She felt movement inside and heard a door slam shut. She leaned out and peered down the side of the trailer. Nothing there. She did the same with the other side and saw nothing. She kneeled and looked under the trailer down its length and to the sides. Nothing there either. There was a window above her head, facing the front of the trailer, so she crouched down to be out of sight. Duster must be inside, possibly with the man named Max.

She didn't have time to fuck around. Her father needed medical attention as soon as possible. And Duster needed dealing with. The same way she and her father had dealt with Monday, the man who murdered her sister. Murdered and ate her, for fuck's sake. Faith closed her eyes and searched her mind for any remorse or regret over blowing a bloody hole through Monday. She couldn't find any. She took a deep breath, relaxed. She felt her mind shift into warrior mode. An icy, calm awareness took over. She opened her eyes and felt ready.

She took another breath and yelled, "Duster! Remember what I told you last time we met? When I kicked your skinny pervert ass? Do you remember? Well, forget what I said. I won't kill you if you come out of there with your hands in the air. I know that sounds like a bad TV show, but game's over for you!"

Crouched on the floor of the trailer, Joey heard her loud and clear and he giggled. That *did* sound like a TV show! He scooted next to the base of the metal table, the kitchen island, and leaned against it. The cop was lying flat on his back on the floor next to him, still passed out. Joey took out his Bowie knife and poked Max's left forearm with the point. There was no response other than a small trickle of blood from the new wound. The guy was truly out of it. A quick search of his pockets yielded Max's keys, wallet and law enforcement badge. Joey looked them over carefully and slipped the wallet and badge into a cargo pocket. He looked down at Max, grinned and said, "Nice ta meet ya, Maxwell."

Joey raised his head and hollered at Faith, "Come in and get me, copper!" and laughed. "Hey, I got some kind of Smokey Bear cop in here and he's still alive but he won't be for long unless you do what I say, and what I say is that you gotta surrender yourself. You do that, and the cop lives. You don't, and he dies, piece by piece! And I toss the pieces out the door, one by one, so you can see I'm serious!"

Faith yelled back, “Goddamn it, Duster. YOU surrender and I won’t kill you. You do anything other than that and I will blow you to hell, just like I did to your partner!”

Joey laughed again. “Beauty, I really underestimated you! You’re so cute when you’re bloodthirsty. You look so beautiful and demure, but you’re some kind of bitch tiger! Where did you learn to fight like you do? Where did you learn to be so tough?”

“Afghanistan! And I’m putting you on notice!”

Joey thought about that and yelled back, “Riiight. Sure. There’s no way. Girls ain’t allowed to fight in combat.”

“Tell that to Josh Monday! And remember what I did to you in Oregon.”

Joey thought, she has a point there. Two points, actually.

CHAPTER 47 — AUGUST 12

Faith was getting impatient with the banter. She crouched and ran along the side of the trailer to the back. The door was closed. She reached up and carefully tried the door handle. It was locked. As she lowered her hand, two muted gunshots punched holes through the door. The bullets just missed her palm. She fell back onto her butt and scooted back a few feet.

From inside, Duster yelled, "God damn that was loud! Shit! Now you get back! Get back or the fed dies!"

"Duster, don't do anything stupid!"

"You mean like you just did? Back off, cunt! Back off and surrender. And by the way, my name's Joey, not Duster!"

"Okay Joey. So what's the deal here? How do you think you're going to get away with any of this?"

She heard laughter inside. "Babe, we've been gettin' away with this for years!"

"What do you mean, Dus . . . er . . . Joey?"

"What do I mean? You don't fuckin' know, do you? I bet Fed-man here knows. I bet he knows Josh and I have been taking women for years and doing whatever we want with 'em. Josh had a thing for someone that I'd guess was your twin sister. He thought you were her. Crazy as shit, huh? It was a long time ago. Yeah, your sweet twin. He told me all about it. They had a hell of a good time for a couple of weeks on the trail, but then she rejected him and that's when Josh found out who he really was. That's when he discovered himself."

There was a pause until Faith asked, "What do you mean?"

"You were gonna find out, sweet cheeks. Oh yes. Josh took your sister and he killed her and he ate her. It took him several days. Ate her! Can you imagine? I bet you don't want to. Your sweet sister, your twinsie, being cut up like a hog and choked down, bite by bite.

Faith felt nauseous. She couldn't say anything. She didn't know what to say. All she wanted to do right now was kill Joey.

"What's a matter, Faith? Cougar got your tongue? Yeah, that's where Josh discovered his passion for cooking. At least he cooked her. Didn't eat her raw like some animal. So whaddaya say to that, Beauty? And she was just the first. Turns out ol' Josh really had a screw loose and kept taking women that looked just like you, like your sister. He was doin' one a year at first, but that wasn't enough. Lucky thing I came along to help so we could do more.

"Faith, I loved it! Did you hear that? Yeah baby, I became Josh's scout and assistant. When I saw you, I thought you'd be perfect. You matched Josh's description more than anyone I'd seen. I took photos of you. Didn't know that, did you? Showed 'em to Josh and boy did he get excited! You were *Her*! It was amazing! He was sure you were Lila, returned somehow to be with him. We were going to take you at Tuolumne Meadows, but you turned down my breakfast invitation. I wanted Josh to see you for himself, but you disappeared.

"Crater Lake was no dice. You with that big asshole and his babe. Besides, we'd already taken someone just a couple of days before. Later I saw you at that place, what was it? Elk Meadow? Elk Lakes? Something like that. Your big guy was scary! I didn't wanna mess with him, so we waited. We were gonna take you at Mount Hood, but that encounter you and I had really slowed me down. I still owe you for that, Faith! I'm gonna pay you back. Don't you worry about that, bitch! You hear me?"

Joey waited for a response but there was only silence. "Faith, you still there?"

Still no answer. He checked the big guy again, jabbing his arm with the knife. Another trickle of blood, but no other response. Joey looked carefully to see that the man was still breathing. He called out again, "Faith, you hear me?"

She answered, her voice muted by the trailer wall. "Yeah, I hear you. Aren't you leaving out something though?"

"I can't imagine what, Faith. Talk to Joey."

"What about the harassment along the trail? Messing with my camp, crapping near my tent, screaming to scare me. What about that?"

Joey thought for a moment and then laughed again. "Oh yeah! That wasn't me. That was that fuckweasel Slowpoke. I talked to him at Tuolumne Meadows. Pathetic asshole said he was in love with you but you wanted nothin' to do with him. So I got him all riled up, told him he should get back at you, teach you a lesson. Man, he tried I guess. I caught up to him and he told me what he was doing. I told him that when he got the chance, he should shit on your tent. Sounds like he missed! Ha ha!"

"And then what? Why did he stop? Why didn't I see him again?"

"You're gonna love this. I did ya a favor and stopped him. The guy was an asshole and he was going to ruin the mission, so I killed him with my trusty knife. Stabbed him in the chest! Made him scream like a girl."

Faith was silent.

"This is great! I wanna tell you more. Feels good to talk about it to someone else, you know? Kind of get this stuff off my chest. Yeah, Josh and I, we processed a lot of women. I helped but I never ate. No sir. I've got limits. The funny thing, the hilarious thing, was that we got rid of the bodies that way. It was a regular meat processin' plant in here. Josh and I would slice and dice, just like with a cow or something. And grind too! That was what we did with most of it. Amazing what you can hide in ground meat! And then Josh would make these great burgers that everybody loved so much! Oh my god!" Joey started laughing. He laughed so hard, he had to quit talking for a minute.

"You ate some yourself, didn't you? And you saw how much people liked 'em! They were finger-lickin' good. Yummers! The fuckin' granolas didn't have a clue. Josh advertised the burgers as free range and organic. I guess that was true. How does that make you feel, Beauty? I'd like to know. Come on, talk to Joey!"

Silence.

"That's what I thought. How does it feel to be a cannibal? I wouldn't know. Probably not so good. But it was the best way to get rid of the evidence. All we had left were bones, and we'd put those in our nifty little incinerator and bury what was left. Turned the bones to ash. Josh said that nobody could ever tell it was from a human. We fucked up at Crater Lake though. Goddamn lightning storm came in, started a fire and we had to leave in a hurry before firefighters showed up. We buried the bones quick and skedaddled, but they got found. When I heard it on the news, I just about shit myself. They got found and I guess the feds must've got some clues. This cop in here, he probably knows about us. The media was all over the disappearance for a week or so. And then nothin' until they found what was left of beautiful Tamara. We thought we'd got away with it until then."

Joey quit talking and waited in the silence, but there was no response from Faith.

He finally hollered, "Faith! You still there? Probably pukin' on the grass right now, I imagine. Take your time, baby. I got more to tell you. And then we need to get down to business."

He waited for another minute and called out again. "Faith, are you there? Talk to Joey . . . Faith?"

CHAPTER 48 — AUGUST 12

While Joey was still talking, Faith ran across the road to the SUV. Her dad was now propped up behind the vehicle, under the open hatch. Faith bent down to check on him. He looked up at her and tried to smile. He was still holding the Ruger .38 Special in one hand, in his other hand he clenched a folded blanket, pressing it over the bullet wound.

"Dad! Dad! Are you okay?"

Mike wheezed, "Shit no, goddamn it. I hate getting shot!"

Faith took his pulse and checked his skin color. His pulse was weak, his skin was pale, cold and sweating. "Dad, we need to get you out of here!"

He patted her hand. He spoke in a frail voice. "Sure as hell do. Fucker destroyed the radios, but my cell phone is over there somewhere." He coughed and pointed to the alders bordering the turnout. His arm was shaking. "He threw it there. I tried to go get it but ran out of steam. Find my phone, call the FBI number. Agents are standing by, close by. Call 911 and get a helo."

Faith nodded and stood up, jogged over to the alders. There was a small ditch there and she started rummaging around in the vegetation. She kept glancing back at the trailer to make sure Joey wasn't escaping. Finally she saw something reflective and reached down, picked up her father's iPhone. She ran back to him and crouched down, showed him the phone. The screen was cracked, but still glowing. There were only two bars on it; hopefully enough signal to get through.

“Dad? Can you make the call? I gotta go contain Duster.”

“Is that what you call him? Makes sense. Stupid coat for a hiker. Okay, dial the FBI guy for me and I’ll talk to him.”

She found the number and hit the call button. The connection was shaky but the other end was ringing. Mike set down his revolver and took the phone, held it to his ear. He waited and then said, “Hey Agent Battles? This is Chief Montaigne . . . yeah. Look, you got our location from Max, right? Okay, get a chopper with EMT’s and some backup here . . .”

Faith patted her dad on the back and looked to the trailer. Still no movement. She picked up the shotgun and walked over to the bloody heap that had been Joshua Monday, The Chef. Frowning, she searched his pants pockets and pulled out a key ring. On it were the Ford keys and what looked like keys to the camper and trailer. She put them in a pocket and moved back across the road.

CHAPTER 49 — AUGUST 12

Joey crawled along the floor toward the back door. Faith still wasn't responding. Was she out there? He wished there was another way out, but there wasn't unless he raised one of the serving window shutters and scooted out that way. But those shutters were loud and she'd hear him, shoot his ass.

As quietly as he could, Joey reached the door and stood up slowly. He leaned to the side to peer out the window, didn't see anyone. He ducked and moved to the other side and peered out that way. Still nobody. He knew she wouldn't go far, that she was probably waiting to ambush him when he came out the door. Well, he wasn't that stupid. He scampered back to where Max lay and nudged him with a foot. No response. Joey knelt next to him and tried to decide which ear to cut off and throw out the door first. He had to do something to show Faith that he was fuckin' serious.

"Joey!" made him jump.

She was still out there. He answered, "What is it, Beauty?"

"I'll make you a deal. You let the big guy go and I let you drive off. I've got the pickup keys with me. You'll have a head start. That's the best I can do."

Joey licked his lips and thought about it, decided, "No, that ain't gonna work, Faith. Here's my deal. First you disconnect this trailer and leave the pickup keys in the ignition. Then I hear you get in that Forestry Service truck and drive off up the road, then I leave the cop here in the trailer and I drive off down the road."

After some more silence, Faith said, "That's not going to work either. I need to know that the cop is all right. You need to send him out so that I can see he's okay."

Joey thought for a moment, finally said, "Fine. Okay, I get out with the cop, gun to his head. You stand way the hell back while I walk with the cop to the pickup, check to see the keys are inside, then I wait while you get in the cop's car and get the hell out of my sight. Up the road and around the corner you go. Then I make the cop drive while I got my gun on him and we head down the road. I let the cop out a few miles down the road and I keep going."

"How do I know you won't kill him? How do I know he isn't already dead? I wanna hear his voice!"

"Uhh, he's not available to take your call right now. Please leave a message after the beep. Ha ha! Guy's still knocked out, hasn't woke up yet."

"Not good enough. I need proof you haven't killed him, or I'm not dealing."

"Beauty, the thing is I just wanna get out of here, right? The cop is knocked out cold and I don't know how to wake up him up. I just want outta here, so you're gonna have to trust Joey."

Faith almost laughed. It was still a bad deal. Any deal where Joey got away was a bad deal. Faith knew she couldn't trust him, but it didn't matter. She had no intention of following through on her end. She had no intention of letting the murdering shit get away. She said, "Okay. I guess there's no other way. You got a deal. I'm going to disconnect the trailer now. And then I'll leave the keys in the pickup."

Faith hated this kind of cat and mouse bullshit. She knew that Joey knew he couldn't trust her and that she couldn't trust him. She knew she was going to either kill or contain him, and try to do it without the cop getting hurt, if the cop was even alive at this point. She was just going through the motions to buy time. Buy time until the chopper and/or the FBI agents could get on scene. She glanced over at the Forest Service vehicle and looked for her dad. He was still there and saw her, raised a hand. She waved back as she walked over to the trailer hitch. She sat down on the wet grass next to the hitch, as close to the trailer as possible so Joey couldn't see her from the trailer's front window. Shotgun in her lap, she started disconnecting the chains and lights, making a lot of noise. While her hands worked on that, she kept an eye under the trailer and waited for what she knew was about to happen.

CHAPTER 50 — AUGUST 12

Joey heard Faith at work and nodded to himself. This was good. While she was busy, he was just going to scoot out the back door, sneak around the trailer and blow her the fuck away. Too bad. He'd been looking forward to raping her first and then slowly cutting her up while she screamed and begged, but you can't have everything. After her, he'd take care of the cop and the old man. Things were working out nicely. To make sure the cop was still out of it, he knelt and poked him with the knife again. No response even as the blade drew blood. Joey smiled and paused. Maybe he should gut the cop now, while he's out, and put one player out of the game. Joey considered it, but reminded himself that he still might need a live hostage. He put the knife in its belt scabbard, picked up the pistol and listened. He could still hear Faith working at the hitch, heard the wheel lift snap into place. She'd be starting to turn the crank to lift the coupler off the ball, raising the trailer. He didn't have much time. He popped out the pistol magazine and checked it. More than enough bullets left. After all, he only needed three or four. He slid the magazine back into the pistol's handgrip until it clicked firmly into place.

He tiptoed to the back door and checked out the window. Nobody there. He carefully turned the handle and cracked open the door, peered out again, eyes narrowed against the sunlight. He put one foot down onto the rear step. That was when he felt the trailer rock and turned just in time to see the big cop rushing toward him. Joey stumbled out of the trailer and onto the grass, pivoted to bring up the pistol just as the big guy flew out the door and slammed into him. Joey grunted and pulled the trigger. The pistol kicked in his hands and the cop swore. The shot went wild. Joey fell to the grassy ground. The cop rolled away from him, groaning, and lurched to his feet. From the ground, Joey tried to bring the gun around to shoot, but the big guy kicked it out of his hand.

Faith ran around the back corner of the trailer in time to see Max lash out with his foot and send the pistol flying. She brought the shotgun up against her shoulder and aimed, but didn't dare fire for fear of hitting Max. He closed in just as Joey was pulling out his big knife. He kicked Max in the groin and lunged at him with the blade. Max crouched over and backpedaled to stay away from the slashing steel.

Faith kept the shotgun on Joey, hoping for a clear shot but the two men were moving around too much. She heard a distant pounding in the air and recognized the rotor beat of a Huey helicopter. She hoped it was the medical crew coming for her father. She watched Max and Joey circling each other, Joey jabbing with the knife, Max jumping back.

Joey chanted, "Come on, pig, come on! Taste Duster's cold steel, motherfucker. Come on . . ."

Faith stepped closer to the fighters, keeping the shotgun muzzle on Joey. Max glanced at her and pulled away from his opponent so Faith could get a clear line of fire. She yelled, "Joey! It's over! Drop the fucking knife, or I'll drop you!"

Joey looked at her, bewildered, and stepped back, slowly lowered the knife. Max waited.

"Drop it!" said Faith. "Drop it now and get your ass on the ground, hands where I can see 'em!"

The thumping was getting louder. Faith wanted to look to the blue sky, but kept her attention, and the shotgun, on Joey. He grinned and dropped the knife onto the grass, then backed up and sat down, hands in the air.

Max turned to Faith and tried to smile. She gave him a quick glance and saw him hunched over from the pain in his chest, where the bullets had hit his vest. He looked pretty beat up. His left arm was dripping blood, one eye was almost swollen shut and there was a knot on the back of his skull.

"Faith Montaigne, I presume," he said with a strained smile, clutching his torso. "Very pleased to meet you. I'm Max, with the Forest Service. Your dad and I have been looking for you and for Josh Monday. I don't know who this guy is."

Keeping her eyes on Duster, Faith smiled in return. She said, "Nice to meet you, Max. As for this guy, he's Monday's pervert partner in crime. His murdering lapdog."

As she stepped closer, shotgun ready, Joey put his hands behind his head and grinned at Faith. "That was unkind, Beauty. I was Monday's equal, even if he didn't realize it." He looked to the sky. "Hey, is that chopper for little old me?"

Max said, "Speaking of Monday, where is he?"

Faith pointed her chin over toward Max's SUV. He took about five steps in that direction, stopped, stared and bent over to vomit. Wiping his mouth, he turned and trudged back to where Faith stood with the shotgun leveled at Joey.

Joey laughed and said, "What's a matter, copper? Got a weak stomach? You shoulda seen some of the stuff Josh and I did!"

Max ignored him and asked Faith, "Where's Mike? Is he okay? He was going to be my backup."

Faith told him what had happened. Max said, "Shit! I better go see how he's doing."

Never taking her eyes off of Joey, Faith said, "I got it covered. One of my certifications is as a battlefield medic. He's in shock but the chopper's almost here. I'd feel better if you stayed here. Besides, you look like you need an EMT yourself."

The sound of rotors slapping the air grew louder. Joey and Max watched as the Bell 212 swooped from the sky. Faith kept her eyes and shotgun trained on Joey. The Huey flew in a low circle around them, a massive, noisy wind machine, whipping up dust and debris from the ground. It swung out and curved west to come in for a landing up the road, sunlight flashing off the plexiglass windshield. Words on the grey and white chopper's tail boom read, "Sheriff, Snohomish County". After a quick glance, Faith kept the shotgun centered on Joey as the chopper's skids gently settled to the ground in a cloud of vegetative debris. It was about 75 yards away. Max stepped over to the side of the trailer and was peering at the ground, looking for his handcuffs. He held one hand up to his face, trying to shield his eyes from the rotor wash and airborne detritus.

Faith risked another quick glance, this time at her father, and caught an eyeful of bits of grass, rotten wood and dust. She squinted and averted her face, one eye open. That was when Joey decided it was time to go. He scrambled up and bolted past Faith. He was laughing, yelled out, "See ya, wouldn't wanna be ya!"

She swiveled to shoot but there was too much in the field of fire and she could only see out of one eye. Tracking Joey, she swept the shotgun muzzle past her father, the two EMT's jogging toward him, Max and then the helicopter. She barely had time to wonder about the civilian rules of engagement and the legal implications of shooting a fleeing suspect in the back.

Squinting and swearing, long black hair lashing in the wind, she lowered the shotgun and started in pursuit. She yelled at Max. He looked up in surprise and she pointed toward Joey, who was ahead of them now, almost to the chopper. A sheriff's deputy had opened the left front door of the Huey and was stepping out, right hand on the grip of his holstered pistol. The pilot sitting in the right hand seat had reduced throttle but the rotors were still turning and making a lot of noise and wind. Joey yelled over the sound of the helicopter, “They’re tryin’ to kill me, officer! Help me! She has a gun!”

At the word ‘gun’, the deputy drew his pistol and kept his eyes on Faith, who was running toward him carrying the shotgun. Joey ran up to the cop, grabbed his left arm and said, “Save me!” The deputy, a large and beefy man, tried to shake off Joey’s grip as he yelled at Faith, “Drop your weapon! Drop it or I’ll shoot!”

Faith faltered and stopped, lowered the shotgun and yelled back, “That man is a murder suspect! You’ve got the wrong person!” She pointed at Joey. “You need to cuff him!”

The cop started to turn toward Joey just as Joey’s fist slammed into his face. He staggered back against the side of the helicopter and raised his pistol but it was too late. Joey wrenched the weapon from the deputy’s hand. The deputy tried to grab his assailant, but missed. Joey kicked out at one of his knees and the cop grunted and fell back. Joey aimed the gun at the deputy’s head, but didn’t fire. He pulled the gun up, grinned, and took off, running by the still spinning tail rotor.

He stopped just past it, bent over, picked up a fist-sized rock and hurled it at the blurry rotor disk. The rock smashed into it, making a horrendous clatter as shards of rotor blade exploded out in every direction. One of the pieces punched into Joey’s lower left side. He staggered backward, screamed and lurched off down the road, the shiny metal protruding a few inches from his abdomen.

Grim-faced, Faith retrieved the shotgun and resumed her pursuit. The deputy yelled as she ran past, “What the hell is going on?!”

Faith pointed back at Max, who was hobbling to catch up, and said, “Talk to that guy. He’s a fed. I’ve got to catch the perp before he disappears into the forest!”

She was catching up to Joey and when she did . . . she wasn't sure what to do with the murderous psychopath. Instinct told her to destroy him; the same instinct that told a white blood cell to destroy a virus. It was a visceral feeling and felt so right, but she tried to think of the consequences, legal and moral. She tried, but all she could really think about was catching up with the psycho and blowing out his fucking brains. She reminded herself that there were witnesses now. It would have to look like self defense.

Ahead of her, Joey was faltering, left hand at his side, right hand brandishing the deputy's pistol. He turned, saw Faith and fired off a loud, random bullet. She ducked down but kept moving. He stopped, turned, gripped the pistol in both hands and fired again. This time Faith heard the bullet zip past her head so she dived for the ground. She wound up behind a rotten stump and heard another shot, felt the bullet thump into wood.

After a couple of silent seconds, she peered around the stump just in time to see Joey disappear over the crest of the hill. He was almost out of the open area, almost to the forest. Once he got in there, the game would become much more dangerous. Joey's pistol likely held at least 12 more rounds. Her shotgun held three at the most. Joey's pistol had an effective range of up to 60 yards, her shotgun nowhere near that.

Faith pushed herself upright and started running again. Glances at the ground showed the occasional spatter of blood. She got to the crest of the hill just in time to see Joey drag himself into the forest, where he vanished.

It was no use. She was in no shape to pursue. Her adrenalin rush was tapering off, replaced by a growing fatigue. She stood there, cradling the shotgun, staring down at the edge of the forest.

The bullet and the gunshot arrived at the same time, the dirt at her feet exploding. Faith ducked down and heard Joey yell, "Fuck you!!"

Keeping low, Faith turned and backtracked. There were more important things to worry about now. She had to see how her father was doing, had to make sure she went with him when he got loaded onto the chopper.

She saw Max and the deputy heading her way. They struggled over the uneven terrain. Max because of his injuries and the deputy because he'd just been kicked in the knee. When they got close enough she said, "He got away into the forest. He's injured but last I saw still moving."

"Jesus!" said Max. "We heard the gunshots but no shotgun blasts. We thought you were a goner, Faith."

"Nope. Still here. Somebody else will have to track down Joey. With that metal in his side, he probably won't get far anyway."

Gasping, the deputy said, "I'll call in for a K9 tracker and more officers. We need another chopper anyway. The son of a bitch disabled our tail rotor with that rock. In the meantime, maybe a bear will do us all a favor and eat the bastard."

CHAPTER 51 — AUGUST 12

When they returned to the vehicles, Faith saw her dad lying on his left side, on a blanket in the shade of a blue tarp that the two EMT's had rigged over the Ford's open hatch. He had an IV in his arm and a white bandage around his head. It was almost noon and getting hot. One of the EMT's knelt next to Mike and took his pulse again. She looked up at Faith and smiled. "You must be his daughter. He was just asking about you. He's gonna be okay," she said. "He's had painkillers and is stabilized. We called for another chopper and as soon as it gets here, we'll transport him to Harborview. That's probably a fifteen, twenty-minute flight? He's experienced blood loss, shock, a possible concussion and has a perforated lung. We've got the blood loss and shock under control. The ER doctors will get that bullet out and patch him up." She looked down at Mike, held his hand and told him, "In other words, in time you'll be fine. Full recovery."

Mike smiled weakly and said, "Thanks. This ain't my first ride on the merry-go-round. Has anyone called my wife, Sally? Does she know?"

Faith said, "I'll call her right away, Dad, and hand you the phone. You can talk to her yourself, reassure her."

The other EMT, a small Hispanic man, looked at Max and said, "Dude, you look like shit. Get over here and sit down."

While her dad was on the phone and Max was being treated, Faith looked around. The scene was getting busy. A black Ford sedan had appeared just down the road and two people, a man and a woman in street clothes, were walking toward the SUV.

Over by the helicopter, the pilot and the deputy were looking at the jagged remains of the tail rotor. Faith noticed a lumpy black body bag stowed in the shade under the craft's belly. She looked to the front of the SUV and noticed that Josh's body was gone. Only blood-stained ground remained.

The man and woman turned out to be FBI field agents Devin Dartford and Brandi Dailey. They first talked to Max while he was getting his ribs wrapped and then turned their attention to Faith. Even though they said they'd been briefed by their boss, Agent Battles, they had a lot of questions.

Faith was trying to answer them, but her mind wouldn't cooperate. She was leaning against the front of the SUV, her arms crossed, staring at the bloody ground at her feet. She finally had to ask the agents to back off for the time being.

Max walked up just then, looking like a refugee from a bomb explosion. His ribs were taped and he had bandages on his arms and face. His left eye was swollen shut and he had an almost comically large knot on the back of his head. Despite a headache, he couldn't help but laugh when he looked in the pickup's side mirror. All in all, he felt pretty damn lucky to be alive and mostly in one piece. That was more than could be said of The Chef.

Yellow crime scene tape was wrapped around the pickup, trailer and helicopter tail rotor area. Those scenes would be processed by an FBI Evidence Response Team (ERT) on its way from Seattle. SAC Battles was traveling up with the team and Max would brief him when they arrived. It was going to get very crowded and very busy. In the aftermath of that morning's events, there would be innumerable phone calls, statements recorded, evidence documented and sequestered, paperwork up the yin-yang. There would be inquiries and decisions, internal affairs investigations, possible court actions. A man had died and his death would unleash an avalanche of paperwork. And that didn't take into account the attempted kidnapping, the suspected murders, the whole jumbled PCT case. Max felt even more exhausted just thinking about it.

He was tired enough already, so he decided to not think about it anymore. He'd already called Bernie as well as Savannah Allen, the Forest Service patrol captain. Although the entire scene would be carefully documented by the ERT, Max took his own photos and made scene sketches, wrote brief notes for a timeline of events and persons. One thing he'd learned over the years is that the bureaucracy needs to be fed. And if it doesn't get fed, things can get extremely uncomfortable. So, despite his pain and discomfort, he did what he could to document the morning's events while they were still fresh in his mind. That documentation would be fodder for both the Forest Service and FBI investigations.

In addition to the ERT, a NTSB team was on its way. The helicopter was grounded pending the on-scene investigation and evaluation of the aircraft tail rotor assembly. Repairs would have to be made before it was air worthy again. Such was the untidy and time-consuming aftermath of brief but incredibly dramatic events.

Faith walked over to Max and said, "Let's talk."

They moved around to the north side of the trailer and ignored the crime scene tape, sat in the cool shade there. Faith leaned her head back against the trailer, closed her eyes and sighed. Her face was haggard, hair tangled and ratty with debris.

Max asked her, "Are you okay?"

Her eyes still closed, she answered, "Shit no, but I will be. The EMT's took my vitals, said I was doing surprisingly well, that my BP was amazingly low considering. I've always been that way though." Faith opened her eyes, looked at Max and said, "So how're you doing, Max?"

He grinned ruefully. "Been better. Headache, ribs hurt like hell, can't stop my hands from shaking. Made it hard to take notes. Other than that, okay. In my line of work, it's never this dramatic or traumatic. Jesus, I've never had a day like today. How about you?"

Faith pulled hair away from her face and looked off into the distance. "Believe it or not, I've actually had worse days than this."

Max looked over at her and was silent for a moment. "Sorry to hear that, Faith. Sorry your trip went so bad here. Christ, what a mess. Could've been way worse for both of us as well as for Mike."

She looked up and gave him a tired smile. "Ya got that right. Dad gave me a quick summary of what you've been up to. Thank you for helping me, for saving me, really. If it hadn't been for you and Dad and the FBI, I'd probably be dead."

"Hell, your Dad and I would be dead if it wasn't for you, appearing out of nowhere. We're damn lucky you showed up. I'm just glad we got to Monday before he had a chance to really hurt you."

Faith looked at him and said, "I haven't told you yet, but I ran into Monday last night." She told him about her encounter with Monday the previous night, what he'd done to her, what he had planned for her and how she'd gotten away, only to return.

When she was done, Max said, "Holy shit. You came back? Back to find out what happened to your sister? I can understand that. So what was your plan? What were you going to do with Monday?"

"I wasn't sure. I had a vague plan and it had to do with my sister and what that bastard Monday did to her and to me. It was about justice. Do you understand?"

Max nodded. "Sure do. 'Nuff said. So who was this Joey character? We weren't sure if he had an accomplice. How does he fit into it?"

Faith told him about her encounters with Duster along the PCT and what he'd recently revealed to her about his role in the murders. When she mentioned the cannibalism, Max almost gagged.

"God, I guess that explains a lot as regards the evidence, and lack thereof, the charred bones with the butchering marks on them . . . Jesus Christ! Did you ever eat any of the burgers?"

She nodded. "Once in Oregon and again last night. But the more I think on it, I'm pretty sure the burger was beef. At least the one I had last night. Sure tasted like it, and it's been weeks since the last known murder, right? So maybe they used up the victims already?"

"Well, the Feebs will find out for sure. I hope word about that doesn't get out. A lot of people have been eating The Chef's food for years. Shit, I wouldn't wanna know about it, that's for sure."

They heard a distant helicopter approaching from the north. As it got louder, they looked up and saw a blue and white helicopter rising from the valley below. It came up fast and roared over the scene, made a big loop to find the new landing zone that the Sheriffs deputy had marked for them. It was further up the road, beyond the disabled Huey. Mike would soon be on his way to the hospital.

Faith and Max got up and walked slowly back to the Ford. There was a wind from the new chopper's main rotor, stirring up more dust and debris. The blue tarp was flapping wildly. The EMT's were prepping Mike for loading onto the new arrival. They already had him in a collapsible stretcher and were arranging his IV. Max walked up and Mike coughed, put out a hand. His voice was tired as he said, "Gimme a shake, partner. It's been a pleasure doing a shift with you. So glad you came by, glad you helped save my daughter's life. Thank you."

Max gripped his hand, dismayed by how cold it was. "Pleasure's all mine, Chief. Thanks to you and your daughter for saving my ass too. We stopped that fucker Monday! I think we saved several lives today."

Mike nodded as the EMT's and deputy began to wheel him down the bumpy road toward the waiting helicopter.

Faith approached Max, her pack slung over a shoulder. She held out her right hand and they shook. Faith said, "I'm riding back with Dad, make sure he gets situated all right. Mom's driving up from Oregon and I'll be there to meet her at the hospital. See ya around?"

"I hope so. Take care of yourself, and your parents."

Max watched as she hurried to catch up with the stretcher. She walked along beside her father, helping to steady the stretcher. It took a couple of minutes for them to reach the idling Airbus H135 helicopter. Once there, the EMTs opened rear clamshell doors and loaded Mike. Once Mike was in, an EMT motioned Faith to climb in. The EMT followed and the doors closed. After a moment, the rotors started spinning faster and began to bite into the air as the pitch changed. Max walked over to his Ford and leaned against the driver's door, watched as the helicopter lifted into the air in a whirling cloud. He waved as it wheeled off west, toward Seattle.

In the growing silence, he heard the crackle of gravel under tires and turned to see a dark brown Chevy Tahoe rolling in to the site. The deputy rushed forward to warn off whoever it was but the Tahoe had federal plates and turned out to contain Seattle Special Agent in Charge Bernard Battles. Max smiled as Bernie and Agent Will Darzi stepped out of the vehicle. A tall, black Dodge van with federal plates rolled up and parked next to the Tahoe. Agents of the FBI Evidence Response Team spilled from it, opened the back doors and started pulling out their crime scene equipment.

Bernie's smile faded into a look of concern as he walked up to Max and stuck out his hand to shake.
"Congratulations, Max! You should be proud of yourself. You solved it and stopped the bastard! But Jesus, you look like shit! What the hell happened here?"

It took about an hour to brief Bernie and Will. The three of them sat inside the Tahoe during the session, engine running and the AC on. Bernie was in the drivers seat, Max in the front passenger seat and Will in the back seat with an iPad to record the conversation. Both agents interrupted to ask questions and Will took notes as Max talked. When he was done, Max turned slightly in his seat to look at Will, grimaced and said, "Ouch. Those ribs hurt. Hey Will, I hope you realize the grand irony in this case?"

Darzi looked confused. "Not sure what you mean."

"I'll give you a clue. Think of the name Joshua Monday."

Darzi shook his head. Bernie started laughing and said, "Holy shit!"

Will looked at Bernie and said, "What? What's so funny?"

He turned back to Max. "Well, what is it? What am I missing?"

Max said, "Joshua Monday the serial killer? Will, he's the guy that wrote the software that helped you write the app that got him caught! The PRS app. He's the guy who built Amenable Solutions!"

Darzi's mouth widened into a broad smile and he said, "That is fan-fucking-tastic!"

CHAPTER 52 — AUGUST 12

Faith was buckled into a fold-down fabric seat and holding her father's right hand. She felt the ship lift into the air and turn. She looked back out the rear door windows and saw Max waving. She waved in return even though she knew he couldn't see her.

The EMT, whose nametag said "Malinda", handed Faith a headset with mic and turned on the comm. Mike was also fitted with a headset so that they could talk over the noise of the helicopter. Faith heard the pilot talking to Seattle Center before the other EMT held up four fingers, signaling her to select channel four for the intercom.

Mike tightened his grip on her hand. His voice on the intercom was very weak as he said, "Quietest, smoothest chopper I've ever been on. Lovin' it!" While they talked, Malinda attached a heart and blood pressure monitor to Mike. She looked over at the monitors and gave Faith a thumbs up.

Faith nodded and smiled. She said, "Enjoy the flight while you can, Dad. It won't be long until we're at the hospital."

"Good! The pain meds are kickin' in and I'm not feeling bad at all. Not a'tall." He paused and said, "Sorry about your trip, daughter dearest. Sorry about what happened back there. Shit, but we did some good though. We saved some lives, Faith. We stopped that son of a bitch. You stopped him, dead in his tracks. Ha ha, get it? And that Max, I would've lost you if it weren't for him. He's a great guy. He latched onto the case and wouldn't let go. Latched on like a pit bull. Did I say he's a great guy? Stay in touch with him. You could look a long time and not find a guy like him."

"Dad, slow down. It's not like I want to marry the guy. We just met. I do owe him thanks though. I know that."

"Hey, I'm sorry. Man oh man, but the pain meds are fuckin' me up, but I'm feelin' good. Don't let me get addicted, okay? Tell the docs not to let me get addicted. I can handle the pain, mostly. Shit. Don't wanna be an addict. Seen too much of that sad shit."

Faith patted his hand. "It's okay, Dad. I'll make sure you're okay. And don't worry about my trip. It was great, right up until yesterday. I did a lot of miles and had plenty of time to work out some things . . ." Faith stopped talking as she realized her father was unconscious. She gave Malinda a worried look and the EMT switched her headset to Faith's channel. "He's doing great. The meds put him asleep is all. How about you? Are you okay?"

Faith nodded.

"Alright. I don't know what happened back there, but it looked bad. If you need anything or start feeling bad, let me know."

Faith said, "Sure will, Malinda. Thank you."

The EMT smiled and went back to monitoring Mike's vitals. Faith kept hold of his hand and looked aft, out the back windows at the forested mountain terrain flowing by below. For a moment, she felt like it was the helicopter that was still and the earth that was moving. She saw trees, logged clearings, sunlight flashing off of creeks, the occasional road and trail snaking over the landscape.

The adrenalin had worn off completely, leaving her feeling drained and bone weary. She looked back at her sleeping father and thought how close it had been, how he'd almost died because of her. Almost died because of her trip, a trip that he'd objected to. What would he say to that? What will he say? She thought about it and realized that he'd say what he already said. That he was glad they stopped a killer and was glad they were both alive. He'd say that he was relieved they finally found out what had happened to Lila, painful and horrible as it was to know, and that they'd been able to dish out their own justice. Lila's family and friends could finally feel that she was resting in peace.

Faith felt tears starting to run down her cheeks and wiped at her eyes with a shaking hand. It did feel better to know what had happened, but at the same time it also felt worse, and it did nothing to lessen the grief. That was something Faith still had to deal with, just as her mother and father had to deal with it.

She looked out the back windows again, saw that the mountains were giving way to hills capped by cell towers. And then there were flat valley bottoms crowded with busy roads, power lines and buildings. Not far now. Her eyes sought out the now-distant mountains, rocky summits streaked with snow under the blue sky. Just minutes ago she'd been there and now she was near one of the largest cities on the west coast. The transition was jarring. It reminded her of her return to the United States after the harrowing battle overseas. There was not enough time to process what had happened, not enough time to adapt to new conditions. Faith wondered if she'd be able to return to the mountains and find again the peace of mind she'd experienced on the Pacific Crest Trail.

Over the intercom, Malinda said, "We're five minutes out."

Faith gave her a thumbs up. She was surprised to see her dad, eyes still closed, do the same.

Chapter 53 — SEPTEMBER 19

He knew he was near the end. The pain was pretty bad, worse than anything he'd experienced before, and he had a raging fever from the infection. He was so weak, so tired, soaked in sweat. It didn't make much sense to keep trying. What if he did find his way out of the goddamn forest? He'd be captured, too weak to defend himself. What was left then? A trial, prison, maybe multiple trials in other states, multiple life sentences, or a long wait for a death sentence. What the hell kind of life was that?

Joey lay back on the damp, cool moss and listened to the creek gurgle a few feet away. He lifted his bloody hands in front of his face and looked at them. Devils club was a bitch to get through but he hardly noticed the pain from the many punctures and scratches. Still, it looked pretty bad. Dropping his hands to his sides, he closed his eyes and breathed deep, which hurt like hell.

It had been a rough week since he escaped from that bitch Faith. He was so tired. Hungry too. Bugs and raw frogs just didn't provide enough nourishment. He tried eating some plants but got scared about poisoning. How far had he gone and where was he? He had no idea. The fucking forest and the fucking mountains seemed endless. He'd kept moving downhill, following the afternoon sun, trying to stay in the big trees where the traveling was easier. But that usually took him away from the creeks and he was thirsty all the time, making constant trips down to water to drink.

It was easier to hide along the creeks. The first couple of days there'd been helicopters overhead and dogs barking in the distance. Joey had staggered down a boulder-strewn creek for a long ways, the water bone-numbing cold, alder branches whipping him in the face. He hoped to throw off the dogs by hiding his scent. Must've worked because even though he'd heard dogs barking after his creek journey, they never seemed to get closer.

It had been a couple of days since he heard a chopper or a dog. Maybe they gave up, figured he'd just die out in the brush somewhere, never to be found. That seemed likely. Maybe that wouldn't be such a bad thing.

Joey used his left hand to explore the wound. It was swollen and painful to touch. At first he thought he'd been lucky. The piece of helicopter tail rotor had lodged between two lower ribs on his left side and hadn't punctured anything vital. What a dumbshit move that had been, throwing that rock! Oh well, live and learn. Or learn and die.

At least he never coughed up any blood. After some initial numbness and the adrenalin had worn off, it hurt like hell to breathe or move. When he walked, the metal pried at his ribs, ripping cartilage. Even though he was afraid of more blood loss, Joey finally pulled the sharp metal piece out. It made him scream and sweat, but the wound felt better afterward. Looking at the shard, he figured it had gone in less than an inch before getting stuck.

Remembering something he'd seen in an old movie, he'd gathered up a handful of moss, mixed it with mud and stuffed it into the wound. In the movie, the moss had soaked up the blood and the mud had some kind of medicinal properties that helped the hero heal. Some old Indian guy had taken care of him until he was well enough to go get revenge on whoever shot him. Joey liked that.

But now, he had to admit to himself that the movie Indian's goddamn moss and mud was probably a mistake. A day or two after he packed it, he noticed the wound turning more red and painful. And then the swelling started.

He washed out the wound with creek water, which started it bleeding again, so he tore off a sleeve from his t-shirt and poked that in. He managed to hold it in as he walked, but had to rinse it out a few times.

It was probably a couple of more days before the bleeding finally stopped. The swollen cut was now a mess of embedded cotton cloth, matted and dried blood, bits of lichen and twigs, dirt. He wanted to do something about it, but figured he better just leave it alone.

At least the weather had cooperated! Joey cackled to himself at that tiny bit of good fortune. Warm days but cold nights. With the fever getting worse, maybe he wouldn't be so cold at night anymore. Maybe he could get a good night's sleep. One that he wouldn't wake up from. Didn't sound so bad now.

Lying in the cool shade next to the soothing sound of the creek, Joey felt a peace unlike any he'd felt before. A nearby bird started singing, its song like the music of the water. Bees zinged to and fro over his head. He brushed a fly off his nose and smiled. The flies would probably eat him. He'd prefer it if a bear or wolf or some other cool animal did that though. He'd rather they took care of his body than a bunch of fucking flies. Still, he wouldn't care. He really didn't care now.

Soothed, Joey started to drift off. And then something started bothering him. What was it? What disturbed his peace? At first he couldn't tell, but something was dragging him from the dark and cool depths of sleep. Didn't he need his sleep? What the hell? He got irritated and tried to figure out what was going on as his mind struggled to consciousness.

Smoke! He opened his eyes. It was wood smoke drifting over him, over the creek. Pale blue smoke that smelled really great. He struggled up onto his elbows and looked around. He didn't see anybody, but smoke likely meant people. Did he really want to die, or did he want to live, even if it meant prison?

Well shit, he did have a gun. Maybe he could control the situation, force whoever it was to help him. His right hand groped for the Beretta and found it. It felt so heavy when he lifted it. He was too weak to call for help so he pointed the pistol at the sky and fired three ear-busting shots, brass shells flying into the creek.

He waited a couple of minutes and fired three more shots, wincing at the sound. Still no one came. Sapped of strength, Joey fell back onto the moss and dropped the pistol. Shit, at least he tried.

At first he thought he was hearing things, but soon it became obvious someone or something was smashing its way through the brush, toward the creek, toward him. He tried to say something, but all that came out was a croaking sound. The noise grew louder and he heard some rocks roll down the cut bank above him. And then he heard a man's voice, rough with age. "Holy shit! Mister, you okay? Looks like you could use some help, pard!"

Joey closed his eyes, smiled and raised a hand in greeting.

CHAPTER 54 — SEPTEMBER 1

"Max! How the hell are ya?" said Bernie as he shook Max's hand. "Glad you could make it, man."

Max looked around as he said, "Good to see you, Bernie. Nice place to meet!"

They were standing on a grassy hilltop in Seattle's Discovery Park, overlooking the choppy blue water of Puget Sound. Across the Sound, rumpled hills faded into the distant, snowy Olympic Mountains. Behind them were tall maple trees and a row of Victorian era houses. It was late morning at Discovery Park and the sun was shining from a cloud-speckled blue sky. There was a slight chill in the sweet air, hinting at the nearness of autumn. Max wore his usual blue jeans, black t-shirt and brown leather jacket. Bernie was wearing his usual dark suit, but had the jacket slung over one shoulder and his tie loosened.

"I love it here! Don't get over here often enough though. Hey, looks like you're healing up well. That nasty knot on your noggin is gone."

Max put a hand on the back of his head. "Feelin' better every day. I'm back at work and trying to get caught up. And I'm very happy to be alive. The headaches are gone and my arm is healed up, but man, those ribs still hurt. The doc over at Harborview told me this morning that they'll hurt for a long time."

Bernie frowned. "Sorry to hear that. But hey, still better than being ground into burgers and frankfurters, right?"

"Too true." After a pause, Max said, "Okay, I have to say something now. I have to say I feel like a complete amateur and idiot for letting Monday bushwhack me like that. I should've known better and not let him get the drop on me. Mike and I should've cuffed him right away. Shit, if he'd aimed for the head, I sure as hell wouldn't be standing here feeling like a fool."

Bernie patted him on the back and said, "Max, at least you're an alive fool. Seriously, don't beat yourself up about it. Place the blame on fatigue. You and Mike were exhausted. Exhaustion and fatigue cause mistakes and accidents. Luckily Monday was in the same boat. Otherwise he might've thought to aim for your head. So don't make yourself feel bad. Just realize you learned a vital lesson and apply that to the future."

Max shrugged, said, "Good advice. Thanks."

The two men started walking side by side across the broad, green hillside.

"Is this another one of your walking venues, Bernie?"

Bernie took a deep breath and looked at the distant mountains. "Discovery Park is way better than the piers, so I get here when I can. Plus," he pointed at two women jogging by on a sidewalk below them, "there's the eye-candy, but don't tell my wife I said that, okay?"

Max laughed. "You got it. So, to what do I owe this kind invitation to partake in the great outdoors?"

Bernie pointed to a bench situated on the meadow's high point. "Let's take a seat over there. I wanted to brief you in person regarding the status of our investigation."

"Sure, but you said there'd be an official report out soon."

"Yeah, yeah, but consider this more of an after-action session. I'm going to tell you some things that won't be in the official report. At least not in the public version."

They sat on the bench and looked out over the water. A large red freighter was slowly heading north, leaving a spreading wake in the ruffled blue. Another ship, a massive, white cruise ship, was heading the opposite direction, toward Elliot Bay. It looked like a huge multistoried cheap motel that had been welded on top of a ship's hull. Two small tugboats were heading toward it. Further out, tiny white triangles of sailboats dotted the Sound.

"Goddamn cruise ships!" said Bernie.

Max looked at him in surprise. "What? What're you talkin' about?"

Bernie waved a hand toward the ship. "Max, those monsters come in, anchor and dump off hundreds if not thousands of people into the city. It's like fucking D-Day all over again. It's an invasion is what it is."

"So why do you care?"

"Well, it sort of ruins my bayside walks. Dodgin' codgers, that's what it's about when those damn ships come in. It gets crowded down along the bay. That's one of the reasons I come here sometimes. Plus, this is amazingly beautiful. But I digress. Please disregard my grumpiness and let me get back to the case. So, what d'you wanna know?"

"Well, I want to know everything. I guess start with the trailer, since that's where I almost got myself killed."

Bernie sighed. "Yeah, the trailer. Some creepy shit, my friend! It's a one of a kind custom-built job. An incredibly well designed and efficient kitchen on wheels. Given what was happening, you probably didn't have time to look around and appreciate it. The day you were there, Monday had the trailer set up for sexual assault and then a ritual slaying, to be followed by butchering Faith, and I assume, from what Faith said that Joey said, eating her himself. We assume this was the pattern for all the other killings too."

"Jesus."

"The ERT people thought they'd seen it all before, but even by their standards, this was something extra disturbing. There were burned out candles, condoms, zip ties, butcher knives. The steel table that Faith woke up on was supposed to be like a kitchen island, but it was more of a sacrificial altar, like the goddamn Aztecs or something.

The metal top had drain gutters for blood and under that metal top, inside the island, was a portable incinerator for disposal of the bones, tissue and victims' personal items. It had a vent that ran under the trailer floor, up a wall and out the roof. Ray, one of the investigators, said he'd never seen something so ingenious. Said that the incinerator was one of a kind, most likely built by Monday himself. Quite the elaborate setup."

"That explains why some of the bones we found were partially burnt. God. Poor Faith. Took some courage to do what she did and escape, and then come back!"

"Yeah. If she hadn't, she would've been dead and probably in the process of being dismembered when you and Mike showed up. And then there were the freezers." Bernie paused and took a deep breath.

Max said, "Uh oh."

"Yeah. Uh oh is right. We found quite a bit of wrapped frozen meat. Chicken, some pork chops, salmon, beef and then . . . well, you know."

"Damn!" said Max. "Does Faith know?"

Bernie shook his head. "Obviously she knows about the cannibalism. Joey told her all about it, but we haven't confirmed to her that we found human meat in the freezer."

Max leaned forward, elbows on knees. "I talked about that with her that day on the mountain. She had burgers on two different occasions but was sure that they were beef burgers."

"We'll let her keep thinking that. No way of knowing otherwise, really, so no need to pursue it. As regards the public, for the time being, we're going to try and keep the cannibalism aspect quiet. I'm sure word will get out someday, but nobody needs to know right now. Faith and the families of the slain women have been through enough. If I can, I want to spare them this. At least while the media is still all over it. And then there's all those hungry hikers over the years. No need for them to know either."

Max rubbed his chin and said, "*Madre di dio*. Wow. Okay, so what about Monday's house on Lopez Island?"

"That was much more productive, even if just as chilling and depressing. It's a beautiful house by the way. The best money can buy and Monday had a shitload of money. Most of the house was clean. On the surface, nothing out of the ordinary for a rich guy, but then we found a shrine in a locked room in his basement. He'd hidden it pretty well, but not much gets past my ERT people and their technology. One of the agents used a 3DRWS unit. That's a 3-D radar unit that can scan through walls to detect open space, movement, the presence of people, etc. She scanned all the walls and found Monday's little shrine. The door was hidden behind a wine rack, just like in the movies."

Max held up a hand. "Wait a minute, Bernie. You guys have a device that can see through walls?"

"Sure, it's nothing new but the 3DRWS unit is much more sophisticated than anything to date. In fact, I'm not supposed to say any more about it."

Bernie tapped on his cell phone and handed it to Max. The phone display showed a photo of a broad, one-story home of dark wood and stone with a roof-top deck, a square rock observation tower on one corner, a flagstone patio overlooking the water and in the distance, a long floating dock with a small sailboat tied to it. Green meadows and groups of fir trees surrounded the property on three sides.

"Pretty nice, eh? Okay, so this shrine? Scroll through to see some photos of it. Totally dedicated to Lila Montaigne. The guy took a lot of photos in the brief time they were together, all of them in the mountains of course, on the PCT. Lila hiking, Lila and Monday hand in hand on a lakeshore, Lila skinny-dipping in a lake, Lila silhouetted at sunset, that sort of thing. Blowups of the photos were plastered all over the room. There's an altar with a huge photo of Lila over it, candles and incense, all that kind of thing. There were some blowups of articles about Lila's disappearance, more of those in a sort of three-ring binder scrapbook he kept. That was how he learned more about her. Fortunately none of the articles mentioned that she had a twin. Faith's status as a special forces operative precluded the press mentioning her. Had Monday known about her, who knows what his twisted mind would've come up with? I'm surprised and relieved that he never contacted the family. Mike said he almost wished he had so he could've found and killed the son of a bitch back then."

Max used his index finger to scroll through the photos. At one point, he handed the phone to Bernie and asked, "What's that about? Looks like a miniature wine rack."

Bernie took the phone and looked. "Oh yeah. Shit, that's a pretty big find, actually. There's 30 slots in that thing and in 20 of them is a small sealed bottle and in each of those bottles is a lock of black or dark brown hair."

"Holy shit! Twenty? Twenty victims? That's almost double what we thought."

"Yeah. Apparently he didn't confine his obsession to the PCT. In a way, we're in luck. Each lock of hair will have the DNA we need to identify some of the victims and maybe close open cases. We'll probably never find their remains. Monday left a book too; another black three-ring binder with photos and dates showing his other victims. Some are named, some are not. The photos . . . well, some of them are highly disturbing. At least they'll provide further help in identification."

"All that violence and death from one rejection? Hard to believe."

"Monday was totally infatuated with Lila. From what we can find out, he'd never been in love before. This despite dating a lot of beautiful women over the years. The media covered his more flagrant affairs with photos and articles. So in a way, the guy was a virgin as far as love was concerned. Monday likely snapped when Lila decided to break up with him. What was it that Joey told Faith? That Monday finally found his true self?"

"Yeah, about that. What would cause this guy, a guy who had it all, to lose it like that? It must be in his background."

"It is. A classic and sad tale of an only child physically and mentally abused by his father Emmet, who also abused his mother, who in turn didn't protect Joshua. We don't know a lot since nobody in the family sought help. Emmet ran an electronics store and made his son work there when he was a kid. As a result, Joshua didn't have any friends, didn't do any school activities, pretty much never socialized properly. And then there was the accident."

"What kind of accident?"

"Warehouse explosion at the electronics business. Monday's store had a parts warehouse attached and one evening there was a big explosion there. Joshua's mother, Arlene, was killed. Apparently she was there looking for Emmet, who was supposed to be doing inventory, but was instead at a local motel with one of his customer's wives. The explosion was suspicious and at first Emmet was suspected, but he had that alibi. So the police turned to Joshua, who was 16 at the time, but he said he was home studying. By the way, this kid studied a lot when he wasn't working. Got a UW scholarship and everything. Anyway, he had a flimsy alibi, but there wasn't much the cops could do. There was no evidence."

Max laughed. "No evidence? You gotta be kidding. There's always evidence."

Bernie grinned. "You're gonna love this, Max. Think about it. What goes into making a bomb?"

"Well, wires, timer, maybe a receiver of some kind, batteries, something to detonate an explosive . . . oh."

"Yeah. Like one of the detectives said in his report, how the hell do you find that stuff in an explosion at an electronic parts warehouse? How do you even prove there was a bomb? Just about everything they found could've been used in a bomb."

"But what about the explosive?"

"Propane gas."

"So no one was ever charged."

"Yep, and young Joshua, smart kid, got his scholarship, left home never to return. He went on to become a computer software mogul, entrepreneur, billionaire, philanthropist, nutjob serial killer and cannibal."

"Wow." Max gazed out over the blue water at the hazy Olympic Mountains. "So what about Joey? What's his story?"

Bernie said, "Ah yes, Joey or Duster. His fingerprints were all over the trailer. We also found some DNA but it'll be a while before we get anything back from the lab. The prints worked though. Found some on file from previous arrests. Duster's real name was, or is, Joseph O'Brian Amadon, age 34. Turns out he was what they used to call a remittance man. I guess he'd be called a trustifarian these days. Rich family has a pervert black sheep, in this case Joey, and they don't want him around, so they pay him to stay away. He roamed the western states, skiing in the winter, bumming around in the summer working odd jobs here and there. The family says his remittance was just enough to live on. Using PRS, we've correlated his travels with rapes and attacks in several states. He was arrested a few times, but nothing could be proved, so he was released each time. We're looking into those. Just like his mentor, Joey was a very sick lad."

"So where do you think Joey is now? Still haven't found him, right?"

Bernie looked grim. "I wish I knew. From what Faith said, and judging by the blood trail, Joey was hurt pretty bad. As you know, we had a lot of people out looking for him, but nothing so far. I like to think the fucker died in the woods somewhere and will remain there forever."

"Yeah, that deputy said he hoped a bear would kill and eat Joey."

"That would be fitting. More likely that the bastard is dead and rotting in some hidden little valley. Still, it would be good to know for sure, have closure. Joey was a highly functioning madman."

"You got that right. Faith, Mike and I are lucky to be alive."

"So, how's the media treating you these days?"

"The media? After the initial shit storm, they moved on to other things real quick. The Forest Service and I underplayed my role in the whole incident, which helped. What about your office?"

"We've got a PR person to deal with that shit. You probably saw the press conference. It went pretty smoothly. Most of the reporters asked smart questions and luckily we had the answers. Nobody has clued into the cannibalism angle yet. There's going to be more interviews and maybe press conferences as outlets like *High Country News*, *Outside* and *Field and Stream* report on the story in more detail. We're ready to provide information to them, minus the cannibalism. Since there's no trial to worry about, we can mostly give the press what it wants."

Max said, "Yeah, uh, my mom wants to write about it too. You remember she's a freelance writer for outdoorsy publications? Well, she's all over this and been bugging me for an interview. Kind of awkward when your mom is part of the press. I told her to talk to you first, so expect a call soon."

"Hmmm. Well, I guess we can work something out, but it is awkward. Before we say much more to the press, we have to finish the investigation, find out who Monday's other victims were, notify the families."

"What about Monday's and Joey's families? Any possibility of lawsuits there?"

Bernie shook his head. "Not this time. Not so far. Amadon's family seems happy that he's gone and want nothing more to do with the case. Monday didn't have much family and as for what family he had, his father saw to it that they stayed away. He was a black sheep himself and he saw to it that his wife and only son were kept under wraps, suppressed. We talked to the father, asked him to come in for an interview, but he declined, so we went to his business in Issaquah. Place is all run-down, no customers, dirty, limited inventory. It's pretty obvious the business has failed. As for Emmett Monday, he was like his store; run-down, unshaven, reeking of booze and marijuana. A ruin of a man."

"What did he have to say?"

"Not much. We asked him if he'd known anything about his son's murderous activities. He said no, but that he was certain Josh had killed Arlene. Didn't have any proof. And then he said that he wasn't surprised about Josh, always knew he was weird and bad to the bone, called him a psychopath. Takes one to know one, I guess."

They were silent for a few moments, staring in front of them at the serene vista.

Max said, "So how did Monday manage to get rid of all those files about Lila?"

Bernie shook his head. "Don't know yet. We're still looking into that. We know what he did, we don't yet know how. I've got Agent Darzi and another tech expert going over Monday's computer and online files as well as trying to determine when the various databases might've been breached. Those guys are working long hours, going back year by year. Monday was a genius with that stuff, and we may never figure out how he did it. As for the physical files, I've got some other people working with internal affairs officers at OSP and National Parks to figure that one out. I suspect that some large sums of money changed hands in exchange for getting rid of those files. Anyone who participated will sure as hell be prosecuted. That kind of shit really pisses me off! The Montaignes restored the missing Lila files with copies sent to OSP and the park service, as well as the online databases. And of course we'll be adding even more after our investigation is completed."

"Well, you gotta admit Monday was smart to eliminate those files. Without knowing about that first case, we'd probably still be spinning our wheels and Faith would be dead. If Ellen hadn't found that SAR report, if she hadn't known about our investigation, if Mike hadn't saved those files . . ."

Bernie waved his hands. "Max, Max, Max! Don't get into the 'ifs'! Ellen did find that report, she was part of the investigation, you did talk to her. Mike had that lone copy. You guys figured it out and stopped that motherfucker. It all worked out! That's the important thing. Leave the ifs alone, whether you succeed in a case or not, just leave 'em and move on."

Bernie put his hands on his knees and sighed, looked around. "I do love it up here. It's a rare treat to be here in the morning. I'm usually here after work and it gets crowded at times. I tell you what, this walking thing? I'm gettin' hooked on it! Gets the blood going, relieves stress and renews one's perspective. Am I right?"

"I have to agree. I'm lucky that in my job, sometimes I even get paid for walking. Speaking of exercise and mobility, I talked to Mike yesterday and he's doing great in rehab. He's one tough hombre. He's still got a lot of weeks of hard work but should be good as new eventually."

"Yeah, I checked in with him too. I really like the guy. We had a great talk. I'm thinking of hiring him as a consultant when we need some outside expertise."

"And what about Faith? How's she doing? Mike didn't say much about her and I didn't want to pry. All he said was she was doing okay."

Bernie grinned. “More than okay, I think. You’re not gonna believe what she’s doing now . . . ”

CHAPTER 55 — September 1

Faith took off her pack and leaned it against a large boulder. She was wearing desert camouflage pattern BDU pants and a green fleece top, her long black hair tied in a ponytail under a green boonie hat. She stood at the edge of the trail, looking north, and breathed in cool, fresh air. The view was stupendous! In front of her, the stony ridge dropped off, plunging over 300 feet to a steep, boulder-strewn meadow that itself sloped down into thick forest. Fluffy white clouds cast dark shadows that slowly flowed across the wide valley below. Ahead of her, the PCT left the knife-edged ridge and continued, contouring through rocky meadows and forest, across steep mountainsides. The meadows were mottled with red and gold as the summer's flora gave way to fall. The air was clear and she could see the thin line of trail as it crossed the meadow headwall of the Gold Creek Valley, traversing Chikamin Ridge and disappearing around a corner of the mountain. Beyond that rose more mountain peaks, grey stone, patchy with snow. She knew that beyond those were even more peaks, mountains all the way to Canada. Mountains all the way to the Aleutian Islands, really. Thousands of miles of mountains, rivers, lakes, creeks, waterfalls and glaciers. It amazed her to think about it.

After the last couple of weeks, it was a good thing to think about. The kind of thing that opened her mind and helped the stress drain away. The traumatic events at the TGI Monday's food trailer were in the past now. What had followed those events had been almost as exhausting and challenging. The flight to the Seattle hospital where her dad had emergency surgery, the FBI interviews and investigation, witness statements, dodging the media, her dad's recovery and the start of his rehab. And then there were sessions with an FBI counselor from the Office of Victim Assistance, long talks with her mom, phone calls and emails to friends and relatives.

Along with all that came the nightmares, back for an encore performance. After being free of them for several weeks, their return demoralized her. She'd felt stripped of any emotional and psychological gains made on the trip. After talking with her VA counselor, the FBI OVA counselor, and her parents, she decided that the best thing to do was to resume her journey, get back to the mountains and complete the trail. Her parents didn't like it, but as before, they understood.

Two days ago, Jenks drove her to the point where she'd left off. They didn't go the extra few hundred yards up the road to where it had all happened. She didn't need to see that place again. The bloodstains were probably still there, along with tattered yellow pieces of crime scene tape fluttering in the wind. No need to see that. Jenks said he'd drive up and take a look, but Faith just wanted to get back on the trail. She'd pulled her pack out of the back of Jenks' pickup, thanked him and gave him a hug. He helped her on with her pack and she fastened the belt, tightened the shoulder straps, turned to give him a smile.

Jenks smiled back and said, "Head on a swivel, Jarhead, and stay in touch, okay?"

She nodded, turned and set off down the trail. It switch-backed downhill through a brush patch, leading her into a cool, shady stand of tall firs and hemlock trees.

A woman's loud voice said, "Um, excuse me?!" and brought Faith back to the present. She stepped back against a rock outcrop to let a group of young day hikers pass by on the narrow trail. She nodded and said, "hi" as they